Kids, Cuddles & Caffeine

Edmund Farrow

Housedad Hero Book 1

Published by DadsDinner
www.DadsDinner.com
@DadsDinner

Printed by CreateSpace, an Amazon.com Company
Available on Kindle and other devices

This book is dedicated to every parent or carer needing a touch of encouragement on the long, hard road to bedtime. May hugs and chocolate see you through.

With immense thanks to my wonderful wife and fantastic children for being funny, delightful, profound and inspiring (and then putting up with me writing about it).

Part 1

Living the Housedad Dream

Message in a bottle

Dear Dave,

I hope this letter finds you in good health. Actually, I just hope this letter finds you. 'Dave, The-dad-who-stays-at-home, Leeds' doesn't give the postie much to go on. Still, it's worth a shot. I'm guessing you're in Leeds because everyone I know in the entire country has heard of you, so you must live somewhere fairly central. As for your name, well, since most guys I ever meet are called Dave, it's a fair bet. Then again, the fact that I *haven't* met you might throw the statistics and I… Oh, never mind, I'm wittering on like a man who was up half the night being vomited on by a two-year-old.

Which brings me to my point.

Seeing as we've never met, maybe I'd better explain who I am. I'm the other one. Yes, the other housedad! I thought we should get a bit of a correspondence going to share our experiences because it's a mum's world we live in and no one really seems to understand. For instance, whenever I explain that I'm a housedad, people look confused and then remember that, in this politically correct age, every individual has an equal right to an outlandish and deviant lifestyle. They stop looking confused, they laugh nervously and then they affirm me. They tell me that housedads are quite common these days. After all, their mother's hairdresser's acquaintance's nephew stays home and looks after his children.

I smile and nod. "Yes, we're all over the place," I say. Then I go home and phone my aunt and tell her to stop gossiping to random hairdressers about me and the kids.

Of course, it's not always me they're talking about – sometimes they're talking about *you* – but I'm pretty sure there are only the two of us. We need to stick together. I'm fed up of just discussing babies at parent and toddler group. I want more. I want to share some meaningful insights on fatherhood, football and *Top Gear*. At the very least, I want to discuss PlayStations as well as poo (or, indeed, Pooh).

Please write back if you are able. If you're too busy searching the house for wooden bricks in an assortment of colours, then I quite understand. We have a tub that claims it contained a hundred when we bought it. At the last count there were twenty-three and the others aren't in the washing-machine. Where do they go?

Yours in a woman's world,

Ed.

The revolution begins

Hi Dave!

Thanks for your email address and the very positive reply to my letter. The revolution has begun. Housedads of the world unite! Let's make people realise that men can look after children too. The time has come for us to march on Downing Street and make our demands for a more equal society:

> 1. Derogatory comments which assume any man in sole charge of a child is a Sunday parent are to be banned. No old lady who walks straight into a male-driven pushchair, causing a pile-up, shall be allowed to get away with saying, 'Looks like you need a bit of practice, dear.'
>
> 2. Baby facilities accessible to dads in public places will smell as nice as the ones available for mums. (And we want the comfy chairs too. We know they're in there.)
>
> 3. Mums are to be forbidden from looking at us sideways when they learn that some misguided career woman has left us caring for her offspring all day.
>
> 4. We want higher prams.
>
> 5. We want bigger biscuits. (Not that mums already have bigger biscuits but it's worth having something to bargain away and, you never know, we might be able to slip it through.)
>
> 6. We want lower…

Oh, who am I kidding? There are only the two of us. We'd have difficulty causing a stir outside Number 10 even if we were wearing balaclavas and speaking with Middle Eastern accents. Besides, we'd have the kids with us. Everyone would merely assume we'd been sent to the shops to pick up a pack of nappies while our wives took a breather.

Maybe we could put the kids in balaclavas…

No, better leave them out of this and struggle on.

I always think that being a housedad must be somewhat like being a female car mechanic. Members of the opposite sex simply don't take you seriously. For goodness sake, it's as if they think we don't know a baby's backside from its elbow and that's the first lesson you learn, believe me… For the full effect, it's best to strap a baby to your front using one of those carriers and then go to the shops. If the baby is facing outwards, then every female you meet will spend the entire time talking to your chest. It's a salutary experience. Maybe we're not the only ones with demands to make. Maybe we should let female car mechanics into the group.

Maybe I should clear that with my wife first…

Ho well, I'll be in contact again soon. I'll leave you with my top tips for telling a baby's backside from his or her elbow:

- If it smells bad then it's probably the backside. No guarantees, though. Where's the baby been? When was the baby last washed?

- If it's in a nappy then, once again, it's probably the backside. Still no guarantees – you may have got it wrong last time.

- If it's sharp and in your eye then it's the elbow every time. Unless it's a knee. Or the TV remote. Or a brick. Or…

Yours in a woman's world,
Ed.

Parent and toddler

Dear Dave,

Thank you for telling me about your experiences with little Sam at the parent and toddler group. It sounds like you're blending in well. (Or at least as well as any man can in a room full of women who don't believe he can really exist. You'll know you've cracked it when someone asks you what your husband does for a living.) I have to tell you, however, that the competitiveness you mention is unavoidable. The desire to come out on top always surfaces whenever any group of children is involved.

Forget the kids themselves – the parents are bound to succumb.

It starts innocently enough as Parent A checks that her kid is normal – that it's not too odd for a child to only have had four teeth at a year, or to still be crawling at fifteen months. Parent B reassures. Her child only had six teeth at a year and only learnt to walk at fourteen months. Parent A isn't reassured. Six teeth is more than four. How about speech? Can Child B say 'tractor'? Ha, no! That's a point back to Parent A. Parent B retaliates. How many blocks can Child A stack? Only twelve? Really? He hasn't built a scale model of St Paul's, complete with dome? Well, I'm sure he'll learn. 3-1 to Parent B.

Then it escalates.

Before long, there are unconfirmed reports of advanced calculus and fluency in five distinct and unrelated languages. Meanwhile, the kids happily sit oblivious, chewing on brightly coloured bits of plastic.

It's very strange. Still, Marie came out on top today. At playgroup she demonstrated her innate understanding of the world's socio-economic system and put the knowledge into practice. She took the brightly coloured bits of plastic from the other children, chewed on them herself and then gave them to the nearest adult. In essence, she took from the little people, gave to the big people and had her own small nibble on the way. There's a bright future ahead of her in the City. That or a beating by a mob of angry toddlers.

Never mind, at least she'll probably grow out of it. When she's eighteen, the chances are that she'll have tie-dye clothes, peace symbols painted on her cheeks and a Communist boyfriend. They'll go off to India together to hug trees. Nonetheless, I'll still be playing the *Progeny Edition* of *Top Trumps* with the neighbours. ('You call your kid a dropout? How many exams did he fail? Ha! And I bet his girlfriend's only a Socialist…')

As I said, the competitiveness is unavoidable. If you think you're not doing it, that simply means you're winning. The important thing is to love the kid even if you're losing.

Oh and by the way, I'm glad to hear that Sam's differentiation is coming along nicely but I have to tell you that my girl can already integrate trig functions.

And she can speak Swahili.

Yours, as ever, in a woman's world,

Ed.

Life after children

Dear Dave,

You're right – I have been getting a little ahead of myself in my correspondence so far. I should probably tell you some more about myself and my family.

My name is Ed, I'm thirty-three, I live in Edinburgh and I'm a housedad. I used to be a computer programmer in a Large Banking Organisation. I met my wife, Sarah, at LBO. She works in marketing. At the point our eldest son, Fraser, was born, I gave up lounging around surfing the internet and drinking coffee all day in order to put in some hard graft looking after him. He's now six. We also have Lewis who's four and Marie who's not long turned two. Most mornings these days, I'm lucky to have an opportunity to check my email, let alone stir up a flame war on a *Star Trek* fansite just for fun. As for coffee, the house is littered with dozens of half-full mugs of tepid Cafédirect I've hurriedly put down for a minute and never had a chance to return to. (Worryingly, last Tuesday, I found one in my sock drawer.)

We get by, though. Sarah is happy with her job most of the time and does well for us. Her boss at LBO is a bit of an idiot who tends to favour those members of the team who go golfing with him (i.e. the men) but, hopefully, he'll do something really stupid soon and get banished to the Swedish office. Fraser's enjoying school, Lewis starts in August and Marie might get a place at nursery in the autumn. (Six months to go!)

People have already begun asking me what I plan to do in my spare time once I've got all three children out of the house. The obvious answer is that I'm going to eat my breakfast in peace while catching up on the headlines on BBC Red Button and then follow that with a spot of cleaning, a chocolate biscuit and an actually hot cup of coffee. Unfortunately, most of my interrogators find it mildly disappointing that I don't have a scheme for world domination ready to put into action during my two hours a day... on weekdays... during term-time... when all the kids are well.

Perhaps they're right. Am I setting my aim too low? Maybe I *can* achieve more than sorting out the wilderness beyond the backdoor or filing the bank statements from the year before last. After all, I no longer have cleaning the windows left to look forward to. (Sarah found stuff growing on the inside of one of them the other day so I had to bring the maintenance schedule forward. They're good until the end of the decade now.) Let's see... What are the possibilities?

I could put more work into the script of *Housedad! – The Musical*. It's a classic tale of one man's struggle to be accepted into the local Women's Institute, featuring nuns on roller skates, performing dolphins, a dream sequence involving Princess Leia in a gold bikini and the music of S Club 7. I see it as a semi-autobiographical work with myself played by H from Steps.

Maybe I could learn a new skill. From taxidermy to Kung Fu, there are a wealth of options out there. I'm sure every single one of them has some kind of practical application for childcare as well. If not, I suppose I could get a job. There must be something available that runs for a couple of hours on a weekday morning. It probably involves being underpaid, overworked and getting filthy, though. I've had enough of that already.

Crime is another alternative, complete with flexible hours, performance related bonuses and low entry requirements. My preference would be for some form of pyramid selling fraud or chain-letter scam. I could send out letters with six names on (mine and five aliases). The recipients would have to send everyone on the list three shares in Nintendo, take the top name off, add their name at the bottom and pass it on. If I ever needed to hide evidence, I'd quickly give it to one of the kids, tell them it was really important and wait approximately a minute for it to mysteriously vanish. I'd have little chance of being caught and I'd own Mario. Excellent.

Or maybe I'll just have a rest. I'll be owed seven and a half years of lunch hours by then – that's an awful lot of *Bargain Hunt*...

Yours in a woman's world,

Ed.

Another child

Dear Dave,

Congratulations! It's great to hear Sam has a little brother or sister on the way. I'm glad the scan went fine and Liz is doing OK. With luck, she'll stop being sick at the mention of broccoli soon.

In your email it sounds like you're somewhere on the border between Excitement and Panic. This is, of course, a fantastic locale to visit, full of unexpected career changes, lifestyle choices and sky-diving taster sessions, but you wouldn't want to live there. Take a deep breath. Resist the siren call of olive farming in Tuscany, of difficult to explain Visa bills and of mysterious women named Svetlana. Come home to the land in which every housedad should start his day – the land of Hopeful Trepidation. You may end the day in Rage or Despair but it's more likely that things will simply muddle along in the eventual direction of A Beer On The Sofa In Front Of *CSI*. (Don't confuse Hopeful Trepidation with Blind Optimism, however – always travel with a pack of baby wipes, a change of socks, three spare nappies and a big stick.)

Which is merely another way of saying don't worry, you'll cope. Trust me. I've got three under-sevens and I'm still sane... OK, I admit I'm recovering from depression and I've just described your emotional state in the style of a housedad version of *Pilgrim's Progress* but I'm not yet *entirely* crazy and I still have my health. Apart from the bad back from lifting Fraser, this flu Marie gave me and a touch of conjunctivitis I picked up from Lewis...

Hmm... I'll come in again.

Two children? You'll be fine. I've got three but I'm still clinging to the last vestiges of reason and I'm not dead yet. No worries.

Perhaps this isn't as reassuring as I'd hoped. The truth is, you *are* going to have your hands full for a while. I used to know a guy who had five kids under nine years old. He was a somewhat busy man but he and his wife sailed around quite serenely in a sea of children. He told me that one child changes your life, a second child changes your life again and, beyond that, there's not much more left to change.

He was probably right. Looking after a baby takes plenty of time. When Fraser was small, I calculated that taking care of him took eight hours a day, nine days a week. It wasn't necessarily hard or constant labour, though. I could sit in an armchair and watch re-runs of *ER* while giving him a bottle, and then get on with other stuff while he had a nap. Lewis made things busier. There was always an awake child to be entertained and I was doing eleven days a week. That may not sound like a vast increase in workload but think of it more in terms of the drastic decrease in time left for anything else, including looking after another child. When Marie arrived, she simply had to fit in.

So, yes, your life is about to change again but not as much as last time and you're on a roll now – you might as well keep going. Nonetheless, having another child always seems daunting. You look at a dad with two children and wonder how he copes. He looks at me and my three in bewilderment. I look at a mum with four kids and break into manic giggling while my eye starts to twitch. She smiles sweetly and glides off with more composure than Mary Poppins on Prozac. Bah...

Don't be discouraged. She doesn't have superhuman powers or an extraordinary level of patience. She's smiling because she's going to be home in fifteen minutes and then she'll be able to lock the little blighters back in their cage, put her feet up and watch some TV show featuring sunshine, make-overs and Peter Andre.

You see, children expand to fill the time you have available for them. If you've only got five minutes, they'll settle for that but, if you've got all day, then they'll take it. One of the most immediate advantages to having multiple children is you quickly learn that a crying child doesn't explode if you leave him for more than ten seconds. Trying to play *Snakes and Ladders* with one, while you change another and feed a third is clearly going to end in some form of misfortune. They have to wait their turn, no matter how much they whine. The more children you have, the more time you will spend ignoring most of them. Once you're good at it, you can spend some of the time ignoring *all* of them and sneak off for a cup of coffee and a quick surf.

Got to look forward to something... (Don't worry, you'll cope.)

Yours in a woman's world,

Ed.

P.S. Wish me luck on Monday – Scary Karen is after me.

Scary Karen

Dear Dave,

Did I tell you about Scary Karen?

We met when I inadvertently sat down next to her during biscuit time at parent and toddler recently. She's older than most of the other mums, big and looks serious. She started a conversation by introducing her toddler. "This is my son, Malcolm. He's named after my dead brother." She followed this up by introducing her baby. "This is William. He's named after my uncle. He's dead now, too." She then proceeded to breast-feed the baby.

Now I'm used to being around breast-feeding mothers. Some are so subtle that I've been talking to them for five minutes before realising there's a baby up their jumper. The vast majority use a certain level of discretion or at least give me enough warning to look away while their human limpet gets properly attached. Not many wap out an enormous quivering boob right in front of me while continuing to fill me in on the details of their deceased relatives. I just about choked on my chocolate digestive. It was scary.

Most people would probably have smiled politely, gulped down their coffee and then whisked their bemused child off for an unexpected nappy change. I, however, have the unfortunate character flaw of being a 'good listener'. If someone starts talking to me, then I sit there in rapt attention, like a toddler mesmerised by a row of flashing lights. I nod and smile and occasionally interject but I'm unable to move as my brain is slowly filled to bursting point by knowledge of what everyone in someone else's family had to eat for lunch in a museum of miniature teapots on a daytrip to Dumfries. Even better, as they consider exactly how many little jars of jam were consumed, my screensaver face kicks in and I'm really in trouble.

When my brain explodes from sheer tedium, it would be nice if I developed a blank gape and a vacant stare. Maybe then I'd get left alone. Instead, my facial muscles slump idly into an expression of sage-like thought and concentration. This makes it look like I'm listening even harder. I get to hear all about the teapots *and* an exhibition of replica steam engines whittled out of railway sleepers from around the world.

So I sat there and quickly discovered that Scary Karen is a 'good talker'. There was no escape. I learnt about her bowel surgery, aromatherapy, her difficult experiences in childbirth, a past life as a torturer and the importance of dental hygiene. She only stopped when the helpers started turning out the lights. Marie had already climbed into her buggy and was straining forwards while holding onto the frame in a doomed effort to drag herself home. We left at speed but I kept looking over my shoulder to check Karen wasn't following us.

The next week was similar, except she hunted me out and sat next to me. Then it was wap, choke, chat all over again. I nodded attentively as I was informed about the wonders of homemade cottage cheese, the variable consistency of cat vomit and the dangers of naked yoga on a bus. As soon as everything went dark, I grabbed the buggy and ran, screams of "You don't push! I pull me!" trailing behind us down the street.

Things have not improved much since. I've considered changing toddler groups but I know lots of the people at St Jude's, it's close, the chairs are comfy and there's nothing much else on a Monday anyway. I've been trying to disagree more audibly with everything Karen says but she doesn't appear to have noticed. Worse still, she's starting another group on a Wednesday morning in the Millennium Centre which is virtually across the road from my house. She's got the hall booked for tomorrow and has invited along a few people she met doing community service. And, you've guessed it, she wants me to be one of the group's founder members.

Another of my character flaws is that I'm not great with conflict. I much prefer to give someone a valid excuse for my reluctance to do something than simply inform them I'd rather eat my only pair of shoes.

I told Karen that I need Wednesday mornings to do my grocery shopping. She suggested using the internet and getting a delivery. I reckoned it was easier going to the store myself. She gave me a computing tutorial. I said that I didn't really trust some random assistant in Tesco to choose my bananas. She told me she worked as an assistant in Tesco. I... I caved in. I said I'll go.

It's going to be me, Marie, Scary Karen, a select band of her scary friends and a gaggle of their no doubt scary children.

I'm a little nervous.

Yours in a woman's world,

Ed.

Cancel the search party

Dear Dave,

I'm still alive. I made it through an hour and a half of the new toddler group and got out with only a few minor dribble stains and a small bruise. Which isn't bad going, considering. Here's what happened:

Scary Karen had asked me to bring along a donation of toys, so I packed up a load of things I've been desperate to get rid of for ages. This included a very noisy Thomas the Tank Engine which whistles tunes, a motorised pig which sings *Old MacDonald* and a pair of electronic maracas. I foolishly forgot to take the batteries out of anything, though.

Then I headed across the road to the Millennium Centre, past reception and down the corridor to the side hall. I was somewhat surprised to find a bouncer at the door. He was a squat, bald-headed guy who had bulging muscles everywhere, even places I'm pretty sure I don't have *any* muscles at all. A wealth of tattoos rippled over his bare arms.

He looked at me suspiciously. "You here for the toddlers?" he grunted.

I had a momentary vision of myself driving off with a cattle-truck full of under-fives. I almost mentioned it but then I noticed the assault rifle inked onto his bicep. It was labelled 'Betsy'. I decided to play things safe. "Er, yes," I said and waved my bag of toys and small child at him. "This is my little girl."

"I like pink!" shouted Marie to back me up.

The bouncer looked at me even more suspiciously. I could almost see the cogs turning in his brain – it was a parent and toddler group, I had brought a toddler, I was a parent, he couldn't justifiably turn me away... but I had showed up to the party one X chromosome short. The cogs spun for a while. I detected a faint smell of burning rubber.

"I go play now," said Marie and walked through the door.

The man's brain re-booted. "'Spose you'd better go in," he said. I smiled and thanked him and went in.

Some mats had been put out in the middle of the room and sprinkled with toys and children. A dozen or so chairs were placed round the edges. Four women had pulled their chairs close together and were having a heated discussion. They, too, eyed me warily as I entered. I smiled at them and followed Marie. She made a bee-line for a toy ironing board and iron. She picked up a baby doll, cuddled it and then proceeded to spend several minutes systematically removing the creases from its face before stuffing it in the trunk of a ride-a-long car. (No more *CSI* for her.)

The women clearly knew each other and were having an argument about who had the worst scar. (Don't ever go there...) I tried not to listen, which was easy, since every child in the room except mine appeared to have a whistling Thomas that they were beating to death with electronic maracas. No one else had thought to remove the batteries either. I stared into space and muttered encouraging things when Marie took the baby out of the car and replaced it with the singing pig.

Eventually, Karen entered the room with a refreshment trolley and the adults drifted towards it and the promise of chocolate-covered sugary goodness. Karen gestured at me and said, "This is Ed." The eyes of the four women widened in a mixture of recognition and awe. Karen introduced them all to me but I instantly forgot their names and which one of them was which. Let's call them Jess, Bess, Tess and Cress. (I've been reading *Meg and Mog* a lot recently.) The bouncer's name was Trevor. He glared at me through narrowed slits.

"You're the housedad," said Jess.

"Karen has told us all about you," said Bess. Tess nodded in a way that suggested this might have been a lengthy process.

"Really?" I said. I couldn't entirely remember ever having had much chance to tell Karen anything about myself.

"Yes," said Tess firmly.

Cress started speaking very rapidly. "You have three children, aged six, four and two. You look after them all day, deal with them at night and then you get up the next day and do it all over again, even when they're sick, or you're sick, or you're all sick. You clean the house, you change the nappies, you wipe up the mess. You take them out in the fresh air, you do their homework with them and you feed them at least five portions of fruit and veg every day. You..."

I interrupted as she took a breath. "So? You do all those things for your own kids."

"Yeah," said Jess. "But you're a man."

"Do you do the cooking as well?" said Bess, jumping up and down a little.

"Kind of," I said. "I don't have much time. These days, I tend to just move food from the freezer to the oven rather than cooking, as such."

"That's more than any of *our* men ever manage," said Tess, irritably, but then softened. "Want a chocolate digestive?"

Things settled down after that. Karen's friends weren't that scary after all. It turned out their community service was merely for getting out of control in a protest around the nuclear base at Faslane. Trevor, however, made me nervous. He lurked near the trolley. He didn't have any children of his own with him. He continued to glare at me. He looked like he should have worked at Faslane, possibly as a missile.

He only stopped glaring when Karen came and sat next me for her normal chat. She wapped out her baby's elevenses and Trevor's brain went into spasm again. He didn't know where to look and then pretended to read the notices on the wall. I forgot about him for a while as I became mesmerised by Karen's account of her attempt to return an item at Ann Summers and I prayed for the world to end.

When the lights went out and I was finally able to grab Marie and head for the exit, Trevor sidled over to me. He wasn't very good at it. "You and Karen," he muttered shiftily.

The cogs in my own brain suddenly clicked into place, then slipped out of gear and whirred away helplessly. Shock, surprise, understanding, fear and incredulity battled for control of my eyebrows. "Karen is merely a... er... friend," I stammered. "I have absolutely no desire to... have any, er, desire. Erm, is that the time? I have to collect my son from nursery. Nice to meet you."

I got the bruise clunking my shin as I ran away. It's still sore.

Yours in a woman's world,

Ed.

PS Next week is an arts and crafts session. All this but with added glue... I can't wait.

What do you mean we're out of wipes?

Dear Dave,

We had a family day on Saturday.

Yes, that's right, I'm talking about one of those occasions where we drag the kids kicking and screaming away from the TV and computer and force them to have an exciting trip to somewhere cold and wet. This lasts from the moment they've finished their breakfasts until a time well after they're supposed to be in bed and long since they have ceased to be civil. The trauma helps us bond together as a unit and is a good excuse to drink a bottle of wine when it's all over.

On this particular occasion, there was a deal where we could buy a special train ticket to Glasgow and then go to various attractions for free once we got there. Being cheapskates, this appealed to us and we set off early in order to visit as many places – and thus save as much money – as we possibly could. Of course, some of the most expensive things in life are free, and our pockets were steadily drained of cash by cafeterias and gift shops throughout the day. Still, we saw plenty of things we would never have got round to seeing otherwise.

We ended up at the Science Centre. This is a fantastic place full of hands-on experiments and exhibits. Our first concern, though, was grabbing lunch. Marie refused everything apart from milk and Hula Hoops but the rest of us tucked in. As usual, the boys finished their food before drinking their drinks – their vast, brimming cups of chocolate milk. There are only so many times I can say, "Drink your drinks before they get spilled," without giving up in despair, however. That's something I need to work on. Quite how Fraser managed to launch his beverage container a foot into the air while still creating enough rotational motion to splatter all of us is a mystery.

After we'd cleaned up the mess, I went and got Fraser another chocolate milk and I picked up some fruit for later.

He gulped the milk down and we headed to the cavernous hall housing the exhibits. Sarah let the younger kids press buttons until they were bored and then pointed them in the direction of something else. I vainly attempted to explain to Fraser the polarity of magnets, the fundamentals of flight and the propagation of sound. He ignored me, pressed buttons until he was bored and then ran off to find something else. I gave up again. I taught him to do a *Towers of Hanoi* puzzle, added a couple of extra rings made from a key fob and a wrist strap, and sat down for a long rest. A very long rest.

Later, we went to the gift shop. It was crammed with brightly coloured, exciting-looking items packed full of educational potential. I quickly tried to hide my wallet in my sock but Fraser was too fast. He grabbed a pack of plastic bobbly things.

"Can I get this?"

"What is it?" I asked.

"I don't know," he said.

"How much does it cost?"

"Five pounds," he replied.

"That's a little expensive for something when you don't even know what it is."

"How about this then?" he said, grabbing a smaller pack of different plastic bobbly things.

"What's that?"

He shrugged. "I don't know."

"How much is it?"

"One pound and fifty pence."

"OK," I sighed. "I guess that's more reasonable. Go and give the money to the man at the till." He went off happily just as Lewis approached, a board game clutched to his chest. From somewhere else in the shop I heard the familiar voice of a little girl scream, "You don't touch it! Pink dinosaur mine!"

Ho hum.

We left as closing time swiftly beckoned and caught the open-top tour bus (another part of the deal) for a scenic return to the station. We all piled upstairs and sat along the back. The boys were starting to wilt and I gave them the fruit to keep them going. This was a mistake. After they'd already gorged themselves, I bit into an apple and discovered it was quite sour. There was nothing wrong with it as such, it was simply not very sweet in a way that suggested it might take some concentrated digestion. I suspected it was not really the thing to give two boys prone to travel sickness while they sat on a bus twisting and juddering its way through the Glasgow traffic.

"Are you feeling OK, Fraser?" I asked nervously.

"Yeah," he replied. "Why?"

"No reason," I said. "How about...?" I began turning to Lewis but I was already too late.

Everything happened at once.

My younger son leant over the back railing and spewed mightily, somewhat to the surprise of the cyclist directly behind us. I called down an apology but I had more immediate concerns: the sight and smell of Lewis' titanic chunder had started Fraser gagging. I grabbed the plastic bag containing our souvenirs, emptied it in Sarah's lap and then held it under Fraser's chin. I was barely in time to catch the geyser of chocolate milk which erupted from his mouth and just kept coming. There was so much, and it was under such high pressure, I expected it to spray out his ears at any moment. Then, finally, the seismic activity eased and I sighed in relief – I had caught every drop. I held the bag aloft in triumph.

Unfortunately, it had a hole in the bottom.

I stared at the hole, my eyes wide in horror, and time slowed. The trinkets falling at Sarah's feet hung in the air, I could hear my own heartbeat and I suddenly noticed the warm, damp feeling spreading across my knees. Reality spun round my outstretched arm...

...then snapped back into place. I dumped the bag on the floor and hunted for the wipes. The earlier chocolate milk incident had seriously depleted our supplies and a couple of nappy changes had left us very short indeed. We had one left. One wipe to last us nearly two hours. One wipe to see us through over three hundred and fifty child-minutes. That's not a lot of back up. I decided to save it in case of a real disaster and cleaned up as best I could with my scarf. By the time we reached our stop, Fraser and I looked nearly presentable.

We were left with that age-old dilemma of whether to leave the leaking bag of sick on the top deck of the bus or to carry it the full length of the bus, down the stairs and out the door, leaking a trail of sick behind us. Tricky. In the end, I put the bag inside my woolly hat and made a break for it. I hurtled to the door, leapt onto the pavement and barged my way to the nearest bin, the crowd parting before me like the Red Sea before Moses. (Though I doubt *he* yelled, "Let me through! I have a hat full of sick!" to get the job done.)

I was tempted to dump the hat with its contents but, instead, I stowed it with my scarf in the net carrier under the buggy, as far from anything else as I could manage.

We cleaned up a bit more in the station and headed home. We'd had a pretty good day, even if some of us did smell faintly of curdled chocolate milk. Marie fell asleep on the train and the boys played with their new toys. I spent most of the journey rescuing multicoloured bits of plastic from obscure crevices of ScotRail seating. Some of these little gaps were unpleasantly sticky but I did score a two pound coin, a return journey from Falkirk and a LEGO Darth Vader complete with light-sabre. Result!

It was extremely chilly when we got back to Edinburgh and, by the time we had walked halfway home, I was freezing. I peered under the buggy in an effort to see if my hat and scarf had gone crusty yet. Sarah rubbed her hands against the cold. "Don't even think about it," she said without so much as looking at me. Marie was snuggled cosily under a blanket, so I stole her pink, fluffy pixie hat and jammed it down on my head. It's possible I may have looked like a lunatic but it's only a real lunatic who walks around with cold ears when they have other options.

It was late. We got home and bundled the kids into bed before putting on a load of washing and settling down in our pyjamas with a bottle of wine and the Sky+ control.

"You did well today," said Sarah as we cuddled up on the sofa.

"You did too."

"Want to go to Dundee next week? I got this leaflet in the Science Centre about... What?"

"More wine..." I muttered. "More wine..."

"Never mind." She kissed me and then poured me another glass. "I'll tell you tomorrow."

"Good idea," I said and reached for the remote. "Now which is it going to be – *Vegas*, *New York* or *Miami*?"

Yours in a woman's world,

Ed.

Part 2

Coping with Everyone's Expectations

Big Friendly Daddy

Dear Dave,

You're right – you do wonder what they're going to remember.

You slave away, day after day. You get them out of bed, dress them, feed them, keep them entertained, undress them and then get them back into bed again. You wash up, wipe down and hoover around. You play games, run about and get head-butted in the privates. You pour your very life and soul into keeping them happy and turning them out right. It's hard work... You kind of want them to remember something of that. If nothing else, it should count in your favour when they're choosing your nursing home.

Sadly, however, Sam's recall of early childhood will probably be so hazy that he will believe that he was raised by Bob the Builder and a crack band of Teletubbies. Your years of sacrifice will be forgotten as he smiles wistfully at happy memories of talking machines, Tubby custard and enormous rabbits. He will build a shrine to Laa-Laa and you will spend your twilight years in a coal shed in King's Lynn.

I'm sorry to say that your future is bleak. I think mine might be worse, though. Not only am I going to be there in that shed with you, my kids will skimp on the extras. You, at least, will get food and a blanket; I will get to starve in my underpants. Every so often, a little goblin will come round and poke me with a stick.

I mean, Marie's two-and-a-half and she already thinks I'm an imbecile. Today, I was talking to her about how we'd been on a bus at the weekend. "No, Daddy," she replied, "we go IN bus." It was a hard one to argue and doing so only made me appear more of an idiot.

I then got a further insight into how she views me. She insisted she wanted to watch something she referred to as *Me & You.* She started hunting through the stack of DVDs but couldn't find it. "We watch *Me & You*!" she shouted desperately. I had no idea what she was talking about so I tried asking lots of questions about the programme – what happens, who's in it, that kind of thing. "We.. watch... *Me*... &... *You*!" she replied louder and more slowly, as if speaking to a foreigner she perceived as slightly dim. This went on for a while.

Eventually, I discovered an animated version of Roald Dahl's *The BFG* (Big Friendly Giant) that had fallen behind the sofa and Marie jumped up and down. "You and me!" she cried. Everything became slightly clearer and I was less than happy. You see, the cover art shows the BFG holding a little girl in the palm of his hand. Plainly Marie associated herself with the girl, so there weren't many options as to how she pictured me. I am apparently an old, balding giant with poor dress-sense, a bulbous nose, ears the size of radar dishes, bushy eyebrows, nasal hair and dodgy teeth.

I paused for a moment and decided that there must be more to it than that. After all, my teeth are fine. I decided it must be something the giant does in the film that made her think of me. Sadly, this didn't help matters much. The giant kidnaps the girl, feeds her horrible food, inadvertently covers her in slime and nearly gets her eaten.

He also farts a great deal.

Then he *sings* about it.

You're wondering what our kids will remember. Well, there are certain things it might be better if they forgot...

Of course, I could have it all wrong. The film does pick up later on. The BFG takes the girl to see the queen, they have some fun and the bad giants get put in the zoo. There are some scary moments but it all works out in the end.

Maybe Marie sees me as a big friendly giant who scoops her up and carries her off to have an adventure. That would be nice. When I'm old and my teeth have gone dodgy, she might even look at them and have a vague recollection of bushy eyebrows, flapping ears and strong arms carrying her along. Maybe then she'll smile and maybe, just maybe, I'll get that blanket after all.

I don't think there's any avoiding the coal shed, though. (Sorry.)

Yours in a woman's world,

Ed.

Keeping up with Supermum

Dear Dave,

You are not a rubbish parent. Just because some mum you met has her kids signed up for three stimulating activities every day, that doesn't mean you are a lazy waste of space. Who knows how much help she's getting, how much she's exaggerating and what potent cocktail of medication she's taking? As a full-time parent with a small child, you are most likely working an eighty hour week and suffering from sleep deprivation. You don't need to add guilt to that. Even good parents need to let Scooby-Doo take some of the burden of childcare from time to time. Look after yourself. Sneak off for a coffee when you can. Have quiet days. Don't worry you haven't taken Sam to a museum for a few months or, frankly, that you haven't managed to leave the house since Sunday. Do the amount of stuff that keeps you and your family sane and happy. Some stimulation is great; too much merely creates tired, crotchety know-it-alls. That's not really something to aim for...

Let me illustrate:

I took the children out Saturday morning. We went to the kid's club at the cinema in the shopping centre. This is fantastic. It's cheap and it counts as getting them out of the house away from the TV, even though it's really just taking them on a bus to an absolutely enormous TV and then giving them sweets.

Marie's still a little young and so I dropped her off in the centre's crèche for a couple of hours. I'd normally leave her at home but Sarah had to go in to work. Manager Steve is trying to impress the top brass and, for some reason, he believes doing stupid overtime will make more of an impact than actually getting the job done without needing to do overtime. Sarah is seriously considering using Voodoo on him.

I went into the cinema with the boys and there was an unusually long queue. That there was a queue at all at quarter to ten on a Saturday morning was fairly strange. We waited... and waited... and waited. The film was almost starting before we got anywhere near the front and found out what was going on. Ahead of us was a group of eleven-year-old boys and ahead of them were a mum and her seven-year-old son. The mum got to the desk and asked, "What's on?" My mind boggled. Who turns up at the cinema with a young child without checking the listings? More than that, the woman had been standing in a queue for fifteen minutes with nothing to look at but a vast bank of brightly illuminated screens telling her what was on. Nonetheless, the man behind the desk patiently listed the options. The woman had a lengthy discussion with her son before they made their choice and bought their tickets and the queue finally moved forwards.

The three boys reached the desk. "What's on?" asked the tallest. The ticket guy patiently listed the options again, although he had to be a little louder than before in order to be heard above the noise of me banging my head against a pillar. The youths then had an argument about whether they wanted to see a Christmas film in March. Eventually they decided they didn't. They bought tickets for a different film and walked off without them.

The ticket guy and I shook our heads at each other. He called them back, gave them their tickets and then it was our turn. After I told him what we wanted to see and handed over the money, the guy politely gave me our tickets and the correct change. I have to suspect they weren't paying him anywhere near enough.

We had a quick (but expensive) stop at the pick'n'mix display, grabbed some popcorn and then hurried into the film. We were just in time to be mildly entertained for an hour and a half by some animated fluffy animals. On our way out, we collected Marie from the crèche and were about to set off for the bus when a gaggle of smiling, highly-scrubbed children rushed over to us, closely followed by their immaculate, beaming mother. It was Julia from our street, and her kids. They all seemed delighted to see us.

Julia is known as SuperMum in our house. (If there was some form of punctuation which signified a roll of the eyes when saying a word then SuperMum would definitely have it. Maybe I should invent some. How about 'Super~Mum'?) She has four children under the age of ten WHOM SHE HOME~SCHOOLS. She also has a successful career as an artist. Last time I asked her how she was, she brought me round a pie to say thanks. Not only had she baked the pie herself, she had grown the apples as a project with her kids. I would have written a thank you note but I was afraid they'd only make me a patchwork quilt in return.

Super~Mum's most annoying trait is that she constantly suggests I perform heroic feats of parenting. Kids bored? Take them on a daytrip to Aberdeen. Kids not eating? Cook them a traditional Bolivian meal. Kids afraid of a bit of dirt? Go on a family pot-holing expedition. Kids watching too much television? Tip the TV out the window and enrol them in an acrobatics class instead.

These ideas are, clearly, insane. The very thought of attempting any of them with my three children makes we want to go and have a lie down in a darkened room. Simply contemplating them sends dizzying tendrils of madness scurrying though my brain. Lamentably, however, these aren't the crazy witterings of an American child-psychologist or of a creepy elderly gentleman on the bus. Julia has actually done these things herself. With *four* children. I know this for a fact – I salvaged a battered flat screen from her shrubbery and fixed it up and now her kids are always lurking outside our lounge window desperately trying to catch a glimpse of *Scooby-Doo!*. Since our lounge is one storey up, I can only assume that the acrobatics class is going well.

As our families caught sight of each other in the shopping centre, there were greetings and polite questions and then it transpired that Julia's lot were going bowling. We were invited to join them. Before I knew it, I was wearing slippy shoes and trying to prevent children from dropping heavy spherical objects on my toes. I don't really know how it happened. Julia didn't seem to understand how an unplanned excursion might be in any way troublesome or tiring. It didn't help that Fraser loves bowling and jumped up and down at the prospect. If I hadn't gone, I would have felt both rubbish and guilty.

It wasn't fun. I had to help the boys bowl while keeping Marie entertained and listening to Julia regale me with the joys of eating Bolivian snacks down a mineshaft. My multitasking skills were tested to their limits. Fraser kept bowling too slowly, the ball drifting to a halt against the bumper halfway down the lane. Fortunately, our lane was right at the end so I could walk down beside it and give the ball a shove. Unfortunately, the final time I did this, I turned round to discover that, despite being told not to several~times, Fraser had taken his second bowl. This was bad. That he'd decided to bowl his sister was somewhat worse. A blur of fluffy pink whizzed towards me, arms outstretched and yelling, "I get strike! I get strike!"

I grabbed a fistful of knitted jumper as it went past and yanked Marie to safety. "You not carry me," she complained. "I am ball!"

We managed to get away shortly after that but I was shattered. I flicked on *Scooby-Doo!* as soon as we got home and lay on the sofa for a rest. A couple of hours later, Julia popped round with a pie to say thank you for the lovely time. I felt the need to stand up to her; to explain that it hadn't been that lovely really; to suggest she consider the feelings of other parents slightly more carefully; to get her to give her own kids a break. I chickened out, though. Instead, I invited her along to Scary Karen's parent and toddler group.

I know this was bad and wrong. I'm hoping their evil superpowers will somehow neutralise each other but there's a good chance that their very meeting will create a rift in space and time that will cause the entire universe to unravel.

Get some sleep while you can.

Yours in a woman's world,

Ed.

Teletubbies save the world

Dear Dave,

I'm sorry to hear that the Teletubbies are destroying your sanity. I remember what it's like. When Fraser was young, I happily got to watch re-runs of *ER* all day, mixed in with current affairs and an occasional documentary about Alexander the Great or quantum mechanics. Then he got a bit older and emergency chest surgery ceased to be suitable background noise for playtime. Not long after that, he realised that I had Dipsy and co. held captive within black rectangles of plastic and could make them perform at any time simply by feeding them to the video machine. Overnight, I went from learning about the fundamental properties of matter to watching a teddy bear tap-dance. On loop.

When *we* were children, television didn't start until nine in the morning, there were just three channels and kids' TV was restricted to lunch-time, tea-time and Saturday mornings. This was clearly to the benefit of parents, giving them peace to get meals ready during the week and to pretend to be sleeping at the weekend. Now, television never stops, there are dozens of channels and kids' TV is only ever seconds away.

That's not to say that my children watch more television than I did as a child, it's simply that most of what I watched ranged from desperate, e.g. the test card, to astonishingly inappropriate, e.g. an Open University lecture on human biology. The problem isn't too much TV, it's that control has been given to the child. By the power of CBeebies, there's no reason for them to put up with boring adult telly. By the power of rewind, there's no reason for them to stay glued to the set and not go disturbing 'sleeping' adults.

Deprived of both TV *and* sex, adults are bound to go slightly crazy. Add to this being constantly bombarded with *Fimbles*, *Tweenies* and *Fireman Sam*, and hallucinations are almost a given. I've found myself dreaming up episodes of *CSI:*

Balamory, *Doctor Who in Toy Town* and *Darth Vader the Builder*. None have ended well. Maybe I should just throw the TV out the window like Super~Mum says...

Actually, that's a little drastic. TV gives kids some of their social identity. I know this because I spent a year in the States as a teenager. There were many times when I felt far away from home but the one that sticks in my head was sitting around in History class discussing shows we'd loved as kids. The Americans were all able to share together and forget their differences. It was as if they were four again. I, however, was more different than before. I'd never seen *Sesame Street* and never cared about Mickey Mouse. They had never heard of *Mr Benn*. There was a new cultural barrier between us.

On the flipside, it turned out that the cutest girl in class had spent a few of her younger years in Britain. We paired off and reminisced about the episode of *Bagpuss* with the chocolate biscuit machine. We bonded. Mutual memories of kids' TV brought friendship and snogging. Kids' TV is good.

Thanks to this experience, I believe that the Teletubbies are in fact the best hope we have for world peace. I know you hate them now but Sam will soon find something else to be fixated with. You will move on to *Pingu*. *Teletubbies*, meanwhile, will continue to be shown all over the world. By adding localised film clips they can infiltrate any nation. There are so many episodes that they will pad out daytime telly forever. No child will entirely escape. In time, these children – our children – will grow up and be in charge.

I imagine a future in which the world is edging towards war and the General Assembly of the United Nations meets for one last attempt to avert disaster. No common ground can be found. Voices rise. Fingers move edgily towards buttons.

Suddenly, Nicole Kidman realises the only way to save the day. (It doesn't have to be Nicole but seeing as I'm imagining…) She races up to the control booth and flicks some switches. BBC children's programming blares out over the public address system.

"Who spilled the tubby custard?" says a well-spoken, male voice and hundreds of interpreters babble out translations.

There is a pause. Then, as one, the ambassadors of the world respond in their native tongues but there is no need to translate. Creed and colour no longer matter. For once, each person understands their brothers and sisters around them with perfect clarity. United, the people of Earth cry out, "It was Po! Po spilled the tubby custard."

Then they give each other a big hug.

From that single moment of shared identity will come new hope. Everybody will have their turn to wear the skirt and there will be tubby toast for everyone...

That's got to be worth a little insanity in the here and now, hasn't it?

Yours in a woman's world,

Ed.

Super~Mum's secret

Dear Dave,

Thanks for asking about Scary Karen's parent and toddler group. Things have been going reasonably well the last couple of weeks. Karen has a new friend in the form of a Polish mum whose English is limited to discussing the weather and cricket. Even south of the border this wouldn't normally make for particularly lengthy conversations but Karen is more than happy to take up the slack. The Polish mum sits and listens, her face screwed up in concentration as Karen rabbits away, and I get to eat my chocolate biscuit in peace. If someone has to listen, they might as well be getting free language tuition at the same time, I guess. The other mums seem to have accepted me. Everything is quite relaxed.

It was until this week, anyway.

As you know, I was expecting Julia the Super~Mum to show and I wasn't sure how well she'd get on with the other parents. I was meaning to turn up right at the start and introduce people but we arrived late. Very late. We all slept in and I had to abandon Marie to the TV while I rushed to get the boys ready for school and nursery. Then, when I did get to her, she refused to eat her breakfast and simply yelled, "I not eat yogurt!" whenever I looked in her direction. This continued long after I'd eaten the yogurt myself, washed up the bowl and shown her the fridge was empty.

The next task was trying to get her dressed. She wanted to go to parent and toddler in a nappy and sparkly pink wellies. I suggested she might get cold. "I not eat yogurt," she said defiantly. I realised it was going to be one of those days.

Eventually I managed to persuade her to choose some other clothes. She selected a red and green top, pale blue trousers, rainbow socks, sandals, pink gloves and a Santa hat. She looked like the bargain rack at Oxfam but at least she was dressed. I opened the door and tried to leave. She insisted on going in the buggy. I pointed out that parent and toddler was across the road and that she could walk. She insisted on going in the buggy... and taking her little dog with her.

She doesn't have a dog.

I pointed this out as well. "It purple," she said. She doesn't have a dog, real or stuffed, purple or otherwise. I offered her every other toy I could think of. She took them all... then demanded her dog. I had to draw her one in the end. She held the picture proudly in both hands as I wheeled her over the road, two dozen soft toys jammed into the buggy around her. She grinned broadly, nodded to herself and, with a satisfied sigh, said, "I not eat yogurt."

It was barely worth turning up by the time we made it to the Millennium Centre and wheeled our way down the corridor to the hall. Trevor, the stocky bouncer, was blocking the doorway. "You don't want to go in there," he said. I laughed politely, thinking he was joking, and tried to go in. "No, I'm serious," he said, raising his hand. "You don't want to go in there. She's got Karen and she's..."

Then the singing started.

I'm used to attempts at group singing at parent and toddler. It normally involves one enthusiastic helper belting out some nursery rhymes, a handful of parents mumbling along and a mob of toddlers clubbing each other around the head with tambourines. The overall effect is seldom melodious. No one in their right mind tries anything fancy. The fact that the sound of *Row, Row, Row Your Boat* was drifting out of the hall in cacophonic three-part harmony suggested that a truly insane person was at work within.

"This is all my fault," I said and pushed past Trevor.

Marie looked at him suspiciously as we went in. "I not eat yogurt," she muttered under her breath.

The scene which greeted us was hard to take in all at once.

The first thing to catch my eye was a huge *Twister* board drawn out on the back of some old strips of wallpaper. There were many brightly coloured handprints and footprints on the board and surrounding area. It was as if players had been forced to dip their bare hands and feet in paint before taking part. This was not an encouraging start.

Then I noticed a table laid out with drying papier-mâché artworks. These were a far cry from the models of my youth, which tended to involve slapping sticky newspaper all over an inflated balloon and drawing a face on the result. It was apparent that the children had been encouraged to use their creativity in choosing items to encase in a giant spit-wad. There was a handbag, a toy giraffe, three shoes, the tea urn, a scooter and one very surprised looking cat.

My focus shifted to the refreshment trolley. It was piled high with healthy snacks. None of them had been touched.

Finally, my attention came to rest on an enormous cardboard box which had been placed in the centre of the room. It was decorated to look like a house. A door and windows had been cut into it but these were shut. Gathered round the box was the most miserable group of bedraggled mums and toddlers I have ever seen. They were covered in paint and glue but were being forced to smile and sing. At least one parent was soaking wet and two of the children appeared to have been stuck together. I sensed that no one had received their normal quota of tea or chocolate biscuits.

Julia was standing with her back to me, conducting.

I decided to retreat but, in my panic-stricken terror, I stepped into a tub of paint, tripped over and landed in a tangle of buggy, soft toys and art supplies. The singing stopped. All eyes turned to me. I picked myself up and tried to wipe away the yellow paint that was dripping from my crotch but my hands were already covered in green. I merely created brown.

"You must be Ed," said the woman who had been conducting. She wasn't Julia. She was an older, greyer, more frightening version of Julia. I realised that I was dealing with Super~Mum's mother. Technically, this might define her as Super~Gran but, believe me, there was nothing 'gran-like' about her. Amidst the chaos she had wreaked, she still stood smart and proud, her expensive clothes and make-up untouched. She was the GrandParent of Doom.

There was a pause as the GPD surveyed me with distaste. Behind her, no one dared move apart from Julia's three-year-old, Marcus. He silently flicked up a piece of paper. On it were clumsily scrawled the words, 'save yorselv'.

"Julia is busy teaching the older children calculus, so I decided to bring Marcus along for her. I'm Julia's mother, Eleanor," said the GPD. Her words were polite but her tone gave the impression she viewed me as an aberration of nature. There was another pause. All the eyes remained fixed on me but I couldn't think of a reply. One corner of the GPD's mouth curled upward in the glimmer of an evil sneer. "Thank you for the invitation," she said.

The assembled eyes narrowed. Sympathy for me drained away. There was dark muttering in Polish.

The GPD seemed pleased by this response. "Seeing as you're so late, perhaps you and your daughter would care to give us a rendition of *She'll be Coming Round the Mountain*." She pointed to a central spot in front of the box. I unstrapped Marie and slunk over, already slumped in defeat.

Marie was oblivious. "I not eat yogurt," she said.

"We'll see about that," said the GPD.

It was a nightmare. The singing was soon over but, a few minutes later, I inexplicably found myself dangling a multicoloured Marie over the *Twister* board whilst trying not to topple over on Tess and her son. Admittedly I was covered in paint already and Marie was keen, but how I got there is something of a blur. I think the GPD must employ some form of hypnosis.

"Where's Karen?" I whispered as we all reached for a yellow.

Tess nodded towards the centre of the room.

"She put Karen in a box? How did she get Karen in a box?"

"She got us to do it," said Tess.

"YOU put Karen in a box?"

"Don't have a go at me. You've only been here five minutes and you're using your daughter as a paint brush. Think what the crazy witch would have you doing if you'd been here an hour. She thought the way Karen was feeding her baby was indecent and, I don't know, it just kind of happened."

"But why did Karen let you...?" My voiced trailed off as I looked about. The devastation in the hall was complete. I would have given good money to have been able to hide from it inside a cardboard box. Worryingly, even a cardboard box with Scary Karen already inside seemed quite attractive. I wondered if the GPD took Visa.

Time dragged on. We painted. We stuck. Eleanor put a straw in some natural yogurt and tricked Marie into drinking it. The girl was almost finished before she worked out what it was. She burst into tears. "I not eat yogurt," she whimpered. The GPD snorted contemptuously at us both and then walked off.

"It's time to go but no one's eaten their snacks," she announced shortly afterwards. "Eat them now or take them with you. They are baked from my own recipe and extremely nutritious." Then she made her error. "What will your husbands say if you don't feed your children?"

Obviously this annoyed me for various reasons but Karen is single and half of her friends are divorced. Most of the rest manage to raise their children despite their husbands' intervention, not because of it. The temperature in the room plummeted several degrees.

"When I was bringing up my children..." continued the GPD, unaware of her mistake.

"Enough!" The cardboard box burst asunder and a towering figure emerged, her hair dyed stiff and yellow with paint, her body stained blue, a baby still clamped to her vast, undulating chest. Scary Karen was transformed into something terrifying – a Pictish queen ready for war. She looked at the gaggle of toddlers huddled by the buggies. They were messy, tired and desperately in need of caffeine and sugar. She pointed at the GPD. "Kill!" she said.

They didn't need persuading. They surged forward, ready to batter her senseless with papier-mâché piñatas and then paint her orange. Luckily for her, Trevor rushed in and held them back with a table. "I think you'd better leave," he said.

"Well, I've never..." Eleanor began but there was a tap on her leg. "What is it?" she said, turning to see who was behind her.

"I not eat yogurt," said Marie with satisfaction and tipped a bowl of the stuff over the GPD's immaculate shoe.

Victory was complete. The GPD grabbed her grandson's hand and marched squelchily away, huffing to herself. Everyone cheered.

I went and collected Lewis from nursery and then came back to help clear up – I needed to earn a little forgiveness. Later, I made Julia a cake and took it round to give her sympathy. It turns out that her mum lives a couple of streets away and has nothing much else to do except come and help with the kids. This explains a great deal. We talked, she cried, the kids ran riot and we ate the cake. I think we'll get on better now.

After that, I had to go to the shops and buy some yogurt. Marie really wanted some.

Hope things aren't as crazy for you. How's Liz doing?

Yours in a woman's world,

Ed.

A new dawn

Dear Dave,

Happy Easter!

I had planned on writing about this being a special Easter for me since things have been going pretty well lately: I've had several months of decent sleep. This correspondence has given me a sense of purpose outside of direct parental action. The days are getting longer. An end to seven years of nappies looks like a possibility. Sunday is here. The stone has been rolled away from the entrance to the tomb. Death is defeated. God is with us! It all feels like a new beginning...

That's what I'd been planning to write, anyway. Then I caught a stinking cold, the kids caught it too, potty training Marie led to a household sock shortage and I felt so tired that I dozed off in a soft-play. I leant against a foam shape and rested my eyes for a moment. The next I knew, I was dreaming of a tortured world of primary colours where small children roam free and there is an ever-present danger of drowning in a pit full of plastic balls. I awoke to a reality that was very similar, except a five-year-old that I had never seen before was barking at me in a Germanic language and prodding me with an enormous padded snail. For one hazy, flu-filled moment I thought I had fallen into a psychology experiment, a foreign arts film or, worst-case scenario, a painting by Edvard Munch. It wasn't good. I rounded up my children and headed home.

Since then, I've been muddling along as best I can until I'm well, looking to get through each day without my daughter leaking too much.

Marie gives me various indicators that everything is not going entirely to plan:

- She points out the obvious. "Your socks wet, Daddy!"

• She exclaims, "Pee!" as if wondering where it came from and what it's doing in her socks.

• She lets out an, "Oh, no," giving the impression she's forgotten to pay her gas bill this month. Or remembered that she has no clean socks left.

• She mutters, "I go to toilet. I not go in shower." This thought is, of course, akin to shutting the stable door after the horse has urinated (in its socks).

• She smiles to herself and then wiggles her bottom as if settling down into a nice warm cushion. *Mmmmmm. Squishy...* (Doesn't require fresh socks, at least.)

• She points at the pee streaming out her shoes.

It's a long time since a toxic spill around the house was a disaster (or even particularly unpleasant) but cleaning up is an effort I could do without when I'm ill. Quite often when I tell people that I'm a housedad, they ask me something along the lines of, "So you enjoy that then?"

There's pressure to justify my existence by saying, "Yes, it's fantastic. It's a fulfilling roller-coaster ride of discovery, challenge, fun and hugs. I'd recommend it to anyone." To say anything else might be to confirm their suspicion that a stay at home dad is against all the laws of God and man. To suggest that children can be ungrateful, hard work and irritating can cause shock and outrage. The truth is, though, that there are days in any job when things could be better. Being ill, dealing with ill children through the night and then trying to hold it all together during the day isn't challenging – it's exhausting.

That said, the trauma should be over quickly this time. A day or two and we'll all be well. Another week or so and Marie will have the idea. Then the changing unit can go and there'll be room for me to have a desk again – somewhere for me to sneak off to in order to write, surf and play *Tomb Raider*. Hurrah!

There have been times in the past few years, however, when it has seemed the cloud would never pass. It was like the despair of a perpetual Good Friday. I went months at a time without a proper night of sleep. I had to cope with a wife with post-natal depression. I had to deal with depression myself. I couldn't see an end to it. Only trusting to God that there would be an end, kept me getting out of bed.

Being a housedad *is* fantastic. It *is* a fulfilling roller-coaster ride of discovery, challenge, fun and hugs. But I'd never recommend it to everyone. Being a dad, never mind a housedad, can be tough. We have to be prepared to admit that, to talk to those around us and to get support when we need it. Just knowing we're not alone can be a great help. Take care of yourself, OK?

All things considered, and fleeting set-backs aside, this is still a special Easter for me. The issues I face as a parent may well become more difficult as the kids get older but a lot of the hard graft is past. (Oh goodness, decent sleep makes so much difference!) I'll get more and more time and space to myself. I'll have some energy to spare. I might even have dry socks. Wouldn't that be great?

All the best to the family.

Yours in a woman's world,

Ed.

Useless Dad

Dear Dave,

I met a Useless Dad yesterday.

You can usually tell them by the air of bafflement surrounding them but there are often other giveaway signs:

- They think three minutes is a long time for a baby to have been crying.

- They are convinced that their partner has magical baby-whispering powers and so looking after children is easier for her.

- They try and read the paper at parent and toddler and have plans to work from home later.

- The baby strapped to their front is upside down and kicking them in the face.

I don't mean novice dads here; I mean perfectly capable men who see having a family as an infestation of little people that the wife deals with. It's not that they don't like kids, it's that they're not entirely aware of them. The other week, I was talking to a mum with two children at parent and toddler (not Scary Karen's one, the one with the great biscuits but hard seats). Her eldest was three years old but she'd only left her husband in charge on his own for a couple of hours ever. "When I came back," she said, "the baby hadn't been changed or fed and my daughter had drawn all over herself with felt-tips. I'm never leaving him alone with them again."

"So you're going to do all the work while he sits around drinking beer?" I replied. "Are you sure that wasn't his plan all along?"

Realisation dawned. "I never thought of that," she said.

"Maybe you should give him a bit of training."

She pursed her lips as if contemplating the possibilities. "Maybe I should," she said in the manner of an evil genius holding a cute bunny and a pair of electrodes, and smiled to herself.

I slipped away to find a chocolate digestive, knowing my work there was done.

Anyway, I was at the same parent and toddler yesterday and saw a guy looking uncomfortable and I went over to chat with him. He was perched on the edge of his chair, holding a six-month-old as if the kid was about to explode. Every so often, he peered nervously across at the drawing table; the rest of the time he looked around shiftily, trying not to make eye-contact with anyone breast-feeding.

"Hi there," I said. "Have you been here before?"

"No. My wife told me to take the morning off work while she goes for a massage."

"Wow," I said, not quite sure where my sympathy lay.

"That's the second time since Easter she's just gone off and dumped the kids on me."

"Wow..." I repeated, suspecting my sympathy had sloped off to the gym for a good rub down. "That's, like, nearly once a week."

"I know. She never did this before. Then she was talking to this guy she met somewhere and decided I should 'take more of an active role'. She said the guy looks after his kids all the time, so *I* should be able to manage it now and then. Calls himself a homedad or something. Can you imagine?"

"I'll keep an eye out for him," I said. The baby was starting to seem familiar and I noticed that a three-year-old girl at the drawing table was busy on a kaleidoscope of felt-tip butterflies that already stretched most of the way up her arm.

"Do you know how to stop this baby crying?" said Useless Dad. "He's been doing it for five minutes and I can't get him to be quiet. He's never like this for Deborah. It's probably the smell. Something smells terrible in here."

I nodded. "Yeah, kind of like an unchanged nappy."

I heard the refreshments being set out and I made to slip away but then I noticed the pleading look on the baby's face. It was the look of a small child who has been screaming to no avail for a while and is in desperate need of a translator (or a t-shirt with the slogan 'I'm sitting in poo, you idiot!').

I sat back down. "You might want to check your son," I said to Useless Dad.

"What?"

"His nappy." The man looked blank. "You know, you might want to check it."

"Oh! Right..." He investigated with slightly less care than was wise and then swore. "Where did that come from?" I stayed quiet, hoping it was a rhetorical question, and he continued, "It was only an hour ago that Deborah changed him. What am I going to do now?"

This appeared *not* to be a rhetorical question. I glanced over to check on Marie. She was dressed up as Bob the Builder and was happily playing with a stuffed toy of Postman Pat, trying hard to saw him in half. I sighed. I could have done with an emergency to be called away to. "Do you want me to talk you through it?" I said reluctantly.

And I really had to. He opened the changing bag like he had no idea what was inside and things went downhill after that. He got there in the end but I had to resist the urge to intervene on several occasions.

"I take it you've changed a few nappies then," said Useless Dad when we were done.

"One or two," I said and decided to come clean. "My wife goes out to work and I stay home and look after the kids."

"Oh, really?" he said, not quite getting it. "I'd rather have a rest at the weekend than babysit. Deborah's thinking of doing something a few hours a week but I'm trying to talk her out of it. It's not like we need the money and, honestly, she's much better with the kids than I am. Doesn't really seem worth it."

"No, my wife works full-time," I said but it was like he couldn't hear me and then he had to rush home. He had some work he wanted to get done. He packed up his stuff and strapped on his baby-carrier.

"That's upside down," I said.

"I know," he said nasally, his son's foot wedged up his right nostril. Then he grabbed Butterfly Girl and dragged her out the door. I shook my head and made my way towards the refreshments.

Marie was still putting her tools to good use as I went past. "I hammer Postman Pat to table," she said.

"Good girl," I replied and hurried to get my tea before the mugs ran out.

The whole experience was quite an eye-opener. Mums give me a huge amount of credit for being a stay at home dad but I only do as much as they do. If they're dealing with partners anything like Useless Dad, I'm doing a darn sight less. Sarah is more than willing to help look after the kids when she's not at work and it sounds like your Liz is the same. They may not know exactly where the pastry cutters are kept or which day the bins go out but they can be trusted to look after the kids for entire days at a time. They don't grudge it either.

We should probably appreciate them more. I'll keep reminding you, if you keep reminding me. Deal?

Yours in a woman's world,

Ed.

In memory of the changing unit

Dear Dave,

The changing unit has gone.

No, I'm sorry, you're going to have to be more impressed than that. I'll write it again. The changing unit has gone. I hope you clapped politely that time. (Count yourself lucky – if you were American, I would have to insist on you punching the air while making a loud whooping sound.)

A chapter has ended. I've been changing nappies on that unit almost every day for seven years. That's a lot of nappies. Three children for two and a half years each. Assuming an average of six nappies a day per child, that's over 16,000 nappies. That's a lot of nappies. OK, I didn't change all of them, but I changed a good load of them. At least 12,000, I'd say. That's still a lot of nappies.

Thinking back, it seems like only yesterday I first placed Fraser on that changing unit and gingerly investigated the small swamp he had wrapped round his nether-regions. So many memories! How about the time I was in the middle of dealing with him and heard a tinkling noise six feet away on the other side of the room but spent several seconds wondering like an idiot what it might be? Or the time he peed in his own ear (and he cried when I laughed)? Or the time Lewis spewed forth copious liquid evil from his backside that went everywhere (and he laughed when I cried)?

Ah, happy days...

You've probably blanked many of the messiest moments of your own experience from your mind but, with a baby on the way, they're all going to come back to you pretty soon. I remember, in the early months of being a new parent, talking a great deal about the contents of nappies. Fraser would produce and then Sarah and I (and any lucky visitors) would gather round and peer closely, trying to discern his health from the splatter. It was like reading tea leaves. ('Ah, yes, I see much tribulation in your future, young man. You will meet a tall, dark stranger. Then you will poo on him.')

Second time around, things are much more routine. You know what to expect.

The first week is the worst. For some reason, babies come supplied full of tar which they exude through their bottoms for several days. What's with that? Then comes fudge sauce, followed by chicken tikka masala. It eventually settles down to something fairly normal on a good day and end-of-term stew on a bad one.

End-of-term stew is the final meal made by hard-up students before going home for the holidays. Every flatmate clears out their cupboard and bungs the remaining contents into one big pot. Typical ingredients include peas, corn, Shredded Wheat, a hairclip, four crushed breadsticks, half a sausage, twenty-three pence in loose change and some raisins. Grated seaweed is added for that extra special aroma and then the whole lot is boiled up in thick gravy. Strangely, the results are less than appetising and the students sneak round to my house and dispose of the slimy mess down the back of a nappy. This is why my children have often been seen waddling around with surprised looks on their faces just before Christmas and Easter.

Well, that's all behind me now. There will still be accidents to be dealt with and I daresay I'll be wiping Marie's bottom for another couple of years but, hopefully, my days of wrestling a stinky toddler are over. There'll be no more need for nursery rhymes to stop them wailing and kicking. (It used to be I could get the kids to calm down by singing to them. Now the only thing which works is promising to stop singing.) We're moving on...

A friend and his mate came round today to take the changing unit away. It has a good home to go to but I found myself oddly sad to see it leave. They lifted it up, revealing dents worn in the carpet, and a tear welled in my eye. It had served me faithfully and seen me through many unfortunate crises. As they carried it out the door, I patted it good-bye and watched it taken from my life forever.

Then I went and washed my hands.
Twice.
Yours in a woman's world,
Ed.

Every child is different

Dear Dave,

Already? Are you sure? I mean, I guess you'd know but... Yeah, thinking about, I suppose you *are* halfway to another child but where's the time gone? Goodness. You're probably thinking the same thing. No wonder you're sounding a little panicked. Still, you'll probably find coping with two easier than you're expecting. You've had plenty of practice with everything like nappies and baths and it won't take long to get slick again.

That said, not to worry you or anything, but...

Every child is different.

Chances are, some of the things that went smoothly first time round will be more of a bumpy ride this time.

Fraser had terrible trouble sleeping and it got to the point where I had to share the spare bed with him and cuddle him most of the night. Since it was a single bed and neither of us is small, I tended to wake up tired and hunched and then lurch around the house like Quasimodo, gibbering about coffee. After a year of that, it was a case of either leaving him to scream himself to sleep or constructing my own bell tower and just going with the whole tormented mutant look. Thankfully, a couple of nights of hard hearts and stubborn wills sorted things and he's gone to bed fine ever since.

After our experiences with Fraser, we were keen to do better with Lewis. He got hankies to clutch for comfort (replaceable and easily portable!), he wasn't allowed to sleep so much during the day, we gave him tooth powder and he was left to get himself to sleep from an earlier age. The plan paid off. He slept twelve hours a night from a year. He didn't sleep at all during the day by that point but I didn't care – we had evenings to ourselves and I'd almost entirely lost the desire to go bell-ringing. We smugly believed that we knew what we were doing.

Then Marie arrived.

She never slept well to start with but teething was disastrous. She wouldn't go to bed until ten or eleven at night and then often woke up and cried for a couple of hours at three in the morning *and then* got up at eight (if not before). I dreamed of the days when I felt as agile as a hunchback. My limbs seized up and I took on the twisted appearance of a gargoyle. I sprinkled coffee directly onto my Sugar Puffs.

Nothing worked. She had muslin cloths to cuddle but she merely grew to need them *and* me to get to sleep. She spat out Calpol. I managed to get the tooth powder in her once but only by tipping it out of the sachet and putting it on a spoon. That took her by surprise. The next time, she saw it coming and blew it all in my face. I couldn't cut down on her daytime sleeping because, well, it wasn't like she ever really slept then either.

There was no alternative but to go for the screaming again. It was desperate, but we were pretty sure it would work...

On the first night, I had to leave Fraser to yell in the cot for nearly five hours before he gave up and went to sleep. (Going in to check on him made things worse, by the way.) Marie only lasted a minute and half before becoming so upset that she was copiously sick all over herself, her sheets and the carpet. This happened every time we tried. It was more work than cuddling her to sleep. We gave up.

My skin turned hard and grey. If I stood still outside for too long then pigeons started to nest in my hair. Passing stonemasons attempted to kidnap me and stick me to a church.

It was only when she was over two and able to be reasoned with that we had any success. One night, when she'd been up for hours, I put her in her bed, told her to go to sleep and then stayed in the room with her. Every time she gagged, I told her to calm down. Three hours later, it was time to get up, but at least she hadn't vomited. After a few nights of doing this at bedtime and whenever she woke up during the night, she got the idea.

Life's been much easier since. I can now walk without creaking. Water no longer pours out my mouth when it rains.

We'll know what to do next time...

(Yeah, right.)

Keep your wits about you. Try different things. Get some sleep now.

Yours in a woman's world,

Ed.

I spoke too soon

Dear Dave,

As I sit here, with my eyes propped open with lollipop sticks, I realise that my previous correspondence about sleep was tempting fate. Either that, or Marie's learnt to read my emails and she felt like having a laugh.

I've been awake for thirty-six hours now.

If this turns into gibberish then you'll know why.

Marie has a cough and we gave her some medicine before bed last night but she sicked it up with some phlegm pretty quickly, so it probably didn't do much good. She tossed and turned for a while, then came down to sit on the sofa and watch some *Little Mermaid* before going back to bed. (She thinks of me as King Triton now, which I suppose is a step up from the BFG at least.) All was quiet for an hour or so and then she woke up and demanded a cuddle. She got a cuddle. Five minutes later she screamed, "I want cuddle from mummy too!" She got that. Sarah and I went to bed.

Twenty minutes later. "I got cough. You make me better." I hadn't got to sleep, so I went through and gave her another cuddle before she woke Lewis in the bed next to her. Then I went back to bed myself.

Fifteen minutes later. "I need my water." I'd almost got to sleep. I went back through and reminded her where her bedside table was (i.e. beside her bed), waited for her to have a drink, tucked her back in and returned to bed.

Ten minutes later. "You fix it. Daddy! You fix it, Daddy!" This is code for, 'I'm lost in my duvet.' I went through and rescued her.

Another fifteen minutes. "Blow my nose!"

Two minutes. "You blow my nose again!"

Just enough time for me to get back into bed. "I need water."

Seventeen minutes. "I need cuddle!"

Three minutes. "You fix it!"

And so it went on... Bear in mind we had elderly relatives staying over last night. They were in our bed and Sarah and I were on the sofa-bed. *On a different floor* from Marie. Just getting to her became an effort as the night wore on. I think I might have nearly dozed off at about twenty past four. Nearly.

"I need water!"

Twelve minutes. "I need water!"

Three minutes. "I need water!"

Her shouting had become louder and screechier by this time, to the point where she sounded like a Dalek. I scurried through, grunting like a member of an oppressed species. This had no effect on the volume or pitch of her voice. "I need water," she shrieked in my face. I moved her cup the fourteen and a half inches from her bedside table to her hand. She took the tiniest of sips and then screamed, "You put it back now!"

I put it back but told her she could get it herself from then on. She might have been tired and sick but I suspected she was also taking advantage. I shouted myself. She whimpered and agreed.

Five minutes later. "I need toilet..."

Give her credit – short of being sick, that was the only plea I couldn't ignore. It also took far longer to deal with than any of her previous problems. She's clever, that one.

Ten minutes. "Blow my nose." I was at least glad that she wasn't asking for the toilet again.

Two minutes. "I need toilet again!"

Argh...

Things never improved. At half past six, I gave up and had a shower. Unsurprisingly, even this had a small intermission in which I had to drip into her room and pick a cuddly toy up off the floor. I don't know whether it fell or she threw it there. Either way, I wasn't impressed. I shivered my way back to the bathroom and finished 'getting up'.

Marie promptly stayed asleep for an entire hour and a half.

I sprinkled some Sugar Puffs on top of a bowl full of coffee granules and had my breakfast while quietly reading gaming news on the computer. Then the boys got up and it was time for the day to begin...

Somehow Lewis had slept through everything. On the one hand, this was fortunate. On the other, we may need to get a louder smoke alarm.

I'm quite tired now. I got through the day surprisingly smoothly. I wasn't much of a conversationalist but that's true most of the time. I was somewhat crotchety but, again, that's not hugely unusual. I wasn't called upon to make any life-changing decisions, which was probably lucky. Sarah came home early to help out, which was lovely. We survived.

Now it's time for some sleep. I think Marie's settled tonight. I'm just holding off for a few minutes to make sure, before going to bed.

(I hope fate didn't hear that.)

Yours in a woman's world,

Ed.

PS Waited until morning before sending this. We all slept through but I appear to have woken with the mental and physical capabilities of a slug. The DVD player may be doing a large portion of the parenting today...

Imagination

Dear Dave,

Thanks for the sympathy over the lack of sleep. Things have been OK the last couple of days but Marie's kicking up much more of a fuss at bedtime than she used to. I can only assume having me at her beck and call all night gave her a taste for power. Speaking of which, she was wanting me to vote for her in the Scottish elections. She's decided she's in the Pink Party. This is kind of like the Green Party but, rather than pushing for a greener planet, the Pink Party's goal is much, well... pinker. I fancy if they ever came to power, then the whole world would resemble the girls' aisle of Toys'R'Us (except maybe with a bit more glitter, if that's possible...)

She's only two-and-a-half and she's inventing political parties! You were asking for more examples of how every child is different and I have to say that if there is one thing which varies wildly between my children it's their level of imagination.

Oddly, this is best exemplified by their attitude towards LEGO.

Everyone knows the entire point of having children is to be able to buy cool toys while looking like an ace dad rather than a hopeless loser geek. (Or is that just me?) I've been biding my time for what seems like an age now, waiting to purchase an enormous programmable robot, but it's beginning to look like none of my kids could actually care less about LEGO. All for differing reasons, of course, but all due to the bounds of their imaginations:

To Fraser, a pile of bricks is just a pile of bricks. He's also a tad lazy, so if he wanted a castle, he'd want it ready assembled and to come with plenty of interesting levers and stuff. If he got it, he'd play with it for five minutes, check how it all worked and then go off and play a computer game. He doesn't have the imagination to make up stories about some bricks. It's not anything to him – it's just LEGO. Prospective careers: Engineer, Traffic Warden, Middle Manager.

To Lewis, a pile of bricks is a pile of bricks but he can be persuaded to stick a few together and make-believe they're a castle or a pyramid. This is all well and good, but he has slightly too much imagination to see the point of LEGO. He can make a car from three small bricks and a wheel. The tiniest semblance of reality will do – he doesn't need a big tub full of weird and wacky specialist parts. (Drat.) Prospective careers: Architect, Journalist, Estate Agent.

To Marie, a pile of bricks could be anything from a selection of apples to a washing-machine. The problem is, if you can stretch reality that far, who needs bricks? (Apart from to weigh down your pockets to stop you floating away.) Prospective careers: Advertising Creative, Public Relations Officer, Space Cadet.

We knew Lewis had a strong imagination from an early age. When he was two, he was constantly making us all imaginary cups of tea (without the aid of plastic cups or anything). One day, Fraser got fed up with the silly make-believe nonsense, however, and decided to play Lewis at his own game. Fraser held out his imaginary cup at arm's length and slowly tipped the imaginary contents over the floor. Lewis burst into tears. He was distraught at all the work he'd have to do cleaning up the mess...

That's a slightly scary amount of imagination. Marie has surpassed him, though. Sarah asked Marie's opinion on a couple of pairs of trousers she was trying on in a shop the other day. On seeing the first pair, Marie shook her head. "They snakes eating your legs. You not wear them." On viewing the second, she said, "No, they have a chicken in them." On the way home in the buggy, she suddenly commented, "The wind turn me into a cat... I not go miaow."

When Marie's a little older, I can see her and Fraser having big arguments while staring at the sky:

Marie: It's a dragon.
Fraser: It's a cloud.
Marie: It looks like a dragon.

Fraser: But it's a cloud.
Marie: What about that one? It's a deep fat fryer!
Fraser: It's a cloud.
Marie: That one's a spaceship. With aliens. And lobsters.
Fraser: That's a cloud, too.
Marie: Look! A pirate made of sausages!
Fraser: IT'S... A... CLOUD!
Marie: He's playing hop-scotch.
Fraser (finally giving in): Oh all right, and that one's a sheep.
Marie: No, *that's* a cloud.

I may have to intervene in order to avoid bloodshed...
Yours in a woman's world,
Ed.

Games night

Dear Dave,

I don't get out much. That's partly because it's an effort finding a babysitter and partly because, by the time the kids are in bed, I'm too tired to leave the house. Then again, it's not like I went out much before we had kids. I've always preferred to settle down in front of the TV anyway. Having kids is merely a handy excuse to surround the TV with gadgets.

This being the case, my social life is somewhat limited but, every so often, a couple of friends, Mike and Rob, come round to play computer games and we blast each other to pieces while failing to talk about anything very significant. Mike's the minister at our church. He's around fifty and has two kids but they've left home. Rob works in the IT department at LBO. I did some of his training and he now has my old job, meaning I feel both sorry for him and somewhat responsible. He's not quite thirty yet.

Sarah has been having to work late again so I decided to organise one of these bloke's nights for the other evening while she was out. Rob arrived just after the children were in bed and made straight for the beer. I asked him how his week was going and he launched into the details of a technical problem he was having trouble with. Vaguely familiar acronyms and jargon spewed forth from his mouth for several minutes. I nodded and smiled. It was like listening to Fraser witter on about Pokémon but I cared slightly less. I drank my own beer and then suggested to Rob that he replace the flux capacitor and then reverse the polarity of the neutron flow. He wasn't amused.

Mike arrived. I asked him how his week was going. He shook his head. "Three funerals and a finance meeting," he said gruffly. "Let's shoot things."

I handed him a beer and ushered them both up to the lounge. "Watch out over there," I said, pointing to a discoloured section of carpet. "There's a damp patch." Rob began edging nervously round it. I rolled my eyes. "Don't worry – it's not radioactive or anything." He didn't seem reassured but found his way to a seat and we launched into a game on the PlayStation. (We can't play the Wii anymore because Mike's been banned for breaking light fittings on two separate occasions. He kept taking it all a tad too seriously.)

Everything went as normal for some time: we discussed the weather and football, we drank beer, we moaned about the news and, every so often, someone got shot. After a while, however, there was a lull and Rob took his chance to change the subject in an unexpected direction.

"So what's being a housedad like?" he asked.

For the past seven years, Rob has been doing his best to ignore the fact that I'm a full-time parent. It's like I'm on an indefinite holiday and he's always hopeful I'll be back at work on Monday. The closest he'd previously come to expressing interest was to say, without a hint of irony, 'It must be nice to sit at home all day eating biscuits.'

I looked at him in astonishment.

Showing greater presence of mind, Mike took advantage of the distraction and fragged me at close range with a shotgun before asking, "Blue line, then?"

"Er, yeah," said Rob, turning to him in surprise. "How did you...?"

Mike shot him in the head with a missile-launcher. "Professional hunch," he said. "Are you still playing, Ed?"

"What?" I'd re-spawned and was standing around waiting for ballistic death to come find me. Strangely, I was no longer looking through my character's eyes but I could see him from a third-person perspective and he was getting larger.

Then I realised I was looking at Mike's corner of the screen.

It was my turn to eat an explosion. "Would you stop that?" I said.

"You can't talk and shoot at the same time?"

"Not when a friend is sharing about how his life has changed forever."

"What?" said Rob. "What do you mean my life has...?" I shoved an enormous gun between his shoulder-blades and pulled the trigger. "Hey!"

"So..." Mike let the pause linger as Rob's character re-appeared close at hand. Sensing what was coming, I charged over to get in range. Nonchalantly, Mike said, "Are you going to get married then?"

Rob stammered. "Er..." Mike and I both let rip at what seemed like the same moment and a hail of bullets turned Rob into sushi. To my consternation, Mike was credited with the kill.

"That's not fair," I grumbled, banging the controller against my head in frustration. "And neither's that," I added as he shot *me* as well. "I'm annoyed now. I'm going to hunt you down and batter you to death with that assault rifle."

"I want to see you try... What were you saying, Rob?"

"Er..." said Rob. "I hadn't really thought about getting married. I'm not sure I'm ready for that."

"What do you mean?" said Mike.

"It's kind of a commitment."

I snorted. "You've bought a house together, you live together, you sleep together, you're going to have a baby together. You've merged your CD collections! Exactly how much more of a commitment do you think getting married would be?"

"There's a little more to being married than that," said Rob defensively.

"I don't know..." I said and went postal with a flame-thrower. "There's a public declaration that you're going to make things last but there's actually quite a lot *less* denial."

"How do I know it's going to last?" said Rob, turning crispy.

"If the two of you decide that it's going to last and always work to achieve that, then there's a good chance that it *will* last," said Mike.

"It's got to be worth a go, hasn't it?" I added. "Let's face it, you're married already, apart from the legal safe-guards in case it doesn't last. What have you got to lose?"

"I don't want to rush into anything," said Rob, running round a corner into proximity with a proximity mine I'd left lying around. He swore. He blew up.

I laughed for at least two good reasons. "At the point you two got a mortgage together, you were still playing games with a wired controller – that's several years and an entire console generation ago! Think how long that's been. Glaciers get together and laugh at how slowly you move."

"Well," he muttered, "there's the expense..."

"I'll waive my fee," said Mike.

"Sarah still has her dress," I said. "Wouldn't take much to make it fit Kate."

Mike nodded. "And the Millennium Centre is cheap to hire."

"I'll do the catering," I said. "I've had plenty of practice with birthday parties. Cocktail sausages and Hula Hoops for everyone. Fraser and Lewis can get a production line of cheese sandwiches going. Marie can help decorate the cake. You don't mind bright pink icing peppered with chocolate buttons and fingerprints do you?" Rob scowled at me. "What? It'd be a talking point."

Mike calmly sniped us both. "I think what Ed's trying to say is that the celebration doesn't have to be expensive and shouldn't stand in the way of the getting married part."

"Maybe... You still haven't answered my question, Ed. What's it like being a housedad?"

I thought for a moment. Mike took the opportunity to smack me about with a brick. "Well," I said, re-spawning faraway, "the hours are long, the holidays are rubbish, the pay's a joke and there's heavy exposure to toxic biological waste. On the plus side, there's plenty of fresh air and exercise, a steady supply of hugs, relatively little stress, strong job satisfaction and an army of amusing minions. You also get to play *Hungry Hippos* and call it work."

Rob perked up. "Really?"

"Yep," I grinned. "And *Mario Kart*."

He glanced sideways at me. "Really!?"

"Yep."

He looked suddenly suspicious. "Is that why you're grinning?"

"No, I'm grinning 'cos I've stuck an explosive mine to your crotch and you haven't noticed."

He had just about enough time to say, "No way!" before his corner of the screen erupted.

I feigned a wince. "That's got to smart."

Time ran out and the game ended. Mike had won by an absolute mile but at least I'd beaten Rob by a point. I did a little victory dance. Unfortunately, I stepped in the wet patch and had to go change my socks.

Rob cheered up a bit at that...

We had some more beer and the conversation returned to normal. It was a good evening. I don't think Rob knows what he's got himself into yet, though. I might let him look through some of these emails, if that's OK with you?

Hope you're well and staying sane. Marie's convinced that you live in this computer. Have you got any photos of you and the family I can show her?

Yours in a woman's world,

Ed.

Marie update

Dear Dave,

Just a quick note to give you an update on Marie:

The potty training is going pretty well now. We haven't had any major disasters in a while. Her sleeping's back to normal too, apart from the need to 'argue' with Lewis every night before nodding off. They lie there counting loudly at each other until one of them needs the toilet.

As for her imagination:

Sarah asked her the other day what little girls grow up to be. She was hoping for the answer, 'Ladies'. Quick as a flash, Marie answered, 'Cats'. Intrigued by this on-going feline fascination, Sarah asked her what little boys grow up to be. Marie thought about it for a few seconds and then, with great satisfaction, answered, 'Lemons'.

Yours in a woman's world,

Ed.

1966 and all that

Dear Dave,

I quite understand the trauma you're going through trying to choose a nursery for Sam. There are so many things to consider: the adult/child ratio, the quality of the equipment and facilities (both inside and outside), the curriculum, the teaching ethos, the discipline code, the evaluation report, the nutritional content of snacks, the colour of the walls and the level of drugs slipped into the milk. We gave up and went for the one at the end of our road. Seems nice enough.

Marie can start when she's three, so I finally got round to registering her the other day. It didn't take long – they copied most of the information from the boys' records. I still had to tell them her nationality, though, and this was harder than you might think. I had three viable options – Scottish, British or English. All were serious possibilities and I tried to peek at the school secretary's monitor in order to see what I'd said for Lewis. I hoped I hadn't panicked and told them he was Swiss. Deftly swivelling her screen away from my prying eyes, the secretary looked at me with an amiable smile plainly reserved for the kind of simpleton who doesn't even know the nationality of their own child.

I tried to think fast. It should have been easy – she was born in Scotland, she lives in Scotland, her mum is from Scotland. There's a pattern there. The only thing is, *I'm* not from Scotland. I'm from the middle of a blackcurrant field in Norfolk and I'm as English as the day is long. Admittedly, I used to describe myself as British but then I moved to Scotland and discovered that in some dialects of Scots this just means, 'I'm English but I want your oil and somewhere to keep my nuclear missiles.'

It doesn't go well.

British would probably have done for an answer in this context but it felt wrong. It would have been like calling myself European – specific enough if I was in rural China but stupidly vague in central Edinburgh. Britain doesn't have a football team. And, realistically, that was what I was choosing – her national identity, her sense of belonging and her level of expectation for progression to the knockout stages.

I have to concede that I found it mystifying when I first moved up here that the Scots have so many fond memories of England losing to Germany in penalty shoot-outs. After all, most English fans are happy to wish the Scotland team success and even to support them if England are already knocked out. Now I understand that this is patronising and annoying. Imagine how Manchester City fans would feel if they won the league and a whole load of United fans turned up to join in the celebrations. Or how Canadians would feel if Americans started taking credit for Celine Dion.

Not pretty, is it?

I've lived here long enough that I'm not entirely sure who I would support if England and Scotland played each other. Probably England... but if they won the World Cup then it would be the main headline on *The Six O'clock News* for at least a week. That would do more for the cause of Scottish independence than almost anything. I'd probably vote for the Nationalists myself if it meant I didn't have to hear about 1966 and 20XX ever again. Independence would be expensive, though. It would be far cheaper holding compulsory classes for English people on how not to irritate their neighbours. Can't see that happening, however, and it would be a shame to break up the Union over football.

As I stood at the secretary's desk, all these thoughts flashed through my mind and I realised that Scotland could do with all the support it can get. An extra cheer here or there might make all the difference. "Scottish," I said.

The secretary nodded. "Wise choice," she said and rubber stamped Marie's forehead with a Saltire. The deed was done.

Of course, you won't have this problem. Unless Liz is French. Then maybe you'd have something of an idea of where I'm coming from. If England and Scotland ever do meet in a World Cup match I'll probably just dig myself a hole in the back yard and hide in it until the entire thing is over, slapping myself occasionally with a wet haddock in an act of ritual penitence for being born the wrong side of the border.

That's what I normally do when the rugby's on.

Good luck with the nursery hunt. Have you started looking into secondary schools yet?

Yours in a woman's world,

Ed.

Worlds collide

Dear Dave,

I'm a dead man.

Sarah is going to kill me. I'm surprised she hasn't left work early and come home to do it already. Maybe she's stopped off at B&Q to buy some bladed garden equipment... Or a nail-gun... Seriously, once I've finished writing this I'm throwing a change of underwear and all the gadgets I can carry into a suitcase and heading for Bolivia. She'll never find me there.

And, to think, the day started so promisingly... I was at parent and toddler and everything was going fine. Then I ended up next to Useless Dad at biscuit time again. Scary Karen was sitting across from us and I waved but she was too busy telling Stefania the details of her colonoscopy to notice.

Useless Dad looked up from his newspaper. "Your wife sent you here again as well?" His baby son was lying at his feet, a rattle having rolled just out of reach. I picked it up and gave it back. The baby smiled and giggled in a transparent attempt to get himself adopted. I could see his three-year-old sister in the distance, filling her shoes with Play-Doh.

I acted dumb. "Yeah, you could say that."

"Deborah threatened to pour away my whisky collection if I didn't take the kids out of the house."

"Really?" I said. I'd met his wife a few times. She'd seemed calm and confident. I was suddenly concerned that having to do pretty much all the child-raising herself had caused her to lose it.

"Yes. This is getting totally out of hand. I'm going to have no end of work to make up. I might only be able to play golf twice this week."

"Really..." She wasn't losing anything. She was taking back what was hers.

Then my day took a rapid downturn.

"My God, what is that woman doing?" said Useless Dad rather loudly. I glanced across to see Karen wapping out one of her enormous bosoms in order to feed her baby.

"Er, that's Sca... er, Karen," I said in a low voice. "She's giving her baby some milk."

No one else seemed to have heard him. I think we would have gotten away with it if Karen's toddler hadn't wandered over to her right then, looking peckish.

"Is that even legal?" squealed Useless Dad as the other undulating meal was wrestled into view and shoved into the waiting boy's mouth.

The conversation around us died. Other parents glared at us. And when I say other parents, I of course mean mums. We were the only men in the room and we were staring goggle-eyed at a breast-feeding woman. Useless Dad was even pointing. This was not the sensitive, enlightened image of fatherhood I have worked hard to cultivate over the years. I reached over and lowered his outstretched finger.

Karen was looking at us with a visage normally reserved for Norse gods who are about to do some smiting. I edged as far away from Useless Dad as I could without falling off my seat. Grinning nervously, I whispered out of the corner of my mouth. "Shouldn't you be leaving? Aren't you going to try working from home?"

He shook his head. "My laptop is still having the vomit removed after last week."

"Oh." I grinned harder and gave Karen a friendly wave. Her countenance only darkened further. Little lightning bolts sparked around her. Everyone was now watching us closely, waiting to see whether we would run or die. Some of them were clearly looking forward to a good smiting.

It was every parent for themselves.

I surreptitiously waved the remaining half of my biscuit at Marie and then gestured extravagantly towards Useless Dad. "New guy, everyone." I couldn't remember his name but it wouldn't have made an impact anyway. I told them what they needed to know. "This is Deborah's husband."

Eyes widened, realisation dawned and understanding swept the hall. Those mums in the know turned to those next to them and began recounting their favourite tales of Useless Dad. Only a handful continued to regard me with suspicion.

Marie ran over and grabbed my half-eaten chocolate digestive. "Thanks. I eat biscuit."

"Good girl. I love you," I whispered so that only she could hear.

"I love you, Daddy!" she shouted back and gave me a big hug.

After that, I was safe. I had an endearing guardian angel sitting on my lap (or a human shield dressed entirely in garish pink, depending on how you want to look at it). There were audible 'Aaawws!' from around the room. The storm passed. Karen finally returned my wave and went back to talking to her Polish friend.

I didn't want to push my luck, however. "We should go now," I said.

"Where to?"

"Er... home?"

"Deborah told me not to come back until lunchtime."

"Why not?"

"She wouldn't say but she'd looked out a leotard, a box of chocolates, the soundtrack to *Pretty Woman*, two cans of paint and some dust covers."

"That doesn't sound good." I would have suggested a trip to the swing park but it was raining. I didn't fancy his chances of surviving a trip to the shops, the library was closed and I didn't want his kids loitering in a damp bus shelter for over an hour. "Er... Want to come round to ours for a bit?"

"Can I check my email?"

"I guess."

"Great. Let's go," he said, suddenly very keen.

"The girls should get on well."

"What? Oh, yeah... Yeah... How fast is your broadband, did you say?"

We wrapped up our various offspring, emptied out their footwear and headed back to the house. Marie led her new friend off to destroy some toys together, Useless Dad logged on and I unearthed an old baby-seat for his sleeping son.

After I'd provided half an hour of free childcare, Useless Dad came through and said, "Your internet connection has stopped working."

"It does that sometimes," I said, kicking the cable I'd just yanked from the router out of sight. "It might be down for a while. Cup of coffee?"

Grudgingly, he followed me through to the kitchen and was somewhat thrown by the confusion of colour. I've put off redecorating by covering all the available wall space with the kids' artwork. He raised his eyebrows at our Nintendo-themed calendar. He perhaps realised that an infestation of children only becomes harder to ignore as they get older.

"What is it you do again?" he asked.

"I look after the children."

"When you're not looking after the children?"

There are many tempting things to say in this kind of situation, such as, 'I'm not telling you my secret identity', 'Sleep' or 'Shh! When they can't see me, they think I don't exist'. All are true but usually take more explaining than is really worthwhile. "No, that *is* my job," I said.

"Oh..." said Useless Dad. "What does your wife do then?"

"She's a marketing analyst."

"Where?"

"LBO." He looked confused and didn't respond. To fill in the awkward silence, I asked, "What is it you do?"

"I'm head of marketing at LBO."

"Oh..." I suddenly recalled Useless Dad's name. It was Steve. Sarah's manager is also called Steve. He's quite useless as well. For there to be two useless managers called Steve in LBO's relatively small marketing department was really quite a coincidence. I mean what were the odds of...

My eye developed a spontaneous twitch. I inhaled sharply, as if someone had stood on my toe. I stifled a whimper. On the list of people not to invite into your home, the wife's evil, misguided boss is pretty near the top, slightly above Dracula and Jabba the Hutt.

"What was your wife's name again?"

"Er..." I decided to lie and said the first name that popped into my head. "Brian?"

I remembered the two reasons why I normally don't lie: a) It's bad and wrong. b) I'm rubbish at it.

"Pardon? Your wife's name is Brian?"

"Erm, it's a pet name I use sometimes. You know, like 'dear' or 'hen' or, erm..." I glanced around the room for inspiration. It was not my day. "Er, or 'Donkey Kong'... Erm, actually her name's Sarah. You probably know her."

He gave the impression of having to think about it but eventually he managed to put all his ducks in a row. He looked over the room with new eyes. Narrowed eyes.

"So Sarah has children then?"

"Yes," I said, biting my tongue. Useless Dad/Manager made the presentation on two of the three occasions Sarah went on maternity leave. On the third occasion, he simply forgot and phoned up after a couple of days to see where she'd got to.

"How many?" he asked.

"Three."

"Three!?" He said it like we were some kind of subversive breeders intent on taking over the world. "Are you sure?"

"Pretty much certain," I said. I took some deep breaths and sat on my hands to stop myself slapping him.

He pumped me for all kinds of further information to do with such things as the kids' ages, schools, holidays and health. I might have thought he was showing an interest but I was fairly sure he didn't know some of the answers for his own children. It was also possible he was trying to gain some understanding of our situation in order to help Sarah maintain her work-life balance. I suspect, though, he has more sinister plans...

I tried not to say anything career damaging and stated several times that I'm the one responsible for looking after the children *even when they're ill.* (Not that I imagine it registered.) Then, at last, it was lunch-time and he hurried off to dump his children with his wife and then go and play squash. I've been chain-eating chocolate bars ever since. Sarah's not going to be happy. I don't know whether to phone her and warn her or wait to see if Steve mentions it to her. Or maybe I should just text – that might be safer. Or maybe it's too late already, and she's in the power tool section of B&Q...

Is Bolivia nice this time of year?

Yours in a woman's world,

Ed.

Balamory, plumbing and vomit, too!

Dear Dave,

Thanks for your letters of concern wondering where I'd got to. (Your list of venomous creatures indigenous to South America was a nice touch and so were the instructions on how to rob a bank in Spanish which you cribbed from *Butch Cassidy*.) As it turned it out, Sarah took the news of my meeting with Steve remarkably well and didn't feel the need to harm me. She was simply glad he wasn't still here when she got home. I didn't have to sit on the naughty step for any great length of time. I did, however, get sent to Balamory as penance. This was like being sent to Coventry but involved taking the entire family with me and having to endure much more singing.

No, really.

Tobermory (where *Balamory* was filmed) is only marginally easier to get to than the dark side of the moon. We spent most of Saturday travelling. We took the train to Glasgow, changed trains there for Oban, got the ferry to Craignure and then rode a fairly scary bus round the island to the land of PC Plum and Miss Hoolie.

There is a point an hour or so north of Glasgow on the train where the world ends. Houses become scattered, mobile phones give up and the sheep start walking about on their hind legs because they think there's no one around to see them. The scenery is beautiful but sometimes desolate. The track becomes winding, hilly and overhung with trees. We were surprised when some branches caught the side of the train and sent wet leaves raining in through the open window. Marie looked on the bright side. "Salad!"

The kids spent most of the journey arguing over whether we were going to Tobermory or Balamory. Fraser was for Tobermory, Marie was for Balamory and Lewis is at an age in between, where he wasn't exactly sure. He understood that they made *Balamory* in Tobermory but couldn't quite grasp why we didn't bump into Spencer during our stay. I think the whole trip messed with his head.

When we finally arrived, we discovered that Tobermory is pretty and there are plenty of restaurants but there's not much else to it. Even half the Balamory houses have changed colour. Worse, the entire place is built on an incredibly steep hill which made exploration difficult. We did find a small swing park but we had to leave in search of plasters after Fraser went down the slide using his brother's head as a mat.

We stayed three nights and any longer would have been stretching things. Waiting to catch the bus home, an old man chatted to us. In the middle of his life story he said, "What do you think of the place. Bit of a dump, eh?"

This was somewhat off-message compared with the official leaflets which advertise a child-friendly town. That said, considering there's very little for children to do and there's a frequent lack of pavements, I'm not completely clear what the tourist board was getting at. I guess 'Tobermory – child-friendly' sounds more appealing than 'Tobermory – *usually* free of ogres, witches, bear traps and Super Nanny'. Apparently, in the height of Balamory fever, the town was swamped with toddlers. Goodness knows what they all did. Tobermory certainly isn't a dump but it's more a place for wildlife spotters and hard-core OAP hillwalkers. It's not really somewhere you'd find yourself passing through, either. The locals must have been highly bemused by a sudden influx of under-fives hoping to stalk Josie Jump.

After we'd discussed Tobermory, I told the old man that we'd taken the ferry across to Kilchoan for a day out.

"Did you go to the place where they sell teas?" he said. "It's quite nice."

This is akin to asking someone who has just come back from Niagra if they went to see the waterfall. In Kilchoan, there are views, a few houses and the place that sells teas. It is, indeed, quite nice.

We returned to the gleaming metropolis of Oban – a place where it is possible to order three glasses of milk at the same the time without a waitress looking shifty and making excuses about the boat/bus/airdrop not arriving until four.

We had a while to wait for the train, so we went and had lunch. Since there was no one else in the restaurant, they put us on display in the window to attract other customers. Unfortunately, Marie took one bite of her food and was promptly violently sick. This was probably not the kind of advertisement they were looking for. The manager didn't look happy. I decided to distract him with a Spanish bank robbery. "Donde esta la caja?" I demanded. He didn't seem to want to tell us where the safe was, however. Sarah pointed a loaded toddler at him. "Manos arriba!" I said, raising my own hands in the air and making for the door. He was suitably confused. We beat a hasty retreat (and left a big tip).

We got home exhausted, only to find water welling up from beneath the floor. Two days later and we still don't know where it's coming from. Marie is still ill as well and having very disturbed sleep. This means *I'm* having disturbed sleep. I think it's some sort of test of parenthood.

Yours in a woman's world,

Ed.

Pub

Dear Dave,

I went to the pub the other night. It felt very odd. Just leaving the house without children was weird. Doing so at night was even more peculiar. I occasionally get to escape during the day at the weekend but I'm usually too tired in the evening once the kids are in bed. The world looked strange. I doubtless looked strange too, bounding along the pavement, unencumbered by buggies or changing bags or screaming children. I seemed to bounce, as if the lead weights had been removed from my boots. It was like walking on the moon (with the added advantage of my head not exploding from lack of air pressure, luckily).

Rob wanted to talk away from the womenfolk and I thought I'd better make the effort and go and meet him. He was panicking again about the prospect of fatherhood.

When I arrived, he was waiting at the bar. He bought us drinks and we settled ourselves down in a dingy corner. At least *I* settled myself – he downed half his pint and then sat and fidgeted. I suddenly remembered to check that the kids hadn't wandered off. Equally suddenly, I remembered I didn't have them with me. I was out in the world as a person in my own right and I wasn't patently a dad to everyone who looked at me. This made me unexpectedly nervous. People let you off with a lot if you've got small children to protect you. They're a distraction, an excuse and a talking point. I felt exposed without any.

I covered by examining my phone to make sure I hadn't missed any messages. "How's work?" I said, which is normally a safe bet – Rob's always keen to talk through his technical difficulties.

"They cancelled the project."

"What? How are they going to manage the new accounts without the IT systems?"

"No, it's the other way about. They decided that giving out scratchcards rather than interest was going to get them in trouble, so they've canned the accounts. We're still working on the IT."

"What?" I'd been looking forward to the scratchcards. "You're still working on the software for a product that's never going to exist?"

"Yeah," he said. "What else are we going to do? There's rumours going round about redundancies across the entire department. We're just trying to look busy."

I nodded. It occurred to me, however, that if I was in charge, people who managed to look busy despite clearly having no useful work to achieve would be the first to find their names mysteriously removed from the organisation chart.

We stared at our pints for a bit. "How's the leak?" Rob asked eventually.

"Put it this way," I sighed, "whenever I go into the cupboard under the stairs now, I take a snorkel and harpoon-gun with me just in case. We've had four different plumbers out to look at it. Mario and Luigi checked the pipes, Mario2 checked the drains and Mario's Friend checked the guttering. Fraser's list of amusing names is getting desperate already but none of them can figure out where the water's coming from. We're talking major work to repair all the damage as well." Rob muttered condolences but he was still caught up in his own problems. "How's Kate doing?" I asked.

"Fine, I think. It's hard to tell – she's knackered the whole time. She comes home from work and goes to bed. Then she wakes up in the middle of the night and eats sausages."

"I take it she's not veggie anymore, then?"

Rob ran his fingers through his hair in agitation. "She reckons vegetables have started looking at her funny. You know, like a nutter on a bus. She's avoiding them in case they try anything. Broccoli – she's sure the broccoli is out to get her. She knows it's planning something."

"O... K... She should get over that in a few weeks, though. Have you thought any more about getting married?"

"To the woman who's considering taking out a restraining order against cabbages?"

"I was thinking more along the lines of 'to the woman you love and who is carrying your child' but that too," I said. "Hormones and lack of sleep are liable to drive you both crazy at various points over the next year or three, so you're going to have to get on and make plans anyway. Is she going to go back to work after her maternity leave runs out? If she is, is it going to be full-time or part-time? And what about you?"

"Me?" He was starting to squeak.

"She's a solicitor," I said. "She earns a good wage working with people in a job she enjoys. You work in a cubicle and spend half your time emailing me funny stories you found on the internet while you were bored. Which of you would cope better staying home? If there are redundancies going round, you could leave voluntarily and escape with a load of free cash."

"And become a deviant like you?"

"I usually refer to myself as a housedad, but yeah. You asked me about it the other day; you must be thinking about it."

"That was the day after I found out," he said, chewing his nails. "I was hysterical. I didn't know what I was saying. I don't know how to change a nappy."

"Neither did I before Fraser was born. You get plenty of practice pretty quick, believe me. Imagine it as a computer game. You gradually gain experience by doing things such as fighting your way through the baby department at John Lewis, braving the terrors of parent and toddler and experimenting with stain removers. You also have to solve puzzles, such as which pram to buy and how to get porridge out of your watch."

This analogy was going down well, so I continued with a small genre switch. "Every so often, your Pokémon level-up, too. They start off with the ability to eat, sleep and expel bodily waste. As time passes, they learn new skills, allowing them to smile, walk, jump, talk and embarrass you in public. Then they evolve into bigger monsters that take more persuading to do what they're told and require totally different discipline techniques."

I was on a roll. "Eventually you're a level sixty wizard with a highly trained menagerie capable of doing all the chores around the house and then going out into the world and bringing back treasure to support you in your old age. An old age in which you get to laugh evilly for no apparent reason while being wheeled round by devoted slaves." I stared wistfully into the distance.

"I don't know," said Rob. "Don't take it personally or anything but aren't women just better at looking after kids? You know, multitasking and all that."

"A man can prepare a meal in between doing the washing-up, while entertaining a baby and at the same time as supervising a game of *Snakes and Ladders*. That's all multitasking is. A woman feels superior because she can do all those things *and* hold a conversation without being distracted, but they're really doing the same number of things."

"No, they're not. She's talking as well."

"Yes, but the man's thinking about sex. It's the same number of things."

"OK," said Rob, "so if it's that simple, why aren't there more housedads around? How come you and that Dave bloke you write to are the only ones I've heard of?"

"I suppose there are several reasons." I scratched my head. "Some people find the whole concept odd. For many couples, both partners have to work. Then again, some men feel it's their duty to be out there winning the bread or don't want to have to go cap in hand to their partner if they want to buy a gadget. There are all kinds of social barriers. The hours are long as well and I only get about five days holiday a year."

Rob shrugged. "That's not so bad. I get twenty-two."

"Ah... No, I don't think you're entirely understanding me here. You get a hundred and thirty-five days holiday a year."

"Don't be daft."

"I'm not being daft. What do you think I do with the kids on bank holidays and weekends? Put them into storage?"

His eyes widened. "Oh..."

"And I don't get sick days, either," I added. "If you became a housedad, there'd be no more rugby-related viruses forcing you to take long weekends in Dublin in order to recuperate."

"Hey! I went into work when I really had the flu to make up for that."

"I *always* have to go into work if I have the flu. Did I tell you about the occasion on which me and the boys managed to throw up twenty-five times between us in the space of eighteen hours?"

"You're not really selling this."

"True," I said. "I'm simply giving you something to think about. You're going to do fine as a dad and you could be a great housedad..." I coughed. "...given a bit of training. I'm not going to tell you it's a sunshine world of domestic bliss and biscuits, though. It's low-stress, fun and rewarding but requires plenty of hard work, patience, diplomacy and organisational ability. A strong stomach is also handy."

"Yeah." Rob nodded but his eyes were starting to glaze over with information overload.

I changed the subject. "Played anything good recently?"

"*MotorStorm* rocks in 3D," he said, looking a little sheepish.

"You bought a new telly?" I said, slightly too loudly.

"Yeah. I was walking home past the shops the other day and it just kind of happened. I needed something to take my mind off things but my credit card's smarting. Looks ace, though."

"Tell me you got a spare pair of glasses."

"It was part of the bundle."

"Then what the flip are we doing here?" I said, finishing off my pint. "Get your coat – you've pulled."

We headed out the door for a night of gaming. As we

left, however, Rob looked at me sideways, a thought coming back to him. "You actually think of them as Pokémon, don't you?"

"Maybe," I said. "Certainly, when people ask Marie her name, she says, 'Pikachu'."

Rob laughed. "I think I'll call mine Squirtle." He laughed again. This time there was just the faintest hint of a cackle...

I wonder what I've started now.

Yours in a woman's world,

Ed.

Part 3

Dealing with Opposition

Conspiracy

Dear Dave,

I think it's a conspiracy.

You only have one child so far, so you may not understand, but I really think it happens. Seriously, I think they get together and plan it. They must have proper meetings with agendas and flip-charts and brain-storming sessions. I keep expecting to find three discarded plastic coffee cups, an empty box of doughnuts and a laser pointer left lying around.

OK, I'm starting to rave but they pushed me to it. I'm going crazy. I realise that this is what they want, yet I can't help myself. I don't know why they want me to go crazy, but they must do – there can be no other explanation, given the persistence of their co-ordinated efforts.

Maybe if I found their documentation, their motives would become clear. Yes, that's it. I'll have to search more carefully. I'd particularly like to see the *PowerPoint* presentation for the stunt they pulled the other day:

Fraser and Lewis had the opportunity to take a tour of the local football ground with Anchor Boys (the junior version of the Boys' Brigade). They have no interest in football, however. They have so little clue, that if forced to play, they might well struggle to know which goal to make for. This being the case, I assumed they wouldn't want to visit an empty stadium.

I hadn't counted on their long-term aim of making me insane.

Fraser was desperate to go look at some seats and a large expanse of grass. He pleaded with me to be allowed to take part. I was bemused. I tried to talk him out of it. The trip clashed with the boys' weekly swimming lesson which was paid up in advance. If they'd both wanted to go to the stadium, then I could have lived with that – it isn't something they'll have a chance to do very often, after all. But Lewis didn't want to go and it was logistically impossible for one to go swimming and the other to go on the trip. If Fraser went on the trip, then I'd have effectively spent money for Lewis to sit at home with me. I was adamant they both had to decide on the same activity.

They argued amongst themselves for a while. Neither would change their mind. I decided to leave the decision until the actual day.

The day came. While Fraser was at school, I tried to persuade Lewis to go to the stadium because I knew that Fraser was determined to go. Lewis wasn't having any of it. He took a big strop, nearly cried and said he wanted to go swimming. Neither of them *ever* wants to go swimming. They kick up a fuss about it every single week. I tore out some of my hair.

We went to collect Fraser from school. I didn't know what we were going to do. Fraser came out and I tentatively asked him if he still wanted to go see the place where they play football. To my surprise, he replied, "No, not really. I've changed my mind. I don't want to go."

I sighed in relief. Then Lewis said, "But I do."

In years to come, I think that will be the moment I will look back on and say, 'Yes... That's when they drove me over the edge...'

There was more arguing but no agreement. I decided to send them both on the trip in the end and, thankfully, they had a good time. Their plan wasn't entirely done, though – Marie took a huff because she wasn't allowed to go. She only got to stay home and have my undivided attention, and, apparently, that just wasn't good enough...

What was it Abe Lincoln said? 'You can please some of the people all of the time and all of the people some of the time but when it comes to your own children you're royally stuffed whatever.' I think that was it.

I'm off to look under Fraser's bed for an encrypted hard-drive.

Yours in a woman's world,

Ed.

Another conspiracy

Dear Dave,

Sorry to hear your neighbour thinks you're moving in on his wife. I take it he believes that because you're both home most of the time, there's more scope for temptation.

Which is mad.

He doubtless goes off in a suit to a workplace full of smartly-dressed female colleagues who he has ample chance to meet up with in his lunch hour. You, meanwhile, are run ragged by a toddler every minute of the day, barely have a moment to brush your hair and are covered in a multitude of minor stains. Also, quite how you'd find the opportunity to get up to something – let alone keep it secret – with three small kids between you, is another matter. *I* can't sneak away for four minutes of shooting aliens on the Xbox without a little person searching me out and demanding some form of urgent assistance or other.

If the guy keeps hassling you, drop Sam round their house one Saturday morning and let him witness how impractical the whole suggestion is at first-hand. I don't know about you, but it can be hard finding time and energy for the woman I already have in my life. I'm not looking to borrow another.

That said, I did have an uncomfortable conversation myself the other day. I answered the phone and a well-spoken and attractive-sounding woman on the other end said, "It's Deborah."

The name didn't ring any bells straight off and I didn't recognise the voice. "Er..."

"Steve's wife." I still couldn't place her. "You know – Useless Dad."

"Oh!" I'd spoken to her briefly at parent and toddler a few times but not for several weeks. I remembered her as intimidatingly confident and pretty. Calling her own husband by the derogatory nickname I'd given him had the combined effect of making me warm to her but also of scaring me. I couldn't recall having mentioned the name in public. What else did she know? More than that, what did she want and how had she tracked me down?

She smiled at me down the phone. "I was wondering if you want to meet up for coffee?" For some reason, I felt like a fly being waved at by a cheery spider. Something didn't entirely add up.

"Er, well..."

"I've got the cleaner in just now but she won't be here long – it's only some tidying up really. Why don't you come round at eleven?"

Normally that would be a rubbish time but Lewis was going to a friend's house after nursery so I didn't have to collect him. I had the distinct suspicion, however, that Deborah was the kind of woman who would remember that I had a child in morning nursery. She probably even had his name, birthday and favourite foods in her mental Rolodex. So why would she suggest a time that she knew I wouldn't normally be able to make? Unless she already knew it wasn't a normal day... But she couldn't possibly know that unless the kids' conspiracy had reached new heights and they were bringing in adults to help them... But that was insane thinking... I was reading too much into things. I... I decided to be non-committal.

"How did you get my number?"

"It was stuck to our fridge."

"Er..."

Being a man in a woman's world has many advantages, such as receiving adulation in the park for being able to reach high enough to unwrap the swings, not to mention having a changing room all to ourselves at swimming lessons. One of the disadvantages is that taking the kids to visit their friends can be awkward. It's socially odd meeting up with a woman in her home without any other adults present. It's not like we're alone or that anything could possibly happen or that I would want anything to happen – it's just strange. I couldn't help feeling it would be even stranger going round to see a woman who was rapidly giving the impression of stalking me.

"Oh come on," she said, discerning my reticence. "I hear the girls get on really well. It would be good for them to get to know each other better. I'll make a cake. We only live ten minutes away."

As attempts to talk me into things go, it was rather persuasive. She made me feel like a bad parent for not wanting to visit and then pointed out the way to be a good parent merely involved a short walk to eat free cake. Genius! After only a little more token back-pedalling, I agreed to take Marie round. Nonetheless, as soon as Deborah put the phone down, I speed-dialled Sarah. Nothing was going to happen but it's always worth informing the wife after accepting an offer of home-baking from a mysterious woman – that way there's less chance of a misunderstanding turning life into an American sitcom. Only less chance, mind:

"LBO marketing department, Sarah speaking. How can I help you?"

"Your boss's wife has invited me round for coffee. I was checking..."

"I can't speak right now, Rebecca. I'll call you back in a few minutes." She hung up and I was left staring at the phone. Somehow I'd found myself in a re-run of *Friends*.

I filled the next wee while encouraging Marie with her drawing while I pondered whether I would rather be Ross, Joey or Chandler. Then the phone rang.

It was Sarah. "She called you already then?"

"What?"

"Steve's still around here somewhere," she said and then lowered her voice. "He's not to know about it."

"He's not to know I'm going round to his house?"

"No."

"But *you* know about it?" I said.

"Yes."

"I'm a little confused."

"Well I knew that before I married you," said Sarah. "Just go round and listen to what she has to say. You owe me on all of this, remember?"

"For letting your boss into our house?" I said. "I thought you'd forgiven me for that. But if you're in on it, no wonder she found it so easy to persuade me. There was no need to go telling her all your secret techniques for manipulating me."

Sarah laughed. "Don't be silly. If I'd told her my *secret* techniques then you wouldn't have known she was doing it."

"That's not reassuring."

"It wasn't meant to be. Oops, got to go. See you later, Rebecca."

I was left staring at the phone again. I felt like such a Chandler.

An hour or so later, with some trepidation, I set off. In contrast, Marie was very excited about the whole prospect, and toddled along at speed. "We go play! I run!" she shouted. I did my best to concentrate on gently steering her through the usual obstacle course of puddles, dog poo and admiring old ladies.

Deborah lives in what appears to be an old, stone-faced hotel that has been expensively renovated into luxury flats. On seeing it, I expected high ceilings, marble finishing and a mezzanine level in the vast lounge.

I wasn't disappointed.

She greeted me with a peck on the cheek and then ushered me through to sit in a bay window where tea and cake had been set out on fine china. There was a table-cloth and everything – the cake was even on a stand. None of this helped put me at my ease.

Marie was oblivious. "I go play now," she said and ran off hand-in-hand with Ophelia. I hoped anything valuable had been put out of reach but I spent the rest of the visit expecting her to come back shaking a Fabergé egg, trying to get the surprise toy out.

Settling into a wicker chair festooned with cushions, I looked about. Whoever had decorated the place had known what they were doing – it was elegant yet welcoming. I was acutely aware, however, that the cup I was drinking from probably cost more than all the crockery in my own house put together.

"Nice place," I said.

"I'm an interior designer," Deborah replied and I instantly wished I'd been a touch more effusive.

"Well, it's really nice. Really, *really* nice." I guess, on reflection, I'm simply not a very effusive person. I pressed on. "Do you get much chance to do any work?"

"Not as much as I want. Ophelia will start nursery after the summer but, since Josquin doesn't sleep for long during the day, it won't help a great deal. A nanny is one solution, I suppose, but I don't like the thought of that. I really need Steve to do more of the childcare in the evening and at weekends."

"Are you sure that's wise. He's a bit... er..."

"Useless?"

"Yeah."

"I am aware of that," Deborah replied. "I phoned him on his mobile yesterday and Josquin's nappy rang. I get the feeling that your wife has some issues with him as well."

"She's not up for meetings on the golf course, she'd prefer to see her family than go down the pub and she has a tendency to disagree with plans which are obviously stupid. This has her marked out as 'not a team player'. She also feels her work is under-appreciated because she doesn't get involved in the testosterone-fuelled bragging his leadership tends to encourage."

"It sounds like she's told you a great deal about it," Deborah said, clearly knowing full well I've had my fair share of angst to sympathise with.

"Sarah's mentioned it on a few occasions," I replied diplomatically.

Deborah raised an eyebrow. "OK," she said, spreading her hands on the table in front of her. "I'll be blunt. I need him to be a better dad. You need him to be a better boss. I think we can help each other. You teach Steve to be an involved father and I'll exert some influence on his managerial style. I can also supply Sarah with any useful information that comes my way, such as when he's going to be out of the office and anything he's planning, so she's prepared."

This wasn't the kind of proposition I'd been fearing. In many ways it was scarier. Still, it was a chance to make Sarah's life better, so I couldn't really turn it down. (I do love her.)

I sighed. "I guess I could give it a try. Where do you want me to start?"

"Go with him to the soft-play next Saturday. I hear you should be free to collect him at ten."

"I thought you were supposed to be supplying Sarah with information, not the other way about."

"We're all working together now," said Deborah.

"Apart from Steve," I said, frowning. "I'm assuming he's not to know about any of this?"

"As if he'd believe you."

"Good point. He hasn't taken in I'm a housedad yet."

"Exactly."

At that moment, Marie and Ophelia entered the room wearing Wedgwood bowls as helmets, and Josquin woke up wanting fed. We turned our attention to keeping children happy and there wasn't much more opportunity for discussion before I took Marie home for lunch.

I'm not completely sure what I'm going to do. I guess I'll meet up with Steve on Saturday and see how it goes. Maybe, simply by being round me, he'll pick up some fathering skills by osmosis. You never know... Sarah's seeming pleased, though, so that's a bonus.

Good luck with your situation. I just hope that this doesn't all blow up in my face like a steriliser full of popcorn. (Don't try that, by the way...)

Yours in a woman's world,

Ed.

All I want for Father's Day is…

Dear Dave,

What are you doing for Father's Day?

I keep getting junk email advertising all kinds of bloke-oriented toys and gizmos that I might want my family to buy me as tokens of their appreciation for my very existence. Remote control items appear to be the thing this year – cars, helicopters, dragonflies, boats, you name it. There are plenty of other bits and bobs on offer as well, from Sat Navs to football-playing robots to little fridges to keep beer in. Bizarrely, one company even believes I might find some digital callipers useful. Still more bizarrely, the only use I can think of for digital callipers is to measure the internal diameter of my nostrils. (I've spent so long around small children, I suspect I'm going native.)

Besides gifts, I've also had suggestions for special Father's Day trips I might fancy. There's a deal on at the museum, for instance, giving a slightly reduced entry fee for families if you eat at the restaurant. Big whoop.

None of this advertising speaks to our situation. It's all along the lines of, 'Remember to take time out from work. Relax, play and celebrate your family. Spend quality time with them. Oh, and drink some beer.'

I get to play with toys all the time, however. We have at least three remote control cars in the house already – one only turns right, one is supposed to turn both ways but only turns right and the other is broken and doesn't turn at all but is a model of Mario on a kart so we can't get rid of it. I have small children to watch play football badly. I don't care what temperature my beer is. None of the stuff really appeals. (I might be tempted by some remote control, football-playing beer. I still wouldn't care what temperature it was, though.)

As for taking the kids for an exciting day out to the zoo... That would be rewarding hard work with more hard work.

Sarah has a similar problem when Mother's Day rolls round. All the advertising involves children thanking their mum for the sweat and tears she's shed looking after them the whole year. It's a time for mums to put their feet up while someone else makes Sunday lunch. This merely causes Sarah to feel guilty for *never* making Sunday lunch. She'd just like a bit of appreciation for being her.

That's another story. The question is how to mark Father's Day. I'm not even wanting any games or DVDs – between renting and the ones I've got already, I've more entertainment available than I have time to fill. Which, I guess, pretty much suggests the solution. Even the kids managed to work it out without prompting. What I could *really* do with is some peace and quiet.

This Father's Day, the children are showing their gratitude for all I do by leaving me alone for a change. Sarah's going to drag them to the zoo and I'm going to stay here and put my feet up. I'll take time out from work. I'll relax, play and celebrate my family being somewhere else. I'll spend quality time with the Xbox. Oh, and drink some beer.

Have a good one.

Yours in a woman's world,

Ed.

PS Three weeks and seven plumbers later, the leak is finally fixed. (There was a crack in one of next door's heating pipes.) I've bailed buckets of water from under the floorboards and things are starting to dry out. There's a good chance we'll have to move somewhere else while the damage to the plasterwork is repaired but, for now, we've just got three large air-blowers cluttering the place and making the house sound and smell like a laundrette. Great.

Educating Useless Dad

Dear Dave,

Everything continues to be entertaining here. The house is still full of air-blowers, I've had a stomach bug, Sarah's off on a course for three days, school finishes for the summer holidays on Friday and the overflow fitting for the bath fell off yesterday for no apparent reason. Hope life is going more smoothly for you.

Thanks for asking how it went with Steve last week. As you'll recall, his wife, Deborah, organised for me to go with him and our combined horde of marauding children to invade the local soft-play and pillage the place. Somehow, during the chaos, I was supposed to nurture his latent fatherhood skills and make him less of a Useless Dad.

Well, I'm not sure I entirely succeeded. He's certainly not the man he was but it's possible he may simply be a different kind of useless...

Anyway, I arrived at their flat on Saturday morning with my happy band of midget barbarians and, to no one's surprise, Steve wasn't entirely ready. The boys raced off to hunt Deborah's cat; Marie clung to me at the sight of Steve – she's seen his childcare abilities at first-hand and wasn't wanting to be his next victim. No one was going to shove a bottle of milk in *her* ear while reading the business pages.

Useless Dad's first mistake on this occasion was in his attire – he was dressed in a suit. He'd gone for a more casual look by not wearing a tie but it really wasn't suitable for clambering around inside giant plastic piping.

I suppose, technically, since he'd needed to be smart earlier in the morning for some kind of business networking breakfast, the suit wasn't actually his *first* mistake. His first mistake was not leaving himself three times as long as he'd expected to get his children ready to go. Temporarily misplacing them altogether was his second mistake. His third mistake was that between them they had a leaky nappy and some Play-

Doh. His fourth mistake, meanwhile, was not restocking the changing bag. So, on reflection, thinking Deborah and I would let him out of the house again without appropriate clothes was probably his fifth mistake. It was the first I was fully aware of, however. (The changing bag fiasco took us nearly two hours to discover. The Play-Doh has subsequently turned up in a pair of slippers, their DVD player and the cat. Half of it remains missing...)

Still, who wears a suit to the soft-play?

Someone who needs plenty of pockets...

"Have you got your smartphone with you?" I asked nonchalantly.

"Of course," he replied.

"You might want to leave it here," I said. "You wouldn't want to lose it in the ball-swamp."

"In? I thought we got to sit and watch."

"And by 'sit and watch' you mean 'occasionally glance up from reading the paper', don't you?" said Deborah.

He looked nervous. "Er..."

I coughed. It was a strange, throaty cough which came out sounding somewhat like, "Frisk him!"

Deborah patted Steve down. The quick search revealed the smartphone, his other mobile phone, a magazine entitled *Middle Management Now!*, a pad of Post-its, a pack of cigarettes, a pre-paid voucher for *The Telegraph* and a half-eaten custard cream. She confiscated the lot.

"Hey! Let me keep the phone," he pleaded. "I need it for... Er... Oh! What if you need to contact me?"

"I'll phone Ed," she said.

"How come he gets to keep his phone?"

"Because no one's going to phone him." She looked at me. "No offence."

"None taken – it's the truth. Anyone phones me and all they get is small children in the background shouting, 'Who is it? Who is it? Can I talk to them?' No one even tries anymore."

"OK, OK." Steve put his mobile away.

"While you're at it," I said, "you should change into something more comfortable for crawling in confined spaces with sweaty children. You probably want to go for old and stained."

"Why?"

"I never know *exactly* why, but the kids usually find a reason before the day's out. Look here." I pointed to a orange smear near the shoulder of my t-shirt. "Marie wiped her mouth on me when I picked her up. And here's where Fraser stood on me while we were playing football." I indicated a black stain on my side. "And all this..." I showed him brown handprints on my back and grass stains on my knees. "Well, let's just say Lewis got into a lot of trouble."

"What's the red one on your front?"

There was splatter across most of the lower half of my t-shirt that I hadn't noticed. "I don't know." I gave it a couple of licks. "Oh, blackcurrant. That could have happened any time."

At that moment, their three-year-old daughter, Ophelia, went past wheeling baby Josquin in a highchair.

"What's that?" said Steve, staring at the floor behind them.

I peered closely. "Looks to me like a trail of gravitational droplets," I said. "Directionality suggests the perpetrator came this way from the kitchen."

Steve went to investigate. The ensuing swearing made me suspect that he'd managed to step directly in the primary crime scene.

It was almost another half-hour before we finally managed to leave. My boys were bouncing off the walls by then but, luckily, they didn't break anything expensive. Once we got going, however, we made brisk pace along the few streets to the soft-play. The four ambulatory children tore off their shoes and plunged straight into the towering, three-storey structure of nets, pipes, platforms and slides. Their ululating battle-cry was rendered unintelligible by the frightened shrieks of those already present. Toddlers poured out the exits like fleas from a sinking rat. Fraser clambered to the very top and did a little dance. Victory was ours.

I left Steve to play with Josquin in an area reserved for smaller children, and I went into the main network in order to make sure that the girls didn't get into any trouble and that the boys didn't cause any. There was no way Steve and I could really sit and talk while still giving the entire horde adequate supervision. My hope was that being abandoned with his son would at least encourage some bonding and that I could talk to him later over coffee.

I got stuck in to chasing children around the brightly coloured wonderland. I don't remember soft-play existing when we were kids so I like to make up for it now. I know from experience, though, not to go sliding down any plastic tubes – I always end up trying to brake with my elbows and friction burns are never pleasant.

After a while, I went and checked on Steve. He was sitting dejectedly, rocking Josquin on a small see-saw. They both looked like they'd rather be doing something else. I offered to swap with him and he shrugged and slouched off to watch the other children. I set to work lifting Josquin onto slides, tickling him and throwing ball-swamp balls around for his amusement. He cheered up a bit.

Sometime later, Marie and Ophelia wandered over and started building towers of squishy shapes while giggling at each other. It took me a minute to spot that Steve hadn't followed them. I couldn't see him anywhere.

"Where's your dad?" I asked Ophelia.

"There," she said and waved a finger about as if indicating he was on the same side of the planet as the rest of the soft-play.

"OK," I said, picking up Josquin and heading off to search. "You girls stay here. I'll be back soon."

Fraser and Lewis were easy enough to find – they were racing each other up and around in circuits of the main structure. They would have been much faster at it if they hadn't stopped every five feet to claim the other was cheating in some manner. I asked them where Steve was. They looked at me blankly. I continued on.

I eventually found him in a corner of the ball-swamp. Things had not gone well for him. He had clearly sat down on the edge of a large, doughnut-shaped squishy shape and then somehow slipped (or been pushed) backwards into the hole. With his muscles atrophied from years of doing nothing but draft pointless memos, he had been unable to break free, his wriggling only causing him to sink deeper into the swamp. He was folded in half, his limbs sticking straight up, his bottom sticking straight down, and the doughnut stuck tight around him. He was trapped.

Scavengers had already arrived. An eight-year-old was trying to prise the watch off Useless Dad's wrist while a three-year-old had liberated his left sock and was using it as a hand-puppet. A particularly portly four-year-old was eying him in the way Wile E. Coyote looks at Road Runner. A speck of drool had formed at the corner of the kid's mouth.

If I'd arrived much later, I'd have found nothing but bones jacked up on bricks.

I rolled my eyes and rescued him.

"I was just having a rest," he muttered.

"Aye, well, you'd be safer smearing yourself with jam and going to sleep on an ant hill. Keep moving about or the little blighters will get you. I'll send the girls back and you can chase them or something."

I left him to it and returned Josquin to the lower slopes. Marie and Ophelia seemed delighted by the suggestion that they go and make Ophelia's daddy run around. They rushed off, still giggling to each other. What I wasn't expecting was for Marie to come back a few minutes later in a huff because Ophelia's daddy was hogging the slide.

He'd got really into it. Not so much the interacting with kids part but the sliding head-first screaming into a vast vat of plastic balls part. There wasn't much I could do about it, though – I was left taking care of the baby. It was then that I discovered the stock issue with the changing bag. I had to fashion a makeshift nappy the best I could out of a muslin cloth, some cotton-wool and two plasters. As an added precaution, I sat Josquin down on an absorbent-looking copy of *Middle Management Now!* that Steve had snuck into the bag.

Our time was up soon after. Steve wanted one more shot but I dragged him off the clamber nets and we hurried home to find nappies. He spent the whole journey arguing with Fraser over which part of the soft-play was the most fun.

I didn't fancy recounting the tale of my limited success to Deborah, and so we parted company at their door. Nonetheless, the torture isn't over. I got a text message from her a few days later, impressed with Steve's enthusiasm about the whole experience and informing me that I'm going back with him in a fortnight. This time he's going to bring some of his friends!

Apparently, he's even thinking of hiring the place for a team-building day.

Sarah is going to hate me.

Yours in a woman's world,

Ed.

Ninja biohazard in St Andrews

Dear Dave,

You're right – you should go on holiday now. You've got one child who is almost three and another due in a couple of months. IT WILL BE YEARS before you have this much freedom to travel again. Sam can eat normal food, doesn't need nappies and can be reasonably expected to sit still and quiet for a couple of hours. In eight weeks time, you'll need to take twice as much stuff with you on a trip to the zoo than you would travelling to Italy tomorrow. It will also be four times as much stress.

Go.

Right now.

... ...

What are you still doing here?

Never mind, seeing as you've continued reading, I'll tell you about our recent trip to St Andrews. (Live with it. You had your chance to make a break for Venice.)

It's a strange place really (even now that Prince William fever is past). It's a small seaside town of around 18,000 but, unlike most small seaside towns, a third of the population is students. Oddly, however, the town actually gets busier over the summer when most of the students have gone away. Tourists and golfers take over. When the Open is on, hundreds of thousands turn up. It's crazy but it does mean that the whole area is geared up for visitors.

St Andrews has plenty of activities for children. Compared with Tobermory, it's Disneyland. There's an aquarium, the castle, the cathedral, a small cinema, a theatre, tennis, putting, two decent beaches, a swimming pool and a dozen charity shops in which to hunt down bargains. There's also a country park on the outskirts of town.

As with everywhere else this summer, it rained a fair amount while we were there but, in some ways, that just gave us a good excuse to lie around in our self-catering accommodation and not do very much. We managed to get to all the places we wanted to but Fraser and Lewis also had ample opportunity to bounce Mario around collecting scores of stars. (Yes, we took a console with us. I had to buy an extra wire to hook the thing up to the hand-me-down-from-the-Flintstones telly but it was soooo worth it – the boys were able to entertain themselves first thing in the morning.)

That reminds me of an unfortunate mix up which happened not long after we arrived. I bought supplies in Tesco and was slightly freaked by the peculiar look the checkout assistant gave me. It was only after I left, I realised she'd heard me answer my mobile and my side of the dialogue had been somewhat incriminating:

"Hello?... Who's going to get it?... Well, we only brought one nunchuck with us... I'm at the checkout just now. I'll call you back when I'm done."

I was probably lucky SWAT didn't show up. Not that St Andrews has a SWAT team but there must be *something* in the back of that police van that drives round town on a Saturday night (besides drunk teenagers, obviously). I certainly don't want to find out what it contains. It could be concealing anything. Maybe the A-Team have found a quiet place to hide in their twilight years. They could be drinking cocoa in the back of that van, ready to leap out at the first sign of trouble and construct weapons from whatever comes to hand. This being St Andrews, the things which most easily come to hand are golf clubs, pensioners and upper-class arts students. The consequences don't bear thinking about.

Of course, I wasn't actually planning a ninja-style contract killing at the supermarket. Sarah was phoning to see whether she should follow the kids' suggestion and purchase the latest Nintendo party game. I was simply reckoning we didn't have enough controllers on hand to make it worthwhile. But I can see now where some confusion may have arisen.

The rest of the holiday proceeded more smoothly. We went swimming, we pottered on the beach and we even had a dry day at the park. It was pleasant to get away from the stress at home.

Marie had a little embarrassment one evening, however:

Sarah took the boys out to the theatre and I was left with the girl. She wandered off into the bedroom while I was working on my nunchuck skills. She chattered away to herself and seemed happy. Then, suddenly, she sounded distressed, as if she'd wrestled a duvet and lost or a pillowcase had eaten one of her cuddly toys. A few seconds later, she emerged from the bedroom with her trousers round her knees. Her pants were flying slightly low and she was trying desperately to yank them up.

This got my attention.

She didn't appear to be leaving a slimy trail behind her but I was instantly prepared for at least a Level 7 biohazard and I feared a Level 8 or 9. In case you didn't catch the public information broadcast, here's the current international scale for biohazard alert levels:

1. Underpants wet but not wet enough to bother changing them.

2. Underpants wet enough to consider changing them if parent responsible is feeling charitable.

3. Underpants undeniably wet. Trousers may also require changing.

4. Trousers sodden. Moisture check recommended in all recent locations of offspring.

5. Shoes need drained. Some fumigation necessary.

6. Underpants contaminated with poo. Clothes may need soaked.

7. Underpants filled with poo. Clothes may need flushed in toilet.

8. Underpants filled with vast amounts of evil poo. Offspring may need flushed in toilet.

9. Containment breach from underpants. Hope you bought more carpet shampoo.

10. Underpants missing. (In some ways, you'll want to find them; in other ways, you won't.)

I got Marie to stop where she was and went over to investigate, my eyes scanning the floor, walls and ceiling for any signs of noxious fluids. Then I noticed she was clinking. Not only that, but the sound was coming from her underpants. This is not normal. She looked at me mournfully. I said some soothing words and advanced cautiously. Kneeling down to cuddle her, I gingerly pulled back the elastic and peered down the rear of her trousers with trepidation, unsure for once of what I might find. I wasn't really expecting seventeen pence in small change.

No wonder she was upset. *I'd* be upset if someone put coppers in my underwear. And, yes, I'd probably be even more upset if I'd somehow managed to do it myself and I had to get my dad to help me retrieve them while he stifled laughter... (One to tell her first boyfriend.)

Hope you manage to get away and find a chance to relax. Not long to go now...

Yours in a woman's world,

Ed.

Letting them win

Dear Dave,

So Sam went in a huff when he lost three times in a row at *Snakes and Ladders*? Then, when you fudged the result of the next game so that he won, he pulled his t-shirt over his face and ran round the house waving his arms in the air and screaming about his own wondrousness?

Yep, that sounds familiar.

Teaching kids to be good winners and losers is a nightmare. You want them to be at least a little competitive, so they've a chance of earning some money one day and moving out. But you don't want to overdo it and have them be too arrogant to live with while you're waiting. You want them to be successful *and* nice. This is the combination that leads to the best nursing home for you, after all.

How to achieve it, though?

I was faced with the problem most recently while having a kick-about in the park with the boys:

Everything started out fine. We found a thirty foot stretch of grass between two benches which we used as goals – a pitch big enough to force them to run around but small enough to make sure *I* didn't have to. I stood in my goal and kept kicking the ball towards theirs. They kept scampering after it and bringing it back. It was all good fun, even if they didn't entirely have the idea.

Playing football with them reminds me of being an exchange student in the States when I was a teenager. I remember playing 'soccer' in PE class and watching almost everyone else on the pitch (including one goalkeeper) form a mob around the ball. Every so often, someone in the middle of the scrum actually managed to find the ball and kick it a few feet. The writhing mass of flailing limbs then duly shuffled in the same direction. Eventually, the ball emerged and one of my team-mates had the sense to boot it up the field to me. I strolled over to the goal and scored. The whistle blew. The mob stopped flailing and peered about in a bewildered fashion. Then we started over from the beginning.

This happened surprisingly often. There were three Europeans in that class and I'm not saying we could have taken on the rest single-handed but whichever team had two of us in was almost certain to win. One of us would go after the ball and pass it to the other one *who was standing somewhere else.* For some reason, this glaringly obvious passing tactic seemed to be beyond our American friends. Trying to be more than a few feet from the ball felt unnatural to them. (Every other sport we did that year, we played every day for a fortnight. After three days of soccer, our teacher gave up in despair. We went bowling after that...)

In a similar fashion, when playing football, the boys run after the ball wherever it goes and so it's easy for me to both (a) get it off them in order to score and (b) tire them out by booting it into the distance and watching them chase after it. At the point they listen to me and take in that they can run in different directions and pass to each other, then I'm stuffed. In the meantime, I have almost total control over the outcome of a match. I can always organise a competitive draw. Everyone has fun, no one gets big-headed because they won and no one gets annoyed because they lost. Patently, this is a cop-out because life seldom really ends in a competitive draw but, if I've got the kids out playing football, my main aim is exercise rather than life-lessons in winning and losing.

On this occasion, however, Fraser scuppered me. "First one to three, wins!" he shouted.

There wasn't an option for a draw and the number of goals required was too low to drag the match out until it was time to go inside without a winner. Either the boys had to win, or I did. Realistically, the result was up to me.

What do *you* do in these situations? How often is it reasonable to let children win? How much is it possible to beat them by without totally discouraging them and making them give up?

We almost certainly got it wrong when Fraser was

young. He received praise for everything. When he was learning to walk, it got to the stage that if he managed to stand up by himself, he'd look around and wait for somebody to clap. If no one did, he'd clap himself. Then he'd clap himself for clapping. These days, his friends at school can be doing cartwheels but he wants attention if he manages to stand on one foot for five seconds without falling over. He's also reluctant to try things he thinks might be difficult because he's worried he might fail and thus not get his fix of adulation. He hates to lose.

Since then, we've learnt that it's more important praising effort than achievement. Basically, if you praise a kid for doing well, then they'll cope badly with failure. Praise a kid for trying hard and they'll continue to try hard and they're more likely to try things that they know they might fail.

So it's OK to reward just turning up and trying, as long as you make it clear that's what you're doing. The thing to avoid is praising mediocre achievement in order to 'encourage self-worth'. Self-worth doesn't come from knowing we can always win – it's what keeps us going when we lose. It's what allows us to persevere and take risks. Trying something, failing and trying again is actually more valuable than succeeding spectacularly at something which comes naturally.

In light of this, we've started praising the kids for trying things rather than succeeding at them. It doesn't always work – often we end up praising them for trying *and* succeeding. Nonetheless, we're trying, too. We're trying to persuade them that practice is important and that being good at stuff takes effort. We're trying to make sure they know that we love them whatever happens and that failing doesn't make them 'failures'.

So how did the football match end? Well, old habits die hard – I praised their effort but I let them win three goals to two. If I hadn't, they'd have simply insisted on making it the first to four or five or twenty-seven, anyway. I was hot and tired by then, and I wanted to go lie down.

It's hard work being a housedad.

Yours in a woman's world,

Ed.

Maternity madness

Dear Dave,

How's Liz getting on at work now her maternity leave is fast approaching? Sarah had some decidedly strange treatment at LBO as her own waistline expanded. By the time there was three months to go, she wasn't being given anything to do, on the basis of her 'imminent' departure. All the good stuff went to one of her male colleagues. He spent about six months doing two-thirds of the analysis badly and then got another job and handed in his notice. He had so much holiday and flexi-time accumulated, he was gone two days later. Sarah ended up redoing the entire project from scratch in three weeks when she got back. It was insane.

Her manager, Steve, really didn't appreciate how much the enhanced maternity benefits and their tie-in clauses enforced her loyalty to LBO. From the moment she was pregnant until the day she had been back at work for a year after maternity leave, it was financial foolishness for her to change job. When she *had* been back a year, Marie's teething ensured we were all too tired for Sarah to go looking for anything else then either. Her incompetent male colleague had meanwhile changed jobs twice more, doubled his salary and come back to LBO in order to oversee a monumental disaster in another department. (Remember that weekend last year when half the ATMs died, a few started spitting out cash and one in Stoke kept challenging passers-by to a game of tic-tac-toe while threatening intercontinental thermonuclear war? His references didn't look so great after that. He's now head of new customer acquisition in Bogota.)

Anyway, it was really Steve I was meaning to write about. The conspiracy centring around him is not progressing according to plan. Deborah isn't having much success in making him a better manager; I'm not having much success in making him a better dad. We're both just trying to hold up our end of the bargain in whatever way we can.

I keep inviting him and his kids to the park so Deborah has some space to work on her interior design business but, somehow, I always end up doing nearly all the childcare while he has a conference call on his mobile or re-jigs his schedule to fit in an extra round of golf.

Deborah keeps attempting to persuade him to run his department more effectively but her suggestions aren't sinking in. He sent out a memo encouraging openness in communication to only half the department. He arranged a discussion on transparent decision-making, then changed the time and location and wouldn't say why. He was sympathetic to the concept of treating those who worked for him as human beings but couldn't create a suitable spreadsheet to automate the process.

Gah!

The upshot is that, most of the time, Deborah simply tells Sarah when that extra round of golf is going to be. Sarah then knows when she can organise her team without interference. Anything which needs clearance is passed back to Deborah, who slips it to Steve and convinces him it's his own idea. Thus, when he suggests it to Sarah and it's already done, she looks scarily efficient rather than like a treacherous usurper.

This isn't ideal. Basically, everyone is taking up the slack for him. In the short-term this is making all our lives easier, but it's going to be hard to maintain. We need him to get a clue and I've no idea how that's going to happen. I'm kind of hoping he'll suddenly have some revelation of his own uselessness and come begging to us all for forgiveness. Like St Paul on the road to Damascus, he will be blinded by the light and his foolishness will be swept away. In a single moment of realisation, all our problems will be gone.

More likely, one of us needs to sit him down and tell him straight that he's an idiot. It should probably be Deborah but that's not really in her nature. He has too much power over Sarah for her to do it and I'm not good with conflict...

Any chance you could make it up here for the day? I'm sure we could arrange for the two of you to be trapped in a lift together...

Hmmm... Thought not.

You wouldn't get here in time to save me from Thursday, anyhow. That's when I'm going with him *and his friends* to the soft-play. I haven't dreaded anything so much since Scary Karen persuaded me to invigilate the sponsored breast-feed she and her mates held to raise money for Children in Need. (With hindsight, I guess I was naive to think she'd mentioned what we were up to when she applied for tickets to the public gallery at the Scottish Parliament. It was almost worth it, though, just to see the astonished looks on the faces of the armed response team... Also, thanks to a bus load of tourists with cameras, I'm apparently now a cult hero in Japan.)

I'll let you know how it goes.

Yours in a woman's world,

Ed.

Useless Dad's friends

Dear Dave,

It could have gone worse.

It could have gone a whole lot better but it could have gone worse...

I should have known something was up when they all arrived wearing raincoats. The way this summer has been going, that wouldn't normally be odd but the sun was shining and the four of them were wrapped up like a quartet of Inspector Gadget clones. I was distracted by the chaos of all our children colliding in a maelstrom of tantrums, greetings and wittering, though. I didn't take much notice.

As I said in my last letter, I was meeting Steve and his friends at the soft-play. They pretty much all turned up at the same time. Todd was an earnest American about my age with scarily perfect teeth and hair. Darren was bright-eyed, fresh-faced and said 'Yes!' a lot. Scott was a burly man in his mid-forties who gave the impression of being a rugby player. I quickly twigged that Scott was Steve's manager. This made him the boss of my wife's boss. Never good. I felt butterflies in my stomach – the kind of evil, misshapen butterflies that three-year-olds draw.

I picked Marie up and carried her around as a human shield.

We had about ten children between us, ranging in age from Scott's eldest daughter, who's around nine, down to Steve's youngest, Josquin, who's under a year. All the kids that could walk kicked off their shoes and charged into the enormous, multicoloured hamster run. Steve handed me Josquin for a moment, as if to take off his coat, and then leapt in after them. The other dads followed. I was left, quite literally, holding the baby.

I stared after them, not entirely believing how easily I'd been duped. I hefted Josquin over my shoulder and set off to give Steve a piece of my mind. At that point, however, he and his friends actually took off their coats. I stopped. I blinked. I turned around and took Josquin back to the area for very small children. I walked slowly, whistling nonchalantly to myself. Facility attendants dressed in red t-shirts ran past me in the other direction. Behind me there were thuds and screams, interspersed with tinny, futuristic sound-effects. It was as if a couple of *Space Invaders* cabinets had turned up and started a fight.

Steve and friends were playing *Laser Tag.*

I knew they couldn't get away with it for long – lights flashed all over their plastic guns and body-armour, and the air was thick with trash-talk and zapping. Not wanting to be shouted at by any council employees, I sat down and wished the ground would open up and swallow me. I promptly toppled over backwards into a ball-swamp and disappeared from view.

I think if I hadn't had my arms sticking out holding a rather surprised looking baby, I might have gone unnoticed. To be honest, I was as surprised as him. I lay there and held Josquin clear of the balls, his face an arm's length from my own, and we stared at each other. Somewhere above us and to one side, out of the corner of my eye, I could see four men being led away by guards in red t-shirts. One of the men was letting out long, low bloops and bleeps like you imagine Frogger would make as he limped forlornly into the path of a truck after being stood on.

One of the guards stopped by the edge of the ball-swamp and looked around while mumbling into a walkie-talkie. I made quiet shushing noises to Josquin. He grinned at me and giggled. I made the shushing noises more urgently. He grinned some more. I grinned back. We grinned at each other. He was quiet and I dared to breathe.

Then a glistening bead of dribble appeared on his lower lip.

My eyes widened. Josquin's mouth was directly above mine but the soft-play guard was still there and I didn't dare move. There was nothing I could do. The bead turned into a drop. It grew bigger. It began to bulge. The guard continued to loiter. The huge, quivering globule of saliva hung downwards, glistening in the light. Still the man would not go away. I tried to hold on for another few seconds. I tried not to think of the warm, sticky ooze that was precariously balanced only inches away from me. I tried to ignore the urge to leap up and run. I tried to think of a happy place. I tried... I...

"Aaaaaaaaaaaaaaaaaaaaaaaaaaaaaaaaaaaaaaaghhh!"

The guy just about swallowed his walkie-talkie as I erupted, shrieking, in a shower of plastic balls right beside him.

Ho well. At least I didn't get banned from the soft-play altogether like the others. I merely got a verbal warning and three points on my leisure card. It did mean, however, that I was left to look after an entire riot of small children while Steve and friends sat in the café and drank coffees.

I'm not sure a 'riot' is entirely the correct term but I've decided this whole collective noun thing is merely a way for English teachers and retired colonels to feel superior. I've started inventing my own. Forget a murder of crows or a pod of whales, how about a slapstick of toddlers or a brood of teenagers? Or maybe an irritation of Tweenies or a prospective-freezerful of Teletubbies? I await your own suggestions... Thinking of such things kept me sane as the rest of the hour passed.

When time was up, I took the sweaty horde for chocolatey snacks and sat down for my own coffee.

"So what do you do?" asked Darren enthusiastically before I'd even caught my breath.

"Steve said you're one of Deborah's colleagues," said Todd in his Texan accent.

"Like she does any work these days, sitting at home watching *Neighbours*," said Scott. The others sniggered sycophantically.

I didn't know where to start. Should I point out how much work being a stay at home parent entails? Should I mention Deborah's ambitions to return to her career? Would talking up both sound contradictory? Should I just tell them my own situation and brazen it out?

I wasn't sure and Steve was desperately trying to signal at me without the rest of them noticing. He looked like the cool kid caught in close proximity to a geek, a thick rulebook, some character sheets and a large pile of twenty-sided dice.

Using my normal line of defence, I decided to make a joke of it. "I'm Executive Vice President of a domestic services partnership," I said and fished out of my pocket some of the business cards I keep for these occasions. "My portfolio includes surveillance, sanitation, education and catering."

"That sounds interesting," said Darren.

Todd nodded. "Do you have share options?"

"He means he's a househusband," said Scott, somewhat contemptuous of both me and them.

"Housedad," I corrected.

Todd appeared puzzled by foreign concepts. Darren let out a long, "Ohhhh!" and then continued with, "Does your wife earn a lot then?"

"No, not really," said Steve. "She's on..."

I coughed loudly. He looked guilty and shut up but I suspected he would tell them all later, nonetheless.

"Still," said Darren, "must be cushy staying home while she goes out to work."

"What do you do all day?" said Todd.

"Wipe bottoms I expect," said Scott. "We can't sit around here finding out. We need to drop the little terrors home and continue the meeting back at the office."

I choked on my coffee. "You're counting this as work?"

Scott mocked me. "Aren't you?" he said.

"I, well, erm..." I'd walked into a trap.

Steve didn't exactly back me up. "We planned several excellent initiatives while you were in there having fun," he said.

(Grrrr.

Are you sure you don't want to come up and give him a good talking to?

Actually... I know exactly who to get to do it. It'll take a week or three to organise but it might work.

Hmmm...)

The four of them collected up their offspring and headed off to their impressive cars before I could think of anything much coherent to say. I was livid.

As a parting shot, they invited me to go paintballing with them soon. I couldn't really say no without looking like a total wuss. I did ask if I could bring some friends of my own, though. They weren't fussed. 'The more, the merrier,' apparently.

Of course, they may not be so convinced about that once they've been hunted down and decorated by Scary Karen and her mates...

Yours in a woman's world,

Ed.

Herding housedads

Dear Dave,

I must have been thinking too hard about inventing new collective nouns – the boys started doing it the other day without any prompting.

They were having an argument over exactly how many cows are necessary to constitute a herd. Lewis thought any number greater than one would do. Fraser was adamant that more than that was required. He settled on five. They got into the kind of legalistic argument that only small children, EU regulators and medieval theologians can really get worked up about. It went on for some time. I mean, how many cows *do* you need for a herd? Is it the same as the number of sheep required for a flock? Maybe, but almost definitely fewer than the number of fish you need for a school. Probably more than the number of lawyers you need for an excess, though...

Eventually Fraser got distracted by a tangential thought that glittered brightly in his brain. He followed it. "Can you have a herd of anything else?" he asked. "How about chickens?"

"Er, I think that might be a flock," I said but I wasn't totally certain. In fact, I was pretty sure that was wrong. Was it a brood? A gaggle? A peck? A Kentucky fry?

I decided to answer his first question. "You can have a herd of elephants."

"What about monkeys?" said Lewis. "Can you have a herd of monkeys?"

"Er..." I said, images becoming crossed in my head, and a herd of giant, hairy gorilla *things* (with trunks) stampeding across my mental savannah.

Fraser replied before I had a chance. "A banana! It should be a banana of monkeys!"

Both boys found this highly amusing. There is something about monkeys that children (and many adults) find instantly funny. The combination of monkeys *and bananas* somehow just adds to the comedy. Fraser and Lewis rolled around the floor laughing. (Luckily, they didn't think of an even more hilarious pairing. If anyone had mentioned a 'fart' of monkeys, for instance, the boys would have wet themselves.)

I started to say that a banana of monkeys sounded strange but I couldn't remember what the right word was and I stopped. Why not a banana of monkeys? It's as good as anything, and they might as well give it a shot – language is the ultimate democracy, after all. Get enough people to use a word and it becomes part of the language overnight; leave a word alone for fifty years and it dies.

If the kids want to try making 'banana' a collective noun, that's up to them. Doubtless a teacher will persuade them otherwise at some point, but you never know. Personally, I have two attempts at dictionary change on the go at the moment. The first is to make the singular of dice to be 'dice' rather than 'die'. Why? I don't know. I'd just prefer it that way. The campaign seems to be going fairly well so far.

The other small change to the English language I'm working on is the popularisation of the word 'housedad'. (You may want to join in this one.)

I've always thought 'househusband' is long-winded and doesn't really describe what I do. I was a househusband back in those distant days before children. I studied, I wrote, I did the hoovering and, on occasion, I sat around playing computer games and ate biscuits.

That is another life. How could I ever have been so idle, working only eight hours a day?

Nope, 'househusband' doesn't cut it. Nor does 'stay at home parent'. My kids don't yell 'Parent!' at three in the morning when they want some attention. (Not yet, anyway.) They yell 'Daddy!' because they know that's what is most likely to get results. They could yell 'Mummy!' but they'd still get Daddy. In fact, they could yell anything from 'I want my cucumber!' to 'Cheese weasel!' to 'I've eaten my pillow!' and they'd still get Daddy (as they know from experience). Yelling

'Daddy!' gives them a sense of victory as soon as I enter the room, however – their first demand has been met, surely it's only a matter of time before they manage to pester their way to the vegetable/ cheddar rodent /emergency medical procedure of their choice.

'Stay at home parent' is no good – I have earned the title of 'dad'.

'Stay at home dad' doesn't really work either, though. I know what it's like to stay at home: before children, I was not just a househusband, I was a 'stay at home husband'. It could be several days until I was forced to leave the front door in search of bread or milk. At that time, my study (translation: cupboard with a computer) didn't even have a window. I would emerge, blinking, onto the street and wonder at the contrast levels and high-definition visuals. If I'd been playing much *Resident Evil*, I would scan the pavement for zombies before proceeding. I really didn't get out a great deal.

These days, with one child at parent and toddler, one at nursery and one at school, I barely see my home. I'm forever trotting up and down the road with some subset of children in tow. And that's before taking into account clubs and classes, shopping trips and visits to the swing park. Stay at home? You've got to be joking.

Of the few remaining options, I quite like 'homedad' – it's more general than 'housedad' and suggests a happy family sitting round the kitchen table. It's cosy and it makes good sense.

Still, I don't call myself a homedad.

The thing is, English isn't about making sense. Try reading *through*, *though*, *cough*, *tough* and *bough* quickly and you'll know what I'm talking about. English is crazy. Most native speakers are used to the craziness, however, and don't notice. New words need to blend. For some reason, 'homedad' doesn't. It makes people do a double-take (in my part of the UK, at least). 'You're a *what*?'

I find 'housedad' simply works better. It sounds close enough to 'housewife' to slip past people's internal made-up-word-detector and it's two or three sentences down the line before the alarm bells start to ring inside their heads. It's too late by then, of course – I might be a nutter but they're already having a conversation with me. All they can do is open their eyes wide and back away slowly. (Top tip: Getting a small child to hug their leg makes it much harder for them to escape.)

So 'housedad' it is. It's a word that describes what I do but doesn't sound too odd. It might just catch on...

That only leaves one further decision. What should be the collective noun for us? I suppose, if it really takes five of us together to justify the use of such a word, then we probably don't need one. Or maybe an 'unlikelihood' of housedads is the way to go? Some old-fashioned individuals might suggest an 'aberration'. Maybe it would even depend what kind of day we'd all had. Perhaps a 'fulfilment'? Or, if we'd been tearing out our hair, a 'baldness'?

Let's face it, though, if someone discovered five of us together in a room one day, I know exactly what we'd be. We'd be a 'surprise'. The only possible way of avoiding that would be if we had our children with us. Then...

Then we'd be a 'pride'.

Yours in a woman's world,

Ed.

Harry Potter and the light switch of chaos

Dear Dave,

Hurrah! I've finally only got two Harry Potter books left to go.

Now I need to resist the urge to read book six. Between me playing catch up and Sarah re-reading them all, the kids are becoming restless with the amount of time we're spending at Hogwarts. Marie in particular is getting annoyed. "You reading Harry Potter!" she says excitedly as she skips over to the armchair. Then she jumps up and down and says, "You stop now," and closes the book on my thumb. I open the book again. She tips her head to one side, says, "Awwwww!" and pouts. I throw her a ball or something and go back to the book.

It's all rather off-putting and I'm wondering what she'll try next when she realises this ploy isn't working. She's taken to claiming that her food goes from her plate to her mouth, down to her tummy, into her legs and then into her socks. I'm slightly worried that soon she's going to cut out the intermediate stages and put the food straight from plate to socks just to grab my attention.

Let's face it, that will probably work.

I should stop while I still can. Things are already out of hand:

We were staying at my parents' house last week. While we were there, I fitted a smoke detector in their landing light. It recharges whenever the light is on and thus, so long as the light is used regularly, the battery should never go flat. The alarm does have one minor flaw, however – testing it involves switching the light off and on again in quick succession. This makes accidental testing rather easy.

The night I installed it, Sarah and I were sitting downstairs in the lounge reading Harry Potter books. My dad went up to bed and switched the landing light out. From upstairs, there was the muffled sound of my mum telling him off – the children might fall down the stairs if they got up and went wandering around in the dark. Dad switched the light back on.

The alarm started going.

There was frantic shouting from my mum about not waking the kids, mixed with muttering from my dad and the sound of the light being switched off and on rapidly. The alarm continued to wail.

Sarah and I both looked up from our books. The light seeping under the door from the stairwell was strobing erratically. We glanced at each other and I shrugged. We returned to our books. My parents continued their private rave on the stairs. The kids did not stir. We went back to reading.

Several hours later, we were still there. My dad went to the toilet. As he went back to bed, he switched off the landing light. He instantly remembered and switched it back on again. The alarm went off. My mum shouted. My dad muttered.

Sarah and I looked up from our books. The light flickered under the door once more. We stared at the ceiling for some time and waited patiently for the chaos to pass.

When it eventually did, we paused for a few more moments, listening out for the children. All that was to be heard was a dark remnant of muttering from my parents' room. It had been a close call. Sarah shook her head, sighed and looked at me. "Muggles!" she said despairingly.

I nodded. We went back to our books.

I think I must have been becoming drowsy by then. Everything went a little strange.

As time passed and the fire burned low in the Gryffindor common room, we continued to read. After all, we had OWLs in the morning and plenty of revision still to get through. "Accio beer!" I called and it flew into my hand (although it did seem to say, "There you go, dear," in Sarah's voice). Minutes turned into hours and the night drifted away...

I was woken for breakfast by a trio of boggarts jumping on my head. I was unable to make them vanish. The day slipped by in a tired blur punctuated with squabbling.

Didn't stop me staying up late again to read some more, though. Which reminds me, I should get to bed early tonight.

Maybe *just one* chapter first...

Yours in another world,

Ed.

Statistics

Dear Dave,

Ninety-three percent of statistics are misreported.

Think about it. Your average journalist is an arts graduate who hasn't studied any maths whatsoever in twenty-three and a half years. Even the four-fifths-forgotten statistics lessons they *have* had will have been to a very low level. The typical journalist, for instance, will only know two and a third types of average and will use the mean in eighty-nine percent of cases. Ask them to calculate the probability of three cases of a ten-thousand-to-one non-contagious illness in a village of a hundred people and they will either answer, 'Small enough to make a big headline,' or run away screaming. Neither of these is the correct answer.

The correct answer runs closer to, 'Is this the chance it will occur in a particular village chosen at random or that it will occur in *some* village somewhere in the United Kingdom? And besides, surely it should be the probability of three *or more* cases? And what are the assumptions again? You haven't even mentioned timescales, for crying out loud!'

An article I read the other week kept going on about the effects of interest rate rises on a typical mortgage. What on earth is a 'typical' mortgage?! Was it the mean value of all mortgages they were talking about or of new mortgages? Something else reckoned that a 'typical' baby sleeps sixteen hours a day. Since I felt lucky if any of mine slept twelve hours out of twenty-four when they were small, I can only assume that some children barely open their eyes before the age of two. What?

Then there are phone-in polls. Don't get me started on those. (No, really – it won't be pretty...)

To be fair, I don't think getting mathematicians to write the newspapers would, in general, be a good idea. (Can you imagine?) I merely tend to view reports of surveys with some scepticism. I saw one that claimed 43% of dads surveyed had 'put their careers on hold' to spend more time with their families, passing up work worth an average of a few thousand a year. What does that really mean, though? Ten percent of all the dads claimed to have gone to working part-time. Surely this must account for the vast majority of the wage reduction? From the information given, it was possible to conclude that over half of the dads had made no changes to their work patterns (maybe they were laid-back to start with!), one third had cut down on overtime a bit and one tenth had gone part-time (but who knows what their partners are up to?).

Does this actually tell us much?

Not really. I probably achieve equally scientific surveys by hanging around outside school at collecting time. On this basis, I'd say there are plenty of couples where both partners are heavily involved in childcare. One or both of them may be working part-time but it's just as likely they're both working strange shifts and granny is filling in the gaps in the schedule. There *are* housedads about but you could probably cram us all into a phone box.

Looking at parent and toddler attendance gives a different picture. Dads are rare. I am 'the man', quite often. Either the percentage of dads staying home and looking after very small children is extremely low or they're all remarkably wary of play groups. Maybe we're as endangered as pandas or female executives or crumple-horned snorkacks. Who knows? Not me.

I think all that the various surveys show is that the number of housedads is on the rise but, obviously, that's not saying much. There won't be vast numbers of us any time soon. More important is that, 'on average', dads are far more involved with their kids than they were a generation ago. Scarily, this makes you and me role models for a revolution where men engage more fully with their offspring. We demonstrate that it's perfectly possible for men to look after children whatever the occasion, not just on Saturday afternoons. We can educate and encourage. We can teach other men that, 'Kids are fun once you know which way up to hold them!' (But, er, maybe we might want to think of a better slogan...)

That may sound like a tall order but the simplest way to start is to walk along the road smiling with a stack of children in tow. If we can do it without everyone treating us like pandas, so much the better. ('Look! Look! There's one. It's a housedad! Aw, isn't he cute with all the little ones. Do you think if I poke this stick at him, he'll eat the leaves off the end?')

Probably best to ignore the statistics and get on with it.

I suppose you may be thinking that if ninety-three percent of statistics are misreported, what about the rest? Should we pay attention in order to learn from the other seven percent of stats we hear and read about?

I wouldn't bother, to be honest – those ones are *entirely* made up.

I'm off to prepare for the paintballing tomorrow. Apparently, Scary Karen has been watching *Rambo III* all week as training. This could get brutal...

Yours in a woman's world,

Ed.

PS I read *Freakonomics* by Stephen Dubner and Steven Levitt recently. Did you know that there's a correlation between having a house full of books and having children who do well at school, and yet reading to kids every day doesn't make a difference to academic performance?

Conclusion: Books are magic! Buy books!

Kidding. It's not what you do that makes you a good parent, it's who you are. Isn't that both reassuring *and* frightening...

Paintball apocalypse

Dear Dave,

There are three kinds of paintball experience that I'm aware of:

- The first I've only seen on TV and involves Americans running around multicoloured inflatable obstacles, shouting and taking it all very seriously.

- The second is more the sort of thing you get at an activity centre – people are assigned to a couple of teams, they're led into a relatively small arena filled with makeshift barricades and fortifications, and then they get to shoot each other for a bit. Half a dozen games, each lasting five minutes or so, and you're done. It's mucky but fun and only mildly like exercise. This is the one to go for.

- The third involves driving to the middle of nowhere and then skulking round a forest for half an hour at a time, before being shot in the back by someone you didn't even see.

The last of these was, unsurprisingly, what Steve had organised.

At least he gave me a lift. We spent most of the journey discussing rugby. I don't know anything about rugby but, then again, Steve didn't really seem to know much either. I think he was trying to pick my brains in order to gain information with which to impress his boss, Scott. Bearing this in mind, I talked up Japan's chances in the next World Cup and mentioned how Simon Cowell was once fly-half for St Helens. I should probably feel guilty but Steve's had Sarah working all hours on yet another daft marketing project that will probably never see the light of day. Even if it does eventually crawl out into the harsh sunshine, he'll almost certainly take the credit for any good which comes of it. Quite honestly, I'd just like my wife home at a reasonable hour and I'd prefer it if she didn't mutter in her sleep about how many free tickets to LEGOLAND a pair of Crocs is worth. (Don't ask.)

We arrived at a muddy expanse of woodland far from civilisation and squelched the short distance from the car park (a field) to the reception centre (a dilapidated caravan). We paid and were issued with face masks, camouflage overalls, guns and about enough paintballs to last us three and a half minutes. We were given the 'option' of buying more paint-balls.

Steve handed over a banknote without particularly looking at it. I don't know if he was expecting change but he ended up with so many little tubs of ammunition he rattled as he walked. Unfortunately, I had to buy almost as many – although Scary Karen and her friends were very keen to wreak some havoc after hearing about the way Steve's buddies had treated me at the soft-play, some of them were on a budget and I'd agreed to subsidise them. I guess if I hadn't spent the money, Sarah would have only put it in a pension or something, so I won't really notice the loss for a while, but I still gulped slightly as I gave the guy the cash. (Ach well, who needs things like shoes or heating when they're old, anyway?)

A long, high wall of netting separated where we were from the game area. We went over to a small cluster of huts, benches and portaloos next to the gateway. Scott was already there. He appeared to have brought most of his rugby club with him, judging by the number of large blokes who were gathered round him laughing. None of them was that young and some of their muscle was turning to belly but they looked like the type of people you want to make sure are on *your* side in a paintball match. They looked like the type of people who would take it seriously and get the job done.

Steve hurried over to join them.

My eye began to twitch. I'd been looking forward to filling Scott full of paint and I'd been hoping he would be surrounded by Steve, a couple of other sycophantic cronies and a horde of scrawny teenagers wearing bandanas and reliving *Apocalypse Now*.

You never want anyone wearing a bandana on your team. They will run around screaming, fire indiscriminately at anything which moves and then get disqualified for being insane (but not before they've shot you). Having a few bandana-wearing maniacs on Scott's team would have made it much easier to get to him. I didn't fancy my chances against an entire scrum of his burly mates.

Scott came over as I was slapping myself in the face in an effort to stop the twitching. He gave me a condescending sneer. "Are your friends showing up? How many of them are there going to be? We need to sort out teams."

"Rob can't make it, so there should be seven, provided they all managed to find babysitters. That's probably them now."

A black van bounced over the rutted grass and pulled up beside us. The tinted windows gave it an ominous appearance, spoiled somewhat by the enormous dents and heavy rust. For a few moments, nothing happened. Then the side door slid open and Scary Karen got out.

She was wearing a bandana.

Bess, Jess, Tess and Cress got out. They were wearing bandanas too.

"Now I think about it," said Scott, "our team's full. You and your friends will all have to be on the blue team." He pointed over to where a group of scrawny looking sixteen-year-olds were loitering nervously around a picnic table. As I watched, one of them hastily hid a character sheet and some dice. Another tripped over his own feet. All the rest were unable to move, transfixed by the very sight of women.

I sighed. At least none of *them* were wearing bandanas.

We also had Trevor and Stefania on our team once they'd taken the van to the car park and come back. Trevor, if you remember, is keen on Karen but hasn't quite plucked up the nerve to tell her yet. More importantly, he's built like a truck, has served in the armed forces and can spit a paintball with enough force to stun a rhino at twenty paces. Stefania, Karen's Polish friend, on the other hand, barely speaks a word of English and looks like she might blow away in a stiff breeze. When handed her gun, however, she pressed it to her shoulder, sighted a number of targets using swift precise movements and then examined every part of the gun closely. She had it stripped down, cleaned and reassembled with a resounding clunk before I'd even got the lid off my paintballs. Then she marched away determinedly, as if off to hunt some Russians.

Trevor and I exchanged glances. "You two stick together," I said.

He nodded and hurried after her.

We were nearly set. A marshal gave us the safety drill, handed out coloured armbands to identify which of the two teams we were in, told us the rules and then lined us up ready to take us to our bases.

I found myself standing next to Steve. "We'll try and go easy on you," he said. Then he pointed his gun at my groin and pretended to pull the trigger.

"Don't do that," I said.

"Don't worry," he replied. "It's not loaded."

Then he shot me in the inner thigh.

From three feet away.

It was a little sore.

He apologised profusely as I crumpled to the ground in agony but then his team got led away and I was left to be given first aid by Scary Karen in a location I really did not want her investigating. It's all very well being treated as one of the mums but I draw the line at massage and healing balm. Particularly there. I had to make a limp for it, just to keep my trousers on.

Nonetheless, the incident did provide an incentive to our team. We headed out to get some payback.

We failed miserably, though. We got gubbed. Half the team ran around screaming, shot anything which moved and then got disqualified for everything from hand-to-hand combat to frightening the squirrels. I was shot by one of my own team on no less than five occasions. The teenagers didn't know whether they were coming or going. I never saw Trevor and Stefania. I was forever trudging back to the area by the gate to clean myself off and wait for the next game. Somehow there always seemed to be plenty of casualties on the red team too, but never enough for us to actually win. It was hopeless.

The day wore on and we got wet and dirty and fed up. We reached the final game and we were becoming desperate. It was capture the flag. We had to get from our base to theirs, grab their flag and get back again, without them doing the same thing to us. We trudged to the clearing which contained our ramshackle, wooden fort and tried to compose ourselves before the klaxon sounded and the game began.

Karen was fuming. She'd thought the squirrel grenade had been a good idea but I'd been standing underneath as the little, paint-soaked critter had sailed overhead. Sure enough, it had looked terrified. She decided to take her frustration out on the teenagers, yelling at them for not working together, her enormous bosoms heaving up and down with fury. The teenagers were rooted to the spot, only their eyes bobbing, as if they were watching vertical tennis.

Trevor and Stefania were still missing. Everyone else sat around looking dejected. I decided that there was only one option left.

"Can anyone lend me a bandana?" I asked.

A minute later, the klaxon went and I sprinted through the foliage, a borrowed strip of cloth tied round my head. I raced between the trees, not stopping to think, shooting anything that moved. I may have screamed.

Paintballs whizzed past my ears. One bounced off my arm.

But nothing splatted.

I kept going. I fired until I had no paintballs left. My lungs burned, stars flashed in front of my eyes. Then I seemed to be through. There were no more enemies about and I blundered on. My running had slowed to a wheezing kind of stagger but, with some elation, I stumbled into the red fort and up the ramp to a little room that I knew would contain the flag.

I almost took Steve by surprise. He hadn't anticipated anyone making it that far and was busy sending a crafty text on his phone. Sadly, I couldn't take advantage – I'd been too high on adrenaline to expect a guard. We both raised our guns. We were only feet from each other in a confined space. Seconds ticked away. It was a stand-off.

"You might as well surrender," he said. "Even if you shoot me, I'll shoot you. You're not getting out of here with the flag."

I lowered my gun slightly, pointing it at his crotch. His eyes widened. "Don't worry," I said, laughing evilly. "It's not loaded."

"OK, OK," he said, putting his gun down.

"Glad you saw reason," I replied, grabbing the flag. "Now give me your sock."

"What?"

"Give it to me!"

"OK, OK," he squeaked, hurrying to pull off his boot and one of his long, woollen rugby socks. I stuffed it in my pocket and ran.

The journey back took longer. I was tired and since I'd actually managed to claim the flag, I felt I had something to lose. I was more cautious on my return. Still, I didn't encounter any resistance and, as I ducked out from behind the last tree, I wondered whether I was the only one left playing.

An entire rugby team was waiting for me.

"It's all over," said Scott, stepping forward from the middle of the pack. "Give me the flag."

I froze. I didn't know what to do.

Luckily, I was part of a team, too.

"Now!" screamed Karen and the air was suddenly alive with paintballs. I dived out of the way. Somehow she'd managed to get the teenagers organised. They emerged from the trees and surged forward like an avenging tide of Ewoks. Rugby players scattered. Mums sniped from the woods.

"Now get the flag home," Karen yelled at me from the maelstrom.

I nodded and threw her back her bandana. "Here!"

"Don't you want it anymore?"

"I've got one of my own," I shouted, grinning, and tied Steve's sock round my head. Then I escaped under cover of mayhem, ran into the trees and tried to find a route to our base from a different angle.

I forced my way through some bushes and I was almost there when Scott stepped out in front of me. I stopped dead. He could have shot me but he seemed to want to enjoy his victory.

"Now be a good househusband and give me the flag. This doesn't have to get nasty," he said, gloating.

My mouth was dry. What could I do? Then I noticed that on either side of him the bushes were edging closer. I tried to hide a smile. "Housedad," I said.

"What?"

"I call myself a housedad."

"Whatever. Just give me the flag." The bushes were right beside him now.

"No."

"Well, you had your chance..."

"Drop it!" said one bush gruffly. The other bush hurled abuse in Polish.

Scott's eyes tried to look both ways at once. Then, foolishly, he went for the trigger. I dived out the way again and ran for our base. Behind me, there was the unmistakable sound of senior management being painted with extreme prejudice by some shrubbery. I didn't look back.

I stormed up the ramp to our base and waved the flag aloft as my team used up the last of their ammunition chasing the enemy into the hills. I was glad I'd bought so much. It was all very satisfying and money well spent. I'll probably regret it in forty years' time when I have to hobble down to the bowls club in carpet slippers but, if nothing else, I'll have the memories to keep me warm.

I gave Steve back his sock in the car on the journey home. For some reason, he wasn't that appreciative.

Let's hope there aren't any repercussions for Sarah...

Yours in a woman's world,

Ed.

Part 4

When Everything Springs a Leak

Pester power

Dear Dave,

Sorry to hear that Sam's constant demands for attention and material gratification are driving you crazy. Let's face it, he probably knows that his entire life is about to go down the pan with the arrival of a sibling, and so he's simply trying to get what he can while the going's still good. Stay strong and don't let him pester you into buying anything other than consumer electronics.

I'm fairly immune to pestering, myself. Actually, that's a lie – it makes me irritable, crotchety and prone to shouting. Pestering annoys me as much as the next dad. What I mean to say is that it doesn't get the kids what they want.

Much of this is down to Fraser. He has a bad case of Alpha Male Syndrome and desperately thinks he should be in charge. When confronted with two chairs and the command to sit down, he will begin by ignoring the command. On the second repetition of the command, he will argue. *Why does he have to sit down? Wouldn't it be better if he sat on the floor? Why can't he witter about Pokémon first? Why isn't Lewis sitting down?* On being shouted at and pointed to the left seat, he will perch on the edge of the one on the right. It's a near certainty he will fall off and injure himself within a couple of minutes and then complain about how he didn't want to sit down in the first place.

He's been like this for a long time. When he was two, I had a big fight with him over a beaker of milk. We both wanted it transferred from his hand to the table beside him; we disagreed on the method in which this goal could be achieved. I wanted him to reach over a few inches and put the beaker down. He wanted me to cross the room, take the beaker from his hand and put it down for him. We were there for fifteen minutes before his arm got tired and he put the flipping thing down. It was all about dominance and control.

The thing is, the endless petty pestering has built up my resistance. If I feel I'm being pestered, I'll even actively delay doing something I was about to do anyway. I hope that, one day, the kids will learn from this and be polite and patient. It's not working so far but, in the meantime, I get to take a little break now and then and claim it's all in the name of teaching them manners.

Of course, it's best to try and nip the pestering in the bud whenever possible. When we go to the supermarket, for instance, the kids are each allowed to choose one special treat. If they've already got something in the trolley but see something else they want, then simply being reminded 'they already have their special thing' is enough to stop them asking anymore. If they *really* want to swap, they can but usually they're too lazy to bother. In essence, they get to automatically win a small battle in exchange for not starting a war.

I like to think this set up teaches them decision making into the bargain but, deep down, I know that's just the deluded longings of a middle-class stay at home parent. They normally go for the shiniest thing they see first. (If I'm fortunate, they'll choose an item I was going to buy anyway, such as crisps. Frequently it's probiotic yogurt drinks(!) or Cheestrings. One time, Fraser pushed his luck with an enormous bowl of trifle – we all ate well that week.)

Lewis has a different pestering technique from Fraser. He tries to grind me down with questions:

Lewis: Can I have a chocolate biscuit?
Me: No.
Lewis: Why not?
Me: Because it's almost tea-time.
Lewis: Why's it almost tea-time?
Me: Because it's five o'clock.
Lewis: Why does that make it almost tea-time?
Me: Because you normally have tea at five thirty.
Lewis: Why?
Me: Because if I left tea until later, you'd get hungry.
Lewis: Why would I get hungry?
Me: Because you wouldn't have had anything to eat.

Lewis: Why not?
Me: Because it wouldn't be tea-time until later.
Lewis: Why wouldn't it be tea-time?
Me: Because... No, hang on, it *is* going to be tea-time at five thirty.
Lewis: Why?
Me: Because that's when you normally have tea.
Lewis: Why do we normally have tea at five thirty?
Me: So you don't get hungry.
Lewis: Why would I get hungry if I'd had a chocolate biscuit?
Me: You wouldn't get hungry if you'd had a chocolate biscuit.
Lewis: Why not?
Me: Because you'd have had a chocolate biscuit.
Lewis: Why can't I have one then?
Me: Because it's almost tea-time.
Lewis: Why's it almost tea-time?
Me: Because it's... Look over there! Something shiny!

All I can do is run away – it would feel wrong to tell a child to stop asking questions. He still doesn't receive what he wants, though. Marie has found a much better way to get round me: if she wants something, she acts as if she has it already.

Marie: I want ride my pink scooter to shops.
Me: You don't have a scooter.
Marie: Yes, I do.
Me: No, you don't.
Marie: Yes, I do. It pink.
Me: Where is it then?
Marie: It in kitchen.
Me: No, it's not.
Marie: Yes, it is.
Me: Show me.
Marie *(going through to the kitchen)*: It not here! It not here! We go look for it.

Me: But you don't have a scooter.
Marie: Yes, I do. It pink!
Me: Er... How about we go to the swing park?
Marie: Hooray! I scoot there.
Me: BUT YOU DON'T HAVE A SCOOTER!
Marie: I do... *(Bites lip and looks sad.)* You help me find it?
Me: I, er...
Marie: *Please...*
Me: Er, I think you might have left it in the toy department at John Lewis.
Marie *(brightening)*: We go get it! It pink!

She's trouble, that one. It got to the stage that she coveted pink Crocs so much that, whenever she saw another child wearing them, she'd run over and accuse them of stealing shoes she didn't have. Credit to her, all the same – while Fraser unwillingly sits on a chair listening to Lewis ask questions about the relationship between tea-time and chocolate biscuits, she scoots round them, happily wearing fuchsia footwear.

I was unwrapping a Mars bar for myself today and she walked up and said, "That's mine." AND I JUST GAVE IT TO HER. It's like some strange form of Jedi mind control.

I think she may have bitten off more than she can chew for her next project, however. Apparently we're all going to Euro Disney. At Easter. In a plane. She's totally convinced this is happening but I'm wise to her schemes now. I will resist.

Good luck with Sam.
Yours in a woman's world,
Ed.

Things you've forgotten about babies

Dear Dave,

You're probably thinking you've got a month to go. You're probably thinking you've got plenty of time to do all those little jobs like fetch the crib out the loft. You're probably even thinking you'll have a chance to pack Sam off to the grandparents for the weekend soon, so you can spend some quality time with Liz before all Hell breaks loose.

Look at it this way, though: by my calculations, you passed thirty-six weeks yesterday. If Squiggly turns up now, the hospital won't even count him/her/it as premature.

Hope you've got that bag packed.

To get you in the right frame of mind, here are a few things you might have forgotten about babies in the last three years:

They're small.

Look at Sam. You know he's three but, truth be told, you still think of him as your little baby. The *actual* baby will make him seem like a pre-school Godzilla, stomping through the lounge, over-turning activity gyms, crushing Fisher-Price playsets and endangering any tiny siblings left in his path.

Dealing with this will require some mental readjustment (and possibly a cage).

They arrive pre-filled with tar.

Yep, nothing says, 'Congratulations! You're a dad again!' more clearly than a nappy full of foul, sticky, black slime.

I'm not sure what the biological reasons are for this stuff but I suspect it's some kind of survival mechanism. It means that no matter what noxious mess a parent ends up in over the following months and years, they will find solace in the fact that at least they're not trying to scrape distilled evil off a baby's bottom with soggy cotton-wool. It makes everything else so much easier to forgive.

They only sleep when *you* have to be awake.

Like when they're being fed or pushed round in a buggy or being driven somewhere in the car or having their nappy changed. Squiggly will wake up at three in the morning, wanting fed and changed. She will sleep through most of this but then wake up crying when placed in the crib, as if the mattress is composed of spiky ice. You will then push her round the kitchen table in the buggy, trying to get her to sleep, before strapping her into the car and taking her for a ride. Upon returning, she will sleep in the crib just long enough for you to doze off. Then she will wake up needing fed and changed.

You possibly don't remember it being this bad with Sam but that doesn't mean it wasn't. It means that sleep deprivation Swiss-cheesed your brain. Be afraid of what else you might have forgotten...

They eat constantly.

I've been told that this is because their stomach is only the size of a walnut and so they need frequent refills but really it's because:

They vomit constantly.

Sometimes it's a little dribble on your shoulder. Other times it's a burp down your back. Often it's a belch over both of you. Once in a while it's a high-pressure fountain of curdled milkiness which erupts over the entire room for several minutes. (Isn't it amazing how much liquid a walnut can hold?)

They go through more changes of clothes in a day than you own for yourself in total.

Between leaky nappies, the dribbling and the vomit, there's always plenty of laundry to be done. The classic scenario is gingerly removing a kid's clothes and nappy because of an escape of toxic chicken tikka, and then having them pee on the clean clothes laid out next to them. It's difficult to know what to clean first in such a situation but there's only one certainty: when everything is scrubbed, the nightmare is over and you're fastening the last popper of the babygro as they lie on the changing mat, that's when they'll vomit down their neck, rub their hair in the resulting puddle and then fill their nappy explosively in surprise.

They smell.

This isn't all that astonishing, given most of the above, but I thought I'd better mention it...

They don't smile.

This is actually the most difficult thing to cope with. It's usually six weeks before babies learn to smile. Up until then, the best feedback you can hope for is no crying. No crying means they're happy. No crying means you're definitely doing your job right.

It's better than the rest of the time, when you're doing your job right and they're crying anyway, but it's not very encouraging all the same.

Just keep slaving on and hold out for that first smile. It makes all the rest of it worth it.

Now go and pack that bag.
Yours in a woman's world,
Ed.

Of mice and Mario

Dear Dave,

Most places it rains water. A few places it rains frogs. Very occasionally, in the American Midwest, it rains cows… I should be so lucky. There's a short season in Edinburgh – it only lasts from late July to the end of August – where local conditions combine with a light headwind to produce a most disconcerting meteorological phenomenon.

It rains acrobats.

This wouldn't be so bad but they're usually carrying sharp knives, flaming sticks or each other. Somebody's going to get hurt one of these days and, let's face it, it's probably going to be me. I'm usually so busy picking my way through the traders and tourists that I don't see the Super Mario Brothers tumbling towards me, and I can't hear them cursing each other in Italian because of yet another bagpipe rendition of *Flower of Scotland* blaring away right next to me. So I always end up getting a slice of experimental street theatre in the face.

The Festival, don't you just love it?

Normally we're far enough from the centre of town for me to be able to avoid the worst of things but we've been moved out of the house while the flood damage is repaired. The insurance company have put us in an apartment right next to the Parliament, close to the epicentre of the chaos. We have to wade through a sea of foreign teenagers and people handing out flyers to get anywhere. It's madness.

The apartment is very swish but not enormously child-friendly. Everything is made of glass. Glass-topped dining tables are not much fun with children. The one here has sharp corners, clatters every time a piece of cutlery is moved and gets mucky the moment a child even looks at it. The only advantage is that when a kid drops some food, you can see exactly where it's gone. Well, you can until the view is obscured by all the fingerprints (and, as it turns out, footprints) on the underside of the table.

On a more positive note, cleaners come in every day. This means the table doesn't get too grotty, but having the toilet cleaned five times a week can't be good for our immune systems.

Nonetheless, it's nice being away from home. After the flood and the air-blowers, there came a plague of insects welling up under the floorboards. Someone sprayed chemicals to deal with them but now we have an infestation of mice.

I found a small amount of evidence we had a problem when we returned home from my parents, so I put out a couple of traps. Nothing happened for a few days. Then I caught the scrawniest mouse you've ever seen. There was much jubilation. I'd never caught a mouse before – they usually nick the cheese and do a runner. Using a bit of chocolate bar as bait seemed to do the trick. I was delighted.

I was less delighted when I caught another. Catching one mouse gives hope that the problem is solved. Catching two *within an hour* suggests that the problem is much bigger than first imagined. I've since caught another two. There's still skittering. All the food is in high cupboards or in tins, so I'm not too worried, but it's been disconcerting sitting in the kitchen waiting for the little critters to sniff out one of my deadly surprises. Our study has been no use because all the furniture's been removed to allow the walls to be repaired and decorated. I've had to sit typing at the dining table, surrounded by teetering piles of junk that has nowhere else to go, and wait for the *SNAP!* of a rodent needing burial.

I'm not desperate to return.

Maybe things will be looking up next week. School is back already and we should have settled into a routine by then. There's going to be a big meeting at LBO, though, and there are mutterings of redundancies. Not good.

Right, the P1 class is only in until lunch-time for the first few weeks, so I should wade off through the street performers to collect Lewis. I was late yesterday because Marie and I got ambushed by some very persistent mimes. Today, however, we should make better time.

I've fitted scythes to the buggy.
Yours in a woman's world,
Ed.

A rough week

Dear Dave,

There is a scene in the first episode of *Desperate Housewives* where the one with the riot of small children (Lynette) runs into a former colleague while attempting to buy groceries. This other woman asks Lynette how things are going and how she's finding being a housemom. Lynette has spent the last several minutes shouting at her children. Behind her they are demolishing what little remains of the store. She obviously wants to reach over, grab the woman by the shoulders and shake her, screaming, "I can't take it anymore. They're driving me insane! Please, help me! Please..." Instead, she forces a smile, says, "Best job I've ever had," and beats a hasty retreat.

There's a lot of truth there. It can be hard for parents to admit that they're not enjoying themselves. I know I have all kinds of fears – fear of being judged, of seeming ungrateful, of betraying my family or of being reported to social services (or worse, to the wife). Maybe in my case there's also the fear of being pitied for being 'a man in a woman's job'. ("Well, what did you expect...?")

This is nonsense. Whatever the job, we all have days, weeks and even years where the going is tough. It's perfectly fine to get some sympathy and support.

I am lucky enough to be able to honestly say that being a housedad *is* the best job I've ever had. Nonetheless, having said it, I have to admit that it's been a rough week.

We're back in our house but nothing much has been fixed. Despite moving us out for a week to a fancy apartment, the insurance company failed to authorise the contractors to actually do the work. The contractors agreed to get started as best they could all the same but weren't entirely sure what they were supposed to be doing. They decided the first job was to remove all the plumbing under the stairs. This allowed them to check more thoroughly for damp patches from the flood and to replace six floorboards which got destroyed during the many fruitless attempts to find the leak. Then they put the plumbing back.

Half of it, anyway.

The plumber broke something in the heating system and reckoned he needed to take it to a blacksmith for repairs. We returned home to find the cold water was on again but the only hot water was from our ancient and very dubious immersion heater.

Several days passed and the plumber did not return. Then I noticed a bad smell from under the stairs. Waste water was leaking liberally every time we flushed a toilet or emptied a sink. Gah!

I phoned the contractors and they sent round a different plumber. He fixed the leak but I've had to bail out my house again. As it happens, the first plumber had already been 'let go' before I phoned. The company had no idea our heating wasn't working. They should have a part by next week but, for crying out loud! And all for six floorboards. None of the plastering or wallpapering has been done. We've missed our slot for the decorators now, so it will be a month before they can start but we've already cleared out the rooms involved.

Besides half the house falling apart and the other half being crammed full of stuff, the mice are taking up tap-dancing behind the cooker. One did a double flip with twist past me down the stairs. I gave it an 8.5. I would have given it more but its landing was terrible. I just found another – it leapt at me from inside the toaster. We've resorted to shaking out our shoes before putting them on.

Thanks to the disruption, Marie has gone from barely having a toilet accident, to needing five pairs of pants a day. She also constantly refuses to do anything she's told.

All this, and Sarah's job uncertainty is getting to me and her both.

It's a little much.

I've had depression before; I know some of the warning signs. I haven't been sleeping well and I've been abnormally crotchety and lacking in energy. I started feeling drawn and just plain debilitated the other day. If you want to know what I mean, stand up, hold one arm straight out to the side and think happy thoughts for thirty seconds. Get someone to try and pull down your arm. Then do it again with the other arm but think about something which stresses you and makes you upset instead. You'll notice a difference. That's how I've been feeling for a couple of days.

Unexpectedly, the thing which really got to me was not being able to play my Xbox.

The tiny room it's been set up in for over a year had to be cleared out for a couple of weeks to allow repairs to be made. Lately, the room has become a study but before that I used to have a small table wedged in the corner next to the end of the changing unit (the head end, naturally) with a monitor on top and the Xbox underneath.

As entertainment centres go, it's never been much. Losing it temporarily shouldn't have been a big deal. After all, I have other games machines and more games to play than I have time to play them. The absence of the Xbox should have been an inconvenience, not a disaster. Nonetheless, I found myself obsessing over it. Once I knew the decorators weren't coming for a while, I felt compelled to blow a couple of hours putting the room back together, despite knowing full well that I'll only have to pack it all away again soon. It was crazy but it had to be done.

As I moved the table back into place and started to set up all the equipment, I began to feel happier and I understood what the problem had really been. I was missing my safe place. That small corner of the house is as far from everyone else as I can possibly get. It's cosy. It's always been free of mice. I've often gone there to play games and wind down late at night. It's my place to not worry. My place to hide. Putting it back together made me smile.

The weird thing is, I don't have to be in the safe place to feel better. I just need to know it's there. I got everything working, spent three minutes shooting aliens and then set about thoroughly tidying the house. Most of it is still in a state because of the water damage but it's much less of a tip than it was. I can live with what's left and that's helped me feel better too.

Yep, it's been a rough week but I'm coping again. Sometimes the only way to stay sane is to admit you're a little crazy (whatever anyone else might think).

Yours in a woman's world,

Ed.

PS One of the great things about this job is that, even in the worst weeks, there's bound to be something to make you smile:

As we went down the vegetable aisle in the supermarket, Marie suddenly screamed, "I want broccoli!"

"We have broccoli at home," I replied.

"I want MORE broccoli!" she yelled.

"Er, OK," I said, hastily grabbing some and giving it to her.

She hugged the bag to her chest like a favourite teddy, rocking it. Then she sank back in the buggy and relaxed. "That's better," she sighed in relief.

Other parents looked on in awe as their children clutched packets of sweets. How on earth, they wondered, had I managed to raise a two-year-old who has a tantrum when *not* given green vegetables? For a brief moment, I was SuperDad.

Blunt, farce and trauma

Dear Dave,

My timing is as impeccable as ever.

As you'll recall, I'm under obligation to encourage Steve to be a more involved dad but I haven't been awfully successful. He's too caught up in work and in impressing his manager to get the message. I think it's got to the point where I'm just not blunt enough for the task. Sure, I can nurture his parenting skills and bring him closer to his inner housedad, but he's going to have to want those things first. He needs to stop seeing his kids as an inconvenience that his wife is dealing with. He needs a revelation.

Engineering those is notoriously difficult.

During the last few weeks, I've considered various options from subliminal messaging on his iPod to fake memos from senior management. I even devised an overly-complicated plan involving a papier-mâché angel, a searchlight and a burning smartphone. These all seemed underhand, however (and too much like effort, to be honest). That said, I was tempted by the idea of giving him a near-death experience. Very tempted.

In the end, I decided my best bet was inviting Steve to one of the games nights at my house so he could meet my friend Mike. Mike is good at being blunt.

Unfortunately, I organised the get-together for last night. Since the big meeting at LBO where they're going to announce the redundancies is today, I was somewhat tense about Sarah's job situation. When Rob turned up, he was in a similar state over his own.

"You OK?" I said, showing him in and leading him up to the lounge.

"Nervous about tomorrow."

"What's the worst that can happen?"

"They fire me, I never work again, Kate dumps me, I have to live in a wheelie bin and the Child Support Agency hunts me down with a pack of rabid dogs."

"You've been sitting in your cubicle thinking about that all week, haven't you?"

"Yep," he said, "it's not like they've given me any work to do. I've be... Aghh!" We were going upstairs and he gave a shriek as a mouse nearly landed on his head, did a triple back flip with reverse twist and landed running in the hall. I pulled out some numerical fridge magnets from my trouser pocket and held up a 9.6. "What the...?"

I shrugged. "We have mice. I think they're training for some sort of Festival performance. Just keep your shoes on and don't accept if anyone offers you any toast."

He nodded but appeared even more nervous than he had before.

"Anyway," I said. "I thought you were trying to look busy completing a project that's already been cancelled."

"They out-sourced it to India."

"Er..."

"It's kind of like a trial run," he explained. "They're testing communications and structures while making sure these guys can really code. Time's cheaper over there, so LBO can waste more of it for less money."

"Yep, you're screwed," I said as we entered the lounge and I handed him a beer. "If it's any consolation, I'll look after your 3D telly to free up some space in that wheelie bin."

"Not funny. How are Sarah's prospects?"

"The last time I saw her Head of Division, he was bright orange and swearing revenge."

"He can't hold losing at paintball against Sarah," said Rob. "She wasn't even playing."

"Scary Karen tied him to a tree and used a roller. He may not be entirely reasonable about things."

Rob grinned. "I'll find a really big wheelie bin and you can share it with me."

"Thanks."

The doorbell rang. I left Rob setting up the Wii and hurried back downstairs. It was Steve.

Conversation was somewhat awkward. Being head of Sarah's department, he knew whether she was going to be made redundant. Sarah had gone to her sister's for the evening to avoid him. I wittered as I took his coat and ushered him up to the lounge. I knew that he knew. He wasn't as abrupt as he usually is, which meant that he knew that I knew that he knew. Then he saw my quizzical expression, his face twitched and I knew that he knew that I knew that he knew that I knew that he knew. And my eyebrows must have raised because it looked like *he* knew that I...

"So is Sarah getting the sack, then?" asked Rob, as soon as we entered the room.

This refreshingly direct approach almost worked. "Ah, well," said Steve, "the details are going to be announced tomorrow but I..." Then he recognised Rob. "You work in IT, don't you? You were one of the people that re-did the data analysis thingies last year. Bob, isn't it?"

"That's me," said Rob. "Are all the, er, thingies going OK?"

"Oh, yes. There are a couple of guys I know at a major insurance firm who are very jealous of the Inverse Customer Retainment Index Calculator. It's an excellent system and so easy to use – our analysts needed less than an hour to get to grips with all the new bits and pieces. They simply got on with the job as normal."

"Oh," I said, knowingly, "I'd forgotten you did that project for Steve."

Rob looked shifty. "Yeah. I had no end of problems, remember? I don't want to talk about it."

I nodded. Steve had read in a magazine about some 'amazing' software that had any number of functions which sounded useful and he put in a request for extra options to be coded into the LBO marketing analysis tools. There were dozens of meetings but none of the people who regularly used the tools wanted the new stuff. Sarah told Rob on the sly to just change the colour scheme and move some of the menus around. It was enough to convince Steve that Rob had done a year's work in an afternoon and it had the added bonus of not breaking any of the code in the process...

The doorbell rang again and I hurried to answer it. As I left the room, Steve was busy asking Rob if he still mentioned *Star Wars* at inappropriate times.

"Steve here?" said Mike when I let him in. I'd already primed him with most of the details of my predicament.

"Yep."

"Good." He headed up the stairs. A mouse flew past his ear and he blatted it out of the air with the back of his hand as it was performing a complicated figure-of-eight spin. It careened off the wall, hit the coat hooks and slid down into Rob's jacket pocket.

"You killed Boris!" I said in the middle of pulling out some numbers.

"He might only be stunned," said Mike, "if you want to take a look."

I thought about it. "Nah..." I said, shaking my head, and we continued to the lounge.

I did the introductions. "What do you do?" Steve asked Mike, clearly excited by the chance to network.

"You'd be surprised," said Mike. "It's usually a mixture of public speaking, management, social work, counselling and teaching."

"Really? Who do you work for?"

"Jesus," said Mike, offering Steve a beer.

"Oh." Steve glanced at me and Rob to confirm that Mike wasn't having him on. Then he realised that he was trapped in a room with a computer geek, a housedad and a minister of religion. He took a couple of involuntary steps backwards.

I decided to make him feel at home. "Golf?" I said and handed him a wiimote. He regarded me like I was on drugs.

"I'll show him how to do it," said Mike, grabbing the motion-sensing controller.

"Make sure you've got the strap on tight," I said anxiously. "I've rearranged the room so you shouldn't be able to hit anything, but short, sharp movements are just as good as..." I was forced to duck as he took an enormous back swing and then dive out the way as he clubbed his virtual ball halfway to Mars. "...lethal arm-waving," I muttered.

Steve was entranced. The possibility of being able to play golf without leaving the house had him hooked. He wanted to know all about the Wii and couldn't wait for a shot. I had visions of him running out first thing in the morning and buying one with a copy of *Tiger Woods*, then never interacting with his family ever again. I'd made yet another error. My only hope was that he wouldn't be able to find the SCART socket on his telly.

As we played, we filled Mike in on the turmoil at LBO. Well, Rob and I did. Steve kept fairly quiet, interjecting only to occasionally defend senior management and their bold plan for the future. He didn't seem entirely clear what the plan was, however. Rob had a couple of beers and relaxed a little. He finally began to see the bright side...

"It's not as if I like the job, is it? I mean, it's OK, and everything. I get left alone to get on with stuff and the benefits are great but... What if there's something better? I haven't looked. There might be something I could really enjoy."

I nodded. "I hear Angelina Jolie is looking for a pet."

He appeared momentarily interested and then took in I was joking. "Seriously," he said. "I need to think about it now before... before..."

Mike sank a lengthy putt. "Before you become a dad, you forget what sleep is, you have no energy for change, risk begins to seem more risky and you start to smell slightly of used nappies?"

"Something like that," said Rob.

"Ach, get over it," said Mike. "There's always the possibility for change."

"It would be easier now, though," I added.

"I'm not denying that," said Mike, "but it's always worth working out what you'd do if you lost your job tomorrow – you never know when you might come up with a plan which is worth doing anyway. What are you going to do if they make you redundant, Steve?"

Steve gave a condescending smile as he tapped one in. "I've been assured that my position is safe."

"By your boss?" asked Mike.

"Yes. Scott and I have worked closely together on a number of projects," began Steve. "I feel that he values my contribution to..."

Mike cut him off. "Have you been completely straight with anyone who works for *you*?"

Steve grunted, shrugged, twitched and looked at me, all at the same time.

"Thought not," said Mike. "Best to at least consider the possibility, if I were you. Would getting fired make you happy or sad? Turn you numb or present you with an opportunity? What do you have outside work to hold onto? Where are you headed? Why are you going there in the first place? What's important? What's your purpose? Who are you and what do you want?"

Steve opened his mouth to answer.

"Heck," said Mike, "don't tell me. Do I look like I care?" He squared up for another big swing. "Tell your wife when you get home." He walloped the ball to within six inches of the hole. "And a fiver says I can beat you over the back nine."

Steve blinked and gaped and then remembered to breathe. Wisely, he declined the bet but he was shell-shocked for the rest of the evening. The conversation turned to lighter things – children, mice, incompetent plumbers and suitable pets for Angelina Jolie. We played golf some more, then moved on to bowling. I made Rob and Mike toasties. Steve had some toast. We finished off with a quick go at *Mario Kart*. I won (thanks to my many hours of being forced to play by Fraser) but Steve was surprisingly good, in spite of his lack of gaming experience. Rob just kept complaining about the unfairness of the blue homing-missiles, as ever.

After that, people started to drift off, agreeing to meet up again soon. Steve went home looking pensive which, I guess, is about the best I could have hoped for. Rob left a few minutes later. I closed the door behind him and there was a muffled scream as he reached the end of the drive – doubtless at the moment he put his hands in his pockets.

Only Mike remained, taking a while to put his coat on.

"Thanks," I said. "You gave Steve something to think about. I don't know if he *will* think about it, but it's better than I've done in several weeks."

Mike rubbed his chin and peered at me appraisingly. "What about you? I know your situation is different but what are you outside your job, Ed? You spend your entire time running around after small children. There's nothing more absorbing than that. What's going to happen when Marie starts nursery and you get some space to yourself?"

I started the mantra. "Not much – not in two hours a day, on weekdays, during term-time when all the kids are w..."

"You've told me that before," he said, frowning. "I'm not asking what you're going to do. I'm asking who you're going to be."

"I, er..."

"Yes, Steve is a pompous jerk but stick with him. He's going to be no more lost if he loses his job than you will be when all your kids are at school."

And with that, Mike was out the door. "See you on Sunday," he said and was gone.

It was my turn to be shell-shocked.

Yours in a woman's world,

Ed.

One-dimensional eating habits

Dear Dave,

Thanks for the sympathy over all the things that aren't going entirely to plan right now. I know you have enough on your own plate to worry about at the moment. (Have you decided on any names!?) Sorry to hear Sam's acting up and refusing to eat anything which isn't long and thin. This does give you plenty of scope for nutrition, however – breadsticks, Cheestrings, carrots, chocolate fingers, crayons... There's a relatively long list of readily available foodstuffs and plenty of other things aren't too hard to cut into linear snacks. Clearly you're going to be struggling with items like baked beans and peas and cake but I'm sure there must be ways round that. Mashing them up and squishing them together might work. Maybe not all at once, mind, but it depends how pushed you are for time...

Marie had a phase where she'd only eat doughnut-shaped food. This was much more awkward to accommodate. For a while she was made of Cheerios, Hula Hoops and Party Rings.

I should maybe just have given her the doughnuts and called her Homer.

Her Simpson-esque traits became even more apparent the other evening at the point I was getting her ready for bed. She was annoyed over nothing and acting up about everything and I asked her if she was tired.

"No," she said, fighting her pyjamas as I tried to get them on her.

I wrestled one arm into her top. "Do you want to go to bed?"

"No!" she said, taking it off again.

"Are you sure?" I said, forcing the garment back over her head. "I think you need to lie down and get some sleep."

"NO!" she screamed and started to cry. She unquestionably and urgently needed some sleep but wasn't having any of it.

I was exasperated, frustrated and tired. I made the mistake of being sarcastic with a two-year-old. "What do you want to do then? Stay up all night and drink beer?"

She stopped. She looked at me. She jumped up and down excitedly. "Yes!"

"Er... I didn't really..."

"I not go to bed," she yelled, her body quivering with anticipation at the prospect of a six-pack, a sofa and a marathon of late night cable TV. "I not sleep. I drink beer!"

At which point Fraser and Lewis appeared from nowhere. "How come Marie's getting beer?" said Fraser.

"We want beer, too," said Lewis.

"Yes, can we have beer?" said Fraser.

Marie started running backwards and forwards along the length of the landing. "Want beeeeeeeeeeer! Want beeeeeeeeeer!" Then the boys joined in.

Needless to say, they didn't get any. But by the time I'd finally got the whinging chancers off to bed, I did have a peculiar craving for a can of Tennent's myself. Funny, that...

Anyhow, as you've probably realised, I'm avoiding talking about the stress in hand:

The good news is that the mouse situation seems to be more under control now. I haven't seen any sign of one for a few days so it's possible they've gone away. Of course, there's every chance that I've just managed to kill the stupid ones and that I'm using natural selection to breed a race of super rodents who will be able to avoid traps, open tins and steal the fridge. At the point they work out how to sell my stuff on eBay, I'm moving house.

The bad news is that the plumbing saga continues. Apparently, our pipework is rather 'unusual'. (Translation: It was designed and implemented by a gibbon.) The heating is now 88% fixed. Making it 100% fixed may involve demolishing the bathroom.

As for Sarah... Things didn't go so well on Friday.

LBO are laying people off left, right and centre. Branches are closing, work is being out-sourced, the final salary pension scheme is no more, services are facing the axe and the directors' bonuses have been linked to how much money they can lop off the operating budget. It's a disaster.

Steve's still sitting pretty, as he predicted. Rob's department is gone but he's been shifted elsewhere. Technically, in terms of leadership and responsibility, it's a promotion. In terms of his annual salary, he's even had a pay rise. He was quite pleased until I pointed out that the changes they've made to his holidays and working week mean his hourly rate has gone down. He's been sulking ever since.

Sarah has been made provisionally redundant. She has a couple of weeks to prepare her case to be kept on and then she has to argue it in front of a special committee set up to give the impression that there has been some consultation with staff over all of this. It's already being called the Inquisition. Handily, each person will be interrogated by their manager and their manager's manager i.e. the people instrumental in picking them for the chop in the first place. There will be an 'independent' member of senior management there from another division too but I don't imagine that that will be much comfort in most cases. Sarah's going to have to pull something extremely impressive out of the bag to make Steve and Scott perform a U-turn. (I'm thinking a bazooka would do it.)

We're coping as best we can. It isn't the first occasion something like this has happened and almost certainly won't be the last. At least she isn't on maternity leave this time.

Yours in a woman's world,

Ed.

PS Mmmmmmm... Doughnuts...

Sugar and spice

Dear Dave,

Yep, might be a girl. In only a couple of weeks you could have a daughter. The three years of on-the-job training in childcare you got from looking after Sam will be out the window as you struggle to cope with an entirely separate species of offspring. All your old tricks for entertaining, feeding, pacifying and cajoling will fail to work. While Sam fell asleep on your chest as you watched repeats of *Top Gear*, Squiggly will insist on being rocked gently while listening to *Take That's Greatest Hits*. On the plus side, the makeshift restraining harness you fitted to the changing unit for Sam will be strangely unnecessary – Squiggly will let you change her nappy without trying to gouge out your eyes and then kick poo in your face.

Well, you can always hope...

Things might not turn out exactly that way but who knows? Whatever happens, Squiggly will be a whole different bundle of joy from Sam, whether she's a girl or not.

It's just that, if she *is* a girl, people will ascribe almost every variation in behaviour to their genders. Everyone will probably tell you that girls are much more demanding than boys for all manner of reasons involving being precocious and awkward. Don't be disheartened. Bear in mind that these are the same people who told you last time round that boys are more demanding than girls because they're always running about causing trouble and getting into everything. Nod and smile.

The truth is, all children are different. As a baby, Marie didn't eat, didn't sleep, had screaming fits and was forever ill. She was definitely more awkward than either of the boys but, realistically, Fraser wasn't much better. In terms of temperament, those two are the most similar. Lewis was a really easy baby. We thought it was because he was our second child and we'd learnt our lessons from Fraser and we knew what we were doing.

But we were wrong.

We used the same tactics with Marie and none of them worked. Lewis was simply a contented baby who liked to eat and sleep, was able to amuse himself and didn't appear to notice his teeth coming in. We didn't appreciate how lucky we'd been until Marie arrived and developed a fondness for waking up at three in the morning to grumble loudly for a couple of hours. I assume last year happened, but I don't particularly remember it.

Was Marie's aversion to sleep due to being a girl? I doubt it. It's not like she was sitting around demurely all day and not getting enough exercise. Fraser chewed everything, Lewis heaped anything he could find into piles but Marie was the baby who wouldn't stay still. She could climb before she could walk. When the boys finally managed to haul themselves up onto the sofa, they sprawled out and watched TV. Marie used it as a staging post on her ascent of the sideboard.

'Boys are more active' – yeah, right...

Obviously, I don't have a very large sample to base my observations on. Maybe some traits *are* more likely in girls rather than boys. I've no idea. The thing is, you can't count on them. Every child has their own personality and needs – it's a case of getting to know them and nurturing them.

Speaking of nurturing, there's the gnarly question of whether to treat girls differently from boys. Will Squiggly get dolls or Duplo for Christmas? That kind of thing.

You think you'll handle them the same but the truth is probably that you simply won't notice when you don't. She'll have the opportunity to take up ballet and dressmaking if she wants, but you won't stand in her way if she decides to go for rugby and car maintenance. You'll even encourage her. There'll be no restricting her 'because she's a girl'.

But what if *Sam* wants to take up ballet and dressmaking?

You may be man enough to let him but don't tell me you won't hope it's a passing phase. You will take him to Six Nations matches and buy him a set of wrenches.

Nope, you will treat them differently. Some things will be your own prejudices, others will be unavoidable. For instance, if Squiggly *is* a girl, then pink will enter your life in a big way.

Babies look alike. Guessing the gender of a baby in a white babygro is next to impossible. They're all bald and wrinkly. Colours vary but that doesn't help much. If she isn't dressed in pink, then people will assume she's a boy. I don't know why – they just will. Admittedly, they may do this anyway but if she's covered head-to-toe in neon candyfloss, at least you'll have an excuse to roll your eyes a bit. You could try purple or lilac but you might as well accept your fate and embrace the pink.

Despite our best efforts, one of Marie's first sentences was, 'I *like* pink.' If she could have added 'actually' on the end, I'm sure she would have done.

Long hair is also fairly essential for little girls. (Again, for reasons of recognition.) Welcome to the world of hairclips and headbands and small, tangled children running away screaming as you approach with a hairbrush. ('It sore! It sore! I want mummy do it!')

What else?

Girls definitely get to trade on being cute. Marie managed to blag some pink Post-its off my optician the other day merely by simpering. The boys would have needed to be charming as well.

Plainly, potty training is a little different with a girl (but not that much).

Looking further ahead, I expect there will be other issues but there's no point worrying about them yet – there'll be plenty of time for that when Squiggly's a teenager. (*Shudder.*) It's never too early to start planning how to embarrass her in front of her first boyfriend, though, or to jot down a few notes for a wedding speech...

Honestly, you'll be fine.

Yours in a woman's world,

Ed.

There's no going back now

Dear Dave,

Things are looking up. Sarah's been given a rundown of the reasons she's been picked for the redundancy list at LBO and they're decidedly unconvincing. As far as we can make out amidst all the business babble, there are three main strikes against her:

She hasn't done the training course for the customer data analysis tools.

This is true but, then again, she helped specify the system in the first place and has been using it daily for nearly seven years. The only reason she didn't go on the course was because it was a fortnight before she went on maternity leave with Fraser and her manager at the time couldn't see the point. She got to stay behind and answer the phones.

Aiding and abetting the competition.

This one's nonsense. Sarah led a project designed to reduce customer turnover. She spent months analysing the data, identifying the customers most likely to leave LBO and formulating ways to get them to stay. It was fantastic. The only problem was, she had to go on maternity leave with Lewis before the mailshot was finalised.

Someone who *had* been on the training course pressed the wrong button and sent the letters to exactly the wrong people – hundreds of thousands of loyal customers received offers of sweet deals and all the customers who were already thinking of leaving got nothing.

They left.

This was disastrous, but clearly not Sarah's fault.

The annelid debacle.

On returning from maternity leave with Marie, Sarah was put in charge of implementing a marketing campaign that was already in the final stages of development. She had had nothing to do with the planning, however, and was dubious about the whole scheme. It was an attempt to persuade financial advisers that although the products of other companies looked attractive initially, they had various legal complications and long-term costs. The campaign involved sending each of these financial advisers *an unsolicited can of worms.*

And, of course, like fools, they opened them.

Believe me, the complaints department received some irate calls that day. Still, not really Sarah's fault. Crucially, when she pointed out the madness of the project, she was threatened with dismissal if she didn't implement it. You can't sack someone for doing something they would have got sacked for not doing. (Not unless you use the kind of logic that can take you from the statement, 'All chocolate digestives are brown,' to the conclusion, 'All brown things are chocolate digestives.' And the people who do use that kind of logic don't last long – they have a tendency to choke to death on their own shoes at biscuit time.)

So there we have it: one reason is illegal, one is spurious and the other is as insane as eating your own boots. Persuading management to see things that way is the tricky part – it might make them look bad. Nevertheless, they don't really have a leg to stand on.

Obviously, the uncertainty has made life slightly subdued round here. We've had plenty of commiserations from friends and family, so we don't feel alone, but there's been some fairly dreadful advice as well, ranging from platitudes along the lines of, 'It will all work out for the best,' to idiotic suggestions that we use the opportunity to go travelling the world.

Hello! Three small children, people! We're entitled to be apprehensive of the future and to be reluctant to go backpacking in Borneo. (Everything else aside, I can't imagine the buggy would cope particularly effectively with the rainforest terrain. And where would we plug in all our handheld consoles to recharge them? Not going to happen.)

Oddly, nearly everyone Sarah has discussed her imminent redundancy with has laughed at some point and said, 'You could always send Ed back to work.'

On the one hand, they're half joking. As if they're sure she won't be able to persuade me to leave the house after what they imagine as eight years of sitting around eating cake and playing the Xbox. Which is, on reflection, a little insulting.

On the other hand, they're half serious. Getting me a job solves the problem of not having any money coming in, after all.

It doesn't solve the *real* problem of somehow securing a job but I guess that's a minor detail. I mean, there's no reason I couldn't get a job. What people don't seem to realise is that I can't compete with Sarah. When I stopped work in advance of Fraser's arrival, Sarah and I were earning similar amounts. Money wasn't an issue when deciding who stayed home to be dribbled on. That was eight years ago, however. Sarah now has eight years more experience than me. She has new and up-to-the-minute skills. She has smart clothes that fit and that aren't all wrinkled from dribble.

She has much more chance of quickly landing a decent job than I do.

I wouldn't go as far as to say that we're now financially trapped in our role-reversal situation but we'd definitely take a big hit in the bank account if we tried to swap back. It's strange how people just don't get that.

Sadly, I suspect they would get it if I was female. It would probably be taken for granted rather than come as a surprise.

And that would be far worse to put up with. I'll stop whinging.

Yours in a woman's world,

Ed.

PS Marie's favourite song at the moment goes:

> *Everybody, everybody, everybody, everybody... everybody likes being a person.*
> *Nobody, nobody, nobody, nobody... nobody likes being a pie.*

It's quite sonorous but does tend to attract some strange looks on the bus...

I'm sure my underwear is around here somewhere

Dear Dave,

Glad to learn you've finally started getting stuff out the loft. Hey, no rush – it's not like *the baby's due today* or anything...

Have you remembered it all? I was trying to think of what you'll need but the whole experience of dealing with a newborn is beginning to blur. Let's see: pram, carseat, biohazard suit, cotton-wool, baby bath, crib (good luck putting that back together again, by the way), more cotton-wool, baby clothes, steriliser, industrial-sized tin of coffee, yet more cotton-wool, play-pen, little blankets, even more cotton-wool than that, mittens, buckets, large vat of disinfectant... The list goes on. There's doubtless a stack of gear I've omitted. (Did I mention cotton-wool?) I have the full list somewhere but I think I'm too scared of flashbacks to take a proper look.

I saw a small baby at parent and toddler the other week being wrapped up for going outside, and it took me back. It was sunny but the kid was being kitted out with a padded coat, mittens and the cutest little pink hat ever. I'd forgotten about the little hats. It was so sweet.

Then again, I was a good ten feet from the little slug and reasonably safe from any stray bodily fluids. At that range there was barely an odour. The thought of going back to nappies and middle-of-the-night feeds and regularly wearing banana porridge makes me feel... tired. In some ways another child or two would be nice, but I don't have the mental or physical energy for it. I'm looking forward to the point where I can sit reading a book while the kids run around outside entertaining themselves. (I can dream, can't I? If nothing more, it will be nice to interact with Fraser without having to constantly deal with/fight off a toddler.) Relatively soon, Marie will start nursery and I'll have a couple of hours a day to myself. Some semblance of freedom approaches. I'll be able to...

Oh, hang on... Maybe you're not really the one I should be telling this to.

Yes, erm, stuff. I was talking about stuff. Our house is still in a state because of the repair work that's going on. We've had to empty out a couple of rooms and stash the contents in other parts of the house. Actually, 'stash' is rather optimistic. All the cupboards were already full beforehand. The beds are now jacked up so we can fit more stuff underneath. Even the loft is full. We would have piled all the refugee stuff in the middle of the lounge carpet but what would we have done with the big pile of stuff which *normally* lives in the middle of the lounge carpet?

We're having to pick our way through teetering stacks of printers and books and towels to find clean clothes. I've given the kids each a hat with a flag on the top so I don't lose them amidst the clutter. It's like living in the version of the Room of Requirement at Hogwarts where everybody hides junk. You never know what you'll find if you go poking around. What will it be? The other shoe you're looking for? Fresh underwear? One end of a cable which could be attached to almost anything? Lord Lucan? Or Scabbers the rat?

It's always worth keeping something blunt and heavy handy just in case.

This chaos is a shame because I had been hoping we'd reached the high tide mark of stuff a few months ago. Marie is at the stage where we don't need much of the specialised baby equipment anymore and she has outgrown many of her toys. We've been able to offload boxes and boxes of baby gear. Before, whenever one child was done with something, we had to put it in storage for the next one. More often than not, we simply left the thing out – the minimal time before we needed it again meant it wasn't worth searching for a space in the loft. Meanwhile, as Fraser got older, we had to buy *more* stuff. Pokémon got mixed in with shape-sorters; a beanbag got plopped beside the bouncy chair. Cupboards overflowed, the carpet disappeared and I had to build a bigger shed. We began to sink beneath a sea of toddler artwork and strange constructions made from cereal cartons and yogurt pots.

I remember, when Fraser was on the way, being offered all manner of useful second-hand items by various total strangers. At first I would find their generosity heartwarming. Then I'd become disturbed by their manic insistence that I take some bulky item of well-worn and smelly baby paraphernalia. By the time they'd dragged me into their home and started piling my arms with tat, I was usually pretty scared. Fortunately, it was always fairly easy to sneak away as they ran round the house opening drawers and tipping the contents into black bin-liners for me.

Now *I'm* one of those people.

We packaged up lots of baby stuff recently, hired a van and drove it to relatives. With hindsight, maybe we should have asked if they wanted it before popping round while they were on holiday and dumping it all in their front room. But, hey, we watered their plants – they can't complain too much. We were desperate to clear some space in our house.

The initial results were disappointing. There was still no spare capacity in our cupboards – it was merely possible to open them without being deluged in bibs and mitts and babygros. We had to do a second trip. Sarah's cousin was apparently very surprised when he got back from Tenerife, opened his garage door and nearly drowned in babywear.

We had slightly more elbow room after that, though. We revealed patches of floor that I'd forgotten we had.

When Fraser was small, I used to pack away his toys neatly at night, sorting them into the correct boxes and tubs. When Lewis was young, I got the boys to help me tidy the stuff into a corner and I checked that favourite toys still had all their pieces. When Marie was tiny, I bought a spade and shovelled the stuff into the corner. Once she was a little older and never went to sleep, I even gave up on that. I cleared narrow paths between the door, the sofa and the telly and left the rest to geology. Over time, erosion and sedimentation from a steady flow of children caused interesting toy formations to take shape. The Teletubbies fossilised.

It was great to clear some of the stuff out at last and have a little room to breathe. Maybe soon things will be that way again. The decorators are supposed to be coming this week and, once they're finished, we can set the house to rights. Better yet, we could even take the opportunity to sift our belongings and fill a few bags for the charity shop. More likely, however, we'll bung everything back where it came from as quickly as possible and leave the sifting until next decade, but it's worth a thought. You never know, we *might* have the time, energy and inclination all at once...

That's still something to look forward to – we can't do much until the house is fixed. In the meantime, I'm reduced to smuggling small piles of toddler artwork out of the house in my trousers while whistling the theme tune to *The Great Escape*. If I can dispose of enough without the kids catching me and throwing a tantrum, I should have tunnelled my way to the biscuit tin in another couple of days.

It better not be empty.

Yours in a woman's world,

Ed.

PS Good luck. Hope it all goes relatively smoothly. Don't forget to pack your sandwiches. Oh, and Merry Christmas.

Yes, I know it's September but you might want to rush out and buy all your gifts now while you have the chance. The first three months of having two children will disappear in the blink of an eye and a mountain of laundry. Or, in other words, if Squiggly is born today, you'll wake up tomorrow to find it's the day after Boxing Day.

Sam will be annoyed you forgot to get him anything.

The List

Dear Dave,

Any news yet? I take it Squiggly has decided to stay put for a while longer. How overdue does she/he have to be before the midwives break out the dynamite? Fraser was nine days late and the more time dragged on, the less likely it felt that he would ever be born. It was crazy but life went into limbo as we waited impatiently for him to do the sensible thing and come out quietly with his legs up. He wasn't having any of it, though. When he finally deigned to appear, he was facing the wrong direction and had to be dragged out by the head. (A pattern of existence we repeat in some form on an almost daily basis.)

Marie was even more awkward. She was determined to stick her toes into the world first, to test the temperature. Nothing would persuade her otherwise and she had to be yanked out through the emergency exit. Stubborn drama queen? My little girl? Never...

Lewis was the sole one to turn up on time and without much palaver. If anything, he was slightly too laid-back and easy-going. We might not have had to rush so fast to the hospital if he'd bothered to fight his way out of his protective bubble and thus given us more warning his arrival was imminent. But no. He wanted to be born in his own private water-bed. He likes his comfort, that one.

Anyhow, good luck and best wishes to Liz. Remember to make the midwives do whatever she wants and try your best to get her whatever she asks for (unless it's sharp and pointy and she wants you to stand close by).

Things are sort of going OK here. Sarah had her redundancy 'hearing' at LBO yesterday – the one where she had to explain to the two managers who fired her why they were wrong. This was never going to go swimmingly but we were pinning our hopes on the third member of the Inquisition who was supposed to be an impartial manager from another department. No one told Sarah who it would be until the day. She phoned me straight away when she found out. It was Gerald, my old boss from when I worked in the IT department. This wasn't good news.

"What do you know about him?" Sarah asked.

I grimaced, glad that she couldn't see my face. "Dinosaurs find him old-fashioned and he can't entirely see the point of women."

"Oh..."

"Yeah, I'm sure they'd have pensioned him off years ago if he hadn't rigged up lots of the code so that only he knows how it works. Not that even he really knows, half the time."

"I need you to be more encouraging here," she said.

"Sorry..." I didn't know what else to say.

There was a silence punctuated by swamp sounds. "What's that squelching noise in the background?" asked Sarah.

"Marie." I glanced over from my seat at the kitchen table to where the girl was stomping around in slime, her trouser legs rolled up as high as they would go. "I've got her doing foot painting."

"Is that wise?" said Sarah, somewhat agitated by this news.

"Almost certainly not, but she's totally into it. I think we're going to need some more pink paint."

"I like pink!" shouted Marie gleefully, and jumped up and down.

I wiped a fleck of paint from my glasses. Then I had an idea. "Yeah, er, what would happen if, for some reason, Gerald couldn't make it?"

"I don't know. It might say in the formal notification they sent me..." There was a rustle of paper as she searched around. "Yes, it has a get-out clause: 'If the named arbiter cannot attend the consultation meeting, then his or her deputy will attend as replacement. In this eventuality, all duties relating to the meeting will henceforth transfer to the replacement.' Which I presume means it's up to the deputy to make decisions and do the paperwork. Do you think Gerald will want to delegate?"

"Nope, he wouldn't dream of passing up the chance to look official and exert some power. Who's his deputy, though?"

"I'll check the org chart..." There was another pause. "Looks like someone called Morag Chandler."

This was much more promising. "She'd be good. She's fair, doesn't tolerate nonsense and bites the head off fools. She'll be more than up for a fight with Steve and Scott. You want her."

"And how am I supposed to arrange that?" asked Sarah.

"Leave it to me," I said.

This didn't come across in the manly and reassuring way I'd hoped. "What? What are you going to do?" Sarah sounded anxious again.

"Woh, calm down," I said. "I think I can get Rob to keep Gerald out of the way for a few hours, that's all. I'm not planning to turn up and send the kids in with water balloons and dung bombs."

"Are you sure?"

"Well, not unless they actually fire you, anyway. Keep on with your preparation for the meeting and I'll see what I can do. Speak to you later. Love you."

"Love you, too," she said. "Just don't do anything silly, OK?"

"OK. Bye."

I hung up and then immediately phoned Rob, my friend in the IT department at LBO.

"I need you to do me a favour," I said, once we'd exchanged pleasantries.

"Sure. What is it?"

"I need you to distract Gerald for the rest of the day. I need you to use the List."

"You what?" he spluttered but then lowered his voice. "Why?"

I explained about the hearing whilst trying to keep Marie on the paper and away from the clean laundry.

"I don't know," muttered Rob when I was done. "There's not much still on there. It's been eight years and I've had a few close scrapes since you left. What if they change their minds about my job and I..."

"Come on. You must be able to do something. *I* gave you the List in the first place."

"It's not like you wrote it," he said.

"I added to it. Have *you* added anything to it? Look, I need your help. What do I have to do here? You want me to lose to you at *Mario Kart*, is that it?"

"Not really. I tell you what – you could be best man at my wedding. How about that?"

I sighed. "I'd rather sit next to the buffet and get mildly drunk while enjoying not having the kids around, if that's all right?" A terrible thought crossed my mind. "You're not inviting the kids, are you?"

"I might do at this rate," he said, sounding peeved. "Aren't you supposed to say, 'Congratulations'?"

"Oh, yeah, sorry. Congratulations! Now, about the List..."

"Only if you agree to wear a kilt and stand at the front holding the rings."

"I have to wear a kilt!? Have you seen my knees?"

"Hang on a minute while I pencil your children onto the seating plan."

"OK, OK, I'll do it," I said, caving in. "I can't believe you're holding me to ransom over this. I am *so* giving you crystal sherry glasses as a gift."

"That's OK," said Rob. "You're getting novelty cuff-links as a thank you present."

"Cheers... Now, the List!"

The List takes the form of a battered and yellowed notebook and has had a mythical status within the technical division of LBO since back in an age when making an automatic calculation involved turning a crank handle. It has been passed secretly down through generations of prospectless techies, hidden from management and any that show aspirations to be promoted to the dark side. Sometimes it has disappeared from view for years, only to be rediscovered in moments of greatest need. It has come to the rescue of many a hapless engineer and some say that if the List is ever used up, then it will be the beginning of the end – hot desking will become mandatory and internet access will be denied, new development will cease and all that will be left is bug fixing...

Once upon a time, the List was in the care of my mentor. He gave it to me when he left the company. I, in turn, gave it to Rob when I left. It records all the subtle technical faults in the system that senior management is blissfully unaware of but that would strike fear into their hearts if they were ever informed. By suddenly 'discovering' one of the problems on the List, an engineer can distract attention from a different disaster that's much more their fault. Be that as it may, there is a price to be paid – all the problems are difficult, dull or time-consuming to rectify. The List is never to be used lightly.

Still, it was all that could save me on one occasion. When a race over my cubicle assault course led to myself, several co-workers and a vending machine falling out a window, the List ensured we got away with only our minor injuries and several weeks of database migration. It was a close thing.

More famously, LBO was years ahead of the game on Y2K because my mentor needed to divert his superiors while he hunted around for the portion of fish and chips he'd lost in the internal workings of the primary mainframe. That incident has become legend.

I started suggesting entries from the List that Rob could use. "How about the Conduit Issue?"

This is one of the items on the List that is situation dependent. The password and access security on the LBO network is very tight. The data, however, travels totally unencrypted between buildings using cabling that runs only a few feet underground. This fact would clearly be a cause for concern at whatever point it was revealed, but is liable to create much more panic amongst the top brass if they peer out the window and see a couple of dodgy looking workmen poking around under a manhole cover. Rob keeps Virgin Media on speed-dial in case of such a circumstance being required.

"No time," replied Rob. "I'll never get a maintenance guy out here before this afternoon."

"You're right." I wracked my brains. "How about the NeverDay Accounts?"

In the early '80s, LBO introduced a fifty year savings plan. Not many people took it up and it quickly died a death. No one would remember it at all, if it weren't for the five customers who signed up on the 29th February 1984. Due to an error in the code, their interest calculations have been somewhat inflated and they now own the company. On the plus side, there's another error which means, since 2034 isn't a leap year, the policies will never mature and the customers will never be paid. Nonetheless, if the accountants ever find out, there'll be pandemonium enough to cover over almost any other catastrophe. (And, yeah, it could be corrected really easily but, unfortunately, that module of code got re-used and now forms part of pretty much every system in LBO. Testing that nothing else got broken by the fix would take forever.)

"NeverDay is overkill," said Rob. "I'm not taking the flak for unearthing that."

I could see his point. "OK, then – the Name Jumbler?"

When a customer's name is entered into the system, it is stored surname first, followed by first names. Each of the elements is separated by a space. John Edward Smith becomes Smith John Edward. This makes it easy to list customers alphabetically by surname. When the system retrieves a name, it looks for spaces and re-arranges the name back to the right order. In the above example, letters would be sent to John E Smith. This works great... mostly. Sadly, the designer had never met anyone with a hyphen-less double-barrelled surname. John Edward Smith Jones gets stored as Smith Jones John Edward but comes back as Jones John Edward Smith. Every time. That's got to be annoying for all LBO's punctuation-phobic customers.

"The Name Jumbler's maybe underkill," said Rob. "Gerald's not going to care. How many customers with hyphen-less double-barrelled surnames do you think we have?"

"It's not the number; it's the importance," I said, becoming impatient. Sarah's meeting was fast approaching. Marie was also running out of paper. "There are a handful of high-profile special cases. See if Her Royal Highness, Princess Enid, Duchess of Anglesey, is still an account holder."

"What? Hang on a minute. Have you got an account number?"

"It's on the List."

"I'll need to get it out from behind the air-vent cover. I'll put you on hold..."

"Wait! No..." It was too late. I was subjected to fifteen minutes of Brahms and irritating reminders that my call was important.

Eventually, Rob came back on. "Right, got it."

"What were you doing?" I hissed.

"It was still in the air-vent in my old cubicle. I had to go buy doughnuts to lure people out of the room before I could get to it. I told them it was Rupert's birthday."

"Who's Rupert?" I asked.

"I dunno. I'm making this up as I go along."

"And no one queried?"

"Who queries free doughnuts?" said Rob.

"True. You might want to add that to the List as another potential security risk."

"Yeah, hadn't thought of it like that," he said. "Where's this account number then? Oh, got it. Hang on while I call it up... Right... OK, they put 'HRH' in as her title so that's fine but, oh, they tried making 'Duchess of Anglesey' her surname which means the system thinks her first name is 'of' and they left 'Princess' in there, which makes her initials... Oh, flip..."

"Yep, she gets letters addressed to 'HRH of APE Duchess'."

"Gerald will go ballistic," said Rob. "I don't see how it's going to keep him out the way, though. He'll get someone else to sort it."

"No, he won't. Check out the name storage and retrieval modules – *his* name is all over them. He'll lock himself in his office and spend the rest of the week hacking up a solution."

"But there is no solution," argued Rob, forgetting to whisper. "All the data's compromised. Even if he changed the code, someone would have to go through about five million customer records to find which ones are knackered. Not that it'll be possible to tell with some of them without contacting the customer. It can't be fixed."

"His pride will make him try. Go tell him."

Rob subsided. "All right, all right. But your speech better be good."

"I'll start writing it as soon as I've got the pink footprints off the telly. Things got a little out of hand while you had me on hold."

"Good luck with that."

"You, too."

I hung up and set myself to scrubbing a small child and various appliances. There was nothing else I could do.

Sarah phoned me a couple of hours later. The List had worked its magic. Gerald had been unexpectedly detained by a technical crisis and Morag had been unceremoniously ordered to the hearing. She had arrived already fuming and clearly spoiling for a fight. Sensibly, Steve stayed pretty quiet through the whole meeting. (His wife, Deborah, still needs my help, so she's been advocating for Sarah ever since the redundancies were announced.) Steve's manager, Scott, meanwhile, was as smug and annoying as ever and Morag told him where to go.

She even drew diagrams.

It's going to be another couple of weeks before final decisions are made but I think there's a good chance things should work out OK.

I'd better start on that speech.

Yours in a woman's world,

Ed.

Part 5

Perseverance Pays Off

Taking the effort out of being ignored

Dear Dave,

I'm sorry to learn that Sam has ceased to listen to a word you say. You're right that he might have picked up some anxiety about your imminent new addition to the family but it's more likely that, since he's three, he simply believes that he knows better than you. Honestly, you're lucky he's listened to you this long.

Take my lot, for example. They were all standing in a line next to a low wall today. Marie wanted to climb onto the wall and jump off. "No, it's wet," I said. So she climbed on. At which point, Fraser sat on the wall. "No, it's wet," I said. Fraser grinned and then Lewis rubbed his sleeve backwards and forwards along the top of the wall. "No, it's wet," I said. They all looked at me blankly. Then they complained they were wet.

Sam will be ignoring you entirely before you know it. You'll have to say everything three times before he even realises you've spoken. This could be annoying but, happily, I have been working on a solution. The prototype is complete. Another couple of weeks of testing and then my Patented Parental rePeater (TM) will go into full production. The Triple-P (TM) will save the voices and sanity of childcare operatives the world over. Hang it round your neck, go about your daily life and then, at the touch of a button, have it repeat the last thing you said. Press a different button and it will continue to repeat the phrase at regular intervals for several minutes, each repetition louder than the last and delivered in a more exasperated tone.

A number of useful phrases come pre-programmed into the Triple-P. These include:

- Look where you're going.
- Don't eat that.
- Say, 'Please.'

- Not up your nose.
- Put your shoes on.
- Take your shoes off.
- Don't do that.
- Sit down.
- Eat up.
- That's not a hanky.
- Do what you're told.
- Not up *my* nose.
- Close the fridge.
- That's my foot you're standing on.
- Leave my Triple-P alone.
- That's not yogurt.
- That *is* yogurt.
- Where did you put my phone?
- For crying out loud, not up *anybody's* nose.
- Turn your hearing aid on. (For use on grandparents who are supposed to be helping but have in fact opted for a crafty nap.)

There is also memory available for the user to record often repeated phrases of their own. From your letters, I suggest that in your case these might include:

- Shredded Wheat is not for shredding.
- Put the PlayStation down.
- Don't feed the hoover.
- You'll be needing those trousers.
- Why's my phone in the fridge?
- Step away from the hamster.
- I'm not a camel.
- Don't eat your shoes.
- Don't use your grandparents as a hanky.
- What's this yogurt doing up my nose?

The Triple-P also has several special modes:

- Stressed Whisper – for use in church.

• Firm but Polite – for use on other people's children.
• Extra Loud – for parties, playgrounds and natural disasters.

The Triple-P is waterproof, shockproof, easily portable, resistant to toxic bodily fluids and has a battery-life of between 3 hours and 7 weeks (dependent on the number, age and behaviour of your children). Look out for it soon in all good retailers (and on eBay shortly after).

Triple-P – taking the effort out of being ignored.

(Go on, you know you want one...)
Yours in a woman's world,
Ed.

It's a girl

Dear Dave,

Congratulations on the birth of Daisy Elizabeth Jane! About time too, I must say. Sounds like it was a bit of a rush in the end, though. When I told you to head out to the shops and buy all your Christmas presents early while you had the chance, I meant for you to do it *before* the contractions had started.

I guess Sam won't forget his first visit to Santa's grotto.

Ho well, it's over now and I'm glad to hear you're home already, safe from overly warm maternity wards and traumatised elves. You should expect a succession of little, pink, knitted cardigans to start dropping onto your doormat any day. If you're really lucky, they'll be in padded envelopes that won't fit through the letterbox, forcing you to go answer the door when the postie buzzes at seven in the morning. Most of this knitwear will be lovely; some will appear to have been measured for a pot-bellied orang-utan by a colour-blind lunatic. The latter will be the ones that Sam will want Daisy to wear. Enjoy.

Oh, yeah, how's Sam coping with having a sibling? Is he proud to be a big brother or is he eyeing his new nemesis warily? Hopefully it's all fine, but I wouldn't worry if he views Daisy as his arch-enemy – Fraser and Lewis hardly got off to the best start:

Fraser was about twenty-two months when Lewis was born but he couldn't say a word. Being our eldest, we didn't know what to expect from him in terms of his ability to understand us. Since he couldn't speak, we assumed he wasn't able to take much in. As a result, we didn't greatly discuss the impending arrival with him. His little brother came as rather a shock.

Everything was going along as normal and then he found himself hastily carted off to a friend's house, abandoned for the day and mysteriously collected by Gran. The day after that, he woke up and came through to Mummy and Daddy's room and there was something lying in the funny swinging basket at the end of the bed. Fraser looked at the 'something' apprehensively. The funny swinging basket had been there for weeks and had remained empty. Suddenly it contained a squishy pink lump. What could it be? Fraser slapped it in an experimental kind of way. The pink lump moved. Fraser jumped out of his skin. They both started to cry. And a life-long relationship was begun...

With hindsight, I think we could have been more up-front with Fraser. It turned out he could understand a heck of a lot. He wasn't talking for a number of reasons:

1. He was late in developing the physical ability.

2. It was too much like effort.

3. Pointing at things and grunting was working very nicely for him.

Some mild speech therapy and a large amount of competition sorted him out.

Marie's integration into the family went more smoothly. Fraser still hadn't quite got over the fact that he didn't have my undivided attention, so one more rival didn't make much difference. Lewis, meanwhile, was two and a half, had a good idea what was going on and was used to being left to his own devices for significant stretches of time.

The boys blithely ignored Marie for about a year until the point she could stand up and get in the way of the telly. Before that, they tripped over her, dropped things on her and only took proper notice of her when they thought she was about to try and eat their stuff. Fraser would frequently complain about the odour of poo that pervaded the house but I eventually convinced him it wasn't usually Marie's fault – Lewis either had a minor milk intolerance as a small child or he just really, really liked farting.

Sam will learn to cope. My boys now consider themselves equals and stick up for each other when they're out and about (despite always arguing at home). Lewis and Marie are partners in crime. They all seem to have some sense of being on the same team. It's reassuring watching them look after each other. When they've finally worked me to death and scavenged the last of the loot from my withered corpse, they'll know to stick together to survive. (If they decide that I'm on the other team sooner than that and join forces against me, I may be in trouble. I suspect that they're big enough already for two of them to grab my arms and the other to make off with my wallet before I have a chance to break free.)

If Sam and Daisy do find themselves as arch-enemies for a while, I'm sure they'll get over it. Just think, in another fifteen years, they'll be setting each other up on dates with their classmates.

Now *that's* something to start worrying about...

Yours in a woman's world,

Ed.

Mice, yaks, tradesmen and a shovel.

Dear Dave,

If there's one thing I hate about this job, then it's dealing with tradesmen. Truth be told, I'd rather clean up vomit.

Erm, not that I'm making a direct comparison here. You know, like they both smell bad and leave a mess on your carpet. All I mean is that handling both is on my list of normal duties and if you arranged the list by ordered of preference, then 'dealing with tradesmen' is at the bottom. There are any number of things I'd rather do, from making packed lunches, to standing outside school in the rain, to watching the same episode of *Tweenies* over and over again until their irritating voices buzz constantly inside my head and I feel the urge to take a large magnet to their animatronics while rubbing chewing gum into their fur.

Heck, I'd rather buy clothes than deal with tradesmen. Considering I only have one pair of shoes and I regularly wear a shirt I bought when I was at secondary school, that's saying something.

The problem is, I'm just no good at it. I can't seem to get them to turn up on the day they've promised, persuade them to do the work exactly as I want or inspire them to ever completely finish the job to my satisfaction. Any tradesman I've found who I *have* managed to bend to my will has gone bust before I've needed their services again. (That or been replaced by their Porsche-driving offspring who do a job that's not quite as good but costs twice as much money.) Coordinating repairs to the flood damage has gone particularly badly because it's my insurers who are paying, so I have absolutely no hold over the company doing the work at all. If I have a complaint, I phone the insurers. After three days of trying, I get through to the person in charge of my case. He emails the plumbers. The plumbers don't reply. My radiators remain upside down. I have to go murder some Tweenies to vent my frustration and then I phone the insurers again. The cycle continues...

Things are finally progressing, nevertheless – albeit slowly. The other morning, a decorator was busily repainting a ceiling on the top floor (the damage was on the ground floor of our three storey house) while refusing to touch up the skirting board on the first flight of stairs (mere inches from where a big patch of plaster had been replaced). Meanwhile, a plumber was merrily removing parts of the central heating (again) but wasn't really committing to a definite time-frame for putting them back. He was also fairly reticent on whether they'd be the right way up.

Looking on the bright side, at least something was happening, which made a change.

The doorbell rang in the midst of the chaos. It was Steve and I was taken by surprise. We hadn't arranged to meet up and get the kids together. He didn't even have his kids with him. He was dressed for work but, clearly, he wasn't at work. He was neither being Useless Dad nor Clueless Manager and, therefore, he was dangerously out of context. I stood and gaped at him.

"Is this a good time?" he said.

"Erm..." I had two tradesmen in the house, Marie was having a strop and I had a live mouse in my hands. I couldn't help feeling that this was stretching any definition of 'a good time'. As if to emphasise the point, there was a clang behind me, the sound of liquid escaping under pressure and muttered swearing. There was an almost desperate, pleading look in Steve's eyes, however. "Erm..." I repeated.

"Good God, what's that?" said Steve, suddenly noticing what I was carrying.

"It's a mouse." It was crouched under a glass bowl which I was pressing down on a thin sheet of cardboard. "I caught it."

"What are you going to do with it?"

"When I catch spiders like this, I normally chuck them out the window. They're less squishy, though. Want to take it home for your cat to play with?"

"Not especially."

"Thought not. That leaves three options: let it go to die a lingering death from the poison it's almost certainly eaten, leave it under the bowl and *watch it* die a lingering death from the poison it's almost certainly eaten, or hit it over the head with a shovel."

"The first two don't sound very pleasant."

"Shovel it is then." I stepped out on the driveway, put my impromptu trap down and fetched a heavy digging implement. "Right, you lift the bowl and I'll whack it."

"That's a very big shovel for a very small mouse," said Steve, not totally sure.

"It's the only shovel I have," I replied, losing it slightly. "They don't sell them in sets like they do with knives – big shovel for allotments, medium shovel for flowerbeds, little shovel for window boxes and miniature shovel for mouse whacking. I have one shovel for all eventualities. What do you want me to do? Brain it with a teaspoon?"

"This isn't a very good time, is it?"

"No, it's not. Now lift the bowl so I can put Mickey out of his misery."

"All right." He very gingerly lifted the bowl. The mouse didn't move. "Are you certain it isn't dead alr...?" He jumped back as I swung the shovel down with a thunk. "OK, it's dead now."

I peered at it closely. "Yep, it's definitely not going to re-route its internal circuitry to its secondary power source and relentlessly hunt us down through a metal-pressing factory."

Steve looked at me blankly.

"Er, never mind," I said. I scooped the mouse into a plastic bag and binned it. Ridding the house of at least one rodent had eased some of my frustration. I felt able to deal with tradesmen once more. It had even been something of a bonding experience with Steve. "Sorry I was short with you – it's been a difficult week. Want to come in for a coffee?"

"If you're sure...?"

"It'll be fine. Just try not to trip over the remains of the heating."

I led him through to the kitchen. The boys were at school but Marie was face down on the floor, screaming, because I'd mixed her yogurt in with her Rice Crispies for her. I'd then tried to make things better by offering to eat the Crispies myself and get her fresh ingredients but no – she wanted the same Crispies and yogurt, not similar ones. She wanted me to miraculously unmix them, solely in order for her to mix them herself. Strangely, I'd refused. She'd been crying for an hour. I guess she's reached that stage... I motioned for Steve to ignore her and take a seat at the table. I washed my hands two or three times and then made refreshments.

"Now, what can I do for you?" I said to Steve, plonking his coffee down in front of him.

He looked apprehensively at Marie. "Is she all right?"

"She'll get over it." I picked up her bowl and offered it to Steve. "Would you like some Rice Crispies and yogurt?"

"No!" Marie yelled. "They mine! They mine! He not eat them!"

"Well," I said, "you'd better eat them quickly then, Marie, before he does."

"OK!" She leapt up from the floor and hurried to her seat in a panic, brushing her hair out of her face as she went. She snatched her bowl from my hand and hugged it close. "My Crispies... Mine."

I put on her favourite *Scooby-Doo!* episode with the sound down low and turned back to Steve. "Yeah, so what can I do for you?"

"Scott's been re-assigned," he said dejectedly.

I was taken by surprise again. Being Steve's manager, Scott was pretty senior, and so there weren't many opportunities for lateral movement in the org chart. Also, having met him a couple of times, I couldn't imagine which division of LBO would want him. "Where have they re-assigned him to? Pensions? Life Assurance?"

"Ulan Bator."

"Oohh..." I sucked in air between my teeth. "Do they play rugby in Mongolia? He can't be happy."

"They called him in, late yesterday, and told him to pack his suitcase. Didn't allow him an opportunity to appeal. They said that after careful consideration, he was the best man to explore new business possibilities in an expanding financial market which required hard-nosed negotiation and the ability to wrestle a yak. They didn't so much as give him time to tell anyone. He's on the plane already and I only found out because his replacement wants to see me."

My worst fears were calmed. For a dreadful few seconds, I thought Steve was going to say that he'd been promoted to fill Scott's parking space. Small wonder he was upset, though – being Scott's favourite sycophantic minion had all but assured him immunity to the job cuts and restructuring. "Who's his replacement then?"

"Morag Chandler. She's an awful woman. She's not even from the Communications Division. She's from IT! She got called in at the last minute a couple of weeks ago to arbitrate at one of the redundancy consultations and argued with everything Scott said and suddenly she thinks she can do better. I'd heard she'd gone to the board to complain but I can't believe they listened to her. It was only by chance she was at the meeting and now she's in charge. I don't understand it."

"Mmmm, yeah," I said, chewing my lip. I was miffed that he didn't remember that it was my wife's redundancy consultation that Morag had attended. He seemed to have forgotten that he'd put Sarah's job forward for the chop and that, thanks to him, her prospects still hung in the balance. I resisted pointing out my lack of sympathy, however, since it might have accidentally emerged that I was more than a little responsible for Morag entering his life. "Any idea what she needs to talk to you about? Presumably all she wants is for you to get her up to speed on everything that's happening in your department."

"Most of my network access has stopped working and my company credit card just got refused."

"Ah."

"What am I going to do?"

"I, erm..." Something about the situation began to trouble me. "Does Deborah know?"

"No, I haven't told anyone yet. I don't know what to do."

My suspicion was confirmed. Somewhere between helping him change a nappy and inviting him round to play *Wii Sports*, I'd been elevated to close friend. I was possibly his only friend outside of work and of the network of business contacts he had attained playing golf and squash. If he lost his job, those other friends might disappear and there was no way that Deborah was going to let him mooch around their flat. I might become his only friend, full stop, and he was bound to turn up at my house every day to do his mooching, probably with his kids along so I could help take care of them.

After a couple of years of wishing a 'career readjustment' on him, I unexpectedly found myself not so sure. I knew it would be pleasant for Sarah to get a manager with more of a clue and that that would have trickle-down pleasantness effects for me but...

I sighed. Maybe I was jumping too far ahead. Maybe he wasn't going to lose his job. Maybe...

I offered him a consoling chocolate digestive. For the first time, I took in how abnormally crumpled and defeated he appeared. In *his* mind, there was no 'maybe'. He had the look of a doomed man and, all at once, I couldn't help thinking that it was me he'd stolen it from. I was out of options. Clearly, I was going to have to start buying biscuits in double quantities.

"It's not so bad," I said. "I hear Deborah's interior design work is really getting going again."

He shook his head. "There's plenty of interest but she doesn't have the time."

"But if she didn't have to look after the children..."

"Once you've taken into account the cost of childcare, she wouldn't make enough for us to live on. Do you know how much nurseries cost?"

"Well, erm, if you did happen to, er, not be working, *you* could look after Ophelia and Josquin."

"Me?" Fear crossed his face. "All the time?"

"Yeah."

"Wouldn't they need fed and..." He seemed to ponder what else children might require but came up blank. "...things?"

"Yep, they'd certainly need fed and, erm, 'things', but you could do that."

"I don't have the..." He indicated his chest. "...things."

"Ophelia's nearly four," I said. "*Those* things are no longer a feeding requirement. Fresh fruit, cheese sandwiches and sausages should keep her going. You could probably manage that."

"Every day?"

"You might want to vary the menu on occasion but you could manage every day, yes. You can make cheese sandwiches, right?"

He was staring into space. "Deborah normally makes my sandwiches."

I decided to lay off on my housedad evangelism. He didn't appear ready to consider the future carefully. He needed reassurance. "I tell you what – go into work and chat to Morag and find out what the score is. Perhaps there's been a misunderstanding or there's some kind of challenging new opportunity waiting to develop your career that she hasn't told you about. You never know. If the worst comes to the worst, you can always polish up your CV and start phoning round your contacts. There's a long way to go yet."

He didn't seem to hear me. "Perhaps..." he mumbled and then looked at his watch. "It's after ten! I've got to get to work to see Morag. Maybe I can convince her to let me help Scott in Ulan Bator. I could learn to wrestle yaks."

"Sure you could," I said and handed him his coat. "It's getting the yak into the spandex that's the tricky part."

He definitely wasn't listening. "Yes," he said, vacantly. "Yes, there's a long way to go yet..." I showed him to the door.

"Are you going to be all right?" I asked, somewhat concerned. He really wasn't all there.

"Mmmm? Yes, I'll be fine. Everything's going to be fine."

"OK. Well, take care. Bye."

He'd already wandered off down the drive in a daze. I watched him along the street for a while to make sure he didn't walk into a lamp post or anything, and then I went back to the kitchen.

Marie had perked up. "I eat all my Crispies. I have dessert now!"

"You don't get dessert at breakfast," I said.

"Awwww," she whined. "I want chocolate biscuit." She pointed at the open packet on the table. "You eat nine."

"I had more like three."

"You eat nine!" She folded her arms and hung her head stubbornly. Another tantrum appeared on the cards.

"Whatever," I said. She had a fair comment in there somewhere and teaching her to count using chocolate biscuits wasn't a route I wanted to follow. I relented. "Would you like one?"

"Yes!" She snatched it from me and grinned. "Thanks!"

I had another myself and we settled down to watch some *Scooby-Doo!*. The plumber broke a couple more things and left. The decorator went off to buy a paper and sit in his van doing sudoku while he worked up an appetite for lunch. I was past caring.

Half an hour later, I discovered Steve had left his briefcase behind. On checking, I found that it contained nothing but a couple of pens and his sandwiches. Either that was all he normally had in his briefcase or he had left home with it out of habit, despite knowing his fate. Both options were depressing.

While I was cheering myself up by eating the sandwiches, Sarah phoned. Steve had been made redundant. On the plus side (or, from Sarah's perspective, on the *other* plus side) she'd been promoted to take his place. (Technically, of course, this meant Steve was being summarily fired rather being made redundant but they'd offered him a settlement to go quietly.) A pay rise, added benefits and the freedom to do the job properly – Sarah was ecstatic. I wasn't as enthusiastic as she'd hoped so I had to explain about Steve's visit. She did her best to understand but, truthfully, her heart wasn't in it. Can't say I blame her – his management made her life a misery on occasion.

We agreed to meet for lunch to talk it over and celebrate.

As I gathered up coats and tried to get my head back on straight, I noticed that the painter *had* touched up the woodwork in the end. Oddly, this felt like the best news I'd had all day. My spirits immediately lifted. In some small way, I'd got a tradesman to do what I wanted. Even if Steve did start turning up every morning, at least the house was nearly fixed. I could cope.

I put Marie's shoes on her and we set off along the street. Sarah's promotion sank in – more money, more holiday and a happy wife. That had to be good. There were all sorts of possibilities...

Soon, I was so busy dreaming of big tellies, I walked into a lamp post.

Yours in a woman's world,

Ed.

Illness

Dear Dave,

I don't remember my parents being ill when I was small. I know now that this is because I was the youngest of four and, by the time I arrived, they had had EVERYTHING already.

Small children – you love them, you take care of them, you give them your energy and your youth. How do they repay you? They go out into the world and bring you back diseases, that's how.

Bleargh. I'm off to overdose on Lockets (again).

Yours in a woman's world,

Ed.

Raising townies

Dear Dave,

I come from a very long line of farmers. There's an absolute stack of them (probably literally) buried in the same churchyard in Norfolk. Half of them even have the same name as me. This is freaky when randomly glancing at gravestones but it means that agriculture and husbandry should flow powerfully within my veins.

As if.

I'm marginally agoraphobic, I can't keep the worms in our worm-bin alive and I look at pot-plants and they die. Truth be told, farming was never my career of choice. It's very fortunate that I'm the second son and so I got to run away to the city.

Growing up on a farm, I felt inadequate as a child because I didn't know very much about the countryside. I struggled to tell a thrush from a starling or a birch from an oak. It didn't help that the *Swallows and Amazons* adventure books I was given to read presented this as moral failure. Turns out, though, that my kids make me look like a born naturalist. Witness the conversation I had with Lewis recently:

"Daddy? What kind of bird is that?" he asked as we sat in the park.

I glanced where he was pointing. "It's a raven," I said.

"No, it's not." He seemed to think I was pulling his leg. "It's a blackbird."

"You're right, it is a black bird, but it's not a blackbird."

"Why not?"

"It's a raven."

"No," he said, realising I wasn't joking but now convinced I was just plain stupid. "It's a bird and it's black."

"Yeah, but that doesn't make it a blackbird," I said. "Ravens are birds that are black."

"Then what are blackbirds?"

"They're... er... different birds that are black."

"Like that one?" he said, pointing again.

I sighed. "No, that's another raven."

"But why isn't it a blackbird?"

Normal logic wasn't working for me, so I decided to stretch the boundaries. "It's not a raven for the same reason you're not a zebra."

This appeared to satisfy him. "Oh, OK," he said and went back to wittering endlessly about Mario. I shook my head in despair.

I acknowledge that in my childhood I didn't know much about the countryside, but I like to believe I had more of a clue than that. If nothing else, I knew where milk came from. (The big vat in the shed across the cattle yard.) Scarily, however, the chat with Lewis was an improvement on the one I had last year with both the boys:

"What is bacon made from?" I asked them.

"Don't be silly," said Lewis, "it's not made of anything." Fraser nodded.

"It's meat. It comes from an animal," I said. This was clearly news to them but I ploughed on anyway. "What sort of animal do you think it comes from?

They shrugged.

"Pigs," I said. "Bacon comes from pigs. How about ham?"

"Cows?" said Fraser uncertainly.

"Good guess but ham comes from pigs too. Beef comes from cows." Things weren't going as smoothly as I'd hoped. I gave them an easy one. "How about chicken? What kind of creature does chicken come from?"

They both looked entirely blank.

"Think about it..." I said.

They continued to look blank. Light bulbs briefly flickered above their heads but then went out. Still blank. The answer was beyond them.

"Chicken comes from chickens," I said, giving up.

I wasn't expecting them to argue. "Don't be silly," said Lewis. "You can't eat chickens. They're covered in feathers."

Quite what the other passengers on the train were thinking by then, I can only imagine, but at that point I had to admit to myself that my children are townies. They'll grow up to hang around on street corners complaining there is nothing to do. They won't appreciate how lucky they are to be able to go to the shops, or the cinema, or a friend's house, without a forty minute car journey. They'll believe foxes are cuddly and that bread grows on trees. I can see it now and I'm not sure I can cope. It will compound my failure.

Half of me wants to run out and buy a book so I can teach them to tell a chaffinch from a rhododendron. That way I could overcome some of my childhood angst through them.

Fortunately, the other half of me can't be bothered. It's probably for the best.

Now I wonder where they think apples come from (other than the supermarket). Maybe I should go and experiment some more...

Yours in a woman's world,

Ed.

PS Just as my children are destined never to be farmers, a career in the military wouldn't be a smart move either. I had to warn Fraser to never become a soldier the other day.

I was examining his hair for lice as he had a bath (there are some going round school) and he simply would not move to the side of the tub when I told him. He kept moving to the end. Then, later, when I wanted him to move to the end, he moved to the side. I kept explaining what I meant. I kept pointing. He slid himself all over the place and then had a lie down, all the while justifying how he was following my instructions to the letter.

"Whatever you do, don't join the army," I said irritably, my back becoming sore from all the bending over. "They'll shoot you."

"Why?"

"They'll tell you to do something but you'll do something completely different and then argue with them. You get shot in the army for doing that."

He wasn't persuaded. "What? If you *ever* don't do what you're told?"

"Well, OK, it depends exactly what you do and I don't know they actually shoot people on their own side anymore but they used to. I'm sure what they do now is still bad. If they tell you to go and fight someone and you don't, then you'll be in big trouble."

He looked horrified. "But the person might be a good person."

"Uh-huh. This is what I'm saying Fraser, this is what I'm saying..."

Wooing Scary Karen

Dear Dave,

Your last letter was very short but it was nice to know you're still alive. I take it that Daisy is being hard work at the moment. Don't worry. It won't be long before you figure out how to leave the house in between feeds, nappy changes, Sam's mealtimes, sleeps and your own intravenous injections of coffee. Meanwhile, if you start running low on food, there's always home delivery. Thankfully, with Liz on maternity, you have extra help and you don't need to faff with sterilisers and bottles. Sleep in shifts if you have to.

How many people have asked if you're planning any more yet, by the way?

We're doing OK. Steve didn't come round here as much as I expected to begin with. I guess losing his job took a couple of weeks to assimilate. That or Deborah decided to go easy on him for a few days. Now, though, it's half-term (or October Week as they call it in the local lingo) and, with no nursery for Ophelia, he's been encouraged to take the kids out and about so Deborah can get some work done. It being October Week, there's no parent and toddler, swimming lessons or other regular activities. 'Take the kids out and about,' essentially means, 'Go round to Ed's house and eat all his biscuits.'

Of course, I'm no longer obliged to make him less of a Useless Dad. He isn't my wife's boss anymore and so my deal with Deborah has expired. I don't need her help to keep his useless management abilities under control. Nonetheless, I feel a bit sorry for him and, also, Ophelia gets on famously with Marie, so I don't mind him turning up too much. It's just that every day is going a little far.

Yesterday I tried getting out of the house before he arrived but the bell went while we were putting our coats on.

"We're heading off," I said as soon as I'd opened the door. I used the buggy and a couple of children to block his way in.

He looked crestfallen. "Where are you going?"

"We're off to meet Sc... er, Karen." I've had to stop calling Scary Karen by that name around the house. Marie started repeating it. This made me afraid.

"Which one's she?"

"Erm..." How was I supposed to describe Karen? "She's an older mum with two children, Malcolm and William. She's fairly large. Got disqualified from the paintballing. Remember?"

Steve's eyes widened. "Oh! The scary woman with the enormous..."

"Yep," I said, "that's the one. She's got something organised in the park."

"But it looks like it's going to rain."

I shrugged. "I'm suspecting it's going to absolutely chuck it down but I said I'd go. It's a case of get wet or suffer Karen's wrath."

"I see what you mean," he said, trying to squeeze inside. "How long are you going to be? I'll put the kettle on, ready for when you get back."

"Nice try," I said, ushering my children out of the house and locking the door firmly behind me. Steve's shoulders slumped despite the fact he was already bent nearly double over a buggy that was far too low for him. It merely added to his general air of despondency. He hadn't shaved and his smart suits had been replaced by casual wear which was becoming ripped and crusty after only a few days of involved parenting. I took pity on him. "If you want to come with us, you can."

It was his turn to shrug. He didn't have many options. We walked round to the park.

There was quite a crowd. I didn't know half the mums there and many of the ones I did know had brought along school-age children that previously I'd been barely aware of. Super~Mum, Julia, had her four with her and they were busily erecting a large shelter from poles and plastic sheeting. Considering her eldest is only eight, it was an impressive sight. I was surprised, though, that the GrandParent of Doom wasn't standing over them sternly, holding a stopwatch and a whistle.

"Is your mother about?" I asked Julia, nervously. The GPD and I have some unpleasant history.

"She's busy cleaning my house."

"That's handy," I said, relieved.

Julia shook her head. "Not really. I had to tidy up specially before she came round."

"Ah. She hasn't lightened up much then?"

"No. She's been even harder to deal with since I told her that I'm thinking of sending the children to school."

"In your situation, I'd never be thinking of much else." (Julia currently home~schools her children.)

She nodded and looked very tired. "I can't keep going with teaching all four of them. Mum's offered to help more but, well..." Julia trailed off at the thought of yet more 'help' from her mother. Then she shuddered and recovered. "I think she's upset she won't see so much of them. She's taken a huff and didn't want to come out today."

"It's probably better that way," I said, holding out my hand to catch the first drops of a light shower. "I can't imagine she copes well with rain."

Julia looked quizzical.

"I'm shrinking! I'm shrinking!" I squealed, contorting myself into my best Wicked Witch of the West impression.

"I don't know what you mean," Julia said in mock outrage as she stifled a laugh. The rain started to fall harder. "I should help the kids."

"Right with you."

We were quickly joined by several other adults and the tent was up in no time. We all squashed in like toddlers round someone else's toy and waited for the worst to pass. Marie and Ophelia ran about, trying to drink the rain, and a few of the other kids copied. Some of the older children started a game of football. Fraser and Lewis stood and complained about the dampness and the lack of computer games until I told them that if they got really wet, we might go home sooner. This encouraged them towards the kick-about. I stood shivering under the awning and dreamed of being back in the house with my Xbox. Then I became suddenly aware that I was crushed up against Karen.

"So? Are you coming on the night out?" she asked.

"Wha-? I... Wha-?" I replied, my tongue making random noises as my brain struggled to take in the horror. "Night out?" I finally managed.

"We're having a parent and toddler night out. Didn't anyone tell you? It's at the Chinese round the corner. We went there for Tess' divorce party but that's OK, they'll have forgotten us by now. We had a lovely meal. I had the duck but I was paying for it for days afterwards. That was the time I had to go to the hospital for... *(I zoned out for several minutes.)* ...Jess told me to put him down but I'd just got the hang of the chopsticks and... *(More sunny thoughts seemed in order.)* ...that's the last time I'm taking the bus to Glasgow, I'm telling you. Unless I really do have a chimpanzee with me. Bloody cheek! Next time... *(Yep. Kids still contented and playing. Everything fine with the world.)* ...Great. So we'll see you there about eight?... *(More dreaming. I... What?)*"

I was evicted from my happy place with a shock. I'd nodded and smiled at a very inopportune moment. It was too late to back out. "Is Trevor coming?" I said in a panic.

"Oh, I hadn't thought to ask him because he's not a parent. Do you think I should? He is always helping out."

"Yes, yes," I said. Trevor might be a hulking ex-soldier who's almost as scary as Karen but I was desperate for any kind of male backup. I didn't want to be the only man around when a dozen mums got their first chance in months to let their hair down. "How about you, Steve? Are you...?" I turned around but he'd disappeared. He's obviously not *completely* daft.

"Oi, out the way." A three-year-old shoved me aside and stuck his head up Karen's shirt looking for elevenses. I was pretty sure it was *her* three-year-old on this occasion but it still seemed like a good opportunity to escape to the football.

Lewis and Fraser were struggling. The makeshift pitch was becoming swampy and their natural aversion to getting messy was competing with their overwhelming desire to go home. They were willing enough to kick the ball themselves but kept running away from it when it was kicked towards them, in case it made them muddy. I joined their team to spur them on. Once they were properly dirty, they got quite into it.

I slipped away to check on Marie. She was with Julia's kids. I was pleased to discover that they were doing my job for me, teaching her the names of various plants in the shrubbery around the edges of the park. I left them to it. I only found out later that it was the *Latin* names they were teaching. Now I've got to tell her to watch out for the *Urtica dioica* whenever she's heading for a patch of nettles. How convenient.

As predicted, it was beginning to chuck it down. Steve had already gone. I went back to the tent to collect my stuff. I passed Karen and Trevor just as a mum raced over and pointed to the other side of the park. A man was taking his dog for a walk. A very foolish man.

Karen instantly rummaged around in her handbag and pulled out a whistle, a plastic bag, an official letter from the council confirming that no dogs are allowed in the park and a chunky, rubber-coated device that, for a second, I thought was a torch. Then she pounded off towards the man, tooting loudly.

"That was a taser," I said to Trevor, once she was out of earshot.

He nodded. "Ach, the bloke's got it coming. It's the little old ladies she catches smoking in bus stops that I feel sorry for."

"She...? No, I don't want to know. How are you doing?"

"Can't complain. Karen's invited me out for a Chinese."

"Er..." I said. Trevor has a thing for Karen. This is part of what makes him so scary himself (along with the knowledge he could crush me like a bug using only his eyebrow). "You do realise all her mates are going to be there? And me?"

"Oh, yeah," he muttered, "but I don't want to rush things. She's a very attractive woman, that Karen. Gives me the chance to use some of my charm with no kids about. Yeah, tell my joke, show her a few tattoos and my shrapnel scar, arm-wrestle if she's up for it..."

I wasn't sure what to say. We both stood in the rain and watched Karen off in the distance chasing a Rottweiler.

"I should go help her," said Trevor but didn't move.

"I think she's got it covered," I said and then had an idea. "If you really want to impress her, though, you could go look after her children. Make sure they're OK and keep them entertained."

"How do I do that, then?"

I shrugged. "You could try showing *them* your tattoos."

"What about the scar?"

"Depends where it is."

He bent over and let me see behind his ear.

"Yep, that'll be fine," I said, without peering too closely.

"You really think..." He sounded surprisingly nervous about the whole suggestion.

I rolled my eyes and pulled childcare rank. "You've seen active service in three different countries. Are you telling me you can't handle two small children for five minutes?"

"No."

"Then hop to it, man."

"Right, yes." I was mildly disappointed that he didn't salute and call me 'sir' but at least he went off and followed orders.

"See you at the night out," I called after him and then gathered up my own children and headed home.

We were soaked. As we opened our gate, I was looking forward to a hot cup of tea, some dry socks and a little peace and quiet. Unfortunately, Steve and his children were huddled by the door under an improvised shelter constructed from our recycling bins. "You took your time," he said. I was about to tell him where to go but he held up a large paper bag and said, "Let's get inside – the cakes are going soggy."

He has learned something, I suppose.

I let everyone in and turned on the heating. We all ended up under blankets watching *The Little Mermaid.* Maybe that will discourage him from coming round today.

Nope. There's the doorbell again...

I should go. All the best with getting some sleep.

Yours in a woman's world,

Ed.

On its last wheels

Dear Dave,

The buggy is dying.

This isn't good – I need it to last another six months. Marie could conceivably walk everywhere already but it's slow going at times. I don't want to be dawdling about in the rain and sleet and cold. After the winter, she'll be better able to maintain a reasonable speed and it won't matter as much anyway. The buggy can be put out to pasture then.

It will be nice to have space in the hall again and to be able to get on buses easily, but there will be a sense of loss too. Where am I going to put my groceries? I'll have to go shopping twice as often or start taking a rucksack with me to Tesco.

Actually, I should buy the kids rucksacks and take *them* with me to Tesco.

That problem is solved but I'll miss the buggy, all the same. It's seen many, many miles of active service as a toddler-carrier and also doubled as a containment unit for unruly children, a bed on wheels and a handy shield to park between myself and people I'm intimidated by. It's a great place for stowing wipes, clean clothes, rainwear and snacks. When I venture forth without it, I feel exposed and under-equipped.

We've had a number of wheeled transport devices over the years: a pram, three single buggies, a double buggy and a buggy board. (That's not taking into account bikes, trikes, scooters, office chairs and storage tubs, but these are more for fun than serious means of getting from A to B. That said, Fraser is convinced that spinning round incredibly fast on an office chair is a good method to travel backwards in time. I'm sceptical. In practice, he seems only able to get as far back as a time before he felt entirely well.)

Each device has had its uses but it's the single buggies which have taken the real punishment. The first got mangled by a car boot and the frame broke when I tried to bend it back. The second was twisted out of shape by over-use of the buggy board when transporting heavy boys – there was no longer any way to get all four wheels to touch the ground at once and it had to be retired. Our third buggy, though, has survived the buggy board, leaking nappies, cobbled streets, rutted fields, steps, snow, constant use and being regularly loaded with a child *and* a fridgeful of shopping.

True, most of these things immediately invalidated the warranty but, then again, the instructions claimed that so did going up and down kerbs. The warranty was effectively out the window the moment we crossed the entrance to a little car park that's just along the road. Bearing that in mind, we've felt free to pile the under-seat storage with six pint containers of milk, loop a shopping bag over each handle and then try to use speed bumps as launch ramps.

It's still going. I suppose it hasn't had to put up with some of the things I've seen other people do. I've witnessed adults sitting in buggies, older children hitching a ride by hanging off the back and one buggy being used to transport an impressively large TV. Our buggy hasn't been abused as badly as that but it is seeming a little past it – its wheels are pitted and worn, it struggles to turn, its raincover is in tatters. Worse, one of the back wheels is in danger of coming off. One day I'm going to take a sharp corner in the electronics department of John Lewis, the wheel's going to get left behind and Marie and I are going to spin off into a display of giant tellies. As we crawl to safety, the buggy will explode, showering us in breadstick crumbs and remote controls. It will be a sad end to a faithful servant (and some expensive TVs). I should really dispose of the buggy before then.

I just can't bring myself to do it.

It's like a dog – an old, tired dog that only has three legs and smells bad, admittedly, but it feels callous not to give it a proper send off. I wanted to catapult it, flaming, off the top of Edinburgh Castle and watch it blow up at the culmination of the Hogmanay fireworks but the council weren't up for that. So now I'm considering something akin to a Viking longboat ceremony. I'm going to pile it high with old baby clothes, set it alight, float it gently out to sea and watch it drift serenely off into the night. If I can get a couple of hundred other people to join in, that could be quite beautiful.

Sniff.

But I'm getting ahead of myself. There's life in the old dog yet. I'm going to give it a wash, spray its wheels with WD40, tighten any loose screws, tickle it behind the ears and then let it gambol around out the back door for a little while.

Then I'm going to load it up with six bags of books to take to the charity shop, perch Marie on top, jump on the mudguards and try to beat my downhill record to the bottom of the street.

If I use enough oil, I might even be able to leave a trail of fire behind me...

Yours in a woman's world,

Ed.

TAB

Dear Dave,

Thank you for your continued interest in the Patented Parental rePeater, my invention which, by endlessly repeating whatever a parent said most recently, takes the work out of being ignored.

As you point out, I did promise that the Triple-P would be available for purchase by now. Sadly, I've run into difficulties and am now in legal dispute with a company looking to produce an item called the Toddler Answer Back (TAB). Here's an extract from some of their marketing material:

Children!!!! TAB is for you. Fed up of repeating yourself because you're not getting what you want? Tired of saying the same thing AGAIN AND AGAIN! Want the power without the effort of actually pestering?

Get TAB (TM).

Hang it round your neck, go about your daily mayhem and then, at the touch of a brightly coloured button, have TAB repeat the last thing you said. Press a different button and keep it saying the same thing over and over and over UNTIL THE END OF TIME!!!!!! The longer it goes on, the louder and whinier it will get. Everyone will hear but only dogs will understand! Your parents will give you ANYTHING just to get THE NOISE TO STOP.

You *need* TAB.

Comes complete with 127 pre-programmed sayings, including:

- No.
- Heh!
- I want it.
- I need toilet.
- Wake up!

• I don't want it.
• So?
• I really need toilet.
• I want Mummy do it.
• I want Daddy do it.
• I want Barney do it.
• I do it myself.
• I REALLY need toilet.
• I'm not wearing it.
• Why?
• You not touch my TAB.
• I don't need toilet anymore.
• I hurt my tongue.
• You rub it better.
• Look at me!
• NOW!
• I need dry socks.
• Turn your hearing aid on. (For use on grandparents who are supposed to be helping but have in fact opted for a crafty nap.)

Save your own annoying sayings and noises:
• Prove to your parents how loudly they snore.
• Play back electronic nursery rhymes slightly out of sync with the original toy.
• Disable voice-activated security systems with ease.
• Drive people insane – set TAB to copy whatever *they* say!
• Record calls for help, hide TAB in common household appliances and watch your parents panic.
• Mimic the phone, the doorbell and the fire alarm.
• Use built-in voice masking wizardry to argue in the style of Darth Vader, Yoda, Beach Fun Barbie or a Dalek!

TAB also has several special modes:

• Extra Screechy – for use in church.

• Firm but Polite – for use on other people's parents.

• Extra Loud – for cinemas, funerals and early mornings.

TAB is waterproof, shockproof, easily portable, resistant to sledgehammers and has a battery-life of between 6 months and 25 years (dependent on the number, age and stubbornness of your parents). Buy it now!

TAB – It complains so you don't have to.

(Batteries not included.)

Clearly, I have a strong case that they've ripped off my idea and subverted it, but things aren't looking good – their lawyers are smaller than mine. The law firm itself is large but the actual lawyers are small and, in my experience, small lawyers are the most dangerous. (Think Tom Cruise in *The Firm*.) Nonetheless, I'm hopeful we can come to some form of mutually beneficial arrangement. I'm thinking a dual pack containing both a Triple-P and a TAB might work. Then both devices could be set going, sealed in a lead-lined box and buried in the back garden. This would leave families free to play together happily without disagreement, knowing all the pointless arguing was being taken care of elsewhere. Peace and harmony would be assured.

If only...

Yours in a woman's world,

Ed.

Parent and toddler night out

Dear Dave,

I'm happy to hear you're well and you're finding your feet with the new routine. It's great news that Daisy is sleeping better.

Thanks for asking how things went the other evening. Apart from the minor bruising to my face, I survived. It was a peculiar night, though. I suppose you want the full story. All right then. I'll start in the middle...

* * *

"This isn't what I signed up for," said Trevor, the silver tinsel of his Deely boppers reflecting off the dome of his bald head.

I could barely make out what he was saying over the blaring of Chesney Hawkes. "I know what you mean," I said, surveying the dance floor. It was full of slightly tipsy women who were old enough to remember a time before Margaret Thatcher became Prime Minister but who were wearing outfits they'd bought when she was still in power. "I think I'm going blind..." Then I caught sight of Scary Karen gyrating as she screamed out the lyrics to *One and Only* and I added, "...but not fast enough." I had another big gulp of my beer.

* * *

To be honest, the parent and toddler night out had never held much promise for me, but I hadn't expected it to go downhill so rapidly.

When I ventured into the local Chinese, there were plenty of mums already seated at a long table. I squeezed up a darkened corner with Trevor and hoped for the time to pass quickly. We ordered drinks while we waited for Karen and a few others.

Then Eleanor arrived.

The temperature around the table dropped so rapidly that it started to snow on the prawn crackers. The only time most of us had met Eleanor previously, she'd forced us to sing in harmony and to paint with our children. (As you'll remember, by 'with' I don't mean 'alongside', I mean 'using'.) I call her the GrandParent of Doom.

"Good evening, ladies. I'm afraid Julia can't make it this evening – her babysitter called off. Seeing as a seat has been booked for her, and I have attended one of your delightful nursery gatherings in the past, I thought I might join you."

There was much muttering. If her daughter couldn't find a sitter, why hadn't the GPD gone to look after the kids instead of turning up at the restaurant to make us all miserable?

Also, why did she have two large bags with her?

"Quiet please," said the GPD, shushing us. "As these events are so rare, I brought some items to make the evening especially memorable." She reached into one of the bags and pulled out a pair of the Deely boppers. She placed them regally on her head and then she reached into the other bag and pulled out t-shirts.

* * *

Did I mention the t-shirts before?

As we sat at the bar of the seedy club with the mature clientele, Trevor and I were wearing white t-shirts that the GPD had obviously prepared well in advance for our humiliation. If they'd had 'Young, free and single' written on them, I could have lived with the irony. 'Worn-out, tied-down & reproduced' was not so much to my liking.

I was desperate to get home and put the offending garment at the back of the wardrobe beside my other emergency t-shirts. These were all 'amusing' gifts from in-laws. One says 'My other toddler is well-behaved' and a second has 'Don't follow me... my children bite'. The third was useful for crossing roads when the kids were small and I wasn't getting much sleep. It's emblazoned with 'Honk if I've got my eyes closed'.

* * *

Eleanor went round the table passing out the t-shirts and came to our corner last. It was an *extra* dark corner by then because I'd snuffed out all the candles I could reach in the forlorn hope she wouldn't see us.

Well, it was worth a try.

She handed me my t-shirt stiffly. "I see that after a hard day encouraging other men's wives to abandon their ideals, you've deserted your own wife while you cavort with... Trevor!"

I blinked. I'd been ready to rebut the put down, to tell her to stop forcing *her* ideals on her daughter and to inform her that Sarah was rather pleased to have me out of the house for once. Trevor really isn't my type, however. I was momentarily thrown by the accusation.

She'd forgotten all about me. "I hadn't realised you'd be here, Trevor. How delightful to meet again. I'm sorry we didn't have much opportunity to chat last time. Now let me see..." She hunted around in her bag of t-shirts before handing him one the size of a small tent. "I brought a couple of extremely large ones in case Karen has a sister." Then she sat down opposite him, put her chin on her clasped hands and batted her eyelids.

* * *

The club seemed to be having some sort of an eighties night. It made me think of school discos and, oddly, Wotsits. A worrying possibility struck me. "What time is it?" I asked. My watch had had a regrettable Play-Doh related accident the day before.

Trevor checked his. "Twenty-five past ten."

"We need to go. We need to go now."

He heard the panic in my voice and, for the second time that evening, I saw fear in his eyes. "Why?"

I searched frantically in my pocket for my cloakroom stub. "We have to be out of here before half-past ten. We can't be here when..."

But it was too late. Wham! had faded and The Weather Girls were already beginning to crank up.

Trevor was oblivious. "What happens at half ten?"

"That's when it's supposed to start raining men," I gibbered, "and if you hadn't noticed, male precipitation is a trifle thin on the ground this evening." I swept my arm to take in the expanse of the room. There were almost no other unattached blokes there. On the other hand, there were quite a few lonely girls who'd left their umbrellas at home. Nearly all of them were looking at us. I reckoned we had until the chorus to escape. "Run for your..."

I turned round and nearly fell over Eleanor.

* * *

The GPD continued to sweet-talk Trevor as we ordered our food. He sat nervously, his mouth slightly open, unable to make his voice work.

Trevor is ten years older than me but Eleanor is a good ten years older than him. It had plainly never crossed his mind to think of her in that way before. And judging by the expression on his face, having had the thought forced upon him, he was terrified by it. Karen might be scary but the GPD is truly frightening.

Karen hadn't showed and no one else was willing to fight.

We put our t-shirts and Deely boppers on.

* * *

Eleanor slowed me down long enough for Karen's friend Tess to grab hold of my arm and yank me bodily onto the dance floor. I abruptly found myself strutting my not-so-funky stuff. Fortunately, it was pretty dark. Unfortunately, that just made my t-shirt glow even brighter purple. We'd walked like an Egyptian and fought for our right to party before I had a fresh chance to escape.

I didn't get far. The exit was blocked by Cress and Jess, who looked like they wanted in on the action. Could have been worse, though. At least I wasn't having to dance with Eleanor.

* * *

By the time Karen turned up for the meal, it was too late. The GPD was all smiles for Trevor but the rest of us had been lambasted about everything from the names of our children to our choice of footwear. We were afraid to speak and shiny tinsel rustled with every movement of our heads. Karen did fight back but the only seat left for her was right at the other end of the table. That end gradually livened up as the evening wore on; my end was reduced to listening to the fun Karen's end was having.

Everyone had plenty to drink.

Trevor didn't get an opportunity to chat up Karen like he'd planned. She was too far away and the GPD wouldn't leave him alone. I shot him the occasional sympathetic glance but he was too shell-shocked to notice. It was a relief when the bill arrived. I thought it was over.

"Let's go to a club," said Tess. "I know a good place that's not far."

There was plenty of merry agreement.

Then again, no one had been expecting Eleanor to come along.

* * *

"Mind if I cut in?" I shimmied between Trevor and Eleanor and then spun him off across the room.

"Hey! None of that!" He tried to bat me away.

I ducked. He'd dragged me along to the club for support. I hadn't wanted to go. I'd wanted to head home to my Xbox. I was going to do my best for him, whether he liked it or not. "Would you really rather dance with her?" I said, pointedly.

"Er..."

"Anyway," I shouted over the music, taking advantage of his confusion, "I'm off to climb out the window of the gents any minute. You won't fit, so you're going to have to come up with another plan. I suggest you make your advances on Karen. It's the only way to get the GPD to leave you alone."

"Who?"

"The GP... Oh, never mind. Who do you think? I had a word with the DJ. The next song should be suitable."

"I..." He was still confused.

"No need to thank me. Just collect my coat on the way out." I pressed my cloakroom ticket into his hand. "I'll get it from you at parent and toddler."

"But what if..."

I remembered that he responds well to being ordered about. "Show some backbone, man! Tell her how you feel. Let her see your passion."

"If you really think..."

"I do. Now, I'll leave you to it. If we dance together any longer at this time of night, then club etiquette seems to suggest that I've got to snog you. I don't think either of us wants that, although I'm sure it would be another way to put Eleanor off."

This he wasn't confused about. "I'd rather tell Karen."

"You'll have to do more than that," I yelled. "You're going to have to show her your moves. Good luck."

We'd discoed towards the toilets. As the song ended, I struck my best Travolta pose, spun round with a flourish and disappeared through the door. I was halfway out into the night air by the time *Dancing Queen* started playing.

I paused, my feet balanced on a urinal. I couldn't bring myself to leave. I slipped back inside and crept over to the door. I opened it a tiny crack to see what was happening.

For an instant, I thought the dance floor was empty. But no! Trevor and Karen were in the centre, tripping the light fantastic. Their t-shirts luminesced blindingly and they were bathed in multicoloured swirls from a dozen disco balls. It was a sight to behold. Everyone else had got out of the way to avoid being injured.

I stood mesmerised until the song finished. Then, to my delight, they went with club etiquette. There were cheers from the other parent and toddler members around the room. I smiled. My work there was done.

I suddenly noticed that not quite everyone was cheering.

Eleanor was livid and her eyes were sweeping the room, hunting for something.

Someone.

She knew. She knew I'd talked him into it.

Her eyes came to a stop, fixed on the gents. I was certain she couldn't see me. The door was only open the merest fraction. She couldn't possibly... And I was in the gents, anyhow. She wouldn't...

She began to march over.

She was coming for me.

It wasn't the softest landing as I hit the cobbles of the alley but my face broke my fall and I was up and running within moments. I dashed off down the street, the heads of passers-by turning to watch me. I didn't look back.

I was almost home before I remembered to take off my Deely boppers.

* * *

I got my coat back today. Trevor and Karen were all smiles. I'll let you know how it works out for them.

I'm not looking forward to my next meeting with Eleanor, however. Could be messy.

Yours in a woman's world,

Ed.

Part 6

The Last Days of Parent and Toddler

Catching up

Dear Dave,

You're right, I haven't told you what happened in the end about all the repairs from the flood damage. I was waiting until the tradesmen were finished. They've been *nearly* finished for a month now.

All they have to do is make the towel rail in the bathroom work again, except they've had to 'order a part over the internet from a foreign gas supplier'. I should really phone them and chase it up but after months of chaos, it's pleasant not having tradesmen in the house. Also, although it's getting chilly stepping out of the shower in the morning, I'm nervous of what else they might break in trying to fix the problem. There's something to be said for quitting while you're not too far behind.

Nonetheless, the decorating is done and, after much effort, most of our furniture and stuff is back where it should be and my safe place is permanently reinstated. Thanks to all the sorting out I've had to do, I haven't had much time to actually spend in the safe place, but it's good to know it's there.

On another happy note, the mice have mysteriously gone away. No more have leapt at me out of household appliances. One day they were high-diving down the stairs and hiding amongst shoes, the next day they had vanished. There was that dopey one I caught a week later but, since then, I haven't spotted any evidence of them. Not a sign. Maybe they were coming in from next door and repairs there blocked up the access hole. Or maybe as soon as I'd closed down the toaster buffet, they simply had no reason to come to our house.

The second explanation begs the question of how often they'd been snacking in the crumb tray before I caught one in the act.

Excuse me briefly whilst I go scrub the worktops with bleach one last time...

We bought a new toaster and we're going through twice as much sliced bread as usual thanks to the novelty value of being able to slightly char it again. I keep a lid on the toaster when we're not using it, though.

Marie went with Sarah on the shopping trip to buy the toaster and was very excited when they returned. "We bought a toaster!" she shrieked, showing me the box. "This one didn't have mice in." She seemed to believe that the other ones in the shop came with the mice presupplied. I didn't correct her. After all, I'm now a man who keeps a lid on his toaster and views open toasters with paranoid suspicion. Who am I to judge what's crazy?

Speaking of paranoia, I did find a mouse-dropping in the middle of the lounge carpet a couple of days ago. I assume it came out from under the TV cabinet when I was faffing with wires to try and fix our wireless router (oh, the irony) but it did cause me to panic at the prospect that there had been some fresh scouting by the rodents. Our stricter than normal hygiene rules will remain for a while yet. I suspect, however, that they will continue to be ignored:

Marie and I were sitting upstairs in the lounge the other evening and she unexpectedly went, "A crumb!" and picked something off her sleeve. It had been a while since tea and I didn't get a good look at whatever it was, so I wasn't convinced her analysis was correct. I was going to tell her not to eat it but I wasn't fast enough. She popped it in her mouth and smiled happily. I was thinking of giving her a lecture but then I looked down and noticed a crumb on my own shirt. Without thinking, I picked it up, popped it in my mouth and smiled happily. I believe it was toast but I didn't really take a good look at it. You know, it had been a while since tea, and I was feeling a little hungry, and it was probably toast and...

I decided to hold off on the lecture. I felt I'd lost the moral high ground.

There's only so much conflict that I can take, anyway. Earlier in the day she'd asked to watch some *Winnie the Pooh*. Now, we have *Bob the Builder*, *Tweenies*, *Teletubbies*, *Bagpuss*, most of Pixar's output, *Tom & Jerry*, *Numberjacks*, *Scooby-Doo!*, *Fimbles*, *Thomas the Tank-Engine*, *Barney*, *Shrek*, the adventures of various Disney princesses, *Mr Men* and goodness knows what else but we don't have any *Winnie the Pooh*.

"We don't have *Winnie the Pooh*," I said. "What do you want to watch instead?"

"I want watch *Winnie the Pooh* instead," she said excitedly.

"We don't have any. You can't watch something we haven't got. You'll have to watch something else. How about *Tweenies*? Do you want to watch *Tweenies*?"

She pulled a face. "No! I don't want watch *Tweenies*."

"How about *Bob*?" I suggested. "Would you like to watch *Bob the Builder*?"

"No. I not like that."

"OK. How about...?" I made various suggestions. She refused all of them. Things went on like this for some time.

"How about *Little Mermaid*?" I asked finally, approaching the end of my tether.

"No," she said emphatically

I gave up. "OK. Tell me what you want to watch then."

"I want to watch..." She paused, knowing I might not take kindly to her asking for *Winnie the Pooh* again. Then she had an idea. "I want watch something we don't have."

I wasn't fooled. This was just a way of informing me she wanted the bear of very little brain without actually saying the name. "How's that going to work?" I snapped. "Tell me something that we have that you want to watch."

It was too late.

"I want watch something we don't have," she repeated but she now appeared rather taken by the concept. At that point, I knew that even if I miraculously found some *Winnie the Pooh*, it would no longer suffice. The second I produced 'something that we didn't have', it would become something else – it would become 'something we hadn't had until recently'. That wasn't going to cut it. She had her heart set on a logical impossibility. She wanted to not have her cake and eat it.

So, of course, she got nothing. She sat and glumly stared at a blank screen for an hour, every so often whining miserably, "I want something we don't have."

It wasn't much fun for anyone but eventually she said, "I want Party Rings now. They make me happy." I gave her the biscuits and, sure enough, she was happy once more.

If only that worked on adults...

Hang on, maybe it does work. Things aren't so bad at the moment but there's no harm in doing a little experimentation in preparation for the next time the house falls apart. I think I'll head over to the biscuit tin to conduct some research...

Yours in a woman's world,
Ed.

They really are silent

Dear Dave,

How are you holding up? It's always tough having a new baby in the family but Daisy is five weeks old now and she should be settling in. You ought to be acclimatised to tiredness, lack of sleep and limited free time. What's maybe becoming more of an issue is that Liz has been on maternity leave for a couple of months.

Have you driven each other mad yet?

The first weeks after Fraser was born were idyllic. I was about, Sarah was about; we learnt together how to be parents. It was different second time round. There was more work to be done, for a start. We were busy. Beyond that, we both felt the effects of Sarah 'invading my work space'. I had my routines and rules and schedules in place but all of a sudden the boss was never far away. I had to consult on decisions and give regular progress updates. Meanwhile, Sarah wasn't sure where she fitted in and often felt a bit pointless as I rushed about getting stuff done and failed to include her in case it slowed me down.

The tiredness, lack of sleep and limited free time didn't help matters.

Remember to work together and discuss your needs over the next few months. If you can talk when you're both relatively awake but the children are both asleep, so much the better. (Good luck with that...)

Thankfully, Sarah and I got by without too many arguments because we're fairly agreed on the general principles of parenting. We're trying to achieve the same goals (happy, polite children who love Jesus and physics), even if the practical methods can vary wildly. Sarah likes to get the kids out and about; I'm keen to ensure they get a chance to relax at home. She maintains discipline using a points system; I tend to employ shouting and banishment. As long as we know who's in charge of the children at any given instant, however, this isn't a problem. We're simply using the methods that work for us.

There can still be issues, though. These days our main bone of contention is the pronunciation of words. It's one of the difficulties of a mixed marriage. The kids' accents haven't become firmly established yet. Will they sound Scottish or English or merely confused?

Fraser brought a book home from school last week to read for homework. I think the idea is that we're meant to find a quiet spot without distraction and he's supposed to read out loud while I correct and encourage. What normally happens is that, wherever we go, as soon as we get comfortable, Lewis comes in wanting to play and Marie needs the toilet. This has a tendency to divide my attention. Fraser steams on whether I'm listening or not. The book was about a naughty boy whose teacher stops him misbehaving by making him responsible for policing the other pupils. Fraser was a couple of paragraphs into the book before I became aware that something was awry.

"What's the boy called again?"

He paused and squinted at the name on the page. "Rage," he said uncertainly.

"Are you sure?"

"Not really. It keeps confusing me."

I took a closer look. "His name's Raj. The book's called *Raj in Charge*. It rhymes."

"Oh, OK." He started reading again. He's good at it and he continued clearly and without hesitation until the next time he got to the name. He paused. He squinted. He made a noise like a revving motor. "Rage?" he said.

"No, Raj. To rhyme with charge."

"Raj, OK." He kept reading. Everything was fine. Then he got to the name again. Pause. Squint. Rev. "Ray... Ra... Radge?"

"Nope. Rhymes with charge."

"Raj, OK." He managed about another half a sentence before he paused for a further revving squint. "Ray-a-arge?"

"Close enough."

He just about had the hang of it by the end of the book. It reminded me of when he was at nursery and had a friend called Conor. Fraser had never heard the name 'Conor' before and couldn't cope. He called the poor kid 'Corner' for months.

The next day at breakfast, Fraser told Sarah about the book he'd read. He waved it at her and was a little way into his account before Sarah stopped him.

"What's the boy called again?"

Fraser paused and squinted at the front cover. "Rarge," he said uncertainly.

"Are you sure?"

"Not really. It keeps confusing me."

Sarah took a closer look. "His name's Raj. It rhymes with badge."

"That's not what Daddy said."

"Daddy's from another country. He speaks funny."

"You can talk," I piped up. "You pronounce the silent 'h's in words like whistle and where."

"For the last time, they ARE NOT silent."

"They are," I insisted. "The old joke proves it. How do you get two whales in a car? Along the M4 and across the Severn Bridge. Doesn't work unless the 'h' is silent."

"At least when *I'm* talking," she said, "everyone knows which witch is which. And *you* can't say bath."

"I can."

"No, you can't," she said. "You say bar-th."

"That's how it's supposed to be said."

"I don't think so."

We did a quick poll of the kids. We got two ba-ths and a bar-th. Then we did the poll again and got two bar-ths and a ba-th. They're evidently confused but it's not the disaster it could have been – we could have called one of the boys Luke. I pronounce the name Loo-k. Sarah pronounces it Look. Having parents who argued over how to pronounce your name wouldn't be that much fun.

As Sarah says it, 'Look at Luke' sounds the same as 'Luke at look'.

That does my head in. Then again, she can't cope with the way I say 'aunt' and 'aren't' alike. She says 'aunt' and 'ant' alike. We can debate how the children should speak for hours.

Fraser returned us to the matter in hand.

"Daddy said it's Rarge."

"Maybe that's how they say it where Daddy comes from but, round here, everyone says Radge like me. Which do you think would be better for you to use?"

I had to concede that she had a point.

"Oh, OK," said Fraser. "Raj." It was somewhere in the middle. Compromise was reached.

I don't really know why we bother, though. He was probably calling the boy Rage again by lunch-time.

We'll have to wait and see what kind of hybrid accent the kids eventually settle on. They've each picked up different bits and pieces. Maybe I should do some more experiments. I think I'll start by getting Fraser to read out, 'Look, Luke, wear ants where aunts aren't," very fast a few times. That should be good for a laugh... (Or is that laff?)

All the best with finding your own compromises and staying sane.

Yours in a woman's world,

Ed.

eBay comes to us all

Dear Dave,

"They want fireworks?"

"Yep," said Rob, sitting across the table from me. "And not just a couple of rockets and a sparkler. They want our names written in flame."

"Oh, goodness." As his best man, I'd gone round to his flat for the evening to chat about the impending celebrations while his fiancée, Kate, was at my house, receiving wedding wisdom from Sarah. "Are you arriving in a vintage car to the sound of bagpipes and then being ushered in for caviar nibbles and the gentle harmony of a string quartet?"

"Something like that. Kate's parents have given up on her brother ever getting hitched, so this is their one chance at wedding glory. Money's no object and it's all going crazy. Have a look at this catalogue."

He handed me a glossy brochure which was half an inch thick and I began to flick through it.

I glanced at my stopwatch. "You've only got a minute left, by the way."

"I'm thinking."

"Don't think too long," I said, "or I'll rip your arms off and feed them to you."

"OK, OK, I'm a little out-numbered here. You won't be laughing so hard when it's my turn to play the aliens."

"We'll see. Forty-five seconds."

Well, we told the womenfolk we were going to chat about the wedding but the table wasn't exactly spread with seating planners. It was covered with squared cardboard tiles representing the interior layout of a derelict spaceship. Up one corner, a handful of small plastic figures marked where Rob's space marines were cowering in fear from an imminent assault by my encroaching horde of four-armed, slobbering aliens. Littered amongst the sections of board were counters, dice, snacks and beer.

I didn't feel too bad about skiving, however. We'd mentioned the wedding on occasion and, if nothing else, I was looking at a catalogue. It appeared to be entirely full of outlandish cakes. Each was peculiarly evocative of a three-way collision between a fairground ride, a flower arrangement and a confectionery shop.

"Gah," said Rob in frustration. "I'll move this guy here and put him on guard. And move flamer guy along..."

"Thirty seconds."

"And then my last guy will panic and shoot blindly down this corridor while swearing loudly."

"Fine," I said, handing him some dice. "You need a six."

He rolled a five. "Do I get a bonus for the swearing?"

"No, but you've got two more shots and fifteen seconds to take them."

"OK," he said. "Give me the dice."

"I gave you the dice."

"No, you didn't. Give me the dice."

"You just rolled one of them. Look. Here." I picked two dice off the table where he'd put them and handed them to him again. "Three seconds." He flung them down and they ricocheted off a tub of Pringles, bounced and flew up in the air. One landed in a jar of salsa dip and the other danced off the table and disappeared under the sofa.

The stopwatch beeped.

We looked at each other and then both leaned forward and peered into the jar. "Chunky," I said. The dice was beginning to sink but it clearly showed a two. "Better go find the other one. You need a four."

"You were rushing me," he grumbled as he got down on his hands and knees and started poking around under the furniture. "Did you see where it went?"

"The dice are your responsibility during your go." I turned my attention back to the catalogue. "There really isn't anything in here but cakes... Oh, my mistake, here are some swans."

"Technically, it's now your go," he said, his voice somewhat muffled from beneath the table. "Want to come help me search?"

I munched on Pringles and sucked spicy tomato from a numbered cube. "It's not my go until that shot is resolved. Is there anything in this catalogue other than cakes and swans?"

"The swans are cakes, too," Rob said, emerging dustily from his hunt and handing me another, even glossier, brochure. "THIS catalogue is for the nuptial livestock."

"You're kidding..." I took the book from him. "You're not kidding. Tell me you're not planning a release of live butterflies."

"Nah. I was thinking more along the lines of white doves. Someone lets a couple go every so often and that's our cue to pull out a pair of Uzis and shoot at each other in slow motion while various bits of scenery explode."

"A John Woo theme," I said, rubbing my chin. "Interesting. How's that sitting with Kate's parents?"

"They're not so keen. Mike's up for it, though."

"He's humouring you. When it comes to the actual day, you'd better be taking things seriously. You've picked the wrong minister to mess with. Any sign of doves and he'd whip a shotgun out of his robes and fill them with buckshot before we could move. Then he'd get on with the service as if nothing had happened. You know it's true."

Rob considered this momentarily. "It is, isn't it?" he said, slightly anxiously.

"Uh-huh," I nodded. "And don't think you're done when the wedding's over. He'll grab you by the shoulder every few months, fix you with a piercing stare and ask you if you're keeping your vows. It's part of the on-going customer service."

"He'll get along famously with my future mother-in-law... Are you going to have your turn?"

"Oh, yeah." I'd forgotten about the game. Rob's under-the-sofa shot had hit (allegedly) but I was in a strong position, nevertheless. As the alien player, I also didn't have to race against the clock. I took my time. "I'm going to move this slavering monster with big teeth up the corridor while your guy shoots at it..." Rob rolled some dice and then swore. "...until his gun jams. Then these other slavering monsters with big teeth..." I moved a counter into his marine's line of sight, flipped it over and replaced it with three plastic figures. "...are going to use their enormous claws to turn him into mince." I rolled some dice. Rob rolled some dice. I banged my head on the table.

Rob smirked as he removed my pieces from the board. "What are the chances of you rolling a total of eleven on nine six-sided dice?"

"I don't want to think about it," I said in between bangs. "Tell me what you're expecting me to do for the wedding."

"You're best man. You've got to organise the stag night for starters."

I moved some more little plastic aliens. They all got shot or flambéed. "Is that wise?" I replied. "My idea of a good evening is going to the cinema, having a couple of drinks and then grabbing a bag of chips on the way home."

"I was hoping more for a weekend than an evening," said Rob, beginning his go. I reset the stopwatch.

"See. I'm bound to get it wrong. If I'm in charge of a weekend, we'll end up knitting."

Rob wasn't having any of it. "Take us go-karting, or something. Come on. A weekend away from the kids! Must be tempting."

I contemplated a couple of days with a group of younger, salaried blokes whom I'd barely met. It's the kind of situation I cope with much better if I have my three small human shields running round me. I couldn't really say no, though. "OK, I'll look into it," I sighed. "When's the wedding going to be, anyway?"

Rob shrugged. "Not sure. After the baby's born, definitely. Kate's getting big already and she doesn't want to look like a fairy that's swallowed a blimp in the photos." He paused in the middle of moving one of his pieces, suddenly worried. "Just don't tell her I put it like that, all right?"

"Wouldn't dream of it..."

My mobile rang and I answered it. "No, this isn't Kevin... Nope, I don't know anyone called Kevin. You've got the wrong number." I hung up. "That's the third time today. It's different people phoning up to offer this guy job interviews. I've had a couple of texts as well."

"Don't think I'd hire someone who got his phone number wrong on his CV," said Rob without glancing up from the board.

"Tell me about it. Two minutes left." He continued dithering over his marines. My eyes wandered around the room. The walls were stacked floor-to-ceiling with books, games and objects of geeky desire. It was like a rift in space and time had opened and half the stock of the local Forbidden Planet store had fallen through. "It's a shame your study will have to go," I said. "What are you going to do with all this stuff?"

Rob looked at me vacantly.

"Er..." I said. "This flat currently only has one bedroom. You're going to need two bedrooms. You have four available options: the kitchen, the bathroom, the lounge and this room. I would advise against the kitchen or the bathroom and your big telly is in the lounge. If, however, you were to replace the desk over there that's covered in computer equipment with a bed, this room would make quite a nice bedroom."

"Don't be daft," he said, concentrating on his marines. "A bed wouldn't fit in that space."

"True. You'd need to move the bookcase full of *Deep Space Nine* videos, the LEGO Star Destroyer and the life-size cut-out of Lara Croft to fit a bed in, but you wouldn't need so much space for a cot. Still, you might want to leave a decent splatter radius. Cleaning vomit out of LEGO is a real pain – you have to use a toothbrush. One minute."

I was hoping I'd distracted him enough but he made certain to finish moving before he replied. His surviving marines had almost escaped and had thrown up a wall of flame behind them. My remaining alien turned into a pile of ash and teeth.

"Hadn't thought about it," he said. "Won't the cot be in our room?"

"For six months or so. Maybe longer. Depends whether you ever want to sleep soundly again... or if you're planning any more kids."

Rob choked on his beer. "Give us a chance. It's months before the first one arrives."

"Three months. Might be less. It'll take you that long to off-load all this stuff on eBay." He appeared horrified but I pressed on. "You could always move house instead but that'll take time as well and, if you're faffing with mortgages, you'll need to consider how much of the next few years Kate is going to be on limited pay. Or if she's going to be off for as short a time as possible and you're going to be home. Or if you're both going to work and you have a wodge of nursery fees to find. How many children you're intending to have will affect all the calculations. Better start thinking."

The shutters of denial went down behind Rob's eyes. "I thought we were supposed to be discussing the wedding. Your go."

I shook my head for any number of reasons. "You've as good as won," I said. "Set things up for a re-match while I go to the toilet. We can talk kilts when I return. But don't imagine that because you can fob *me* off, you can do the same with Squirtle. He, she or it isn't going to go back in for a few days while you get round to auctioning off your *Magic: The Gathering* cards and Bobba Fett lunchbox."

Rob grinned. "You're just jealous I have them."

"Well, yeah," I said, heading out the door, "but that's not the point."

I left him to it. As I was washing my hands, I caught the distant but unmistakeable sound of an electronic rendition of *The Ride of the Valkyries* turned up loud enough to hear above traffic and three wittering children.

"Did my phone go?" I asked when I got back.

"Yeah," said Rob, putting the last of the plastic figures into place. "It was for Kevin. I told the woman I was his parole officer and that I was wondering where he'd got to, too. I don't think she'll be bothering you again."

"Cheers." I sat down and reached for my beer and a pile of dice. "Now it's time to snack on fiery death, big-teethed alien scum." I went for a warm-up roll. I got five ones and a splattering of salsa.

"Or maybe not..." I added.

* * *

Hope you're keeping well, Dave. Everyone I meet seems to be suffering from something. Lewis is croaky from a sore throat, Fraser has an infection (don't ask where), Marie's been exposed to chickenpox and Sarah has come into contact with scarlet fever.

I'm feeling nervous.

If we all get through this week without seeing a doctor, I'll be amazed...

Yours in a woman's world,

Ed.

Protective perspective

Dear Dave,

You're right. Kids make you worry. Two kids is twice the worry and you only have half as much available time to fit all the worrying in. You need to concentrate your worry on major risks.

If only I knew what those were...

I seem to spend a great deal of my life shouting warnings about imminent catastrophe:

'Don't do that!'

'Look where you're going!'

'Watch what you're doing!'

'Don't stand there!'

'Don't touch **that**!'

Unfortunately, my voice usually carries the same sense of urgency whether 'that' is a sweet on the ground, my glasses, a python or an electrical substation. If the kids are doing something liable to cause injury, I will often throw in, 'It's dangerous!' If they're doing something hugely stupid, I might go so far as to say, 'It's *very* dangerous!'

This really doesn't give them a particularly clear picture of risk.

'Stop waving your fork around. It's dangerous!' isn't much of a step up from, 'Watch out! Careful with your milk!' In fact, the latter is actually likely to create more of an impression, thanks to the words escaping my throat in a frantic scream as I lunge across the table to catch a teetering cup. My kids probably live more in fear of giving me extra cleaning than they do of impaling their siblings with kitchen utensils.

I guess this will make them normal. It's hard to realistically determine probabilities and to weigh likely rewards against possible disasters. It's not surprising the kids don't have a clue. *I* don't know what the most likely calamities might be and how badly they could go. Running with scissors doubtless is fairly dangerous (if they have a pointed end) and so is hopping with knives but how dangerous is dancing with a spoon? What level of warning should I use? Does it depend on the size of the spoon? The style of dance? The proximity of crockery?

Or should I let the poor kid enjoy herself for a change without me prophesying doom?

The media doesn't help. I saw an item on the main evening news the other week that was all shock and horror about the dangers of hazardous drinking. A large glass of wine every night is a hazardous level of consumption! Well-to-do rich people are drinking too much! Shock! Horror! Not once was it mentioned in what way this level of drinking was hazardous, nor to how great an extent. They did, however, imply a causal relationship between having an expensive house and drinking too much. This means that it's not the drinking that's the root cause of danger – it's buying a mansion.

As I said, the media isn't much help.

Then again, neither is personal experience when it comes to assessing most risks. I know from experience that if we go to the swing park there's a high probability that some-one will scrape a knee but what's the chance of one of the kids getting snatched? Considering I'm not in the middle of a custody battle, vanishingly small, most likely, but all I've got to go on is hearsay and media reports. And I've already estab-lished that the media isn't much help.

Nope, it's very hard to tell what's truly worth worry-ing about. Still, based on the amount of thought and effort I put into preventing disaster, these are the dangers I feel most threaten my children:

> 10. Food. Between obesity and food poisoning, additives and E numbers, E. Coli and bird flu, there are any number of food related scares in circulation. I'm considering moving the kids over to a diet of lime juice and crackers, just to be on the safe side.

9. Going to hospital. Hospitals are full of germs and sick people. Must avoid.

8. Dirty hands. Dirty hands are covered in germs and cause sick people. Must wash.

7. My old Xbox. The instruction manual contains only one warning about photosensitive seizures but FOUR about not dropping the thing on a small child. Do the maths.

6. Dog poo. We have some inconsiderate dog owners round our way. I'm constantly telling the kids to look where they're about to put their feet. Strangely, this usually makes them look behind them, peering over their shoulder to see if they've stepped in it already. This is not hugely safe or convenient. I see dog poo on the pavement and shout at the kids, they look behind them, step in it and then walk into a lamp post.

5. Coffee. It's hot and spillable, which is a dangerous combination. Luckily, it's usually gone cold by the time I get a chance to drink it.

4. Traffic. The boys have got the hang of the 'Stop' part of 'Stop, Look & Listen' but haven't yet realised that the other two are quite tricky if they're talking at me. A couple of days ago, while we were halfway across a road, I told them to cease wittering about Mario and look for cars. This merely led to even worse distraction. Fraser promptly shouted, "Look! There's a car," and pointed at a vehicle that was not only in the wrong direction but also on a different road. Handy.

3. Each other. When the boys were younger, I turned round from the washing-up to find Fraser stabbing Lewis in the head with a fork as they sat quietly eating their tea.

2. Themselves. On closer examination, the number of triple puncture wounds suggested that Lewis had been letting him do this for a while. (Ho well, at least they weren't making a mess...)

1. Zombies. I watched *28 Days Later* recently. Since then, most of my spare brainpower at any given moment has been devoted to locating emergency exits and suitable materials for barricades, in case of the unexpected arrival of a horde of the living dead. It may not be a very likely threat but its consequences would be catastrophic. Best to be prepared.

That's the list. Essentially, if I gave each of the kids an eating utensil and a turkey sandwich while I was drinking coffee and we all followed a dog along beside a busy road on the way to the hospital, that's the most dangerous situation imaginable. Unless it started raining Xboxes... or zombies.

I suppose I could take comfort in the fact that we all had clean hands.

Right, I'm off to purchase emergency plastic bags, a chainsaw, some bear-traps and a shotgun in readiness for the inevitable undead apocalypse. Got to keep the kids safe! And it beats worrying about which secondary school to choose...

Yours in a woman's world,

Ed.

Bleargh!

Dear Dave,

We're all suffering from one illness or another, the mice are back and I'm fed up.

I've been coughing for three weeks and I'd just like to feel better, thank you very much. Fraser has some virus that's making him tired, achy and argumentative. (Well, more argumentative than usual). I don't think he'll be at school tomorrow. As I write, it's late at night and, over the baby-listener, I can hear Marie sounding choked up. This could be a long one...

On a positive note, Marie has a place at nursery after Christmas. I can barely believe it – it's even a morning one. I'll have two and a half hours each weekday when I won't have *any* children to look after (during term-time, anyway). The possibilities seem endless. It's not a case of not knowing what to do with myself. It's a case of not knowing what to do first. I hardly dare imagine it.

Interestingly, Marie *can't* imagine it.

"What should I do once you're at nursery?" I asked her.

"Come and collect me," she said.

"Yes, I'll collect you from nursery but what should I do all the time you're there?"

She looked confused. "Play with me?" she ventured.

"No, I'll be somewhere else."

She considered the thought that I exist when she isn't there and reluctantly accepted it.

I asked her again. "So what should I do?"

She laughed. "Go to work!"

I wasn't impressed.

Yours in a woman's world,

Ed.

References

Dear Dave,

Steve hasn't coped well with redundancy.

He had been coming round here most days to mope and mournfully steal my biscuits but then, last week, he stopped. I didn't hear from him at all. My initial relief turned to concern as I thought back over the past two or three months. I realised he'd gone from smartly dressed, bright-eyed businessman to exhausted, dishevelled housedad without me really noticing. The talk of CVs, contacts and interviews had faded. He no longer laboured under the recurring delusion that he was doing his wife, Deborah, a favour by 'taking the kids for a few hours' – looking after the children had become his job.

Under other circumstances, I'd have been delighted with another housedad in the area but (a) this is Steve we're talking about and (b) it's not something he would ever have chosen.

Sarah and I decided together that I would be a housedad. We planned for it. We looked forward to it. We made it happen. Steve, however, hadn't been prepared for the housedad life when it claimed him. As a result, rather than embracing it, he was holding onto an image of himself as a businessman – a businessman who couldn't get a job.

I'm dishevelled because I don't care; he'd become dishevelled because he'd given up.

When he didn't show at parent and toddler yesterday, I thought I'd better pop round to his flat and check he was OK. Marie was delighted at the idea. She'd missed playing with Steve's daughter, Ophelia.

Steve didn't look good when he answered the door. His eyes were bloodshot and his movements were slow and accompanied by little groans. He regarded me vacantly. For a moment, I thought my worst fears had come true, and I scanned the stairwell for available weapons. I'd blundered into a zombie outbreak.

Marie didn't seem too fussed. "I'm Marie," she said. "I'm three. Can I play now?" Without waiting for an answer, she ran past him, the bobble on her pink fluffy hat bouncing up and down merrily. There was a great deal of mutual squealing as she disappeared into their sitting room and found Ophelia.

"Right," said Steve but didn't move out of the way to let me in. He hadn't shaved for a few days, his hair was wild and he was wearing his dressing-gown. It had a selection of milky stains down the front. I relaxed slightly – he looked a bit too shabby to be a zombie.

"I can come back and get her later, if you like," I suggested.

"What?"

"Marie. My daughter. You can let me in or I can come back and get her later."

"Oh."

That seemed to be the closest to an invitation I was going to receive, so I plastered over the social awkwardness with a grin and followed after her.

The sitting room was not as I remembered it. The ceiling was still high and the stairs to the mezzanine level were providing a great deal of excitement for the girls but nothing else was as it should have been. Cushions were strewn everywhere, the bay window had paint handprints all over it, brightly coloured toys festooned the furniture, half-eaten bowls of cereal booby-trapped the floor and what appeared to be a sausage was sticking out of the video player. Josquin, Steve's nearly-one-year-old son, was imprisoned in a play-pen in the centre of the room, rattling a beaker against the bars.

"I'd let him out," said Steve, reflecting his own guilt off me, "but I'd need to tidy up."

I nodded. "Maybe a little. Tell you what, I'll take the bowls through to the kitchen. You go sort yourself out and then let him crawl around in the cushions. Girls! You get off those stairs – there are plenty of toys to play with. Josquin!" He started with shock at the attention. "You giggle. I'll be back in a minute. Drink your milk." He duly giggled and took a long swig from the beaker. I hoped it was reasonably fresh. "Tea?" I asked Steve.

"Thanks," he said and then, as if in explanation, he added, "Deborah's away for the week, overseeing a project."

"Uh-huh," I said, failing miserably to look amazed. I quickly gathered up the bowls and headed through to boil the kettle.

I needed a coffee. Which I guess is synonymous with saying that I was awake, since I always need a coffee, but on this occasion I really, *really* needed a coffee. Scary Karen had cornered me at parent and toddler and regaled me with accounts of her trip to the doctor and of her latest date with Trevor. Both these stories were long, dull and filled with horrifyingly inappropriate detail. What's more, I'd been unable to escape long enough to grab supplies from the refreshment trolley. I desperately needed some caffeine and biscuits.

I put the kettle on and began to hunt around. There were two mugs on the drainer that only needed a quick rinse, I found a clean teaspoon in the drawer and the teabags had all been inexpertly stapled to the notice board in a flower pattern. I carefully removed a couple. I couldn't locate the coffee, though. I rifled through the cupboards near the kettle, scanned the work surfaces, peered at the shelves and checked on the table but I couldn't see it anywhere. The dirty crockery, abandoned food and Weebles covering everything only made the task harder.

I sought further afield. There were some biscuits in the bread bin (plain digestives, lamentably, but better than nothing) and the cupboard under the sink had the expected cleaning supplies in it. Unlike everywhere else, that cupboard appeared neat and untouched. Rolling my eyes, I checked the cupboard on the wall above.

A cat exploded from it.

Oddly, it was painted pink and lightly sprinkled with glitter.

The cat screamed, I screamed, it bounded off my head, the teaspoon flew up in the air and the creature streaked off out the door in search of a new hiding place.

I paused to take a few deep breaths and let my sudden adrenaline-high fade. No one else in the flat seemed remotely disturbed by the clattering and screaming. I took a few more breaths and considered examining the cupboard more closely but, on reflection, I decided it would be wiser just to close the door and move along. If the coffee was in there, I didn't want it.

My search became more cautious after that. It took me some time before I found the jar of Gold Blend in the fridge. The water was long since boiled and I made the drinks. I take my coffee black but Steve has his tea with milk and sugar. This was a problem – I couldn't find a supply of either. In the end, I had to go with a dollop of yogurt and then rub two stale doughnuts together over the top of the mug. It was the best I could do...

Steve was sitting in the lounge where I'd left him. Josquin was still in the play-pen. The girls had vanished. I took Josquin out of the play-pen and let him crawl.

"What's up?" I said, offering Steve a biscuit. The state of the flat went beyond incompetence. I was genuinely worried about his mental health.

He reached into his dressing-gown pocket, drew out a crumpled letter and handed it to me. "I thought the interview went very well," he mumbled, staring at the wall. "I really did. They're a respected company with an excellent product. The benefits were good and I felt I connected with the management team. They liked my ideas. We could have moved forward together."

He'd been turned down for another job. Nonetheless, it sounded like he'd got a long way through the process with this one. They'd gone as far as requesting references – the rejection letter mentioned some issues with one of them.

"What...?" I began but Steve cut me off.

He reached into his other pocket and drew out a second piece of paper. "I phoned them in an attempt to make them reconsider, and they faxed me this. It's what Scott wrote about me."

The mention of Steve's arrogant and vindictive old boss immediately made my hackles rise. I'd wiped his existence from my mind the instant he'd been transferred to Mongolia. That had been a very happy day. (Obviously, I didn't mention this, since it had been a much less happy day for Steve, what with him being Scott's head crony and getting briskly fired by Scott's replacement and everything.) I skimmed the reference letter, hoping that it wouldn't stir too many memories, but I had to stop halfway through and go back over it more carefully. I couldn't believe what I was reading. It was scathing.

Seriously, *Attack of the Clones* had better reviews.

"Wow," I said, finally. "Turns out that it wasn't just me he didn't like."

"I don't understand it," said Steve. "I always supported him. I carried out his plans. I did what he said. It's not *my* fault he ended up in Ulan Bator. Why did he write that?"

"I dunno. Maybe he's convinced himself that it *is* your fault, or he was frustrated and couldn't find a goat to kick. Hey, maybe he thinks he's got a chance of a job with these people and thought this might impress them."

"If they'd employed me, I could have put in a good word for him. How does this help?"

"Well, er..." The honest answer was that if they'd hired Steve, they might have discovered what a clueless manager he was and been none too pleased with the guy who'd provided them with a glowing recommendation. I wasn't sure Steve was ready for quite that much truth, however. I stalled. "Who knows what was going on in his head?"

Steve shrugged. "It doesn't matter. I'll have to get someone else. It's almost certainly too late but perhaps if Sarah wrote me a reference, I could convince them to take me on." His voice was pleading. "You could phone her right now and ask..."

"Yeah, I could..." I should have seen it coming. As Steve's most competent former underling, Sarah was always bound to be high on the list of candidates. I didn't fancy letting her know, though. She didn't need the stress and I didn't need a stressed wife. Having a stressed wife makes me stressed. Me being stressed, makes Sarah stressed. The thought of her getting stressed because I was stressed about her being stressed, made me stressed.

Which was stressful.

I tried to think. There was a way out. All I had to do was not phone her. If I took the stress of dealing with Steve myself, she wouldn't need to get stressed. Sure, I'd be stressed, but I might be able to internalise and ignore it before I spoke to her again. That would prevent her from getting stressed about it. If not, at least I'd have removed one layer of complexity from the problem. Rather than being stressed about her being stressed about me being stressed about her being stressed, I would only have to be stressed about her getting stressed about me getting stressed.

Result!

Er, maybe...

I started to run it by myself one more time but then became aware that no one had said anything for a couple of minutes.

Steve was still looking at me expectantly, begging me with his eyes. There was nothing for it but to tell him the truth. I felt like I was approaching a baby seal with a big stick.

"There's no point Sarah writing another reference," I said. "It would be the same. Kinder and with less swearing but, fundamentally, the same. Productivity has trebled since you left."

"What?"

"You're not a very good manager."

"Oh..." The silence stretched on for a while again. It was broken only by an enormous eruption in Josquin's nappy.

Shoulders slumped, Steve picked his son up and carried him to the changing unit out in the hall. I followed, in case help was needed.

To my astonishment, it wasn't. Steve had been practising. He gave the mobile above the unit a spin to distract Josquin's attention, made lots of soothing noises, whipped off the dirty clothes and nappy, wiped everything clean, contained a surprise second delivery without incident, wiped everything clean again, fastened a fresh nappy, slipped on clean clothes, put the kid in the play-pen, tidied and disinfected. Then he washed his hands thoroughly. He could have done it in his sleep and, if my own experience of small children is anything to go by, he probably had. It was a master-class in nappy changing. I almost clapped.

Steve went back to sitting dejectedly in the lounge. I checked on the girls. They were hiding happily under a duvet so I left them be.

"Maybe you should try something different," I said when I returned to my seat.

"Like what? I don't have any skills."

I pretended to consider this for a few seconds as all my mental energy went into not saying, "That never stopped you before." I managed to contain myself but the thought was so loud that everyone in the building abruptly got a headache. A pigeon flying past the window was temporarily stunned and dropped out of the sky. A moment later, a car alarm went off in the street below.

I did my best to ignore it. "Six months ago," I said, "you couldn't change a nappy. I had to talk you through it. Just now, you carried out one of the smoothest nappy changes ever seen, without any help and without even thinking about it very much. That's a skill right there."

"I can't put it on my CV," said Steve, rubbing his forehead, as if in pain.

"Depends what you're wanting to do. Deborah's business is doing great and she's enjoying it but she'd rather the kids didn't spend all day in nursery. If you got another nine-to-five job, that would leave her with some difficult decisions. You might want to..."

"Stay in the house and look after the children?" he interrupted, glumly.

"You don't have to stay in the whole time. Actually, I'd advise against it. But, yeah, look after the children."

"I couldn't."

I tried to reassure him. "Sure you could. A little more practice and..."

"No, it's not that. What will everyone at the golf club say?"

I shrugged. "All kinds of ignorant things, probably. Tell them you're taking a career break to consider your options and explore new avenues, or something. Tell them you're prioritising your family. I don't know. Does it matter?"

"Yes."

"Oh." I guess I've forgotten what it's like to be socially embarrassed about being a housedad.

"What if they found out that I had to get Deborah to pay my membership fees?"

"Tell them it's part of your benefits and compensation package," I said.

"How do you mean?" he asked, sounding more interested.

I remembered to speak his language. "Think of yourself as a team player. You're empowering Deborah to complete the task and supplying her with back-office support. Without your cog, the family machine would fall apart. As such, you're entitled to a share of the profits." It seemed to be working, so I pressed on. "Re-analyse your goals, step back from the plate and, er, take a fresh look in the mirror."

He shook his head. "Maybe you're right but..." He motioned around himself at the bombsite that was the room. "Where do I start?"

"Somewhere."

He looked sceptical.

"Anywhere. Come on. Whatever you decide to do in the long run, you need to concentrate on the job in hand until Deborah gets home. This week, you're a housedad, whether you like it or not. Now, you go and get dressed, and me and the girls will get started with tidying in here. I'll do the washing-up; you feed the kids and put some laundry on. Then I'll entertain them while you give the kitchen and bathrooms a quick wipe around."

Spurred on by my feigned enthusiasm, Steve perked up somewhat and went to have a shower. I extricated the girls from the bed linen and set them to work. I won't let Marie help at our house – there's far too much chance of spills or breakage – but the opportunity to give her some training with other people's valuables was too good to miss. She quite enjoyed herself. Once Steve had dressed, he explored the cupboard full of cleaning stuff and the next couple of hours passed swiftly.

There was one moment of concern after lunch. I was sitting in the lounge with the girls when Steve screamed and I nearly jumped out of my skin. The girls went on with their colouring as if nothing had happened. Marie merely looked up briefly from her scribbled, pink masterpiece. "He found cat," she said cheerfully.

We had to leave soon after that to go and collect the boys from school. Steve was happier by then and the flat was in a hugely better state. I was reluctant to leave him to fend for himself for the rest of the week, though. As we stood there in the doorway, my eye started to twitch. We'd said our good-byes but I was stuck there. I felt an involuntary urge to...

"Why don't you bring the kids round tomorrow? We could have coffee." It was out of my mouth before I could stop it.

Predictably, Steve readily accepted and I made a mental note to buy more biscuits on the way home. I couldn't believe I'd invited him round. I'd had more than enough of him moping in my kitchen over the previous weeks. As we headed down the stairs and out of view, I valiantly restrained my desire to kick myself.

My efforts were undone shortly after that, however, as Marie's voice echoed shrilly up the stairwell. "You're silly. Don't hit walls with your head."

Hopefully Steve didn't hear that.

Yours in a woman's world,

Ed.

PS Thanks for the sympathy. We're all feeling much healthier since my last letter and I haven't seen a mouse recently. Hooray!

The vanished

Dear Dave,

Marie starting nursery has been a tantalisingly close prospect for a long time now. Back at the beginning of the year, I thought there'd be an in-take after the October Week holiday and, since Marie's birthday is late September, I was expecting she'd get in then. Shortly before the summer holidays, I found out she wouldn't be eligible for a place until after Christmas. More recently, I began to hear rumours of place shortages at the nursery attached to the boys' school. There were tales of kids having to wait months despite already being three; accounts of parents having to beg, plead and shout to get their children in; whispers of vast hordes of Polish four-year-olds invading the area and demanding pre-school education; suggestions that Marie might have to wait until next August...

I got used to thinking nursery was several months away – nearly in sight but too distant to really plan for. All of a sudden, I know she has a morning place in January. I'll have a couple of hours or so each day without children. In five weeks. It's truly going to happen. I can hardly believe it. I'm BobBIng UP aNd DOwn aS I tYPe. There are limitless possibilities.

I can barely wait but, now it's more of a reality, I can't help experiencing a mild pang of fear. I will no longer have a small child in my care every minute of the day to justify my existence. On occasion, I will have to be a person in my own right. That's going to be strange.

Stranger yet, there will be no more parent and toddler.

Admittedly, I've been feeling like I'm serving out my time there for a while. I go along and drink my hot drink, eat some biscuits and stare into space while Marie entertains herself. I chat a bit but if no one I know is around, I'm not desperate to introduce myself to new people.

The idealised image of these groups implies that I should have a core band of friends to go to the café and talk toilet training and exhaustion with by now. It's not happened, though. I haven't collected a little clique of coffee-drinking companions.

Part of this is down to being a man. Place thirty mums and a dad in a room and tell them to make some friends, and the dad is almost bound to be at a disadvantage. Throw in another dad, and the two of them will stick together but there's no saying that they'll have anything more in common than being trapped in a room full of sleep-deprived women and children with potty issues. This is not necessarily a recipe for long-term friendship.

Oh and, chances are, the second dad will only be giving his partner a break on his day off from work and the first dad will never see him again anyhow.

Grrr.

Yep, some of the reasons for not having a coffee shop clique are down to being a man but, let's face it, some of them are down to being me. I'm shy, I struggle to start conversations and I'm not much of a coffee shop person. On top of that, when Lewis was young, I had depression, which doesn't make meeting people any easier. When Marie was small, there simply wasn't time in the schedule between changes, feeds and school runs for any caffeine-based socialising.

I suppose it's not been a total washout. I have made a few friends who live close by – just not very many of them compared with the number of people I've chatted to. I've made far more acquaintances. In most cases, at the point I was starting to get to know them better, they disappeared. One week they were at parent and toddler and the next they weren't... ever again.

At one of the groups I attend, the other parents have all changed three or four times. Even the helpers have changed twice.

Often they've gone without me noticing. It's normal for people to be off sick or on holiday for weeks at a stretch. It's only after a month that it becomes clear they're not coming back. And there's no way of contacting them. The organisers aren't allowed to hand out personal details (if they so much as have them) and, by then, two-thirds of the other parents are liable to struggle to remember who I'm talking about, let alone where they live. (My descriptions don't usually help. 'You know, that tired looking mum with brown hair and a couple of kids. She used to wear a scarf a lot...')

Where have these people gone?

It's impossible to tell. Have they moved house or got a job? Have they fallen out with someone or found a better group elsewhere? Has the kid taken to napping in the middle of the morning? Has the parent taken to lounging around in coffee shops? Are they all OK? Has there been a disaster? Was it anything to do with zombies?

It would be nice to know. Sometimes the family shows up again at nursery or with another child or when the kid starts napping in the afternoon once more. Other times, they're just gone. Disappeared. Vanished.

I wonder where they all went...

New people ask me, "Have you been coming here for a while?"

It's interesting watching their reaction when I say, "Six and a half years."

There's nearly always a double-take and some nervous laughter. New helpers realise that I know a great deal more about how the group works than they do. New parents realise the length of journey they might have begun.

And now my own journey is about to change course. In a few weeks, I will be one of the vanished.

The thought makes me a little sad and, as I said before, a little scared. What happened to those six and a half years? What mark have I left? Will people wonder where I've gone and then struggle to remember my name?

I have to assume so.

Still, I've given plenty of advice and sympathy during my long attendance. I like to imagine it's done some good. More than that, parent and toddler has got me out of the house, given me the chance to talk to people old enough not to idolise the Teletubbies and provided me with a steady supply of hot drinks and biscuits. I've been very glad of it... but it's time to move on. I have a different life ahead of me.

I'm kind of hoping that it involves coffee shops rather than zombies...

Yours in a woman's world,

Ed.

We've got to let the mums win at something

Dear Dave,

Yeah, I know how you feel – Christmas seems to have crept up on us. Sounds like you're mostly on top of things, though.

We're getting there. We've converted the lounge to 'Christmas Land' (as Marie calls it) with the aid of plenty of shiny baubles, an explosion of tinsel and a very irritating musical snowman. We should get our cards sent soon. We've given the kids a gift or two each already to spread things out. We're having a mulled wine party in a few days. (Scary Karen has promised to bring her accordion!) The shopping's almost done. I've been to a couple of carol services. Everyone keeps asking Marie what Santa's bringing her. Fraser keeps impatiently explaining to them that Santa isn't real. The school nativity play was yesterday. There's Christmas music everywhere. Christmas adverts. Christmas food. Christmas lights. Christmas. Christmas. Christmas. Christmas. Christmas. Christmas.

Too much Christmas.

And there's over a week left to go. Goodness. I'm going to be burnt out before the day arrives.

Must think of something else...

Oh, there is one thing I've been meaning to write about for a while and it's kind of related to Chr... that other thing... in a roundabout sort of way:

I recently chanced upon a study which indicates that boys who have been cared for by their fathers a significant amount as toddlers perform less well at academic assessments upon starting school than boys who have been looked after by their mothers.

There are many obvious questions thrown up by this. Why boys and not girls? Exactly *how much* less? Were the dads who were surveyed looking after their children out of choice or circumstance? How does this compare with children who are looked after by their grans? What sort of assessments? And what's all this got to do with Chr... er, the time of year?

Maybe the actual study answers some of these questions. (Well, perhaps not the last one.) As per usual, the press coverage didn't even *ask* most of them. It was all, 'housedads could be damaging their children's future chances!' Men don't give children as much mental stimulation as women, apparently... or, that's to say, possibly. The study didn't have any definitive reasons for the discrepancy.

Of course, the instant reaction is for us to jump up and down in annoyance. How dare journalists accuse us of not stimulating our kids? They do fine at school. What are the researchers talking about?

Sadly, this is twisting facts to support our own agenda as much the newspapers have done. Men and women are not the same. There are numerous situations and problems that, on average, men and women will deal with differently. Whether this is due to upbringing or genetics doesn't really matter – it simply is the case. This is bound to apply to childcare too, and thus it's bound to affect the kids in some way. Maybe what this study has discovered is true.

But don't hurriedly rush out to find a job and order Liz back home to stimulate Sam and protect his future...

There are a million things you could measure about a kid to evaluate good parenting. These include nutrition, behaviour, happiness, fitness, curiosity, dental health, vocabulary, politeness, bravery, cleanliness, stubbornness, resilience, knowledge, empathy, hand-eye coordination, kindness, imagination, road safety awareness and biscuit decorating ability. In all probability, dads are better than mums for encouraging some of these. Working out whether it's men or women who come out on top for a majority of the list would take rather a long time, and even then, it wouldn't necessarily help very much in determining who should look after the children. Is a slightly higher chance of the kid being resilient more important than a slightly higher chance of them being polite, for instance? That could be quite a debate and, in the end, the childcare duties in any given relationship will still come down to finances and temperament. Which is how it should be. Having parents who are solvent and enjoying their roles is going to do more to encourage a child's long-term development than anything else.

Bearing that in mind, I'm perfectly happy to accept the results of the study. There was always going to be *something* that dads aren't so good at. I'm pleased that it turns out to be this. You see, I'm not certain that children doing less well in academic assessments upon *starting* school is such a disaster. Surely the whole point of schools is to teach children how to do well in academic assessments. I wouldn't want to interfere with the teachers' jobs and, besides, being a little behind the curve gives plenty of room for some quick confidence-building improvement. Even the papers pointed out that the research didn't investigate whether 'the damage to the boys' prospects' is permanent. There's every possibility the boys in question caught up in a very brave and resilient manner after a couple of months. Perhaps the other ones, the ones who'd been taught to read by their mums, got bored, burnt out by the end of the second week and dedicated their lives to politely decorating biscuits.

Who knows?

And you're still wondering what this has to do with Chr... the current up-turn in sales of turkeys and Brussels sprouts...

Well, I guess my first point – that housedads aren't an abomination against nature – doesn't have anything to do with Chr... Frosty the Snowman... but, given the context of this rant, it's not really much of a point, either. You probably saw it coming. My second point, however, is about stimulation:

I grew up somewhere so dull that I used to sit watching the test card for entertainment. Maybe if my mum had sat with me and taught me to spell then I'd be a genius now but I doubt it. I'd most likely just have been a know-it-all who made life difficult for my teachers in primary school. I might also have lost a very useful trait. As it stands, I have a very high tolerance for tedium. This makes my job a whole lot easier. I can play *Snakes and Ladders* for hours at a time without going mad and watch the same episode of *Tweenies* endlessly without gibbering. I should really thank my mum for neglecting... er, leaving me to my own devices so much as a child. (I'm not going to, though. You know, in case it comes out wrong...)

So remember, next time you sneak off to check your email, you're not ignoring the children, you're building resourcefulness and self-reliance. After all, there is such a thing as over-stimulation.

If you're in any doubt, think of Christmas.

Yours in a woman's world,

Ed.

PS I've got a peculiar ringing in my ears now. I suspect it's jingle bells...

Mince pies and mistletoe

Dear Dave,

It was the Christmas party at Scary Karen's parent and toddler group today. When I turned up early with Marie to help decorate, there were some streamers in the hall already and a decent-sized tree complete with baubles and lights. If I'd been running things that would have been enough but Karen adheres to the 'more is better' philosophy of holiday décor. This holds that you simply can't have too much gaudy tack stuck to the walls when the festive season rolls round. In her case, it doesn't even have to be relevant tack. She emptied out the Millennium Centre's store cupboard and we hung up everything we could find. Soon, amongst the tinsel and stockings, the Easter Bunny stood atop a heap of grinning pumpkins. It had flashing red eyes and was wearing reindeer antlers.

I set up the spinning disco lights. Trevor inflated huge numbers of balloons with a single breath each. Karen's friend Bess put on some suitable musical accompaniment. It was the CD that all the shops have had on loop since mid-November. I immediately felt a compulsive urge to buy piles of junk in a mad panic and I had to do my best to blank out the jaunty melodies. I didn't do too badly until Slade came on and Marie started running round the room shouting, "It's Christmas!" at everybody.

She knew it to be true because Noddy Holder had told her so.

"Well, sort of," I said, when she got to me. "It's a Christmas party. It isn't actually Christmas until next week."

She pondered this momentarily and then ran round the room again, shouting, "It sort of Christmas! But not really!" at everybody. Then she came back to me and said, "Can I have a mince pie? Pleeeeeeeeeaaaaaaaase..." She made her eyes wide and pouted mournfully. She gave the impression she hadn't been fed in a week. I knew, though, that only half an hour previously she'd taken one small bite of toast for breakfast and then declared herself finished.

"No," I said.

"Oh," said Marie. Her lower lip quivered and tears welled up. "But I'm huuun-greeee..."

"You should have eaten your breakfast then."

She started to sob. "You made me sad, Daddy," she wailed and buried her face in her hands.

"Tough." I got on with wiring up the lights. The other adults nearby looked at me like I'd told Tinker Bell to her face that fairies don't exist. I ignored them (and Marie) and before long the room was bathed in multicoloured swirls. Marie lay face down on the floor for a bit and then gave up. "I have mince pie later?" she said hopefully.

"OK," I replied.

She grinned, wiped her eyes and ran off to dance. I scarcely had a chance to grab a cup of coffee before she ran back and gleefully exclaimed, "It later now! I have mince pie?"

"Nice try," I said, sitting down amongst a group of mums.

"Awwwwww..." She tipped her head to the side, tucked in her upper lip and tried to drown me in eyes that were deep, pleading wells of sorrow.

"Not just now," I said.

"You made me sad again, Daddy," she said and threw herself to the ground once more. The mums gave the impression that I'd just given Bambi the bad news in a rather callous fashion.

I ignored the looks (and Marie). "You all ready for Christmas?" I asked.

This brought various tales of shopping woe and festive mayhem that distracted everyone. Marie got up and returned to dancing. The conversation moved on to advent calendars.

"Yeah, we got the kids a chocolate-filled one each last year," I said. "They kept forgetting to open them and we ended up with a stockpile of little edible Scooby-Doos that lasted halfway into January. They've got one between them this year and we're still three days behind. The only one who's organised is Lewis. He's on the bottom bunk and has taken to suspending an additional stuffed animal from the slats above him every day in the run up to Christmas. It's less of an advent calendar, more of an advent toy lynching."

"Christmas sounds like fun in your house," said Jess.

"Shouldn't be too bad. We're off to Sarah's sister's for the day itself. Her husband will make a few snide comments about my place being in the kitchen but apart from that, it'll be fine. How about you?"

It transpired that they would all be experiencing a mixture of custody wrangles, bickering with relatives and *Angry Birds*. The first two were speedily glossed over in favour of comparing which family members they were getting a handheld electronic device for Christmas. They all reckoned *Professor Layton's Brain Training* was ace and wanted a version on their mobiles. I sat there, perplexed. By rights, I should have had a great deal to say on the topic but, after years of not having anyone to talk to about computer games at parent and toddler, I was dumbfounded to unexpectedly find myself surrounded by women promoting gaming as both entertainment and mental exercise. I couldn't figure out whether to be supportive or to correct all their factual errors. It was as stupefying as if my mum had suddenly admitted she was thinking of becoming a Jedi and had asked me where she could get hold of one of those 'lightswords'. I simply looked bemused, wishing I'd bought shares in Apple or Nintendo a few years ago.

Marie broke me out of my trance by shouting in my ear. "Is it later yet?"

"No."

She didn't even blink. "And now?" she said, smiling endearingly.

"Nope."

Pause. "And now?" She did the cutest little jig you've ever seen and, still smiling sweeter than a Sugar Puff dipped in saccharine, she asked, "Can I have a mince pie, nooooooooooooooooooooow...?"

"In ten minutes," I said. She threw herself at my feet and cried into the floor again.

The mums frowned at me like I'd flushed the Andrex puppy down a toilet.

"Oh, look," I said, directing their attention elsewhere. "Santa!"

I don't normally picture Santa with tattoos. Or bald, for that matter. Nonetheless, the red suit and fake white beard certainly gave the impression that Trevor was attempting a Father Christmas impersonation. He didn't look too happy about it, though. I can only assume that Scary Karen had used her feminine wiles to talk him into it. She'd slipped on a slinky, fur-trimmed, scarlet outfit complete with Santa hat. It was surprisingly fetching in a scary sort of way. It also appeared liable to burst at the seams at any moment in an even scarier sort of way. I had visions of an explosion and nothing being left but the hat.

I hastily focused myself on Trevor. He really wasn't looking too good. I imagine he'd be totally up for catching bullets with his teeth but he's quite agitated by kids. Still, all he had to do was sit on a chair, pull the gifts out of a sack, read the labels and call over the children to take their presents. How hard could it be?

It was regrettable that the first three gifts he pulled out were for Mateusz, Enkhjin and Joao. Karen had to bend over to help him make out the names. Each time, I tensed myself in preparation for the velvet and ermine shrapnel, and then sighed in relief when the catastrophe never came.

After that, it was Marie's turn.

I picked her up off the floor and gave her a shove. She trotted over to Trevor, who held out the parcel to her at arm's length. He was deaf to the creaking bodice-work beside him and seemed worried that it was Marie that might explode.

He may have had a point.

She looked at the parcel briefly, clearly torn over whether to take it. She glanced at the sack to see if there was anything more promising in there. She gazed suspiciously at Trevor's fluffy beard. Then she made the eyes and pulled the face. "I reaaaa-leeeeeee want a mince piiiiiiie..."

"Er, I don't have mince pies," said Trevor. "Just this." He shook the parcel and grimaced slightly.

She threw herself to the ground and started to cry again.

I rushed over, grabbed her and the parcel, and whisked her out of the way.

"Santa doesn't have any mince pies!" she wailed.

"It's OK," I reassured her. "That's not really Santa." Then, in the interests of openness, trust and honesty, I added, "And Santa's not really real anyway."

It's possible I may have said this a little too loudly.

Every adult in the room scowled at me like I'd stood on Tinker Bell while wearing fluffy slippers made from Bambi and the Andrex puppy. Luckily, every child in the room remained transfixed by the sack of presents.

"Would you like a mince pie?" I asked Marie hurriedly.

"Yes, please!" she said and we beat a retreat to the refreshment trolley. The whole thing was a close call... but I think we got away with it. The gift-giving resumed and everyone relaxed again. Before long, toddlers were dancing once more and I was being offered something warm and spicy in a mug. Jess had mulled some of her homemade wine.

I've never had green mulled wine before. I peered at it apprehensively.

"It's the spinach," Cress whispered.

I shrugged and tried some. It tasted kind of all right – not disagreeable as such, but you wouldn't ask for it specially. I guess a lot of Christmas is like that. I had a second helping for no other reason than it was there. I guess a lot of Christmas is like that, too. It seemed to make Jess happy, though.

Marie opened her parcel. It was a box of pretend medical supplies containing a stethoscope, a rectal thermometer, a pair of scissors, a hammer and a spoon. All the essentials of a home surgery kit, allegedly. She was delighted and set about listening to my knees as she took their temperature.

The time slipped away and then, all at once, it was half-past eleven. We had places to be but I was reluctant to get our coats. The Millennium Centre is still going to be closed for the holidays at the beginning of January so Karen's toddler group won't be on again until after Marie has started nursery. Today was our last one. It was odd looking around at the familiar faces and toys, knowing that (barring sanity-threatening contraceptive accidents) I'd never be back. I lingered, finding it hard to leave, not knowing quite how to say good-bye.

Then I noticed that Scary Karen had found some mistletoe.

I wished everyone a merry Christmas and headed out the door.

It was time to go.

Yours in a woman's world,

Ed.

Hopes and fears

Dear Dave,

Merry Christmas! Well, almost... Christmas seems to have been going on for three weeks already this year. The kids are worn out from a constant stream of parties and relatives and Santas. I'm somewhat confused the actual day hasn't quite arrived yet.

That said, I'm putting off wrapping a big pile of presents by writing to you.

One thing I am still looking forward to is singing plenty of carols in the next couple of days. There's the Christmas Eve Christingle service tomorrow. (Forget offering hope, love and forgiveness – the Christingle is where we entice families with young children into church with promises of oranges and sweets.) Then there'll be more carols on Christmas Day. I like them because most of them have decent tunes that even tone-deaf people like me can manage to belt out.

We got a taster at church on Sunday with *O, little town of Bethlehem*:

O, little town of Bethlehem,
How still we see thee lie.
Above thy deep and dreamless sleep,
The silent stars go by.
Yet in thy dark streets shineth
The ever-lasting light.
The hopes and fears of all the years
Are met in thee tonight.

(Phillips Brooks 1835-93)

It's my favourite carol. ...*The hopes and fears of all the years...* That line always arouses emotions and normally makes me think about God becoming human to show us how to live, to fix our relationship with him and to give us a glimpse of the world beyond.

This time, however, my mind turned elsewhere.

Spare a thought for Joseph on that first Christmas night:

He'd had to live through months of gossip, thanks to the wedding date and due date not entirely adding up. That had been followed by a lengthy trek with a heavily pregnant wife in order to register for a census which was almost certainly an excuse to stiff him with a hefty tax bill. Then he'd failed in his first task as a dad – finding somewhere decent for his child to be born. (This isn't ordinarily the first task, but he'd missed out on the usual one and that was a completely different issue entirely...)

As we join him, he finds himself in the stable, surrounded by animals. He's managed to get the rowdy shepherds out the door at last, along with all the townsfolk made curious by the talk of angels and saviours. Mary is passed out from exhaustion in the corner. He wouldn't mind joining her. He wouldn't mind simply going and lying down beside her and giving her a cuddle.

If only the little Lord Jesus would flipping lay down his sweet head.

No crying he makes? Yeah, right. Newborn babies are generally pretty frustrated and irritated. This one has recently gone from holding the whole world in his hands to not being able to find his own thumb without sticking it in his eye. That's one *very* frustrated and irritated baby.

Chances of a silent night: slim.

So Joseph sits there, bleary-eyed, rocking the baby in his arms and he finally has the opportunity to wonder what he's got himself into. He suddenly realises he's a dad. Never mind the dreams and prophecies, he has a tiny life to take care of. A son! A son to teach and love, to provide for and protect. Terror and pride mix together at the prospect.

...The hopes and fears of all the years...

At that moment, he feels the truth of these words more than anyone.

Then he discovers his sleeve is warm and wet. He sighs and starts hunting around for more swaddling clothes. It's going to be a long night...

Best wishes to you and all your family. Have a great Christmas. I'd better go wrap those presents.

Yours in a woman's world,

Ed.

Almost there

Dear Dave,

Happy New Year!

Have I told you that Marie is starting nursery soon? I think it might be that I've mentioned it in passing. You know, in an offhand kind of way. It's not like it's a major event or anything but it's just possible I might have alluded to it once or twice. I doubt it was more than a sentence or two. I certainly haven't gone on about it.

What? What's that you say?

Really?

Every other email for weeks?

Oh...

Ho well, get over it, I'm not going to stop now. She starts tomorrow. Excuse me while I pirouette serenely around the kitchen on tip-toes, showering myself with flowers to the tune of *The Blue Danube Waltz*:

Yah da da da DAH, da-da, da-da. Yah da da da DAH, da-da, da-da...

...and then cut abruptly to an energetic interpretation of *The Time Warp*:

It's just a jump to the left...

...only to finish with an overblown rendition of *The Final Countdown* complete with air-guitar, a straggly mop stuck to my head and fireworks: Cue big-haired, leather-clad, Swedish men erupting from the cupboards in a blaze of pyrotechnics.

It's the final countdown! DUH-duh, duh, DUH! DUH-duh, duh, duh, duh!

DUH-duh! Duh, duh, DUH-duh! Duh, duh, du-du, du-du, duh-duh duuuh...

Actually, no, I think I wandered off into *The Flintstones* there, but who cares? My youngest child starts nursery tomorrow! I'm not fussed if my kitchen ends up full of European rock stars or Fred and Barney – all that matters is that I'm going to get regular time to myself without children.

Yep, the fabled two or so hours a day, on week days, during term-time, when all the kids are well, are almost here. That's over ten hours a week, thirty-five weeks a year, during which I might simultaneously have both the time and energy to achieve something. The very thought consumes my mind. I can barely contemplate anything else.

Then again, maybe Fred would bring Wilma...

...sigh...

Er... Where was I? Oh, yeah, free time once Marie starts nursery. I'll have some. That's going to be odd.

In the past, I've laughed at those who've said that I won't know what to do with myself. I have a hundred things I want to get done:

Clean the house.

I make the house *look* clean on a regular basis already but there are certain out-of-sight areas, like top shelves and at the back of the TV cabinet, that are so dusty you'd think a vampire had crawled in and died. They could do with some TLC.

Visit all the poky little shops in the area in which there isn't room to swing a screaming toddler.

For years, I've only dared venture into supermarkets and department stores, unwilling to risk navigating a buggy through cramped aisles of breakable goods. Even then, it's seldom been pleasant. One time, when Fraser was small, I took a wrong turn into the crystal department of John Lewis and he immediately decided the only way to travel was with his legs stuck out to either side as far as he could stretch. Steering a path to the exit became a nerve-wracking test of skill and concentration, akin to those games where you've got to move a metal ring along a wiggly wire without making contact and setting off the very expensive smashing noise. Ever since, colourful little stores selling knick-knacks have seemed out of the question.

I want to go and browse pointless trinkets again. I also want to go into one of the four Polish delicatessens that have recently opened within a few minutes' walk of my house and see if anything looks tasty. Hopefully a lot will – soon, a third of the shops round here are going to be Polish delicatessens and I won't be able to buy food anywhere else. (The other two-thirds of the shops have become internet cafés and barber's. The neighbourhood is apparently now full of Polish people who want to get their hair cut and then blog about it.)

Fix some of the things around the house that have been broken so long that I no longer even notice that they're broken.

Like, erm...

Go round the house looking for broken things.

See above.

Meet friends for coffee...

...and talk about topics other than children and things around the house which need fixed.

Play those computer games I've been meaning to play but haven't.

These are mostly PC games I picked up years ago, only to discover my computer at the time wasn't powerful enough. Doubtless they still won't work for some reason but I'd like to give them a try.

Zombie-proof the house.

If they climb on the wheelie bin, they'll be in the bedroom window before we know it. I need to sort out a spring-loaded booby-trap that will catapult them into next door's garden. The neighbours may not be too pleased when zombies start raining on their crazy paving but I assume that will be the least of my worries...

Have a proper mid-life crisis.

I had a minor one shortly after Marie was born but I never felt I had the time to get into it satisfactorily. I was too busy changing nappies to buy a motorbike; I was too tired to do anything else because I wasn't getting enough

Sleep.

Write a book.

I have a great idea for a haunting, Celtic fantasy novel set in fifth century Scotland, stuffed full of myths and heroes, and played out against the backdrop of the growing conflict between Druidism, the old gods and Christianity. It's totally awesome.

Alternatively, I could cobble together all these emails I've written to you and see if anyone's interested. Got to be worth a shot...

Buy clothes.

Much less awesome but it has to be done. It's years since I bought any clothing other than underwear. The trick, as ever, will be going to the shops and coming back with trousers rather than a PlayStation. Gah, who put GAME next to John Lewis? It's too tempting. Before long, I'll have to fashion myself a new coat out of DVD boxes.

The list goes on...

And that's merely off the top of my head. I'm beginning to understand what those people who said I won't know what to do with myself were talking about. There's so much I want to get done and only a couple of hours each day to do it. The problem is where to start. I don't want to waste any of that precious time and I may find myself paralysed with indecision. How best to maximise my productivity and enjoyment? The planning itself could take weeks.

I'm having to keep a lid on my own expectations. Even tackling one a day, I'm not going to achieve all of the above list in the first week. In fact, I'll be lucky if I manage to do more than lie on the sofa groaning for the first week. The second week, I might manage to lie on the sofa groaning while eating crisps. For the third week, I'm looking at a little light TV, less groaning and maybe some pretzels.

There's no point working myself up to anything more – the week after that, the kids are off school. To be honest, keeping to the schedule as it stands might be pushing it. Although Marie starts tomorrow, she's being broken in slowly. Tomorrow is really only a chance to look around; after that, on Friday, she'll get to stay longer but I won't be allowed to leave the building in case she has a titanic tantrum. (As if...) Depending how she copes, it could be a week before I get to leave her at nursery all morning.

The pretzels might have to wait until nearly March.

Let's face it, if I get half the things on my list done before the summer then I'll be doing extremely well. If I get three done, that'll still be impressive. Failing that, merely getting my regular cleaning, grocery shopping and a few chores done so I can pay more attention to the kids the rest of the time will be a result.

Drat. Now I think about it, maybe my life isn't going to change that much. Nonetheless, at least I should have enough time to dream about that mythical day, nineteen months from now, when Marie starts school. I ought to go get a calendar and start crossing off the days!

No, hang on. I'll wait a fortnight and buy one in a colourful little store which sells knick-knacks. Then I'll eat something Polish and get my hair cut while everyone stares at my jacket made of DVD boxes.

You never know, I might even start a blog...

Yours in a woman's world,

Ed.

What I really wanted them to get for Christmas

Dear Dave,

Listen!

Can you hear it? That lack of noise. Shhh...

...

Yes, *that* lack of noise.

It's the sound of an empty house. Sarah's at work, the boys are at school and Marie's at nursery. It's weird. I'm sitting in the kitchen, feeling perplexed. What now?

I should probably tidy the lounge but I can't be bothered. It's full of the kids' Christmas presents.

I suppose, all in all, they haven't done too badly this year. The unexpected drum kit from the in-laws has been successfully smuggled to a charity shop without the children noticing but, apart from that, the gifts have generally been appropriate and reasonably appreciated. The question is how to store the loot amongst all their other stuff?

The boys got a huge construction set consisting of scores of wooden wheels and poles and joints. It's not bad but it comes in a tin the size of Wales. On seeing it for the first time, I gave a sigh, unsure where on Earth we were going to keep it and fairly certain that none of the kids would show the slightest interest. We've had Duplo and K'Nex for ages – stacks and stacks of both – that they've hardly touched. It's filling up cupboards that could be better used to house their board games and the army of cuddly toys. This new set is very like K'Nex. I expected them to ignore it.

To my surprise, however, they've had great fun building rockets and robots and towers almost every day. Maybe it's the novelty of it being wood rather than plastic... or maybe it's simply that the tin got left out in the middle of the lounge because we couldn't think where else to put it. Whatever the reason, they've got quite into it. Perhaps there's hope they'll like LEGO yet. As I've mentioned before, securing a legitimate excuse to play with LEGO again is one of the prime reasons for having children.

I had a LEGO moon base when I was a kid that I played with constantly. I designed various extra vehicles and buildings for it myself with the help of cannibalised parts from other sets. I loved that moon base. If I were to see another one in a charity shop, I'd buy it instantly, even if it had teeth marks all over it like my old one did. (My dog was frequently hungry and permanently stupid.) The new Mars Mission sets call to me whenever I wander through a toy department. I drag children along with me, hoping they'll attempt to pester me into buying some, as they do with every other shiny lump of plastic in the store. Doesn't happen, though. The girl wants to play with the pink, sparkly trikes and the boys want to know when we're going to the computer game section.

Annoying.

I guess it's for the best. It might not be as much fun as I imagine. The children would get me to do all the work putting it together and then they'd muck about with the moving parts for a bit before leaving it lying around to be stood on. Unless they were prepared for some construction and make-believe themselves, there wouldn't be much point to it.

Disappointingly, the children haven't taken a second look at Playmobil stuff either. I had the mobile hospital set of that when I was Lewis' age. It was superb. As for Action Man, I had a tank but I was desperate for the submarine and the death-slide. I tried to make my own death-slide tower out of cardboard but over-specced the project and never completed it. With hindsight, I could have just tied one end of a length of string to the latch of an upstairs window and the other end to the back gate, cuffed Action Man with a bag-tie and sent him screaming across the garden to splat into the woodwork. (He could take it. His normal experience on exiting an upstairs window was having his parachute fail to open and then plummeting head-first onto the patio.)

One of my boys got an Action Man a while ago that I would happily have bought any number of gadgets for but the poor guy's long since been left lying in a twisted heap at the bottom of a drawer, abandoned to spend a hundred thousand years biodegrading in his injection moulded underwear.

It's distressing. Maybe the kids will get into LEGO now but I can't see it ever occurring in a big way and although Marie might soon want Playmobil stuff if I suggest it often enough, the Action Man submarine is a lost cause unless there's a lilac version which comes with fairies. (The Barbie covert infiltration and assassination range!) I feel I'm missing out on one of the perks of parenthood i.e. the chance to buy all the toys I wanted when I was a kid but didn't get.

In reality, it's all rather silly. Do I *really* want to play with LEGO? These days, if I want to create, I can make something more lasting and more useful. Shelves, anyone? If I want to imagine, I can write. If I want to play, there are plenty of computer games.

What I really want *is to be seven* and play with LEGO. I'd like the freedom to run around with a LEGO spaceship without people staring at me. I'd like to be able to create and imagine without feeling the responsibility to produce something useful; to be able to relax without feeling pressure to recharge before the end of my scheduled downtime.

That's not going to happen, unfortunately. Not even if I buy the totally enormous space station thing. I should stop hankering after it and start directing the kids towards stuff that I would find fun in the here and now.

The boys already play computer games, so that's a beginning. Our taste and ability occasionally overlap. One day we'll be able to play co-operative *Halo*. In the meantime, I need to start getting them interested in games involving little plastic figures and dice with an improbable number of sides.

Is there a Pokémon version of *Risk*?

A readily available supply of strategy game opponents – that would genuinely be fantastic and might be achievable. I should go hunt around in the loft and see what games I can get my little minions playing.

Being an adult is actually pretty good sometimes.

Nevertheless, there's one thing I can fairly easily do for the part of me that will forever long to be seven again. I'm off to find that Action Man, a bag-tie and a very long bit of string...

Yours in a woman's world,
Ed.

Part 7

Enjoying the Moment

Coffee

Dear Dave,

Thanks for the congratulations. I'm still somewhat confused by the whole free time situation, though. It's hard to explain. I tried to explain it to Rob yesterday but, between his new phone, the curtains and the... No, I'm getting ahead of myself. I'll tell you what happened:

Rob looked around suspiciously. "When you suggested meeting up for coffee, I was thinking Starbucks or Waterstone's. I would have settled for the Debenhams cafeteria or even that dodgy place at the end of your road that does all-day breakfasts. This is... What is this place?"

"It's very cheap," I said, pointing to a chalkboard with the prices on. "I thought you were broke."

"Well, you know, wedding and baby and stuff, but doesn't mean I can't drink proper coffee." Rob squinted. "Flip, that is cheap!"

"Exactly. Now quit complaining."

We were in a little community centre housed in a converted church. It was all stone pillars, stained-glass and gravestones set into the floor, but the pews had been removed to make way for a café, a gift shop and a lounge area where some elderly people were dozing in a selection of tired old armchairs. At the far end, the altar remained intact and the area around it had been left as a chapel. The café was empty apart from a couple of mums who were sitting at a table with hot drinks and cake while their small children played with battered toys from a tub in the corner.

Rob had the day off work to get organised for the imminent arrival of his first child but, with only a week to go, he was in denial and more than happy to meet up to chat rather than buy nappies. It was ten o'clock in the morning. I had two children at school and one at nursery. I had no children with me. It was strange. I felt liberated and exposed. I was able to leave the house on my own but, on the other hand, I had no young children around to explain my dishevelled appearance, the bags under my eyes and my permanent manic grin nor why I kept inadvertently humming *Old MacDonald*.

"Would you stop that!" said Rob.

"Was I doing it again?"

"Yes."

"Sorry. It's in my head. Especially the verse about subsidies. You know, *With a ching-ching here, and a ching-ching there. Here ching, there a ching, everywhere a...*"

Rob looked at me sadly. "You've finally lost it."

"I'm not sure you're wrong." I sighed and tried to shake the nonsense out of my brain. "What are you having?"

"A cup of tea and a doughnut." He examined the price list again. "Hang on, make that two doughnuts and a scone. These prices are just mad."

"Yeah, that sign over there says this place costs £1200 a week to run but I don't know whether we're supporting them or they're supporting us. Maybe if you eat enough doughnuts it'll cost them £1400 this week."

"I'll give it a go."

We went up to the counter and ordered. I had a black coffee and a scone. The man found a mug and immediately put some milk in it. "Ah, you said black, didn't you?" he muttered. I nodded. He found another mug, held it ready to pour water into and then hesitated. "It was tea, wasn't it?"

"Coffee."

"Oh, right, right." He put a spoonful of instant coffee in the mug and then filled it until it overflowed and he had to mop up with a tissue. He put the mug on a saucer and then had a similar level of success with Rob's tea. He put the doughnuts on a plate and told us the scones would be brought to our table once they had jam on. We picked our way through the sleeping old people and found a table that, according to the inscriptions on the floor, was situated above a particularly large concentration of dead people.

"I think I know why this place is so cheap," said Rob.

"Well, when you're doing the buying, we can go to Starbucks, Mr Two-Incomes-And-Not-Quite-Any-Kids-Yet."

"I do have a new iPhone to support."

"Seriously?"

He whipped it out and took a photo of me looking incredulous. Then he uploaded the picture to Facebook.

"Honestly, you have more money than... than... Oh, I don't know..." I grabbed it from him for a quick play. "...than is probably good for you."

"Cool, though, isn't it?"

I shrugged. "I doubt this will survive being tumble-dried as happily as my brick-like old handset does."

"I'm not going to let the kid near it."

"Not even if it turns out to be the only thing that stops him or her crying?" I asked.

"No," said Rob, very definitely.

"Uh-huh," I said, trying to make my derision clear, "whatever..."

At that point, the manager arrived with one scone and informed us that our order had been misread but she assured us that the other scone would be with us shortly. Her large and conspicuous name badge was on upside down.

After she'd left, Rob gave me a look. "Don't be too hard on them," I said, handing back his phone, "I'm assuming they're all volunteers."

"Next time – Starbucks," he mumbled through a mouthful of doughnut.

I changed the subject. "You got the bag packed yet?"

"Bag?"

"Kate's bag for the hospital."

"It's on my list," he said.

I couldn't believe it. "Please tell me you're joking."

"What?" Rob said defensively. "I've been busy. Some of us have work to go to, you know. The weekends are taken up with buying things like cots and buggies and cotton-wool, and I've been spending evenings eBaying my stuff after you told Sarah to tell Kate to tell me to get on with it."

"You need to get the bag packed. If you have to do it at the last minute, who knows what you'll end up throwing in? You'll get to the hospital with your DS, two *Star Wars* action figures and a packet of biscuits but without the TENS machine. It won't go well."

"I..." He stopped as a text message arrived for him. "It'll be Kate. I saw a set of four matching bridesmaid dresses in a charity shop this morning – only a tenner each. I sent her a photo." He showed it to me. The dresses had a muted, floral pattern and an excess of pink ribbon.

"My aunt used to have curtains like that twenty years ago," I said. "I always wondered what happened to them."

"Wearing curtains didn't do the girl in *Enchanted* any harm..." He read Kate's message. "Oh."

"Let me guess," I said. "She wasn't thrilled?"

He pulled a face. "That's an understatement."

The other scone arrived and we tucked in. "How are things, now that Marie's at nursery?" Rob asked. "I bet you don't know what to do with yourself."

I resisted the urge to slap him. "Everybody keeps saying that but it's only a couple of hours a day and I've got plenty of stuff to do."

He chuckled, as if humouring me. "Still," he said, "you must be enjoying the chance to put your feet up."

"That's another thing people keep saying. It's driving me mad. If you ask if I miss the children really, and then argue when I say no, I'm afraid I *will* have to kill you with..." I grabbed the first item which came to hand. "...this!"

"Don't be stupid," said Rob, chuckling some more. "You can't kill someone with a sachet of sugar."

"Want to risk it?" I said, waving the sachet at him menacingly. "It's amazing what can be achieved with limited resources. Remember the time I saved your career with a packet of Polos?"

He rolled his eyes. "How can I forget? I had to hide the flipping things from a Dell service technician only the other week."

"They're still there?" I flicked the sachet at him in irritation. "That was supposed to be a temporary fix. I told you to get it sorted. Haven't you managed to replace one pack of mints in eight years?"

"It's not just the one pack now."

"What?"

He looked sheepish. "It's possible I might have got drunk one night with the hardware support team and told them about it. They thought it was an excellent solution I'd come up with and they liked it so much..."

"*You* came up with? I... No, wait a minute, I don't think I want to hear where this is going. I still have a pension with LBO. My future financial security depends on the IT equipment not dying in a super-heated eruption of breath-freshening caramel."

"As I was saying," he continued, "the hardware guys liked the solution so much..."

"I'm not listening! I'm not listening!"

"...they've gone and used it all over. Every time we get a new server we have to send a trainee to the newsagent's to buy some mints. The last guy was useless. He came back with Extra Strong rather than Polos."

I took my fingers out of my ears and stopped humming. "How was that going to work?"

"Exactly!" said Rob. "Too big, too thick and no hole. Never going happen."

We both clicked our tongues and shook our heads. There was silence for a few moments as, in mutual despair, we contemplated the incompetence involved.

"No really..." said Rob eventually. "How's it going?"

I gazed into my coffee. "It's all a bit weird. I had lots of plans as to how I was going to celebrate when Marie started properly but nothing much has come of them. I guess this is it." I gave a sweep of my hand to take in everything from the dubious coffee to the comatose octogenarians. "Not exactly wild, is it? I got thrown on Friday and I haven't totally recovered. I was expecting to have to hang around in the building in case the girl had a strop. I took along a pen and some paper to write to Dave while I waited. I wasn't prepared when they said, since she'd settled so well on her first day, I could just leave her. They took my number and I wandered off."

"Freedom," said Rob. "What are you complaining about?"

"Except I had to go back to the house," I said, taking off my glasses and rubbing my eyes. "I couldn't remember my mobile number offhand so I gave the nursery my home number. I spent a couple of hours sitting in the kitchen, feeling confused and slightly ill."

Rob smirked. "See! You do miss them really."

"Right, that's it!" I grabbed a fistful of sachets and made to lunge.

"Woh!" He threw up his hands to ward me off. "Sorry! Sorry! Calm down. You were the one who spent the whole walk here going on about how exposed you felt without them."

I slumped into my seat. "I hadn't thought about it that way. Maybe you're right. Maybe I do miss them a little. But it's certainly not like I get to the middle of the morning and hanker after a long, complicated explanation of the life-cycle of the monsters living in my child's elbow."

Rob raised his eyebrows.

"Don't ask," I said. "If you want the full story, I'll send Lewis round to explain."

"He's the one that spent three hours telling me about level five of *Super Mario Bros*, isn't he? I'll pass, thanks."

"Good call – I'm glad of the break myself. It's just... I don't know." I drank some of my coffee and tried to think how to explain. "Have you ever lost your ID badge from work?"

Rob nodded. "Dropped it in a shredder once."

It was my turn to raise eyebrows.

"Don't ask," he said. "If you want the full story, I'll send Geoffrey from Corporate Regulations round to explain."

I passed. "Anyhow, not having the kids about is like having lost my work ID badge. It makes me feel the need to explain who I am, what I'm doing and why I don't have my ID."

"Yeah, know what you mean," said Rob. "If nothing else, it must be odd not being able to wave them in the right direction and have doors open for you automatically."

"That's perhaps taking the analogy a little far..." I said.

"Perhaps." He leant back and munched on his scone. "So did you do *anything* exciting on your first day of peace then?"

"I killed an Action Man in a freak death-slide accident."

"Er..." Before he managed any further questioning, his phone went again. He checked the message.

All the colour drained from his face.

"You OK?" I said.

"I've got to get home." There was panic in his voice.

"Is everything all right?"

He opened and closed his mouth several times before saying, "I've got to get that bag packed."

"Yep," I said, standing to leave. "You'd better go."

"Uh-huh." He didn't move. He continued to stare wide-eyed at his phone.

"Would you like me to call a taxi?" I offered.

"No... No... I'll flag one. I, er... Do you want some Mars Mission LEGO?"

"Excuse me?"

"I haven't got round to eBaying it yet," he said, sounding faraway. "I haven't sorted through my books, either. Or painted the spare room. Or bought any nappies. Or completed the new *Tomb Raider*. I can't do them all this afternoon."

Having recently convinced myself that I really wouldn't like some space LEGO, even though in some sense I really would, this put me in a quandary. Suddenly I was being offered some for free. Being free is always a big plus. Also, Rob has the deluxe set. I was tempted.

Still... Really, really...

Ach, I don't need any and I didn't want to take advantage of Rob in his deranged state. Besides, I felt he could do with a happy thought to hold onto.

I made a difficult decision.

"You should save the LEGO for Squirtle," I said. "He or she might want to play with it. It'll be a few years till then but I'm sure you can find some storage space somewhere."

"Oh... Oh, yeah. That's an idea. Yeah, we could play with it together. I..." He wasn't entirely in his right mind.

I hauled him out of his seat. "I tell you what, let's go flag that taxi together." I dragged him across the room. He stumbled along in a daze, a doughnut in one hand and a half-eaten scone in the other. Once we were outside, I bundled him into a taxi, wished him luck and sent him on his way.

I made sure to remind him where he lived first.

Hopefully he was OK and didn't try to pay with the doughnut. I haven't heard any news yet; I'll let you know when I do.

Regards to Liz and the kids.

Yours in a woman's world,

Ed.

PS Marie's at nursery again just now and I'm still feeling strange.

Looking back

Dear Dave,

Can you believe it? An entire year. We've been writing to each other for an entire year. It's a milestone in our friendship. If this were an American sitcom, there'd be two possible ways we could mark the occasion:

> **The expensive option**: I could draft in a celebrity correspondent to guest star.
>
> **The cheapskate option**: We could sit on a sofa and reminisce via flashbacks while everyone laughs at how our hair used to look.

Guess which one you're getting.

Not that I can remember anything much from before last Saturday to reminisce about... One of the consequences of parenthood is that you rapidly end up living in the here and now. The kids' bedtime looms so large in the future that beyond it is a mystery. Repetition and lack of sleep make the past a woolly fog in which events swirl without context or chronology. Some occasions stand out clearly but I have lost whole months and years in that temporal soup. If you ever find out what became of my youth, let me know...

I am aware, however, that a few things have changed for me since I started writing to you. For instance, the baby department at John Lewis now feels like a forgotten world. I was there yesterday, searching for a suitable present for Rob and Kate and Squirtle. (Turns out they had a false alarm on Tuesday. Nevertheless, any day now...) As I stared at all the shelves and shelves of gadgets and gizmos, it was like opening a drawer at home and finding flared trousers, a vinyl LP and a ZX Spectrum. Although the stuff brought back fond memories, I was heartily relieved I didn't need it anymore. Marie still uses a cup with a spout, the buggy continues to cling to life and carseats will be with us for several years yet but almost everything else is behind us. There's no more faffing with sterilisers, nappies, folding toilet seats, musical mobiles or high-chairs. Twelve months ago we were getting there but now we're very definitely past the baby stage.

My sympathies to you and Liz as you prepare for all the fun of breast pumps and frozen milk when she heads back to work. It's good to be able to feed my kids any old junk that's lying around in the fridge rather than spending my time stopping them from feeding themselves any old junk that's lying around under it.

Unexpectedly, as I hunted about amongst the baby stuff, I observed that technology has already moved on from 'my day'. Double-decker buggies are now much more common and someone has finally made rubbery ice-cube trays specifically designed for freezing portions of home-made baby food. The foldable baby bath didn't look very convincing, though. The foldable potty, meanwhile, would have collapsed under the weight of any of my remarkably large children.

I'm much more cynical about these things than I was back when I was a fresh-faced prospective parent. I've bought my fair share of baby gizmos that didn't work, from a baby-listener that kept losing signal to a portable bottle-warmer that used an exothermic chemical reaction to turn cold milk into almost tepid milk in the length of time it took for a hungry baby to give up and fall asleep. I've had non-spill cups that leaked everywhere and others that my kids couldn't get liquid out of even when they were trying. Neither of these was ideal. I was particularly fond of the plastic bib with a lip at the bottom that caught half-chewed food in one handy place as it fell – all the better for Fraser to swivel the bib round and tip the contents in his ear...

It's for the best that I'm done with parent and toddler. Before long, I would have been the grumpy old man in the corner. 'When I was looking after babies, we didn't have any of this new-fangled video-on-demand nonsense. We had to make do with CBeebies, no matter what was on. I lived through the great Tweenies Bank Holiday Funday, I did. You young'uns wouldn't understand, but I was there. I still have the mental scars. You hear me? I still have the scars!'

As the recollections began to overwhelm me, I decided to choose something quickly. I got them the same clip-on carseat toy arch I get everyone and beat a hasty retreat.

Yep, Dave, plenty has changed since I started writing to you. Not least, the kids are growing up. Lewis is at school now and it feels like he's been there forever. I can scarcely remember what it was like when he was at nursery. Fraser *has* been at school forever but his reading ability has come on hugely in the last year. Marie, however, has matured unbelievably. She's sleeping properly, eating properly, generally using the toilet and has become quite a talker. A year ago, she could say simple sentences along the lines of, 'I like pink!' and, 'I go kitchen.' Now she can express concepts as complicated as, 'We're having a party in the lounge, so we need to be tied up!' She can also grin mischievously and say, 'Babies aren't nice... for eating,' before laughing in a scary fashion.

These conversational gambits do have a tendency to worry and confuse visitors but I only have myself to blame:

Sarah: What do fairies make?

Marie: Cakes!

Me: Yep. From teeth.

Marie: OK.

Ho well, she'll grow out of it soon. It's ages since she believed everything I told her and it won't be long before she starts arguing with absolutely anything I say. *Sigh.* Enjoy having a tiny one while you can. Daisy will be stomping around whining before you know it.

I suppose if it ever gets to me, and I pine for the simple days of caring for a baby who only complains about basic, physical needs, I can borrow one of the slimy little critters from Rob. Then I can hand it back, go home and sleep without being disturbed.

Bliss.

It's been an eventful year. All the best for the next one. Thanks for the emails, advice and encouragement.

Yours in a woman's world,

Ed.

Nobody expects the Spanish Input/Output error

Dear Dave,

Plenty of things are different from a year ago, but others are the same as they ever were. Certain aspects of my life have remained constant since way back before I quit paid employment to become a housedad. Bringing up kids is very like running an IT project – for some reason, I'm routinely behind schedule.

With IT projects, the difficulty is that there are always unexpected snags. Typical issues range from a logical inconsistency in the specification (i.e. you've been asked to do the impossible) to a discovery that the highly paid contractor brought in to handle the tough stuff was bluffing all along and has spent six months playing *Minesweeper*. If you're really unlucky, the project will simply open up a vortex in the very fabric of nature that sucks in time and money and dumps them out beyond the galactic rim. (That's never good.)

Obviously it's possible to figure some leeway into the production timetable but if you don't know what the problem is going to be, it's difficult to know how much time to allow for solving it. Maybe it will only require someone nipping to PC World for a cable. Maybe it will send the entire project back to the drawing board. Who can tell? Probably sensible to allow twice as long as you're really hoping...

Of course, putting vast amounts of blank space in the schedule 'just in case' gives a bad impression, so it doesn't usually happen. Then, halfway through the project, someone leaves the team or the customer suddenly needs the product in a hurry, and management has to cut corners in order to get the job done. The easiest thing to do is remove from the schedule the time and manpower set aside for contingencies. Voilà! The whole project is back on track... provided nothing goes wrong. Management may argue that this is the kind of emergency that the padding in the schedule was for, but the truth is that these are management problems that should have had padding of their very own. In reality, what's gone is the time required to cope when it transpires that the software bought in from another company doesn't do all the things the salesman said it would, doesn't work at all or has manuals that are written entirely in Danish (apart from the sections in Braille).

Strangely, management is surprised when the project overruns...

Maybe it's an unwinnable battle. If by some quirk of fate a project did ever come in early, the customers would merely start trying to think of 'minor' bits to add on. These would inevitably involve starting again from scratch and the project would end up overrunning anyway.

Similarly with children, being late can be unavoidable. If on a good day it takes ten minutes to get everyone's shoes on and get them out of the house for school, there are going to be other days when it takes twenty. Setting aside twenty minutes is asking for trouble, though. You don't want to be waiting outside the school for ten minutes in the rain. Equally, you don't want to be hanging around at home for ten minutes – the kids will complain loudly about being bored, take their shoes off again and then lose them. They will arrive very late for school, wearing their slippers. Leaving too much time for a task can make you later than leaving too little. You'd be better off allowing fifteen minutes on a regular basis and accepting the fact that you're going to be five minutes late on any day that one of the children gets distracted and tips his milk into his ear rather than his mouth.

That said, forewarned is forearmed. With a little knowledge and planning, it's possible to avoid being horrendously late on most occasions. To help you along, here is a selection of tasks I've found unexpectedly hard in the past. You'll have encountered nearly all of them yourself already but they may not have seemed like that big a deal. Please remember, however, that the time taken to resolve these issues is proportional to the square of the number of children you have. Thus, now you have two, you need to quadruple the amount of space in the schedule reserved for:

Getting them to wear appropriate clothing.

I tell my kids that it's raining and they'll need to put their raincoats on.

Without looking out a window, they say, "No, it's not."

I argue for a bit, they don't put their raincoats on and we step out of the door. They instantly start screaming that it's raining and run around in a tizzy like they're the Wicked Witch of the West and someone's dumped a bucket of water on them.

I say, "It's almost stopped. You'll be fine."

They argue and demand their raincoats. Eventually I give up and they go in and put their raincoats on.

The rain stops, the sun comes out and they complain it's too hot in their raincoats.

They refuse to take them off.

When we finally arrive at our destination, people wonder why we're wet, late and sweaty. I just shake my head and sigh...

Getting them to do stuff for themselves.

Marie kicks up a huge fuss about drying her own hands. She's currently lying on the hall floor yelling for help because a small part of her lower arm is wet. She's holding the towel in her other hand but wants me to go through and combine the towel and arm with some gentle rubbing action. Suffice to say, she'll be yelling a while longer – probably for several minutes more than it takes the water to evaporate of its own accord.

Getting gloves on a toddler.

Their fingers go everywhere apart from the right place

Getting them to stop doing stuff for themselves.

If we're in a big hurry and I pro-actively decide to dry Marie's hands for her, she'll absolutely insist on doing it on her own... very... very... slowly...

Going to the shops to buy milk.

Between getting them dressed and toileted (including the washing and drying of hands) and persuading them to leave the house, going to buy milk can take lengthier organisation than a trip to Paris without children.

Going to Paris with children.

Like going to buy milk but with added luggage.

Keeping gloves *on* a toddler.

It doesn't matter that it's freezing and you've just spent five minutes teasing the things on, the kid wants to see her fingers...

Feeding them five portions of fruit and veg a day.

It's not so much getting them to eat it, it's supplying it:

5 family members x 5 portions per day x 2 days = 50 portions.

We also require around 8 pints of milk and a loaf and a half of bread. Hang on a minute while I nip to Tesco again...

Cheering up a toddler whose hands are cold.

If you can coax them to calm down for a minute, you might be able to get those gloves back on. (Briefly.)

Working out if they're ill.

When my kids were small, it was easy to tell how ill they were from the number and amount of toxic substances oozing out of them. These days there's often less to go on. They'll complain of aches and pains, cough a couple of times and then sneeze. Questioning them uncovers that they've been feeling 'not that great' for 'a bit'. Taking their temperature reveals that one ear has a mild fever and the other is dead. (Repeated attempts cause the symptoms to swap randomly between ears. Shaking the electronic thermometer produces a rattling sound.)

Since I've now spent nearly eight years clearing up the toxic substances despite having had various strains of plague myself, I'm low on sympathy for minor cases of the snuffles. Then again, I don't want them going rapidly downhill the second they leave the house. I can do without being summoned to school halfway through the morning to explain why I sent in my highly contagious child. (Teachers are scary.)

Coming to a decision takes forever.

Explaining the difference between live-action TV drama, cartoons, documentary footage, the news, CGI and real life.

As for theatrical adaptations of kids' shows, well: 'Yes, those are real people pretending to be the real people who normally pretend to be the pretend people on TV and if that one falls off the ladder it will really hurt them. And, yes, it is just a story, but listen to what they're saying – real vegetables really are really good for you… er, really…'

Avoiding drowning in Fimbles.

Soft toys. Everywhere. Stuck now. Can't... make... it... to... the... door...

Being understanding.

This takes an astonishing amount of effort. What I actually want to say is, "I told you you'd get cold hands."

There we go. With this information, you should be able to leave enough time (but not too much) to achieve most goals. I wouldn't count on it, though. The kids are bound to find some new way to slow you down.

Take consolation from the fact that you're not in charge of the software for the government's latest tax scheme. I hear that's created a vortex that's *spitting stuff out*. They're having to deal with giant space spiders, unicorns and intermittent downpours of odd socks.

Whatever happens, we're never going to be as late as them.

Probably.

Yours in a woman's world,

Ed.

Squirtle

Dear Dave,

There's a theory that the manner of a individual's birth affects their personality. A traumatic birth creates an anxious little person; a relaxed birth leads to an easy-going child.

For my own part, I have a different theory. Having witnessed three children make their grand entrance into the world in their own inimitable styles, I can't help thinking that things are the other way about and it's the personality that affects the birth. Easy-going children relax and enjoy the ride; anxious children dither and get stuck; awkward children brace their arms and legs and dare you to come in and get them...

Bearing this in mind, Rob shouldn't have too hard a time of it. Kate gave birth to a nine pound baby boy on Saturday and, by all accounts, delivery went as smoothly as you could reasonably expect given the basic logistics of squeezing an object that large through a hole that small. It's somehow fitting, however, that the contractions started for real during a heated game of *Guitar Hero*. Rob saw it as a good excuse to avoid losing. Through gritted teeth, Kate told him to go eat his own whammy bar, and then riffed him into the ground.

They were lucky that Squirtle didn't come out holding a controller. (Yep, he's still called Squirtle. They haven't entirely decided on a name yet.)

I went to visit on the second evening they were in hospital. The ward had four beds in it. A selection of tired looking mums and dads were showing their new offspring to enthusiastic relatives. It was a chaos of flowers, balloons and teddy bears. It was also far too hot. Prepared for this eventuality, I'd slipped into Bermuda shorts and my Mr Incredible t-shirt on arrival. Kate was off having a shower and Rob was left holding the baby in a slightly tense manner.

"Who chose that outfit?" I asked.

"It was some of the guys from work."

Squirtle was wearing a brown towelling robe, a white cloak and a green hat with large, pointy ears. "Know you well, they do," I said.

"Yeah, maybe," he said, gently rocking his little baby Yoda. "They weren't totally sure, so they got a couple of others too. There's a Darth Vader one for days when Squirtle's feeling evil and a Princess Leia one for days when I am."

"You can't dress the poor kid up as Princess Leia."

"It's not as if he's going to care," said Rob, "and you should see the hat. It's superb. Have a look in the bag. There. See!"

He pointed to a bag overflowing with cotton-wool, nappies and babygros and I had a rummage around inside. After a lengthy search, I pulled out a dark brown skull-cap with snake-like coils of fabric on the earflaps. I stared at it. "That *is* quite something," I managed eventually, ready to beat it with a bedpan if it started to move. "You might want to save it in case the next one's a girl."

"Give us a chance."

"Well, now you've got the costume... And you definitely can't put it on Squirtle. Someone will take a photo and he'll never live it down."

Rob looked slightly crestfallen. "Like you're a fashion guru."

"Hey, at least I'm not melting," I said and pulled straight some of the creases in my Incredi-shirt. "Are you any closer with a name yet?"

"Traditionally, all the men in Kate's family are called Robert but that's confusing enough as it is. Kate's kinda keen on Ben but neither of us is that convinced. I had Frodo shot down in flames earlier. I dunno. We'll work it out – we've got a few weeks."

"Three. Less than three now, in fact. If we were in England then you'd have longer. What are the rest called?"

Rob nodded his head in the direction of the other babies in the room. "Jack, Jack and Lewis. The next ward is Lewis, Jack, Sophie and Jack. I'm thinking, not Jack."

"Wise."

"You want to cuddle him?" he said, offering Squirtle to me.

I held up my hands to ward off the snotty little Jedi. "Been there, done that. Besides, let sleeping babies lie."

"If only," Rob sighed. "The minute I put him down, he wakes up and starts screaming."

"The ones that keep screaming even when you're holding them are worse."

Rob nodded but gave the impression that that wasn't exactly what he needed to hear. He was looking exhausted already.

"How are you doing?" I asked gently.

He couldn't speak for a second. Emotions wrestled with each other across his face. Then he sort of shrugged and said, "I'm a dad." There was a mix of fear, joy, astonishment, pride and confusion in his voice.

"I understand," I said. I remember very clearly that's how I felt when I first held Fraser. Heck, I still feel like that if I think about it. "If you ever need help or advice..." The words trailed off. The rest didn't need said and, besides, we might have ended up hugging or something...

"Thanks," said Rob and then, after an awkward pause, he added, "He does need his nappy changed, if you're interested."

"Forget that," I said. "It'll be full of slimy tar. Dealing with that stuff is a rite of passage for new parents. I wouldn't want to deprive you."

"Some help you are."

He was close to starting to think about opening the changing bag just as Kate returned. She was clean and refreshed. Rob handed Squirtle over. Squirtle woke up and was immediately a little sick on her. She didn't appear ecstatic. Then she gave the baby a sniff and realised she'd been duped into the bargain. At that moment, Rob's parents arrived.

I decided it was a good time to make my farewells.

Wish I'd thought to switch out of my shorts before leaving the building. I didn't half look a fool waiting for the bus…

Yours in a woman's world,
Ed.

Being there

Dear Dave,

I'm sad to hear that Sam has lost his cuddly green cat called Blue Rabbit. Have you checked inside his wellies, behind the sofa and under his mattress? How about coat pockets and the freezer? (Yeah, sorry, I know you're an old hand at this and you've already scoured every feasible location twice but sometimes it's easy to overlook the obvious places.)

Before Christmas, Marie lost a pink hat by posting it through the gap between the back and hood of her buggy. She thought it had landed safely in the shopping net underneath but, in reality, she'd cunningly dropped it on the pavement behind us. The next day, when we discovered it missing, we went searching but it had vanished. She was distraught. She wanted us to go door-to-door asking for it. In the end, I had to tell her that it had 'gone to live on a farm' and it was happy frolicking through the fields. "No, it's not," she whimpered. "It's crying because it's lost *me*."

What can you do?

I hate not being able to fix things. It's particularly vexing when children go out of their way to create insoluble problems. The other day, Marie burst into tears because I'd brought her raincoat rather than her umbrella when I collected her from nursery. We got soaked as she shuffled slowly and miserably home. All the way, she whined that she wanted her umbrella. Since the umbrella was at our house and that's where we were going, I'm not sure exactly what she wanted me to do. She was simply determined to be annoyed.

Usually in these situations, she gets a handful of Extra Strong Mints to cheer her up. She loves having a 'fiery mouth'. Unfortunately, the day before, she'd received a public health DVD from nursery. It detailed the best method of brushing teeth and tried to persuade us to avoid sugary snacks. She'd insisted on watching it half a dozen times. It made her feel hungry and me feel guilty. Now, when she's not whining about me having brought the wrong waterproof equipment, she's whining because I won't give her Extra Strong Mints in case her teeth fall out.

Nevertheless, for a while, it was convenient being able to put almost anything right with a touch of minty freshness.

Dental hygiene aside, I suppose it wouldn't have lasted anyway. The boys have already encountered emotional issues that are too hard to deal with by simply fobbing them off with sweets. For instance, when Lewis was only four, he was inconsolable for weeks after he learnt his best friend was moving away.

Fraser gets upset if certain kids won't play with him at school. He comes out of the gate at the end of the day and wants me to talk to their parents. I explain that adults can't force other children to be friends with him but he doesn't seem to understand:

Years ago, when he was in nursery, I asked him who his friends were and he laughed and said, "We're all friends in nursery. That's the rule." I kept trying to find out who he was especially friendly with but he merely persisted in repeating, "We're all friends in nursery," in a Stepford kind of way. All the kids had plainly had this drummed into them. It's an attractive concept but, you and I both know, it's institutional short-hand for, 'We will peacefully tolerate one another's presence and not whack each other senseless with Duplo.' Fraser took it rather more literally, however, and hasn't totally recovered.

I try suggesting different children in his class he could play with but they won't do. He wants everyone to be friends with him but reserves the right to be selective about returning the affection. (Which I guess is normal – it's just a shame for everybody involved.) My instant desire is to fix things for 'my little boy' and make the issue disappear. That's not possible, though, and maybe it's not even a good idea. Coping with loss and disappointment is an important skill he should learn. I can help by acknowledging the hurt and giving him sympathy, but there's no use pretending that everything's OK and it doesn't matter really. He needs to know that it's all right to be sad sometimes.

That said, sometimes he needs to get a grip – in my book, it's not acceptable to burst into tears because you got the wrong type of bedtime hug nor to kick your brother in irritation because he doesn't want to play the same game as you. These situations require patience, respect and negotiation rather than emotional outbursts. Still, there are occasions when he has a right to feel genuinely upset and I shouldn't expect him to shrug it off. Being rejected isn't fun.

All I can do is tell him we love him no matter what he does or achieves, and encourage him to explore and control his emotions. Providing him something to look forward to doesn't do any harm either. A Pokémon card battle is a great healer.

Good luck finding a replacement for that cat/rabbit. Will Sam be happy with a brand new one or will he insist on it looking, feeling and smelling the same? Hopefully he'll accept the explanation that you've 'given it a wash'. If not, at least you can vent your parental frustration by administering the flipping thing a good battering with a shovel.

Yours in a woman's world,

Ed.

PS Don't forget to pour some milk on it and leave it in the sun for three days before wiping it on the nose of a passing dog. That should get the scent and texture just about perfect...

That would be an ecumenical question

Dear Dave,

When this housedad existence is over, all the kids are grown up and I no longer have any purpose in life, I'll presumably have to find a job or something. By that point, of course, I will be a withered husk of my former self with outdated qualifications and atrophied skills. On paper, my employability will be severely compromised.

I'm not too worried, though. If I can blag myself an interview, then I should be fine. I'll have had years of practice responding to unexpected and awkward questions in high pressure scenarios. Nothing will phase me. After all, what could compete with being asked (loudly) on the bus, 'Why is that man so fat?' or being interrogated in the playground as to how exactly the baby-seeds get from the daddy to the mummy? In comparison, sitting in an office and having to answer some nonsense about what I can contribute should be a breeze. I'm reasonably confident of talking my way into senior management within a couple of weeks. That, or landing a position as PR rep for the nuclear power industry.

Yep, I have to deal with difficult questions all the time. Lewis has an insatiable desire for information, no wish to think things through for himself and a complete lack of tact. Fraser is becoming intrigued by the mechanical details of child production. Marie, meanwhile, has developed a preoccupation with theology.

Fraser was the same at her age, asking all sorts of questions like 'Where is God?', 'What's he made of?' and 'Will I get to play computer games in Heaven?'. We were impressed until we realised that he was timing these questions for twenty-eight minutes past seven in the evening and his main aim was to avoid going to bed. This was impressive in its own fashion but nowhere near as gratifying. Marie, however, seems to be looking more for a good doctrinal debate. She's equally uninterested in what we have to tell her but is keen to share her personal theories with us.

Recently, she's been wandering around with a pink, sparkly teddy bear. "This is my toy Jesus," she says, holding it out in front of her and then letting go. "She likes being dropped."

Strangely, she doesn't get to take this particular bear to church.

Then she picks up the bear again and says, "The real Jesus is inside." It's hard to disagree, since God is everywhere.

Well, almost everywhere:

Sarah is taking the boys to Aberdeen for the weekend soon. Marie isn't too pleased at the prospect of staying home with me. She demonstrated this to Sarah the other day.

"God is here! He's in our house!" Marie shouted excitedly. Then her eyes narrowed and she muttered, "When you go to Aberdeen, he won't be there. He's going to stay here with me."

Does this say more about her understanding of God, I wonder, or about her knowledge of Aberdeen?

Hmmm... That's maybe one question I won't answer...

Yours in a woman's world,

Ed.

Consider the penguins

Dear Dave,

So much for my new found freedom. Just as I was getting used to a couple of hours without children every weekday morning, the February Week holiday has arrived. More than that, it turns out that the name is misleading. It's actually the February Week-and-a-bit holiday.

Ho-hum.

I was back to steering a trolley and three under-eights round the supermarket today. It wouldn't have been so awful but they've all reached an age where they're eager to help. Between one pushing, one loading and one sitting in the seat and yelling, 'Charge!' we tend to leave a trail of mangled groceries and scattered discount signs in our wake. Most other shoppers get out of our way but we occasionally scoop up random (very surprised looking) children by mistake. Thankfully, it's been a while since we've knocked a granny into a chest freezer. (They're always so polite and apologetic as they lie there surrounded by frozen peas, with their feet and Zimmer frame sticking up in the air – it makes me feel bad.)

Oh, that reminds me: I may not have achieved much with my extra time but I have managed to defrost our deep-freeze. That's right, in the three weeks Marie has attended nursery, I've successfully done all the chores I normally do, gone for coffee once and melted some ice.

Big whoop.

As it turns out, in my most recent plans for world domination, I forgot to figure in time for the things which I used to do while Marie was having her toast – things like routine tidying up and eating my own breakfast. They still need done even though she's not around. I also failed to appreciate that weekday mornings have previously been an opportunity for relative relaxation. I'm accustomed to spending them sitting about at parent and toddler, chatting and eating biscuits. Now, if I spend the mornings getting stuff done, I don't have much energy left in the evenings to do extra stuff. Drat. Looks like JK Rowling's lawyers can rest easy for a while. It doesn't appear I'll get around to my unofficial eighth Harry Potter novel (in which Harry deals with the trials and tribulations of being a stay at home dad) until Marie starts school. The world will have to wait an extra year or two for *Harry Potter and the Nappy of Disaster.*

As far as the holiday goes, it's been fairly quiet. The kids have had a couple of friends to visit but, in general, they've been glad of some peace. The boys have been honing their hand-eye-Mario coordination and Marie has glued lots of pink, sparkly bits and bobs to coloured paper.

The other day, we went to the zoo with Steve and his children. He's been doing much better recently. He seems to have come to terms with being a housedad. I suspect that if a vaguely decent management position came up, he'd have his offspring into day care faster than a toddler-powered trolley into a precarious display of eggs, but he's giving fatherhood his best shot for the time being.

He's not entirely adjusted yet, however.

"Here's our timetable," he said once we'd arrived, and he handed me a print-out. It was colour-coded to correspond with stickers he'd stuck to the map. "We're two and a half minutes behind already. We should be at the flamingos by now. Let's go."

I wasn't prepared for such zealous levels of organisation. "Shouldn't we check to see if any of the kids need the toilet first?" I grumbled.

"There's a scheduled rest-break at eleven. Toilet and snacks then. Come on."

He began striding up the steep hill on which Edinburgh Zoo is placed. Josquin was in the buggy and Ophelia skipped along beside him. I straggled behind. The boys were feeling queasy from the bus journey and were making a big show of holding paper bags under their chins as they walked. Marie wanted to go to the gift shop and buy a live penguin. I had to drag them all along.

The expedition was arranged because Deborah needed Steve away from their flat for the day so she could get a stack of business calls done. I don't think she trusts him to manage out and about for that length of time on his own yet, so she roped me in. Our destination was selected on the basis that there were some hands-on exhibitions taking place – spider fondling and snake cuddling, and suchlike. If I'd known this, I might not have agreed. I hate spiders and snakes.

Helpfully, Steve tried to instruct me in the error of my ways.

"They won't hurt you," he said when we reached the door of the building housing all things that slither or scuttle. "Snakes aren't slimy, you know. Come on, man."

"I have phobias," I said. "I *could* go in there but it wouldn't be fun."

He laughed. "Confront your fears."

"I go outside all the time. Doesn't stop me feeling agoraphobic on days when the sky is clear and there's a light wind."

"Like today?"

"I... er..." I looked up into the cloudless blue and I felt a tingle down the back of my neck, along with a familiar feeling of foreboding. I shivered. "I tell you what," I said, "Fraser's not too keen and Josquin's too young to care. How about I take them to the monkey house and we wait for the rest of you there? It's always nice and cosy."

"It's not very well lit," Steve chuckled. "There might be all manner of snakes and spiders hiding in the darkness."

"Cheers for that," I said and hurried off to find somewhere that had a low ceiling and was inhabited by creatures with more than no legs but less than eight of them. I was highly relieved when I finally wheeled Josquin into the dim, musty, tropical confines of the monkeys' home. It's one of my favourite parts of the zoo. Various primates were visible playing behind the glass panels which let us gaze into the indoor sections of their enclosures.

I'd have been better off going to fondle the spiders, though.

In his excitement at seeing a macaque eat a grape, Josquin brought forward the scheduled rest-break and created a nappy so disastrous that even Harry Potter would have struggled to overcome it. Being out of practice, I made something of a hash of things. I wasn't aided by having to change him on a bench in the gloom while being watched by a family of chimpanzees.

As I was bent over my grim task, I heard the sound of something venomous approaching from behind me.

"Now, children," said a cold, female voice, "can anyone tell me where these creatures are from?"

This time the tingle of fear wasn't in my neck. I huddled down lower and hoped Fraser was adequately entertained elsewhere. I was fairly sure she'd never met him. He would attract her scrutiny only if he rushed over and started clamouring at me...

I fixed my attention on dealing with the nappy and concentrated on not looking round. On the one hand, I couldn't believe my misfortune in choosing the same day as her to go to the zoo. On the other, I cursed myself for failing to realise that she would never pass up the prospect of educational workshops complete with added arachnids.

I felt the air chill behind me as she passed by, and I held my breath. Since I'd already been holding my breath for some while to avoid the smell from Josquin, I came close to passing out. I was terrified that the unduly loud beating of my heart would give me away.

Luckily, one of her grandchildren broke ranks at the sight of a lemur and ran off for a closer look. She was forced to follow, threatening all manner of chastisements as she went. I chanced glancing up.

Eleanor was disappearing into the murky distance, unfolding her portable naughty step as she went.

I let out a sigh and finished dealing with Josquin, getting him back in the buggy just in time for Steve's arrival.

The chimpanzees clapped.

"Daddy! Daddy! There were spiders!" shrieked Marie

when she saw me. "Big spiders with hair and legs and eyes and they walked around like this!" She did a little dance that induced adoring glances from other visitors. I'd rapidly become very conspicuous.

"Let's go and have that snack and you can tell me all about it," I said, ushering everyone towards the door.

Steve began wandering off towards the monkeys. "It would be more efficient for us to re-arrange the schedule and..."

"It's eleven," I hissed. "Ice-cream. Now."

"In February?"

"I..." Ice-cream was the only thing I could think of that the kids would find more enticing than staring at monkeys. "She's coming this way! Move. Move!"

I shoved Steve and the kids out the door and marched them round the corner to the café.

"Eleanor was in there," I explained when we were safely settled at a table with the kids busy melting frozen milk over their clothes.

"Who?" said Steve.

"I must have told you about her. She's the mum of one of my neighbours and I call her the GrandParent of Doom. We really, really don't want to run into her. Seriously, she's like a Sith Lord in tweed and she's got it in for me."

He nodded but he was clearly humouring me. Having dodged The *Twister* Incident and the parent and toddler night out, he didn't understand what she was capable of. I tried to fill him in on the details but we were both distracted cleaning our children. Afterwards, we set off for another look at the monkeys. I was confident she'd have moved on by then, so it was the place she was least likely to be. I began to calm down. Nevertheless, I spent the rest of the day peering over my shoulder.

The problem came after lunch when it was time for the penguin parade. Every day, the penguins get the opportunity to leave their enclosure and go for a short, circular walk on the path round the grassy area outside. If none of them are interested, then it doesn't happen, but there's usually a few. Just about all the visitors in the zoo turn up to watch.

Eleanor was certain to attend.

I'd already promised the kids that we'd go – it was one of the things that had persuaded them to put up with the expedition in the first place. This made avoiding her much more difficult. There was a chance she wouldn't notice us in the crowds (particularly as she was unlikely to recognise Fraser and Lewis) but I wasn't feeling lucky. We needed disguises. I contemplated plucking a llama and making us all false moustaches. It wasn't much of a plan, though. Fortuitously, as we got to the pool, I saw exactly what I was looking for in the window of a little shop full of penguin merchandise. They had a selection of cheap, waterproof hooded ponchos. These were black and white with orange visors. I hastily kitted out my family.

"It's not raining," complained Fraser as I put one over his head.

"It's to make the penguins feel safe," I countered.

"Why isn't anyone else wearing them?" said Lewis as we took up position by the parade route.

"They must be here to scare the penguins," I said, scanning the area behind us for hostiles.

Sadly, I was peering completely the wrong way.

"Look! It's Darth Granny!" squealed Marie.

I whipped round, only to discover I was facing my nemesis directly across the narrow path. I suddenly felt very conscious that I was dressed as a penguin. Eleanor fixed me with an icy glare. I pulled all my little penguins in close to me for safety.

"Oh, hi, Eleanor," I said. I wasn't sure how much of the previous conversation she'd heard. I remained optimistic she hadn't picked up on the whole interstellar evil witch reference.

"I know her," said Fraser. "I've seen her out our window. Is she the GPD?"

"Good afternoon," said Eleanor stiffly. "What, exactly, is the GPD?"

"GrandParent of Doom, of course," Lewis chimed in cheerfully.

Sometimes children are paying more attention than they let on...

"This is Eleanor," I said to Fraser. "She's the gran of Marcus and the others." Eleanor's four young grandchildren waved back politely but they knew something was up and were noticeably edging away from her.

"I suppose this is one of your housedad friends?" said Eleanor, indicating Steve with tight-lipped distaste.

"Er..." I said. It was a tricky question. Strictly speaking, Steve is my currently-out-of-paid-employment acquaintance who's filling time by taking care of his kids. Under the circumstances, however, 'housedad friend' was close enough. "Yes?" I ventured.

"Can *he* not get a job either?"

"Er..." It was another tricky question. I could have defended myself easily enough. I know full well that I have a job already – a job I've chosen, I'm good at and I'm happy with. Steve was more of an issue. Everything I'd normally say in such scenarios was bound to only make him feel worse. "We came to see the snakes," I said.

"They went hisssssss!" said Marie, spitting all over Josquin who was in the buggy in front of her. Josquin burst into tears. Steve unstrapped him and picked him up, only to discover that his nappy had leaked copiously. It just added to the whole air of tongue-tied, poncho-wearing incompetence we were generating.

Eleanor was unwilling to hide her contempt. "I pity your poor wives and children."

"Er..." I said again.

Then the penguins arrived, flanked by their keepers. The ungainly birds waddled past, squawking. Cameras flashed, children shouted and the crowds pressed in around us. I concentrated on keeping hold of my kids in the crush. When the mayhem was past, Eleanor had gone, her humiliation of us complete.

I was seething. Any number of things I wanted to say to her sprang to mind. Few of them were civil.

Then I took a deep breath and tried to let it go. Realistically, I don't care what she thinks about me. It's not like I'm a big fan of her grandparenting (or even parenting) style. The encounter had been unpleasant but we'd all survived and it meant the GPD probably wouldn't bother us again for the rest of the day. We could relax, take photos, break out some more snacks and then press on up to the safari area.

By the time I'd helped the kids off with their disguises, I was feeling much better. If I could whistle, I would have whistled.

Then I noticed that Steve was missing. I was worried he'd taken Eleanor's words personally and skulked away somewhere in a funk. Who knew what he might be up to? I started to look for him but then Fraser and Lewis 'helped' by running off in all directions to search, and I had to concentrate on not losing *them*. This slowed me down. I was at the point of becoming concerned and phoning Steve's mobile when I finally found him and his children watching the penguins on the other side of the pool. It turned out he'd been off fumigating Josquin and the buggy. He did look glum, though.

"Sorry about that," I said. "I told you she's not hugely keen on me. Still, at least none of us ended up breast-feeding in a box this time."

He shrugged and grunted.

"Look," I continued, "don't let anything she said get to you. She has very strong opinions about raising children and thinks everyone else should go along with them, no matter how inappropriate it is for their situation. We don't fit in with the way she sees the world and she can't deal with it. She doesn't want to. Ignore her."

"But she's right," he said, struggling to keep it together. "This isn't normal. This isn't how it's supposed to be."

"What do you mean?"

"I can't do this. I'm a man. I can't even put a nappy on properly."

I shook my head. "*I* put on that nappy, remember? Maybe I messed up; maybe it was one of those things. What counts is that you handled it well. You had spare clothes, wipes and nappies and you got on with it. A woman couldn't have done better and I've seen plenty do worse."

"But I shouldn't be here. She's right. I should be at work, providing for my family."

"What? Because the guys at the golf club say you should?"

"How did you know?" he said, embarrassed.

"Because I've met some of them and they're rather opinionated, if I recall. They approach life with certain preconceptions. If you can't look at the world differently, then you're going to go crazy. You need to change your perspective."

Sudden fear gripped him. "You're not going to tell me about God, are you?"

"Er, no," I said, "I can, er, do that if you like but I... I was actually going to tell you about penguins."

This cheered him up and confused him in equal measure. "Pardon?"

"If you want to understand about perspective, you need to know about penguins." I pointed over to where a particularly rotund penguin was clumsily waddling down to the water. "Penguins are funny birds with an ungainly walk. They can't even fly. A bird that can't fly – what's the use of that?" At the last minute, the fat penguin slipped and did an enormous belly-flop into the shallows. "As we see them, they're comical and a source of slapstick but I doubt they perceive things that way themselves. They probably think of each other as ninja fighter-pilots. That one's the Red Baron to his friends."

"But they can't fly," said Steve.

I snorted. "Of course they can. You just need to witness life from a penguin point of view. Follow me."

With the children close behind, I led him round and down to the enormous observation window in the side of the penguin pool. Initially there was little to observe but soon the Red Baron came into sight and dived towards us, then fluidly banked and swooped upwards again, effortlessly gliding away. He was quickly joined by a couple of buddies, the three of them swirling around each other in an unbelievable acrobatic display. They were simply flying through the water.

"Don't be put off because other people can't see or appreciate what you're doing," I said. "You may not have some of the opportunities you want right now but you've got different ones. You can spend time with your children, for a start. Make the most of it."

We stood and watched the swimming some more. Steve appeared deep in thought. When he didn't say anything for nearly five minutes I became concerned again. Had my analogy crashed his brain? I contemplated telling him about God after all. Then, at last, he said, "Isn't it the male penguins that look after the young?"

"They certainly take their turn," I replied.

He considered this a little before saying, "Glad I don't have to waddle around with an egg on my feet."

"Amen to that," I nodded.

Steve seemed a great deal happier. He fished out his schedule and we headed further up the hill to see the zebras and kangaroos and big cats. Marie and Ophelia shrieked excitedly at every sparrow we passed. The boys, meanwhile, were beginning to lose it. They took the briefest glance as each creature went by, and then returned to bickering. They barely grunted at the sight of a tiger.

Then, unexpectedly, they started bouncing around and pointing.

"It's a Raichu!" screeched Fraser.

"Bless you," I said.

"No! It's a Raichu – the evolved form of Pikachu! Look! Look! That boy's got one."

The four-year-old in question did, indeed, have a small cuddly toy that looked like a deformed version of Pikachu. Fraser insisted on having his photograph taken with it. Luckily, both the boy and his mum were very understanding.

"There's a lion over here," I said when the photo session was done.

The boys scarcely acknowledged me. "Whatever..."

Marie ignored me entirely and danced round some litter. "It's a crisp packet. It's empty! It's not in the bin!"

I decided it was definitely time to go.

We called into the gift shop and bought a plastic penguin and similar assorted tack, then headed home. Steve and his lot had their car with them, so we said our good-byes on the steps. He shook my hand warmly but slightly awkwardly. Marie and Ophelia gave each other an enthusiastic, jumping hug. Josquin gurgled.

We waved them into the distance and waited for the bus. It began to rain.

Handily, we had shiny, new waterproofs.

(Some things work out well in the end.)

Yours in a woman's world,

Ed.

Safe operating procedure

Dear Dave,

I was removing the packet of a new screwdriver the other day when I noticed that the instructions contained the warning, 'Do not insert in ear.' As I set about loosening the screw holding shut the battery compartment on a plug'n'play computer game, I noted that the batteries came with the helpful advice, 'Do not open.' The game itself suggested the user should play in a brightly lit room, rest for fifteen minutes in every hour and never play when tired. I thought this was being rather hopeful. The additional advice to cease playing in the event of losing consciousness did seem sensible, nonetheless.

All this was for a child who came with no warning labels whatsoever and is, without doubt, the most dangerous thing in my house! It's time to redress the balance. The following should be distributed in maternity wards everywhere:

Your child. Care and safety information.

Congratulations. You are now the proud owner of a new human being. We wish you many years of happiness and satisfaction with this product. As with all complex biological systems, however, your offspring will require some care and maintenance to ensure optimum performance. Please take a moment to look over these instructions and familiarise yourself with safe operating procedure. Thank you for your cooperation.

Non-compliance with these warnings may cause malfunction of the product and/or injury or distress to pets and soft furnishings. It will also invalidate your warranty. No returns can be accepted and there are strictly NO REFUNDS.

- Keep away from fires, sharp objects and open tubes of toothpaste.

- Hand wash only.
- Product may emit strong odour. This is not a defect.
- Slippery when wet.
- Cross-border transfer may be restricted.
- This product can cause nausea, drowsiness, irritation, despair, anger, vexation or fatigue. If symptoms persist, seek help, prayer and beer.
- Caution: Contains vomit.
- Not dishwasher safe.
- Slippery when covered in sun cream.
- Do not throw out with bathwater.
- Risk of high noise levels. Wear ear protection.
- Do not combine with alcohol, excessive sugar, wet cement or fragile valuables.
- Slippery when covered from head-to-toe in purple paint. Note: Also messy.
- Not for use as a flotation device.
- Danger of choking: Product may feed you LEGO while you are sleeping.
- Just plain slippery.
- Warning: Product may contain traces of its grandparents.
- Do not tumble-dry.
- Children in mirrors may be closer than they appear.
- Prone to incessant wittering.
- Do not leave in direct sunlight, cars or trifle. (Cages are fine.)
- Contents may stain clothing.
- Requires love, attention, support and university tuition fees. (Not included.)
- Splash-proof, shockproof and resistant to reason.
- Store in a cool, dry place.
- Do not refrigerate.
- Handcuffs are not a substitute for parental supervision.

We hope this fresh addition to your family brings you much joy and pleasure. Good luck.

Did I miss any?
Yours in a woman's world,
Ed.

PS I took a look at the list of possible side-effects of some travel sickness pills we have – one of them is vomiting. Hmmm....

This *is* normal

Dear Dave,

I guess you don't have long to go now. Another fortnight and Liz will be back at work. Your life will be a whirl of sterilising bottles and defrosting milk. You'll have to figure out how to fit all Daisy's feeds and nappy changes around ferrying Sam to nursery and clubs. It'll be a constant rush to keep up with the timetable and you'll have to do it all while suffering from broken sleep and whatever illness the kids have brought home this week. It will be long and tiring.

Enjoy it while you can.

I'm not kidding. I think I miss it a little.

Yes, yes, I know I'm mad. I've blanked the repetition, frustration, exhaustion and endless *Teletubbies* from my mind. There is something to be said, however, for the simplicity of survival. Eighteen months ago, my horizon was firmly fixed at getting through the day to a can of beer and some *CSI*. Every evening that I made it to the sofa, turned on the telly and cracked that ring pull was a triumph. (Apart from the odd occasion where the can had been shaken and I got a lapful of Murphy's, obviously.) No one was sure how I managed it. Friends and family applauded me merely for keeping going.

Now things are different. The children are older. They can all sleep through the night, use a spoon, fire up a DVD and go to the toilet without too much intervention. My services are becoming obsolete.

Since I no longer need to be chasing after toddlers 24/7, there's scope for longer-term goals. There's even some expectation (both from other people and the craziness in my own head) that I'll achieve them. I can start educational projects with the kids, attend to neglected chores, study, work, keep fit, meet social obligations and generally look beyond bedtime. Except I can't do *all* those things – I don't have that much time or energy. I do have time and energy for some of them, though. This means I have to make decisions and I'm not used to those kinds of decisions anymore.

This was brought to my attention the other morning when I heard a knock at the door. It was Mike. He was wearing his dog-collar and he was carrying a Bible and his ring-bound personal organiser. I wasn't expecting him but he looked like he intended business.

"I'm here for lunch," he said bluntly.

"Er... Do you have a reservation?"

"No," he said and came in anyway. "Where's Marie?"

"I'm in the lounge!" came a shrill cry from upstairs. "I'm cooking Bagpuss!"

"Mmmmm, fried cloth cat," I said, taking Mike's coat. "Are you certain you want to stay for lunch?"

"Sandwiches will be fine," he said, going through to the kitchen and taking a seat.

"Cup of tea?"

He shook his head. "I've had seven already, thank you."

"Seven!"

He sighed. "I spend much of my time visiting elderly ladies. Overdosing on tea and biscuits is one of the hazards of the job."

"How about a beer then?"

Unusually, Mike was lost for words. This didn't seem to be an offer he'd often received in his two decades of ministry. He pondered it for a moment. "Just a small one," he said, trying not to appear too pleased. "With my lunch."

"Right you are." I set about preparing the food.

"How are Rob and Kate and the baby?" he asked. "Have they thought of a name yet?"

"They got to the registry office in the nick of time on Friday," I said, rolling my eyes. "The poor kid almost got called '[To do]'. They settled on Luke Robert in the end."

Mike chuckled. "You've been living in Scotland for fifteen years and you still can't say Luke properly, can you?"

"Don't you start," I said, my head in a cupboard. "I think Rob chose it simply for the chance to wind me up. Apparently, if I can pronounce the kid's name correctly five times in a row, then I get to be a godparent."

"Much luck?"

"My high score's currently two and a half. So, no. Not much."

I put a sliced loaf on the table and dumped most of the contents of the fridge beside it. There was cheese and sliced meat, salad and a tub of hummus. "Tuck in," I said. Then I began cutting up some fruit for Marie.

"I'll need a knife," said Mike.

"Oh, yeah." I grabbed one from the drawer, rubbed off a couple of fingerprints with my shirt and handed it over.

"Thanks." He made himself a sandwich and waited for me to sit down. It took him a few seconds to twig I wasn't going to. I went to find that bottle of beer under the shelves, switched on the kettle as I went, poured a child-sized cup of milk on the way back, opened the bottle and put it in front of him. Then I returned to chopping.

"How's life?" Mike asked and started eating.

"Busy. Marie's settled at nursery but I've been spending the free time sorting out the house and stuff. The boys have been having lots of friends round. Sarah's got extra work to do at the moment. All being well, the last of the repairs from the flood will be completed tomorrow – if the plumbers turn up, they can fix the pipe in question, and they don't break anything else in the process. Once that's over, we're looking into getting the kitchen done, so that'll be more chaos. At some point, I'm planning to do some writing. Next month we're going to..."

Mike cut me off. "That's what you've been filling life with. It doesn't answer my question. Stop what you're doing, come over here and talk to me."

"Er..." I was almost finished preparing Marie's lunch. I only needed to spread margarine on some crackers... I reached for the packet.

"Now."

"OK," I said, suitably abashed. "Can I wash my hands and get my coffee?"

"All right."

I gave my fingers a quick rinse, dried them on my trousers, poured my drink and hurried to sit opposite Mike. I rested my elbows on the table and held the mug up with both hands, trying to act natural and relaxed rather than as if I was using it as a steaming shield to fend off any cross-examination.

"So?" said Mike.

"So?"

"So how's life?"

I looked away, uncertain what to say. Sunlight was streaming in through the patio doors and it was an almost nice day outside for a change. Beyond our back fence, I could see Julia playing *Tig* with her children in the park. They were wrapped up warm against the wind but they were enjoying themselves. She still hasn't put the four of them into school... Maybe she will soon...

I watched them for a bit, imagining the laughter that I couldn't hear past the double-glazing.

"I don't know," I said eventually. "It's a few years since I've properly had time to think about it. There's been one distraction after another. Well, one child after another, anyhow. It's just been a case of keeping on going. Life feels like an endless game of *Tetris* sometimes. I used to be able to clear the screen every so often and take a breather. Now it's like I've had too many of those 'S'-shaped blocks in a row and I'm forever scrambling simply to keep the last few lines from filling up. Things are getting better but I don't believe I'll ever get the screen clear again."

Mike didn't say anything as he considered this, then he changed tack. Or perhaps he didn't. It's hard to tell with him. "How's Dave?" he asked.

"He's OK. He's got two kids now, so he doesn't have as much chance for email, but we're keeping in touch. It's odd remembering back to when I was in the situation he's in. Having a tiny one seems like so long ago."

"It's about a year since you started writing to him, isn't it?"

"Yeah. It's weird how much has changed. I'm getting proper sleep, Sarah's job has settled down, Fraser can almost take care of himself, Lewis is at school, Marie's at nursery and we've been able to pass on the baby equipment. I keep thinking that life will return to normal soon. Then I realise that Marie's nearly three and a half. Even when she starts school, life won't be that different. These days, looking after them all often entails nothing more than keeping an ear out for trouble while getting on with something else. We're past the stage where I had to be constantly physically involved with the children merely to keep them fed, clean and rested. This *is* normal and it's going to be the way of things for a while."

"Uh-huh," said Mike, making himself another sandwich. Then, offhand, he added, "And how are you coping with that?"

He didn't so much as lift his gaze from his plate. I'd been expecting to have to deflect a piercing stare with my coffee. I was taken off-guard. "Er..." I said, lowering my mug in surprise. "I'm... maybe..."

Then he looked me in the eye. I was trapped and defenceless. There was no avoiding an honest answer.

I just struggled to think of one.

"My world is different and I'm not used to that yet," I said, after a lengthy pause. "I'm not sure what I am or where I fit in. For years, I've been able to introduce myself as a housedad and be confident that that covered everything. It doesn't any longer. Then again, I'm hardly close to getting my old life back. I'm somewhere in between."

"Does it matter what you are?"

I shrugged. "If you're wanting me to figure out *who* I am, it's going to take more than one visit and I'll be needing some of that beer."

"We can arrange that," he said, flipping open his organiser and unscrewing the lid of his fountain pen. He poised the nib over the page. "A week on Thursday, in the evening?"

"Well..."

He wrote the appointment down before I could reply. "I'll bring the beer; you provide the PlayStation. It's been months since I got to embarrass you with a shotgun."

"Er, can I invite anyone else?" I asked, giving in.

"If you don't mind sharing your angst with them."

"I'm long past caring," I muttered.

Mike snorted. "We'll see."

Marie bounced into the room. She had a toy saucepan in her hands. A pink and white tail trailed out from under the lid. "Lunch-time!" she squealed.

"Almost," I said, jumping up to finish piling her plate.

Then she caught sight of the park and Julia's children. "It's Marcus! He's playing a game on the grass out the back door! Can we play?"

I glanced at the packet of crackers and at Mike. It wasn't exactly a convenient time but another twenty minutes and Julia was bound to have gone in. It would probably also have started to rain.

"Please..." said Marie.

"It does look too good to miss," said Mike, leaning back in his chair. "I'll sit here and watch, though, if you don't mind."

I dithered. There was stuff to be done and I had a guest, but, nonetheless, there was something to be said for blowing the cobwebs away...

"OK," I said at last, "we won't be long." Marie and I got our shoes and coats on. "Help yourself to crisps," I called over my shoulder as we stepped out into the sunshine.

"I was going to," said Mike, sipping his beer.

Julia waved us over cheerily and we joined in with the running about and screaming. It was cold enough to see our breath and need our gloves. My ears were soon ready to fall off.

Still, it was fresh air and exercise.

It was also a chance to play with my little girl before either of us grows up any further.

We had fun.

Yours in a woman's world (for now),

Ed.

About the author

People meeting Edmund Farrow for the first time tend to think of him as tall, quiet and generally harmless. Then they learn he's a housedad, has a physics degree and is a lay preacher in the Church of Scotland. One way or another, this usually makes them afraid...

Edmund has been staying at home looking after his three children since they were babies. He codes educational apps and writes books whenever he gets the chance to sneak away to his computer. Only old school friends, double-glazing salesmen and Glaswegians call him Ed.

Housedad Hero Book 2
Toys, Teenagers & Tantrums available 2014

You can find out more at:

www.DadsDinner.com
www.MathsWarrior.com

or follow Edmund on Twitter:

@DadsDinner

Legal Disclaimer

All advice in this book is offered for entertainment purposes only. Every child is different and requires different care. For better or worse, your children are your own responsibility. Love them, nurture them, encourage them, treasure them, enable them and occasionally ignore them... but use common sense. Also, don't drop games consoles on them, and watch out for zombies.

21942207R00200

Made in the USA
Charleston, SC
09 September 2013